Demons  s:

Luctus

Jay Britton Fisher

CONTENTS

Part 1: The Research   3

Part 2: The Artifact   129

Part 3: The Grief   203

Questions for Readers   304

Acknowledgements   306

Death
(only a few days in the future)

Staring at the lifeless flesh lying all around me, I wanted to think that it was over.

I ached. I could do little more at the moment than sit, crumpled on the floor, just breathing. I'd nearly passed out when I'd hit the wall behind me, and with no immediate threat nearby, I wasn't going to try to stand. Sitting in a vaguely upright position was enough for now; it didn't help my sore shoulder, but at least I was able to rest.

I didn't want to stay here for long, though. In this strange place, filled only with horror, I was too tired to recognize any sadness, but I was suddenly very lonely, if no longer scared. I regarded one figure on the floor not far from me, both somewhat familiar and uncomfortably foreign at the same time. The body had appalled me at first sight and still left me sickened.

As I made the mistake of breathing too heavily, the stinging and soreness in my shoulder intensified and I cried out and leaned away to try to ease it. For a moment all I could see was the dirty floor as I hunched over it, trying to stay awake but feeling that I would collapse into darkness any second.

With effort I lifted my eyes again.

I wanted to think that it was over. But as I stared at the wretched fiend on the floor I knew that instead, for me it was a disconsolate beginning...

Part I

The Research

1

Some things are forever lost. Four thousand years ago a man came through this land, lived and laughed and fought and cried and had his own story and for years people passed it on, but now, no one knows that story. It is forgotten. One day a group of anthropologists will find his skeleton, and despite all they may be able to divine from their discovery, they won't really know his story either. Maybe he wrote his story on a rock wall, but most of his inks faded into nonexistence, and only part remains for viewers to interpret. The rest is gone, with no way of ever getting it back.

Today, most people's stories are available to the whole world through a vast computer network, but like a needle in a needle-stack stories are lost in a different sort of way. Amid an ocean of diverting triviality the most important stories usually don't get the most attention. So far, the part of my own story that I was comfortable making public was also trivial, but not entertaining or inspiring enough to draw any notice. I was okay with that; I liked to appreciate other stories when I could find good ones. That's why I was at my local bookstore again today.

In my hand I held a newer book that mentioned several archaeological sites, some recently discovered in my own locale, which gave new clues about an old civilization. I had flipped through it and was actually quite interested until I checked the back cover and saw the price. Too high. For being from a wealthy family, I didn't like to spend a lot of money. I got that from my father, and I can only assume that a big reason why he had so much money was that he didn't spend much of it.

Maybe frugality was common, but if it wasn't, it was the least of many ways in which my father was unusual. *He* certainly had a story worth reading, but while he had a habit of recording it in hopes that it wouldn't ever be lost completely, he kept it in an old handwritten journal that I expected to stay private for a long time. When I'd asked him about it, he'd said only that one day it would be interesting to me, and then he'd put it away. But while there was still a lot about his past that I didn't know, I could tell that it had shaped him into someone quite unlike anyone else in the world.

The strangeness of his manner had affected me as well: I never hesitated to be different, to take another path, to choose other music, to try (most) new foods...I was okay being the odd girl. Usually. Sometimes it was also a bit lonely, but most of the time I was perfectly content to be lonely in exchange for being my own agent. I knew I didn't want to just sway and flow along in the current of consumer appetites and popular culture, as some people seemed content to do. I wondered inwardly if strangeness might be a necessary precursor to greatness. Most people were probably too normal to achieve true greatness, and maybe to even know what it was, thinking they could be happy with celebrity or wealth. I wasn't sure I knew what true greatness was either, but I meant to take a path that hadn't seen many footsteps already.

Anyway, my father was weird, and it had rubbed off on me. I set the book back on the shelf where I had found it. I decided to only buy one item that day—a magazine on hairstyles and product usage that I had seen upon entering the store and had been holding since. A girl's got to take care of herself, and good hair care was essential.

Evidently some of my mother had rubbed off on me as well.

I figured that I'd spent enough time shopping for one evening and began to move toward the front of the store to make my purchase. As I approached the register from the side I saw that I wouldn't have to wait in line for very long; only a single young man stood by the counter. He was probably about my age, though I couldn't see him well at first. From where I was I could mostly only see his longish hair, which was a glossy black, and in passing I noticed that he was wearing a grey long-sleeved, collared shirt, a black vest, and black, lightweight gloves. But instead of scrutinizing his apparel, I took notice of the unusual book he was holding: *Demons and Dark Essences*, by someone named Drake. It made me laugh to myself. *Well, now*, I thought, *if you really want to learn about that kind of thing I could have you meet someone I know.*

At the same time, I was curious—the book was large and leather-bound, and it looked old. It wasn't the sort of thing I expected the store to sell. Having almost reached the counter I craned my head to see the book from a different angle.

The boy turned so I could see his face, and I halted mid-step.

His eyes hit me. I felt like they held me and stopped me from moving any farther. They were a deep blue that seemed to be somehow both dark and bright at the same time. The similarity of the luster with the shine of his hair was enough to be distracting by itself, but for a moment I could do nothing but stare right at his eyes.

Of course, when I realized that he was looking right back at me I flushed with embarrassment and turned my head away. I peeked back once more and then turned away again quickly and ran my free hand through my hair, biting my lower lip on one side. I waited with nervous impatience, and then tried to sneak a glance back at him. His expression was almost one of playful disbelief, as if sizing up the situation. I didn't keep eye contact.

While I reached for and held some nearby object on which I could pretend to focus, he must have continued onward. After turning the thing over a couple of times I heard the door to the store open. I turned around but only saw the boy's back for a brief moment before he was out of sight beyond a narrow window next to the door.

I looked down at the object in my hand. It was a small daily tear-off calendar showing cats and intentionally misspelled captions. Definitely not for me. I set it down and walked to the purchase counter.

The cashier, a plump woman of about thirty, regarded me with a raised eyebrow as I approached. "Find everything okay?"

I gave a brief exhale. "I found a bit more than I bargained for." I handed her the magazine. "The boy who was here just a minute ago—have you seen him come in here before?"

She scanned my purchase as she spoke, smiling faintly. "Nope. Haven't seen him here or anywhere else, and I'm good with faces."

I frowned at that.

She put my magazine into a shopping bag that I normally would have rejected if I had kept more presence of mind. "Good choice, by the way," she said. "Do you dye?"

I squinted and arched an eyebrow, as if she knew too much, and answered with a measured, "We all die someday..."

In response she simply lifted the magazine partway out of the bag again so that the title and part of the photographs on the cover were visible.

"Oh, right! No, this is natural." I flicked my hair out with one hand as I said the word "natural". She watched it rise and fall. "Actually, I don't think they make dye in this color. I couldn't be sure, though. I've never paid much attention to color options. My mother would kill me until I was dead if I dyed my hair." She didn't answer back.

I paid, thanked her, and turned to leave the building. As I turned I ran straight into a man who must have been standing nearby. "Excuse me!" I stammered as his eyes went wide. "I didn't notice you there!" He stepped back, muttered something under his breath, and hurried away into an aisle of books. I glanced around to see who had observed the little accident, giving a quick blushing smile to the cashier.

Stepping outside, I peered off to the side where the blue-eyed boy had gone, but I saw no sign of him.

Sighing gently, I looked back again to this bookstore I'd visited many times before. On many occasions I'd left the place with new books, but today, unexpectedly, I was taking something else away—something within me. I felt some new fuel inside myself, waiting to flare up if I could only find a spark.

I began walking home in the light of the setting sun.

1.1

Walking down the familiar path from the front gates to the great doors of my father's house, I took only a short moment to appreciate the atmosphere created by the sentries. Along either side of the walkway, facing inward and opposite each other in pairs, stood statues of six life-sized ceremonially armored guards. The style of the armor seemed like it might have been Greek or Roman, though a bit more grandiose. The first two guards were armed with sheathed swords; their hands rested on the hilts of the weapons as if ready to draw them. The next pair of sentries held spears, angled slightly inward, as if prepared to lower them and bar passage. The last two guards held great shields in their near hands and tall halberds further back. Even though they were just statues, I always felt as if nothing harmful could ever pass them. I assumed that unwanted visitors would find them foreboding, or perhaps be instilled with a sense of awe, but either way they gave me a sense of security whenever I returned home.

The statues that immediately followed always gave me a sense of welcome, which I'm sure was their purpose for any visitors as well. They were of four women, who all wore dresses gathered at the shoulder and were crowned with a thin wreath of some vine-like plant. The first two held plentiful baskets of fruit and wore warm but calm smiles. The others held bouquets of flowers and also had tranquil expressions. They gave a feeling of peace that one can only embrace when in a place of strength.

That was surely what my father's house was for me—a place of strength.

At each of the other entrances to the large house was another pair of sentries, all with spears crossed above the doorway, and at various intervals on the grounds more solitary armed statues were positioned. None of these were visible from where I was now, but I knew each of their locations by heart. I supposed that I was a bit spoiled, being waited on constantly by sentries and maidens, but I relished the feeling of security. It was perhaps a bit strange that statues were my only continual attendants; neither the groundskeeper nor the maid or her assistant lived on the premises, but were only present intermittently, sometimes only as often as once per week.

Opening the front door of my father's house to step inside, I heard the tinny but elegant sound of our harpsichord. The distant notes moved up and down smoothly, belying a graceful set of fingers on the keys. Thinking of the musician made me smile. I followed inward, toward the source of the melody, taking care to walk softly so as not to let my footsteps send echoes through the halls.

The door to the music room was ajar, as usual. I remained outside, listening. My father sat so that I could see his profile. His long, silver hair (much like my own) ran down behind his shoulders. I always preferred it when he didn't keep it contained.

His presence in this room completed it. It was mostly occupied by a small assortment of instruments, tables, and chairs, many of them antique, but all of the highest quality; however, while the room already possessed a classic elegance, he himself seemed the perfect finishing touch. He had taken a brief glance in my direction when I first appeared in the doorway and then turned his attention back to the music.

The piece he was playing was one I'd heard from him many times: the Wood Carving Partita. While it was a decent music, it wasn't my favorite piece by any means, though it must have been one of his. "A good piece for a library," he had once said of it in his resonant voice. Whatever that meant.

He didn't play often, but when he did it was evident that he'd had many years of practice. He was the sort of person that excelled at everything he did, from martial arts to business to music (though I'd never heard him sing). His hands moved as if in liquid form over the harpsichord's keys. For as still and somber as he was most of the time, occasionally he was surprisingly fast, and not just on a keyboard; I'd seen him move from one place to another with almost alarming swiftness. It was a thing of beauty to see his hair whip out behind him as he leaped forward in a flash or turn suddenly. Similarly, it was inspiring to watch his fingers strike the keys of this instrument, or our piano, with such precision and speed.

I wondered, as I had often before, if I would ever have that kind of conspicuous grace and beauty myself. I doubted it—in fact, I figured it was impossible for anyone else in the world to match him in that respect—but it didn't matter; I just loved my dad and was proud of him.

"Hi, Daddy!" I said to my father in the middle of his playing. My voice was bright with a smile. It was the sort of smile I gave readily now, having gotten used to it in high school, but which in my childhood and early teenage years I had otherwise often used only when we had no company. I tended to be more formal when others were around, which was largely a reflection of my father's behavior. With age I'd picked up more of my mother's sociality and her vivacity, though I still had serene moments.

In response to my greeting he added a signature trill to the song he was playing, nodded his head once, and then continued without breaking rhythm.

Even if he hadn't been in the middle of operating the instrument, I wouldn't have asked him about the old-looking book. I thought he might know something about it, but we were peculiar enough already, and I tended to want to keep our life together in the realm of the normal whenever possible.

That had never been difficult, somehow. Though we kept a secret that no one else would understand, and that strengthened the bond between us, we only rarely discussed it. Each time was the same; about a half hour of solemn admonition mixed with periods of silence, followed by a change of topic to school or friends or church or music or anything else.

Yes, church. I imagined it would perplex most people if they found out who he was and discovered him to be religious also. Our local bishop knew his secret, and, though he was initially shocked, had been supportive. Somehow, though, despite our regular attendance at services, we remained aloof from most of the congregation. Perhaps they could sense something, or perhaps they just weren't terribly friendly, but more likely I think it was just the introverted habits of my father that found their way into my personal customs.

It was almost the same at school. I'd had many acquaintances but few close friends. Sadly, most of them had moved away; it made for a somewhat lonely summer but also gave me a greater appreciation for those I still saw occasionally.

While I cherished my friends, the people in my life with whom I had the closest relationship were my parents. I supposed that was normal, but as I got older I also began to consider them my best friends as well.

I stepped noiselessly away from the music room, leaving my father to his playing.

Not far away, in the conservatory, where she could still faintly hear my father's music, my mother was busy with her hobby of painting. She actually wasn't very good, but she got into it every once in a while. Again I stopped in the doorway to observe. She stood in front of an easel, holding a palette in her left hand and a brush in her right, just next to her mouth as she shuffled a pensive expression on her face. Her deep, dark red hair fell in waves around her shoulders. My father must have had some very dominant genes for me to have no trace of my mother's red in my own hair. She stood framed by several lush, green hanging and potted plants; she always felt as if she was more artistic when surrounded by life.

My mother said she called that room the "conservatory" because it reminded her of a room in the board game Clue. For added effect she kept a candlestick, rope, and wrench on a table in the corner. I was pretty sure they'd never been used for either murder or mystery, but I loved my mom just a little tiny bit more for them being there.

"Hi, Mom!" I called.

She smiled at me and waved the last few fingers of her brush hand, then cast a measuring gaze back at the easel before striking it twice with the paint-coated bristles.

She tended to attempt what she called "modern art", which ended up being an assortment of splotches and inconsistent strokes that were never very appealing to me. As often as I possibly could, I gave her sincere compliments on the parts that I liked in any way. She knew that apart from what I said in those simple assertions I didn't enjoy her work much, and no one else did either—the only people who ever bought anything of hers were friends—but she enjoyed painting and she painted merely for enjoyment, so overall it worked out just fine for her.

Not that she sold many paintings in the first place; she'd had some limited success in the past, but now she tended to give them away as gifts that always caught the recipients by surprise and often tended to confuse them. *"Is it an animal? A deer, or maybe...a duck?"* My mother's brief explanations of the art never quite left them confident about it and they tended to squint a lot while trying to discern the subject she described. Sometimes it was about nature, but often enough it had to do with my father, and my mother never felt embarrassed about it.

She wasn't as complicated as my father, not as deep…and I had wondered, inwardly, sometime before, if that lack of depth of character made her inferior somehow. Not that I realized at the time what I was thinking; on the contrary, it was only with introspection and hindsight that I realized what horrid doubts I'd had about my mother. It was the sort of doubt that would have blinded me to the true value she had, the same as a great many other people surely had been blinded to the innate goodness and value of those around them. But I had rejected my doubts fiercely once I looked past them properly, and I loved my mother more than anyone, with the exception of perhaps my father. It was difficult to say whom I loved more, but regardless, there was no one quite like my mother, and I was sure that when I looked at her I could see her *true* beauty.

I watched her for a few moments, as I had with my father, and then wandered back toward my own room, reflecting on the rather picturesque life I led. My parents spent many evenings together, but it was also nice to see them taking time to pursue personal interests in the arts.

On other days I might have joined one of my parents for a while, either listening to my father or maybe trying to play a duet with him using my meager skill on the piano, harp, or cello, or alternatively taking an hour alongside my mother to create paintings of even less talent than hers. But today I was glad to just say hi and then let them take some personal time.

On the way to my room I glanced down a broad hallway toward a largely unused wing of the house. In most of that wing, dust had gathered in thick layers. My father wanted it that way; we could have easily had our housekeepers clean it up or attended to it ourselves, but my father seemed to be comfortable with the sign of time passing, and stillness. I think it was partly a sense of frugality as well; his house was much larger than the space needed by a family of three, even if living comfortably. It was somehow a statement for my father, albeit one I didn't entirely understand.

Furniture in the well-trafficked areas was spotless, though; I never thought of my parents as vain, but they did take great care with both personal and domestic appearance. According to them, while vanity was self-centered, their efforts to look proper were motivated by respect for others. I believed it.

"Maria," came a deep voice from behind me.

Startled by the suddenness of the voice even though I recognized it immediately, I jumped just a bit. I turned to see my father, who must have come to find me after finishing his song. "How are you?" he asked.

"I'm fine," I answered, shaking my head at his innate ability for stealth. "I've just been enjoying a slow summer."

He cocked his head. "Not too slow for too long, I would hope."

"Oh, Daddy." I stood on my tiptoes to kiss him on the cheek. "I'll get a job soon. Maybe at a bookstore...that would be fun."

He sighed, and I could see that he wanted to smile but was restraining himself. "And what of autumn?"

"You know I've been accepted."

He regarded me silently.

I answered the unspoken question. "No, I haven't registered yet. There's supposed to be a freshman orientation a few weeks before school starts, and I'll register then. Don't worry about it!"

He continued to observe me.

"Dad, I'm really enjoying not being in school right now. I'm not going to be lazy forever, but graduating from high school is a big accomplishment! Don't I deserve to relax a little?"

"You deserve everything, but prolonged relaxation will be less rewarding than you may expect."

"I'm liking it so far," I said with a smile. "I tell you what. I'll start looking for a job. Will that make you happy?"

"You make me happy."

Knowing what I did about my father in his past life, that statement reached deeply into my heart with warmth. I didn't have much to say back, but I smiled. He reached one hand behind my head, pulling it forward so that he could kiss my forehead. Then he turned and left as quietly as he'd entered.

1.2

I found a letter on the small table just outside the door of my room. I knew right away who had sent it, because I only got mail from one person. The last of my female friends had gone to Europe as part of a foreign exchange program, or, more correctly, had been invited to Europe by the family of a Swiss student named Aline who had previously come to the U.S. in the program. Before she left, my friend and I both agreed to correspond by regular mail. There was something about letters on paper, especially when written by hand, that said, "I care enough to do this." They were, perhaps, a bit longer in the writing, but more fun to read, and there was a certain anticipation and excitement when receiving a letter in the mail.

Sure enough, the name in the upper left corner of the envelope read "Noviembre Solis". *What's the latest, Nova?* I wondered as I picked it up and carried it into my room.

Nova was a strange one in her own right, starting with her name and nicknames. I didn't think being named after a month was particularly common in any culture, but the mother of the Solis family had named her daughter after her favorite. Noviembre, or even "November", which she sometimes got from schoolteachers or others who couldn't handle a bit of Spanish pronunciation, was still a bit of a mouthful for her siblings and friends, and while she was still quite young she earned herself two shorter versions that had stuck with her ever since. First, she had wanted to point out every item of interest to anyone near her, and when people told her, in Spanish, that they had seen it or often hadn't ("No vi!"), an abbreviated form of her name became her nickname. Also while she was still a little girl, she stubbornly wanted to stay home with her ailing father instead of going anywhere her mother, aunts, or uncles wanted to take her, and in repeating multiple times that she didn't want to go ("No va!"), her aunts and uncles took to calling her that. That one caught on more with some of her school friends, and when I was particularly pleased with something she'd done she even became "SuperNova". If she was ever bothered by the nicknames she didn't show it; I'd never once heard her insist that anyone call her by her proper name.

After opening the envelope and removing her letter I flopped onto my bed to read it, propped on my elbows with my feet crossed above me.

Dear Maria,
  Así se va:

That's how all of our letters started. "So it goes" (or "así se va" as Nova translated it) was most of the title and a repeated lyric from a Billy Joel song about sad romance. I had started using it early in our letter writing because of Nova's preoccupation with boys.

She'd responded in kind, with those few words written in Spanish, when she'd written her next letter back. I didn't have to explain where the words came from; she knew. She certainly knew that I was making fun of her a bit by using them, but Nova was the sort of person that accepted herself and wasn't injured by some good-natured ribbing from a friend, even when laced with a bit of truth that might have cut another person more deeply.

One of the last lyrics of the song was, "and you can have this heart to break." I'd never known that kind of heartbreak myself, and I knew I never wanted to—if I was going to know true love, I wasn't going to let it go—but the sentiment seemed powerful to me, and in any event, repeating it was tradition now for us, and we would probably keep using it even when she got back and we were no longer writing letters to each other.

The first part of her letter mentioned recent touring she'd done. Apparently the Matterhorn, or Mont Cervin, as the French-speaking Swiss people called it, was a lot cooler than one would be led to believe by visiting amusement parks. She had a trip across Lake Geneva (Lac Léman) to Italy, even though she didn't care for boats. Then, naturally, the topic changed to boys:

The man in the picture I sent is someone I might date. He's cute, right? I met him because he's Aline's brother's friend, I think. We waited in a long line together for a movie. I thought maybe I talked too much but Aline said it's okay because I'm American and they expect that. I might try to get stuck waiting in a line again with him.

Most of the guys here aren't that cute, though. Maybe it's their clothing? Maybe they're just too European for an East Washington chica like me. I'll leave them for the girls from Seattle.
I still can't believe you aren't dating anyone! I don't know why the men don't ask you out more often. A babe like you could have four boyfriends at once. I'm surprised you're not dating more than one guy right now! Just killing! I know you're cautious with boys, but someday you need to find a good-looking guy. You must be torturing all the boys right now, but I also don't think you should rush things.

"Just killing" was a way of having fun with our Swiss pal. Aline had used it many times before finally learning that the Ls were supposed to be Ds. We always thought it was cute, but she ended up being upset with us that we hadn't corrected her sooner. Nova and I didn't want to tease her, so we'd stopped saying anything about it in front of her, but between the two of us we still brought it up sometimes.

The boy in the photograph Nova had included was cute in a way, but probably not my type. More power to her, though, if she liked him. As for myself, I knew I wasn't torturing any boys, and I was okay with that. I strongly shared her sentiment about not rushing things.

Anyway, I've got more adventures tomorrow. I'll chat you later!

Noviembre

I could all but hear her voice with her over-pronounced but very American-sounding Rs during that last line. Nova just had her unique ways of saying things.

P.S. My time here is almost up! I'll be home coming home soon. This might be my last letter. I'll make sure to send a postcard before I fly home. We'll have a race to your house. Say hi to Hansen.

I put the letter back in its envelope and then into place on my short stack of her previous letters.

Sometimes I hurried to write back, but not tonight. It wasn't the late hour—that never stopped me from reading or writing when I was on a roll—but rather just an impression I had, a sort of inner sensation. As I became aware of it, I had a hard time identifying it exactly. I was too relaxed to be anxious, and too calm to be excited, but only barely; it was almost like a premonition, or at least anticipation, of something coming. The thought of something interesting about to happen, even if I couldn't put my finger on it or even guess much at what it might be, made me think that I should wait a bit before sending word back to Nova, just in case I had bigger news soon. I could pay more for faster delivery if her travel day was getting too close.

I lay in bed wondering for a little while, with varying thoughts about events from the last several days. I gradually became more and more sleepy, and I couldn't remember where my thoughts had last fallen and gone still when I dropped into a heavy sleep for the night.

2

As we get older and the world changes around us, we grow quiet.

Some places, like bookstores, are supposed to be quiet, but the world as a whole is so much noisier than it used to be. Or it seemed that way to me. We get caught up in the noise too, but older folk grow weary of it and become quieter and quieter with time. I was still young, but being attached to books made me feel old sometimes. Books—relics of the past that had shaped civilization but were fading into obsolescence—no matter what new devices came along, I knew I would never give up regular books. I had hope that there were enough others like me out there who would also keep their printed treasures long after the newest generations forgot the feel and the smell of printed paper. As we read them, we'd all be quiet together and let the noisy world rush on by.

I was quiet all during the next day; in hindsight, I felt like a storm was on its way, though I didn't identify the feeling quite as such at the time. While in the moment, I simply noticed that I was hushed, and meditative. Something had started within me the day before, like a hot coal smoldering without a flame. I had sensed when it began, and I knew it had something to do with either that boy or the book he had purchased. (Though I wasn't going to fully admit it to myself, I wanted it to be the boy, but the thought embarrassed me too much and so I tried to attribute it to the book.)

To begin, I was reserved during breakfast, cutting my speech well below even my father's normal conversational pace, though it could have been easily overlooked because my mother was almost chatty enough for the three of us. Eventually she asked if something was wrong, to which I responded, "Oh, no, nothing; I'm just pensive." And then I went back to saying basically nothing. My thoughts strayed to many places throughout the day, touching mostly on memories that didn't seem to be connected—my dad teaching me about weapons, a visit from one of his friends, the time I found a special flower to place in my diary—nothing that seemed immediately relevant. If my father noticed my unusual quietness, and I can't help but assume that he did, he didn't say anything to me about it.

Partially to distract myself, I began writing a resume. I soon found that I didn't know what I was doing. I'd seen resumes before, but I just couldn't quite get a feel for how mine was supposed to work. I finally decided that, not knowing if I would even need the resume, I shouldn't worry about it for the moment. Later in the day I could pick up the job hunt by looking for places in town that were hiring.

I spent the rest of my morning outside tending to our gardens, which was an unusual activity for me but which afforded me some privacy and further opportunity for reflection. I was a bit careless as I worked, but I was too distracted to worry about several instances of improper pruning or what the groundskeeper would think of them later.

At one point, as I was moving about the gardens seeking plants that needed trimming, I passed close to the northern border of my father's property, and Hansen called out to me through a break in the hedges where a gate sat. Hansen was a neighbor my age that I had known for many years, and who had become a reliable friend. At times I thought the brawny, sandy-haired, and freckled "Handsome" was good looking in a careless, shaggy sort of way. For a friend. Today I responded to his greeting with a surprised, "Oh, hi!" after which I moved on and ignored him in order to return to my own ponderings, taking no more than a second to hope I wasn't being rude. He'd probably be irritated at me, but he was too good of a friend to be truly offended.

As it happened, he was too persistent to let me get away with that. He hustled to the gate, which he opened before calling over to me. "Trimming hedges today?"

I just shrugged and smiled.

"How you feelin'?" he asked.

"Contemplative."

"I like talkative better. Maybe because I'm more used to it recently."

I shrugged again.

"Okay, so, whatcha thinkin' about?"

A pair of blue eyes came to mind. "Books," I answered.

This earned me a surprised look from Hansen. "Yeah, I completely space out thinking about books all the time."

I stuck my tongue out, but then smiled and clipped another small branch.

He laughed; I didn't need to look at him to envision his good-natured grin. He was one of the few people I was close to, and I figured I knew him as well as anyone. He started walking back into his own yard. "When you float back down to Earth, let me know."

I called out to him. "I'm not spacing out!"

He leaned back over the gate to smile and wink at me before disappearing behind the hedges again, securing the gate on his way out.

Later, my mother almost overcame the silence; at lunch she succeeded for about ten minutes in engaging me in a discussion about some of my favorite music and lyrics, but the wave of conversation passed, and I became introspective again as I washed my dishes. Each time I broke the silence and re-entered it, it became more profound.

In the afternoon I wandered the halls of my father's house noiselessly, pacing slowly so as to make no sound with my feet. My *father's* house—it was always my father's house, not mine. For some reason I could never identify it as mine or as my mother's. It was the age of the house—despite my feelings of personal maturity I knew he was far more suited to the house than either of us. Not that we were uncomfortable; on the contrary, it was entirely comfortable for us, but we always felt more like guests, like we were staying in a grand hotel (where we still had to wash our own bed sheets).

Here a drape of cloth muffled ambient sounds, there an old suit of armor challenged my silence with a quietness of its own; it made me feel almost as if my very motion of walking was causing offense against some rule of the house. Tables and vases provided more instances of inert presence; paintings with peaceful scenes contributed to the stillness.

Yet, other paintings brought energy to the atmosphere. If I ever needed something to highlight the difference between my mother's happy hobby and true art, there were numerous examples in the house. One in particular caught my eye this evening. In my meanderings I came to a tall painting that I had seen many times before but with which I had never spent much time. On this day, the instant I glanced over at it, it gripped and held my attention.

I halted mid-stride and then stepped back to regard it.

Depicted in it were various figures, some heroic but most demonic, and all of them quite small except for two. Central amid the skirmishing creatures and people stood one warrior, clad in chain mail and wielding a bright sword, who cast his regard up beyond the fray around him to a massive figure in the sky, whose face was scarcely visible save for the eyes—eyes which burned a crimson red outline around malevolent blackness. The form of this gargantuan fiend was indistinct; at once it appeared to resemble the folds of a great, dark cloak while extending outward into dragon-like claws and a tail. The warrior looked upward without fear or hesitation in spite of the hellish apparition before him, and in spite of the grave wounds his comrades suffered on either side. Somehow I imagined that he was neither ignorant nor uncaring of the carnage inflicted on his companions, but that he simply knew they were all willing to make any sacrifice necessary to combat the evil they faced.

As inscribed on a small plaque, the painting was titled, "The Final Struggle of Viorel". My father had once given me a brief explanation; Viorel was the man with the bright sword.

I was captivated for a moment, seeing the demons as more evil than I ever had before. For several seconds I couldn't look away from the burning voids that were the demon's eyes. I wondered why the artist had chosen to depict this moment when some noble man had chosen to fight a monster but suffered defeat at its hands, or claws, or whatever it had. I had always taken it as mere fantasy, but as I considered it again the image seemed vastly more real than it ever had before. Not that I had a problem believing in fantastic creatures—with a background like mine, I had to have an open mind—but I had always taken it for granted that this work of art was merely that and nothing more— just art.

I was aware that very few people in the world had seen this painting. I didn't feel particularly privileged. I understood my father wanting to keep some things—many things, even—to himself. The feeling changed inside me, though, as I looked on, to make me think that there was some key here in this "Final Struggle", something that was important for me to see…something that was clearly there but which I hadn't seen before, possibly because I had not been ready…something that would tip a balance… something so significant that my life might depend on it.

I scrutinized the painting, trying to find that key. It eluded me for quite some time as I inspected the depicted beings. Scrutiny provided the same deduction as my initial glance; the answer was not in the smaller battling creatures. As I regarded one falling warrior after another and finally came back to the stalwart Viorel, who was bound to fall as well, I came to the obvious conclusion: sometimes the monster wins.

At that moment, when the alarming idea struck me, I was also overcome with a feeling of being watched. I spun on my right toe, expecting to see my father as I came around, but the hall was empty. The feeling didn't make sense: I was wary, but without any evident cause. It took a moment to convince myself that no one else was present, though eventually I accepted it. All the same, I held my peace for a long while, searching out the empty corners of the hallway with my eyes.

The discomfort remained. With the painting at my back, I now felt almost as if the demon was watching me, and, peering out of the corner of my eye I was tempted to turn and verify that the painting hadn't somehow changed, but instead I abruptly stepped forward and strode down the hall.

Eventually coming to my own room, I entered, taking comfort in the confines of my own sanctuary. But I didn't throw myself onto my plush bed as I otherwise might do upon reentering. A flicker of a thought lingered in me, and I wanted to learn more. I wanted to learn more about mythical creatures and the people who fought them—not just Viorel, but the long line of combatant heroes who battled sinister and shadowy forces. Then again, it was more than that—instead of learning the stories of the heroes, perhaps I was even more curious about the monsters. I wanted to know of their power, their evil…I wanted to learn about all of them.

Checking the time even though I knew it was late in the afternoon, I made a quick decision and threw on my backpack and walking shoes, then made my way speedily from my room to the front door of the house without announcing my departure to anyone. The world felt alive as I rushed out the door and along the long walkway toward the front gate.

I was going to buy a book.

2.1

The walk to the bookstore from my house only took about fifteen minutes, but after arriving I spent another twenty searching around before admitting to myself that I couldn't find the book on the shelves and eventually walking back to the front of the store. A tall, thin man with short but wavy hair stood behind the counter today. "Excuse me," I called as I approached him. "Can you help me find a book?"

He smiled, mostly just on one side. "Indubitably. I can help you find lots of books. But if you have a particular title in mind..."

I clasped my hands lightly. "Drake's *Demons and Dark Essences.*"

"*Drakes, Demons, and Dark Essences,*" he repeated dramatically.

"Sorry. Drake was the name of the author; the title is just *Demons and Dark Essences.*"

He paused for a second before turning to his computer. After typing the title into his system and hitting Enter, he studied the screen briefly, typed something again, hit Enter again, and furrowed his eyebrows. He glanced up. "What was the author's full name?"

"Just Drake. That's all I know."

He typed again, and examining the result, made a quiet, "Hmm-mm." He typed yet again, then turned the screen toward me so I could see it more easily. "You're sure this is the exact title?"

I verified what he had typed, and nodded. I had no doubts about the title; I had excellent vision and had seen the book clearly.

He used his computer mouse to click "Search", and I watched various results populate a list.

Dark Shadows...Demons of the Heart... Dungeons and Dragons...many of the books that were listed had similar words, but what I was looking for wasn't there. "I don't see it," I said.

"It looks like if it *was* in print, it's not anymore."

"No, someone bought a copy here just yesterday."

"I don't think so. If it's not in our system, we wouldn't even be able to order it."

Curious. Curious and vexing.

I trusted the employee to know his business, but I had a good memory, and I couldn't make sense of this. Conveniently, just at that moment, the woman who had been behind the counter the previous day entered the building. "Hi, Steven," she called. "I think I left my wallet here last night."

"Excuse me, ma'am," I said, walking toward her. She stopped and regarded me. "I was here yesterday, and I saw a boy buying a book and I was hoping you could help me find it."

"It's not in the system," Steven offered before she could answer. "I already checked."

"Well," the woman replied, "I'm on my own time right now, but what was it you're looking for?"

"*Demons and Dark Essences*, by someone named Drake. It was leather-bound."

She shook her head. "I remember seeing that book—very old-looking. He didn't buy that here. He carried it in with him. He was actually looking at our selection of dictionaries, but I guess nothing we had was good enough."

When I didn't respond after several seconds, she turned back to her co-worker. I felt embarrassed for not speaking to her, and said, "Thank you anyway." She smiled at me and continued on to rummage around behind the counter. I took one more vague, futile glance toward the bookshelves as the woman found what she was searching for and left, and then I departed also.

Just outside the bookstore, I nearly ran into a poorly-groomed young man I thought I knew from high school. Stepping back to avoid bumping into me, he eyeballed me, down and up, then said, "Whoa. Hey, girl. How you doin'?"

Then I noticed his t-shirt. It was black with bold white lettering that read, "FBI: FEMALE BODY INVESTIGATOR".

I rolled my eyes and held up one hand to ward off any potential advance, then glared at him straight in the eye as I spoke back. "Your shirt broadcasts the message, 'I'm a jerk' about ten times as well as a shirt that actually said, 'I'm a jerk.' It's boorish."

Then I walked away swiftly while he was figuring out how to respond. As I marched on, I wondered if I'd been too rude, but he'd started it and I had no patience for that sort of thing. Even with the distance I kept from most people I'd already had too much of that sort of attention in my teenage life.

As I walked home I remained unsatisfied, but at the same time the book was more interesting now; the fact it was unattainable for the moment made it even more intriguing. I was impatient to seek it out. I walked at a brisk pace even though I wasn't really in a rush to get anywhere.

Back at my father's house, in my bedroom, I lay on my bed for a few minutes with my hands behind my head, but didn't stay there long before standing again. I felt defeated, and I didn't like that. I left my room, crossed the house, and found my mother sitting silently in the greatroom. "Hi, Mom," I said as I entered. "Where would I go to find a really old book?"

"Have you tried the library?"

That's what mothers are for. With anyone else I might have been embarrassed by asking a question that merited such a simple answer, but here I just smiled, and was about to rush out the door when I started actually paying attention to the expression on my mother's face. She seemed uneasy. "Is everything okay, Mom?"

"I think so." She looked forward again, away from me. "Luc is away." "Luc", pronounced like "Luke", was an abbreviation of my father's name. I followed her gaze to the corner, where I now noticed something highly unusual. My father's traveling gear, including an old-fashioned cloak and pair of boots, were missing from their display. "He must have left while I was running an errand. It's odd for him to go away in the evening like this."

"Um, did he say anything before leaving?"

My mother shook her head without looking my way.

"Did he leave a note?"

"No."

This was indeed unusual. "Are you worried about him?"

"No, no, he knows how to take care of himself, but I feel...strange. A bit cold—a little bit empty."

I wasn't sure what to say. It took me a moment to come up with words I thought might be sufficient. "I'm sure he's fine, Mom. He'll probably be back in just a little while."

She looked at me, then away again and nodded. "Yes. Probably not very long."

The way she said it, distantly, and the way she sat still in her chair made it clear to me that it was weighing on her. "Well, he's not in any danger. You know that. I'm sure he's fine."

She nodded again.

If my father was gone, we could only wait for his return or some sort of communication from him. Having nothing else to do about it, I decided to get back to my own business. It occurred to me that even if I didn't want to ask my father about the book directly, I should have asked him for permission to examine his personal collection, just in case he happened to have a copy of it. It was probably unlikely, but I should have checked while I could.

I started to turn back toward the entrance. "I'm going to hurry to the library before it closes."

"Be safe."

Before stepping out, I again contemplated the bare display in the corner. My father had used his traveling gear only rarely, and had never worn it for an outing in any place so near as the city. His traveling gear was intended for *traveling*. He might not be coming home for quite some time...

2.2

Dodge!

I had to leap forward in the darkness and roll on the sidewalk to avoid being hit by a figure flying toward me with outstretched arms. I moved in time; whoever it was struck the fence post next to the sidewalk with some force and seemed to be momentarily stunned.

I turned over into a sitting position to get a view of my aggressor, and took a good look at the grey body in front of me. I'd never been particularly tall, but it was smaller than I was, or at least shorter; with my keen night vision I could see clearly that it was malformed and possibly not even human. The thing snarled, and when it turned its head toward me I recoiled at the sight of the crooked fangs and distorted features.

A shock of fright ran through my heart; seconds ago it had been a normal night on a normal city street, but now I felt a silent alarm sounding within me, a wordless signal that my world had just changed forever.

I had little time to wonder what the thing was before it attacked again; with an angry cry it lurched down toward me.

But my surprise wasn't so great that I couldn't react.

I kicked out, landing my foot squarely on the thing's face. The impact jolted me, but my attacker reeled backward, clawed hands cupping its nose. I rolled backward over one shoulder on the sidewalk, coming to a crouching position. Slipping my left hand down to my boot, I felt for my only weapon—a dagger my father had given me two years before. Reassured by its presence, I withdrew it and curled it behind my hand as I moved my arm behind me. I raised my right arm in a defensive gesture.

The beast in front of me now slowly advanced with an open-mouthed frown and claws raised in front of its face. I stared into its black eyes, trying in vain to discern if it was intelligent and what it intended to do with me.

It advanced one step, then another, shifting a bit to each side as it did. I matched its first two steps, then held my ground.

It stepped forward once, quickly, and grunted when it saw me flinch. It began to breathe more heavily, and took two more steps. Then, faster than I had anticipated, it lashed out with its left claw.

I reacted without thinking; the beast seemed frozen with confusion as my right hand caught its wrist and held its claw suspended in the air. I didn't let the fleeting pause pass unused; taking advantage of the beast's stupor, I lifted its arm slightly and lashed out with my dagger, bringing the blade across its exposed chest, then spinning fully around to follow through with the cut and facing the creature again, having released its claw as I spun.

With a howl it pulled backward and stumbled away, clutching at its cut chest. I now raised the dagger high and took two quick steps toward it, much as it had done toward me before. I bared my teeth, hoping that the sharpness of my canines, however minimal, would be apparent.

The beast seemed to see the gesture, and it retreated slightly before suddenly turning and loping away on all four limbs.

Watching it flee, I wondered briefly if I could outrun it. I doubted it. I was also pretty sure that I didn't want to follow it anyway; in fact, I was quite sure that I didn't want to be anywhere near the thing.

I stood for a minute longer, trying to help my heart rate drop by taking intentionally long breaths.

The fairly cool June night would have otherwise been quite comfortable, but I felt hot. I lowered the dagger to observe a thin line of dark liquid along the edge. A single drop fell to the sidewalk. The color wasn't quite a reddish hue, but closer to purple or black. I felt strange, seeing the inhuman blood and being a bit repulsed by it. I wiped the blade on some nearby grass. Then, seeing that it wasn't clean enough, I found a bit of the inside of my jacket that I didn't think would ever be normally visible and wiped the blade again there, hoping but unsure that the stain would wash out, though at the moment it was hard to care much.

I stared at the dagger for a moment longer. This was the first time I had ever used it in combat, and the first time I had ever been in a real fight of any kind at all. It seemed like no time had passed. The encounter had been so brief that I wasn't sure what to think. Maybe I had watched too many movies; I expected fights to be long and drawn out.

I replaced the dagger in my boot sheath and stood again, still peering down the street where the creature had disappeared.

My first real fight had taken only seconds.

This was also the first time I had ever seen a supernatural creature—other than my father and me, of course, but I felt like we didn't count. We were so normal. We appeared mostly normal and acted mostly normal and it was easy to forget that we were part of a world most people believed was fictional. It was easy to share the spirit of their ignorance. So it was something of a shock to actually see a real monster.

I turned and continued down the street, not thinking much about where I was going but intent on moving on. After taking several steps I stopped again, and once again stared back.

Where had that thing come from?

Why was it here? Why did it attack me?

Does this sort of thing happen all the time, and was it now just luck that I was the one to have a bad encounter? I doubted it. I didn't know why, but I felt that it was coming after me specifically.

What was that thing *doing* here?

Amid the shock and questions I at least had one reassuring thought: I'd handled myself well. I'd won.

But would I have to fight something like that again?

A light wind blew some of my hair across my face.

I heard a voice behind me. "Are you all right, milady?"

I turned and backpedaled at the sight of the young man with sharp blue eyes. I was partly startled because I hadn't noticed anyone else around before, partly flattered to be called "milady", but mostly surprised to see the same dark-haired boy I had seen in the bookstore. He wore a dark overcoat, but underneath it I saw a collared shirt and black vest much like he'd worn before. The fingers of a pair of gloves dangled from one of his coat pockets.

"You seem ill at ease," he said with a strangely soothing tone to his voice. He was standing closer to me than would normally be comfortable. I thought I smelled a fragrance, something he must have been wearing. It was nice...something between spicy and sweet, and almost earthy.

"I...I was just attacked by some...one."

He looked at me, then behind me. "Are you hurt?"

"No, I'm fine. I fought back, and he ran away."

He frowned slightly. "We should tell the police."

I shook my head. "No, that's okay; it won't be necessary."

He regarded me firmly and repeated, "We should tell the police."

I couldn't help but notice his eyes again. A dark blue, but a blue that glinted in the moonlight. I knew he was right, or would have been right under normal circumstances, but I was sure there was nothing the police could do about the creature that had attacked me. "I'll talk to them later. Right now I just want to sit down."

"Of course. I have a spot in mind. This way." He led me to a small restaurant that was nearby. I was impressed when he opened the door and held it for me before entering. He held a steady gaze on me as I walked past him, somehow entering my personal space without being intrusive. Maybe by keeping eye contact I was inviting him to stare. My mother had told me many times that she had been "simply spellbound" by my father's hair. She was wrong; eyes could be so much more mesmerizing.

No one greeted us immediately when we entered, but he led me to a table by a window, offering his hand to me as I took a seat. I had to look away a bit while our hands touched as I sat down, hoping that my cheeks weren't flushed.

"Would you like something to drink?"

I almost hurried to decline his offer, out of a habit of trying to be polite and independent. Instead, I thought about it for a moment, figuring that it might be helpful. "A hot chocolate would be very soothing."

I could see him raise an eyebrow just slightly, but without great delay he turned and approached a server. I didn't remember his hair being quite so long; I had always rather liked long hair on men when it was done well. This was surely because my father wore his in such a dignified way. While the boy spoke to the server I retrieved a small mirror from my jacket and checked my appearance.

It was suitable. I generally did well for myself, and my genetics seemed to render makeup mostly unnecessary. The makeup I'd applied earlier still seemed fine. I ran my fingers through my hair to smooth out a few frazzles that had shown up when I'd rolled on the ground.

When he returned I tried to look casual.

"Are you sure you're feeling quite all right?" He spoke comfortably, as if he could not only see but also sense somehow that I hadn't been harmed.

"Yes, I'm fine. Really. But if you please, I don't know your name."

He sat back. "My apologies; that's quite discourteous of me. My name is Bastian Greywall."

I offered my hand. "I'm Maria." I refrained from giving him my last name; he was cute, and he was being quite a gentleman, but I still didn't know much about him. One can't be too cautious, I felt, especially with people who read about demons.

In light of recent events, though, demons were not such a strange thing anymore.

He shook my hand across the table, standing and leaning forward just enough to keep the handshake from being awkward. "It's a pleasure to make your acquaintance, Maria." Instead of pumping my hand repeatedly he shook it once and held it for a couple of seconds. I withdrew my arm somewhat reluctantly when he released my hand. "I had been rather hoping for pleasant company this evening. To meet a beautiful woman like you is as much as I could have hoped for."

I wasn't used to receiving direct compliments from boys that weren't also immature and objectifying. I liked it. "Well, with the terrible company I'd just had, I'm glad you crossed my path."

"I'm similarly content. Delighted, in fact."

I hoped my curiosity wouldn't bother him. "Do you...do you always speak like that?" It almost reminded me of the way my father spoke.

His eyebrows raised. "Ah; not strictly, no." Suddenly I could hear a more normal, comfortable tone. "I like to be well-mannered. It's something I do to become more...refined. Am I making you uncomfortable?"

I laughed. "I'm fine. I just wondered if it was normal for you."

He smiled. "Well, it's more normal every day."

The server came with my hot cocoa and a similar mug for him. I tested it, found it to be not too hot, and took a sip. "Do you mind if I ask you a question?"

"Not at all." The formal tone to his voice crept back in. "Go ahead."

"What was that book you had in the bookstore the other day?"

He smiled again. This smile was a bit different; he was satisfied. "Ah, you remember me then. And you remember my book. It's something of a special interest."

"I'd say. Do you study demons often?"

He paused. "I study a lot of old things, actually. Are you at all familiar with my book?"

"No, but it caught my eye." I was having a hard time measuring his expression.

"I wouldn't expect you to know it. I don't believe there are many copies available." He took a sip of his own cocoa. "What about you? Do you take an interest in such things?"

I also took a drink before answering. "Yes. I mean, I don't want you to think I'm weird...but I guess you probably wouldn't."

He gave a short laugh. "I was concerned that *you* would be the one to find *me* strange."

Now I allowed myself to smile a bit. "Oh, I do, but I'm okay with strange."

"Good." He drank again. "Would you say you had a strong interest in my book?"

He was getting at something. "Yes, yes I would."

He shifted in his seat. "Well, if you're sure that you're quite well, then I suppose it's acceptable to speak of such things. I've...I've been doing some research, and part of my studies include investigating the contents of that book. I'm looking for research partners, but of course, given the subject matter it's not easy to find the right kind of people."

I didn't want to seem too excited, but something was drawing me to this boy and the book, and I was sure that the excitement showed. "I think I could make myself available for a bit of studying."

He set down his mug. "Excellent." After retrieving a pen from his vest, he began writing on the back of a small card. As he gave it to me I could see that he had written *Greywall Castle* and an address on it. His handwriting was elegant and crisp. Turning it over, I saw that the other side had his name printed on it in fancy gold lettering. "That's where I live."

A castle? Near here? I read the address again. "Your parents' place?"

His smile was almost a smirk. "I live alone."

"Oh," I said, pulling the card back with one hand. "I'm sorry. You sort of look too young for that."

"I am a ripe old twenty-four."

"Oh!" I was simultaneously surprised and mildly pleased by this news. He wasn't much older than I was (by some standards), but he had his own house. His own *castle*. I put the card in my jacket.

He leaned forward and placed clasped hands on the table. "Are you available tomorrow?"

That was sooner than I expected, but I was free all week. "Sure."

"Perhaps you could come by in the afternoon. Say, two o'clock?"

"Come by your house! Oh...well...I've only just met you, and if you live alone, I'm not sure I should be going to your house, or castle." Truthfully, after fighting off a brutish and unnatural creature I felt completely capable of taking care of myself, but it still struck me that it would normally be unwise to visit a stranger alone.

He looked surprised. "Surely, you don't th—no, you're right," he conceded. "It is just a bit abrupt. Perhaps you'd be more comfortable if we got to know each other a bit more first, and a day's wait won't hurt. You would accompany me for dinner tomorrow evening, then?"

Dinner! I didn't do this sort of thing often, but it was probably better than going straight to his house. "Okay."

"Eight o'clock?"

That sounded a little late for dinner, but in the summer the sun hadn't even gone down by then. "Sure. Do you have a place in mind?"

"How about Romano's?"

"The little Italian place by the old train cars?"

"That would be it."

"Okay. Romano's at eight. I think I can do that."

He stood. "Good. Then if you are quite well, Miss Maria, I will be on my way, and I shall await your arrival tomorrow."

"I'll be there."

He nodded, and I waved lightly. He walked over to the server, spoke briefly, and then exited the restaurant without looking back.

I was left with somewhat mixed feelings. I certainly liked this boy—this man—but everything was happening so strangely. Two days before I'd been having a normal summer, and now in rapid succession I was dealing with a compellingly mysterious book, a supernatural attacker, and a polite and appealing young man. I could still feel the excitement of the fight, and I felt strong and capable, but a sense of uncertainty remained in me.

I suddenly wished I could talk to my dad about it, and remembered that he was gone.

After a last sip from my mug I stood and looked inquiringly at the server.

"He covered it," he said to me with a sideways nod toward the door, correctly gauging my questioning expression.

"Thank you," I said back, and I retrieved a bit of money to leave as a tip. After setting it on the table, I left.

What kind of person carries calling cards like that? Not a business card; a calling card. And what kind of person that young—even if he's not as young as he appears—owns his own castle? I supposed I would find out.

As I stepped outside, I was just a little bit irritated. *He might have at least escorted me home,* I thought. Was I already starting to feel a sense of connection to this boy, a sense of ownership? Strange...but not unpleasant. Anyway, I was by myself now. I no longer needed to go to the library. I also didn't want to go back the way I came; choosing a detour, I made my way back to my father's house.

Back at home, as I walked through the halls I passed by my father's library, and I paused at the doorway. Oddly, I hadn't thought of investigating the back chamber. There were rooms in my father's house that were rarely opened, and the back chamber of the library was one of them. I'd had a glimpse of the room before; the books inside were much older-looking than the others in the larger main library. I supposed it was possible that my father had a copy of the very same book. I didn't bother to investigate the possibility of checking that at the moment, though; I didn't have his key, and at this point I had another option that included a personal guide through the text.

I continued on to my room, but met my mother in the hall. "Did you have a nice time at the library?" she asked.

"Oh, right, actually, no, I didn't end up going to the library. I stopped at a restaurant for cocoa instead. I met a nice boy."

She arched an eyebrow. "At this time of night? What's his name?"

"Bastian. Bastian Greywall." I hoped my voice didn't sound wistful as I spoke his name. "It turns out that he has the book I was looking for at his home. It's very convenient. I'll probably go over sometime to see it." I pulled out his card and showed it to her.

She seemed both puzzled an impressed. "Greywall Castle? I've heard of it. His family must be quite wealthy."

"I guess so." I was uncomfortable saying that he lived there alone, given that I'd already said I'd be visiting him. "He seemed to be well brought-up."

She squinted at the calling card. "What's this book about again?"

"History." Hmmm…now I was clearly misleading her, and even though it seemed innocuous I was starting to feel guilty all the same. When she looked back at me without saying anything, I offered up a little more. "Well, history and legend. I guess I'm interested in the stories."

"How old is this boy?"

"Oh, about my age…just a little older."

"Is he someone I can trust with my daughter?"

"Yes, mother, he was actually very polite."

She folded her arms and frowned. "That doesn't reassure me much. I've seen it plenty of times before. A lot of men out there act like perfect gentlemen while setting the hook, but inside they're really swine."

"Mom, I'm not a fish, and Bastian isn't a pig. Really. We spoke and he's really a nice person. I appreciate both your concern and the mixed metaphor, but if he wanted to take advantage of me he could have already tried."

She raised one eyebrow and gazed hard at me for a moment. "Maria, I honestly do want to trust your judgment. It's just hard for my little girl to not be so little any more. I don't want to try to shield you from all the young men out there, and I don't want to assume that this particular young man is one of the swine. Just be guarded with how you cast your pearls."

"What does that mean?"

"It's a biblical reference."

"I caught that, but I still don't know what you're saying."

"Maria, you're a beautiful young woman. You're very pretty, if I may say so as your biased mother, but what you have within you is much more important. And at some point you'll gain a real affection for some young fellow, but there are all sorts of people out there, and while some would treat your affection as something special, others would trample it like the pearls under the proverbial swine's feet, and use you for their own petty wants."

"Mom, you're making a big deal out of this. It's just a study session."

"Okay, I'm sorry. I'll try to suppress my fear of you growing up. It's still good advice, though, so remember it: guard those pearls fiercely."

I had to laugh. "Okay, Mom, I will."

She handed the card back to me. "Good."

I thought I could detect a bit more cheer than I had seen earlier. "You seem to be in a better mood."

"Mmmm, yes, well, I don't like your father being away, but you know him—his perpetual sense of purpose leaves little room for doubt. He's so strong. I'll be glad when he returns, though."

"You don't think you'll hear from him before then?"

"I don't think so." She sighed. "I hope he comes home soon."

"Me, too." I kissed my mother on the cheek and went on to my room.

As I got ready to go to sleep I brushed my hair for several minutes, and my new acquaintance's name ran through my mind. Bastian. I had never met anyone else with that name. I'd never met anyone like him, either in appearance or in the way he struck me. He had a sort of familiarity to him, as if I'd known him sometime in the past, though I was certain I'd never met him before. Still, he was different in some indefinable way.

Well, "Miss Maria", I thought to myself, *we mustn't make too much of all of this. Plenty of girls out there have thought they've met Mr. Perfect and then gotten burned.* He was courteous, though. That counted well for him.

What an interesting young man. I'd find out more about him tomorrow.

2.3

"Miss Maria!" Bastian's voice called from off to my right.
I'd spent the day feigning an attempt to investigate
employment opportunities. It was less out of a desire to follow
my father's counsel and more because I was impatient and
wanted to distract myself with something. Now that this
charming new young man and his intriguing book were available
to me, I was perturbed with myself for delaying. But I had no
way of contacting him other than simply showing up
unexpectedly at his doorstep, and that seemed far too brazen. So
I'd done what I could to focus on something else, and decided to
arrive early at Romano's, but then lost track of time for a while
when I was trying to find the right hair clip, and I ended up being
almost half an hour late.

Bastian was waiting outside the restaurant and called to me
before I entered. He carried what distinctly looked like a picnic
basket. He walked closer to me with the handles of the basket in
the crook of his left arm.

He wore a long-sleeved shirt again with the sleeves rolled up
to his elbows and a vest. On his head he wore a short-brimmed
fedora; the hat, vest, and his slacks were all in a matching shade
of dark blue that was almost charcoal grey. I wasn't sure if the
vest-and-hat combination gave him an appearance more like a
classic businessman or an old-time mobster, but either way it
gave him an air of being both sharp and sophisticated.

Then I had a distinct feeling that I had seen him just like this
before. It was an absurd thought—I had only met him for the
first time a day ago—but I couldn't deny that the image in front
of me felt like an echo from a long time ago. The clothes, the
hair, the eyes, the expression on his face...all of it.

I tried not to be too distracted by the odd notion. "Mr.
Greywall. Hello!"

With his free arm he waved off my greeting. "Please. Call
me Bastian. Don't worry about going inside. I thought an
evening picnic might be nice, so I ordered a few things to go."

"Oh!" I was a little embarrassed now and wished I'd been
timelier in my arrival. The idea of a picnic so late was odd, but
also kind of appealing, so maybe it would work out just fine.
"How nice! Where are we going to eat?"

"There's a park just down the road."

"Well, then, let's go."

He stepped forward and lifted his right elbow. It took me just a moment to realize that he intended to guide me with it. I found the gesture charming, and I happily let my fingers curl around his arm, finding a spot for them in the crook of his elbow. We began to walk toward the street and then along the sidewalk. It wasn't quite dark yet, but the moon was up, fading into the sky.

"Do you eat at Romano's often?" I asked.

"Not infrequently. It's one of the finer eating establishments in the vicinity. It's not necessarily the ambiance, but they have superior Italian food. What about you?"

"This'll be my first time. I know of the place, but I've never eaten there."

"Then I'm glad to introduce you to it. Do you enjoy Italian?"

"Sure, as long as there isn't much garlic. I like it meatier, heartier."

"My selection should be suitable, then."

We continued down the street without saying anything for a while. I was content to follow along, guided by my companion for the evening. I watched for any pair of eyes we passed that might be momentarily appreciating a handsome couple strolling along. I couldn't be too sure of myself, though I hoped I would be fetching in my peasant blouse and circle skirt.

The wind was strong today, if intermittent. It whipped my skirt annoyingly, and I was sure that my hair flipped against Bastian's face a couple of times with a few silver strands. "I hope the park is close."

"It is."

When the wind blew harder I released his arm and he held more steadily to the picnic basket. It died down again, but afterward it seemed awkward to reach for Bastian's arm again, so we only walked side by side for the short distance remaining to the park, turning down a side street along the way.

The park itself was small but pleasant with everything I might expect: trees, grass, a few tables, and swing sets off to one side. "Table, or grass?" Bastian asked.

"Grass."

He withdrew a thin blanket from the basket and spread it flat on the turf, then set the picnic basket down next to it and gestured for me to sit.

As I sat, he crouched and lifted the basket's lid again on one side, then propped it open. He set his hat next to the basket. "Romano's makes excellent sandwiches. Normally it's not what I would choose for dinner, but I hoped that you would find them delightful this evening."

"I'll eat a sandwich."

"I have a small assortment, but if you trust my judgment, you can try this one." He withdrew a small box and handed it to me. "It has prosciutto ham, a slice of apple, Brie, and some sort of sauce. I made sure they put on plenty of Brie."

I had some particular tastes in food, but nothing in that list sounded objectionable. "Sounds great."

"I'll go with the sausage. I find that they season it just right." He lifted a second box from the basket and set it on the blanket. He then got out a bottle, opened it, and poured some of its contents into a champagne flute, which he then held out toward me. "Sparkling cider?"

I suddenly felt embarrassed. "Oh, no, thank you. I'm not very thirsty." He looked disappointed. "Maybe later," I added with a smile. "I'll try the sandwich."

He gave a bemused grin, then sipped the flute once before setting it on the closed side of the basket.

I opened the box and inspected the sandwich inside. It looked delicious. Taking a bite, I found that it tasted even better. "Good choice," I said before I realized that I was talking with my mouth full. I covered my mouth as I swallowed. "Delectable."

"It's a favorite of mine." After setting his hat on the grass and sitting on the blanket he sampled some of his own food, then gazed skyward. "The wind has stopped, at least for now."

"I'm glad for that."

He looked back at me, and again I had the same strange impression as before, like I'd already seen this boy the same way I was seeing him now. I couldn't imagine why I would think so. It was unsettling in a way, and agreeably mysterious in another.

"So, the point of the evening was to acquaint ourselves with each other," he said. "Are you from this area?"

"I've lived here all of my life. Never wandered far from it."

"Oh? You seem like the type that would have traveled."

"Why do you say that?"

He paused, smiling. "I don't know."

"What about you?"

"My family has lived here for my whole life, but I've had some opportunity to see the world." He drank from the glass again. "Do you have siblings?"

"No," I said, swallowing before speaking again. "Just my parents."

"What does your father do for work?"

"He's a businessman. He's done quite a bit, actually; no single enterprise or venture. I think he only owns most of his businesses these days, but has other people manage them. He's done quite well for himself over the years."

"What about your mother?"

"She raised me, and keeps herself busy with hobbies. She used to be a hairdresser, but she never cared for steady employment outside of the home."

"She's happy to let your father bring in all of the family's income?"

"Oh, yes. She had plenty to do at home, though." I sat up straight and turned to show my profile. "Producing a fine member of society like myself is quite a full time job."

He made a soft noise; when I looked back at him he had a strange expression on his face.

"What is it?"

"Just a bit of déjà vu. Do you ever get that?"

Other than twice in the last hour? "...Sometimes."

He chewed a bite of his sandwich. "You know, you're not what I...what I would expect."

"Oh? And what would you expect?"

He chuckled gently and took another drink of cider. "You really should have some of this. I guarantee it's better than any you've had before."

"I believe you. I'm sorry; I'm not thirsty."

"Suit yourself." He emptied the glass. "Could I meet your father?"

"Of course!" Then I remembered. "When he gets back. He's away." Bastian nodded. I was about to ask about his parents but he spoke again first. "What are your hobbies?"

"Oh. Reading, music, and fencing are my top three."

"Swords, or chain-link?"

I laughed. "Swords. My father is sort of an expert in old weapons, and he got me started."

"Fascinating. Do you mean listening to music, or making it?"

"Mostly listening. I don't have my father's skill with instruments. I've been told I have a nice voice, but I don't have any real hope of being a gifted musical artist. I think I've learned combat from my father pretty well, though."

"Not just fencing?"

"A little bit of hand-to-hand combat also. A little. Mostly just fencing. I doubt there's any weapon in history that my father doesn't know how to use."

"Sounds violent."

"Oh, not at all. I mean, he knows a lot about fighting, but don't think of him as violent. He certainly doesn't want any violence in his life." I tried to sound playful as I asked, "Will you let me finish my sandwich already?"

Bastian nodded and obliged me, taking a bite of his sandwich also. We took a couple of minutes just to eat; he stared into the distance, contemplating something I couldn't know, and I watched him, curious about him and hoping the sound of my eating wasn't too awkward but also thoroughly enjoying my food. He'd chosen well.

"Would you like to try another?" he asked, seeing that I was finishing.

"No, this was great—worth coming back for. Thank you." An idea occurred to me. "Let's take a different route back."

He sipped from his flute again, then set it down and stood up. "That means a longer route. It's getting dark, but where do you want to go?"

The sun was down now. "Dark is fine." I also stood and glanced behind me. "Let's just choose a direction and walk for a bit."

"Lead the way."

"What about the picnic basket?" I asked.

He shrugged. "I'll pick it up later."

"Okay. Come on."

Instead of following the road, I chose a different walkway out of the park. When we hit another road, I motioned for Bastian to continue along the sidewalk. "So what about you? What are your hobbies?"

"*My* hobbies? Like you, I also like reading and I enjoy some music, but I confess that I know basically nothing about combat. So I won't be challenging you to a duel any time soon."

I smiled.

"I enjoy theater, and have thoroughly delighted in learning that art, and in an informal sort of way I study people. I like to figure out how they work."

"Huh. You've had a few minutes; how do I work?"

"Oh, you're more complex than I anticipated, but I'll be happy to take more time to discover that."

I felt myself blushing. Although I'd never thought of myself as particularly complex, I liked that he'd said that about me. More time—I could handle that. Wouldn't it be nice to have someone figure me out...

He was right in what he'd said before, though; it was getting dark. One of my mother's sayings came to mind: "Good judgment goes to bed with the sun." I didn't want to ignore that echo in the back of my mind, but I didn't plan to be out too much later.

We approached a large yard bordered by an ornate metal fence. Many gravestones beyond were visible in the moonlight. We both peered into the graveyard as we passed by quietly. We came to an entrance road and an open gate, where I turned and took a few steps beyond the fence line before stopping to regard nearby headstones. I was sad that we only had a crescent moon, and that the markers were illuminated mostly by the yellow street lights. I had a memory of light from a full moon reflecting off gravestones in some other cemetery in an almost pretty way, and I wished it were so right now.

Bastian stepped up next to me. "You like cemeteries?"

"No...not really...well, in a way I guess I do, because they're peaceful places dedicated to honoring and respecting people, but I never thought about that until now. Before you asked, I was just thinking that death hasn't ever been part of my life."

"You feel like you'll never die?"

"No, it's more that I feel like no one will ever die. I know it's not true, but so far people around me tend not to die. It gives me a weird feeling, like I have a hope that seems real but I know it can't be."

"None of your extended family members or your friends have died?"

"I don't really have many extended family members, but no, I've just never had to deal with it." We looked out over the cemetery together.

"I'd say it's just as well," he said, "but unless somehow you go first, or go early, you'll end up seeing a lot of death."

That was kind of a downer. I'd been enjoying the moonlit scene until he said that.

Maybe he saw me frown. "Let's keep walking," he said. "Let's follow the driveway to the next gate."

"If you like." I stepped down the driveway and he followed.

I had to acknowledge that what he'd said was true, but I couldn't fathom how a friend or family member's death would impact my life. I tried to imagine what it would be like if my mother died…and I couldn't.

Gazing out at the gravestones not far away, I was struck by how some were similar, and some were quite different. They varied in shape, size, type of stone, and engravings, probably a lot like how people vary in many aspects, though I doubted that the headstone reflected much about the person whose body rested under it.

Not having known people who ended up in cemeteries, I'd also never spent much time in any. I had to acknowledge that I was unexpectedly comfortable among the low stones, small monuments, and occasional crosses.

After a short walk we exited the cemetery again. The gates, open at such a late hour, seemed to be just ornamental, even if not terribly lavish.

"Maybe it's silly of me," I admitted, "but when I first saw the cemetery I thought I'd see how you reacted to a late-night walk through it."

"We didn't go very far in, but did I pass the test?"

I pondered it while still walking. He had gone along with what I wanted even when it was a little weird. He was obliging. "Yeah. You passed."

"This route back to Romano's actually isn't much longer than what we took to the park. Our evening will shortly come to an end."

"They always do. I'm sleepy, so it's just as well."

"So next time, you'll meet me at my home, so we can really get down to business?"

I blinked before answering that. "Yes." I cleared my throat. "Old books about monsters. I'm up for it."

"Very good." A few paces later he stopped, looked upward, folded his arms, and said, "Do the stars please you?"

Again, the way he stood looked like it was in a picture I'd seen somewhere; I tried to keep my wits about me without being too distracted by the impression. "Why, did you order them just for me?"

He grinned. "No. I'm just asking about you."

I shrugged. "I guess I don't particularly like the stars. They're fine, but I suppose I just see them as background." We simultaneously started walking again. "With such pale skin, you probably don't have to ask whether I particularly like the sun."

"You think I have pale skin?"

"No, I meant me."

"Ah-hah. Actually, I normally favor dark skin, but yours is uncommonly pretty—like a porcelain doll, especially at night. I'd hoped it wouldn't be obvious that I've been admiring you, but to be frank, the tone of your skin in this light is eye-catching."

"Oh." I tried not to smile too blatantly.

"Your hair is also accented beautifully in the moonlight. Strikingly so."

I involuntarily added a little sashay to my step before catching myself. Not knowing how to respond to his compliments, I said nothing and focused on remembering the delightful words of the handsome young man next to me. There was a warmness in the air despite the night having cooled. I savored it as we strolled.

He suddenly stopped walking, and I saw that we were back at Romano's. "Miss Maria, it has been a pleasure."

"Mr. Greywall, thank you for a pleasant evening and again for the delicious food."

"It's okay if you call me by my first name."

"I know."

"You have a ride home?"

"I drove."

"All right. Then I bid you a good evening."

"You, too. I'll see you tomorrow."

He nodded. I turned and started back toward my car, glancing back once or twice on the way. Bastian waited for me to reach my car before leaving. I waved as I left, but I didn't think he saw it.

In my mirror it looked like another person approached Bastian's shrinking figure, but it was too dark and he was too far away to be sure. As late as it was, I worried for just a moment that someone might be assailing him, but I quickly dismissed my concerns. The movement was too slow to be an attack, and if he had been in trouble he could have run away.

It would have been nice if he'd offered to pick me up tomorrow, I thought. Still, I was excited just to go there.

A short drive later, I was back at my house. My mother met me just inside the door when I got home. "Did you have fun?"

"Yeah!" "Fun" wasn't the word I would have chosen, but it would do. The walk, the picnic…they were fun enough activities by themselves, but it was the company that had made the evening remarkable. Thinking back on the events of the evening was enchanting.

My mother was watching me with narrowed eyes, her head turned just slightly.

"What?" I asked.

"Nothing…" she replied, still staring.

It wasn't "nothing", but I didn't care to figure it out. "I'm going to have to take you to the restaurant we went to."

She raised her eyebrows. "Good food?"

"*Great* food. Did you wait up for me?"

"Of course I did. Not that I was overly worried, but you are my daughter and I take an interest in you, and my bed is lonely when your father is gone."

"Well, you didn't need to do that, but thanks. I'm tired. I'm going to get right to bed."

"There's nothing else you want to tell me?"

I was confused. "No…should there be?"

She sighed. "No, just asking. So, you'll see him again sometime soon, this—what was his name again?"

"Bastian. Yeah. Soon." I smiled as I saw him in my mind again. "I mean," I said, focusing on my mother again, "he has that book."

"Just keep your guard up."

"Mom, take it easy. You know you don't need to worry about me."

"Okay."

"I'm going to bed now."

"Me, too." She didn't leave until after I did.

I went to my room, lazily brushed my teeth, and got in pajamas. A quick bedtime prayer later and I was getting into bed recollecting the events of the evening. Maybe it was shallow of me, but my favorite part was when he had complimented my looks. I'd heard a few catcalls before, but they weren't like what I'd heard tonight. Compliments coming from Bastian were a completely different thing. I pictured him again in his hat, with his arms crossed, gazing up at the sky.

I could get used to compliments from him.

With that thought I lay down for what I was sure would be a peaceful night. My last waking thoughts were of Bastian.

2.4

Murky and sinister creatures were chasing me. I couldn't see them, but I knew they were there...I could feel them getting closer to me.

I ran down a deserted city road, weak and unable to distance myself from my pursuers. Side streets vanished into shadow. The lights near me faded, leaving only an ambient glow that grew dimmer with every sluggish step I took. Each door I passed was shut and unyielding; each window was dark. I searched for someone to help me, but found no one. I called out, but heard no answer or echo. The unseen things chasing me grabbed at my heels, at my arms, at my hair...I ran on and on, but they stayed with me, and their claws gripped my limbs. The claws were ghastly, rough, and inhuman. I turned and squirmed but couldn't get away.

As I twisted away from a fiendish grasp, I saw a hooded figure standing off to one side, motionless, watching. I couldn't see its face; it was lost in shadow, only perceptible in outlines of a brow, eyes, and a mouth. I called out for help and reached for it, but it did nothing, seeming to watch my distress dispassionately but almost with a scorn barely visible in the darkened features of its face.

I lunged this way and that, pushing away at shadows that seized me, and I began to run again. They pulled at me, and held me, but with a great effort I spun on them and pushed away with all of my strength. As if a great wind had come, they raced away, outward and upward, farther and farther, though I felt that some still lingered around me. Where I stood I was visible as if in a spotlight, but all around me was dark, a swirling mass of smoky dimness. Various sets of hazily glowing eyes materialized to gaze on me from time to time before fading away again.

Then the hooded figure sat in front of me on an indistinct throne.

It spoke to me in a voice I couldn't understand. I waited, and it spoke again in a mysterious tongue. I stood cautiously still, but it beckoned me, then rested motionlessly as I slowly approached. When I halted before it, it stood and then extended one closed hand as if to give me something.

I took another step forward to see what it held; as I looked closer, it reached with its other hand and took hold of my wrist in a rigid grip. I fell back to one knee to escape, but could not move or break away from its relentless hold. The figure held its open hand in front of me, palm up; wisps of tarry smoke churned above it as I watched. Without warning, black flames erupted, surrounding and engulfing me. I covered my face and head with my free arm in a futile attempt to shield myself. The flames also covered the hooded figure, who threw up its arms in agony, then fell to the ground, rolling and grasping. I also flailed but couldn't free myself from the blaze. Farther and farther away from me, the figure burned until it was no longer visible in the black fire.

"That was weird," I said to no one in particular as I opened my eyes.

I stared at the ceiling for a few minutes, enjoying the dimness and the comfort of my bedding. It seemed to be very early morning, and I must not have been resting well during the night, because I was still drowsy.

I had spoken aloud in a meager attempt to dispel the uneasiness brought on by my dream. I didn't want to remain in that lingering fearful atmosphere. I shouldn't feel that way in the place that was *mine*. Lifting only my head, I examined my room and found everything as I would expect it. Closing my eyes again, I turned and curled back into my pillow, then tried to think of nothing at all.

In just a few seconds, I felt myself fade back out.

I was in my palace. This was my home, where I had walked the halls and dined at feasts in a grand dining hall many times. I moved about swiftly, all but flying from one room to the next. I was happy. The carpets and tables were bright, and fireplaces glowed and brought me warmth. Now I walked; as I had done so many times before, I moved from the dining room to the throne room, up the tower stairs and to the top of a turret. Walking out into the warm, starlit night, I saw someone at the edge of the turret. I had never seen anyone here before, but he was as natural where he stood as anything else. I walked slowly toward him, and as he turned to me I saw the dark hair and deep blue eyes that I knew so well.

He reached out and caught my extended hands. "I've finally found you," he said in a whisper. Retaining my right hand in his left, he turned me and brought me back inside, where we entered the ballroom and he took my other hand, leading me about the floor and spinning me frequently to accent the steps of our dance. Then he spun me one final time and I twirled away slowly, looking up to a starlit sky...

Sunlight lifted my eyelids, bringing me back.

I could never make sense of my dreams. I'd heard other people say they took great meaning from their dreams and sometimes even based major life decisions on things they saw or otherwise experienced while sleeping. For myself, I rarely felt that any of my dreams corresponded much with reality, but what I'd just woken from was definitely one of those rare instances.

I would have expected to be frightened by the nightmare that came before, but while it was uncomfortable for me earlier, I didn't feel scared at the moment. I wasn't sure what it meant—if anything at all—and I didn't want to devote much imagination to trying to figure that out.

Instead I preferred to think about the second dream—the one that had a very real and very positive connection with events in my life. I was quite content to just picture Bastian in my mind. Of course there was more to him than his looks; aside from his appearance, he was both charming and intelligent. But he also had such intense blue eyes. I liked his hair, too—it made him look dark, strong, and even enigmatic. And there was something almost troublingly pleasing about the phrase he had spoken to me in the dream—as if for some long time I was what he had been searching out.

I sighed to myself. *Don't get carried away, now.*

I thought again about how he seemed familiar in a way that I had never noticed with anyone else. I felt as if it wasn't the first time I had seen his eyes and hair, and that it wasn't the first time I had spoken with him. I felt, inexplicably, as if I knew him from many years before.

I couldn't think of any other time when I'd woken up thinking about a boy. I'd known some that I liked, some that were cute, but this was entirely different. I stayed in bed for a while running scenarios through my mind about how our encounter might go, what sweet things he might say to me...

Then I began to feel nervous. I was going to meet him alone at his home! Sure, I was an adult now, barely, but it still felt like this would be a bad idea...normally...for most girls, anyway. He seemed like a wonderful guy, but the seclusion of a private home could be problematic. Out in the open, anyone would be hesitant to do something improper, given that many other eyes could be watching. But the privacy of a home was different, especially if he lived alone.

If I hadn't been confident in my ability to take care of myself without an escort I would have refused his offer. Such as things were, though, I figured I wouldn't have any problem even if he did try something bad, which I highly doubted would happen anyway. I exhaled and stood up out of bed, eager to get ready for the day. I made sure to brush my hair extra well.

3

Just as knowledge can only be gained one idea at a time, truth can often only be found in bits and pieces, hidden among translations, interpretations, and retellings. I'd always been fascinated by ancient myths that held obviously common threads, and wondered which culture's version of the story was more accurate. Invariably, most accounts, either old or new, contain a lot of inaccuracy or "enhancement" depending on the memory, honesty, perspective, and communicative ability of the person telling the tale. Thus, when attempting to see things as they truly are, or truly were, while looking through someone else's eyes, one has quite a difficult task of discernment.

I also often wondered which ancient culture provided the original tale. Sometimes it's easy to attribute a symbol to a given group that used it frequently, labeling later peoples as copycats, whereas the "original" group may well have taken those same symbols from someone else. Who could ascertain the true origin, and who could provide a certain meaning for the symbol? Those questions sometimes couldn't be answered with certainty. Ultimately, though, I didn't care too much who did the writing first as long as I could glean something from it.

The question now was what Bastian was hoping to glean from this book of his. I'd been so intrigued by him and the book itself that until I approached his home (the castle) I hadn't taken a moment to wonder why he was doing this research in the first place. I had to accept that among the things out there in the world that were considered mythical and supernatural, some had to exist (my father, for example, and the strange thing that had attacked me), and even the more exaggerated tales likely had their roots in truth—but how would a knowledge of such things serve the average person? Most people never encountered any "demons" or "dark essences". I hadn't, in any significant way, until yesterday. Had Bastian? What did he already know about such things?

Whatever he knew, I wanted to know also, and now I would have the opportunity. That thought gave some pep to my step as I walked to my car and later from my car to the front door of Greywall Castle.

The castle itself seemed a bit of an anomaly. It was clearly much older than anything nearby but neither truly hidden away in the city nor on display. It was simply there, another feature—an out-of-the-way place whose existence the locals likely acknowledged and mostly ignored. Behind it was an orchard, and in front of it another smaller but forested chunk of land mostly obscured it from vehicles passing by. I had to circle a bit at first to find the right place to enter the property with my car. It gave me a chance to appreciate the size of the estate; it was not so large as to make the building inaccessible, yet large enough to provide quite a bit of privacy.

The castle was large and built from dark stone. On my way over I'd passed another old castle, not distant from here. It was much smaller and had been converted into a flower shop. Though I didn't know its origin, the building's size was appropriate and the stone-block construction lent to a quirky old-fashioned vibe for the shop. This castle in front of me now, however, was built on an entirely different scale. As I approached the front door, I saw a vast wing of the castle stretching out to my left; behind and to the right of the main entrance an immense square tower rose up, with an angular red roof like that of the rest of the building instead of battlements.

As I walked forward I yearned to touch the stone of the walls to make the place real to me. I hadn't expected to see genuine castles around here, in an otherwise normal and essentially modern town. To me, and probably to most people, castles had always seemed to be relics of not only another age, but another hemisphere. When I thought of castles I always tended to think of Europe and great battles with armored knights and archers, or even medieval Japan, but not the American frontier with Lewis and Clark and people of the Nez Percé or other local tribes.

But regardless of my preconceptions, here I was with the massive stone structure in front of me. Someone, at some point, had wanted a castle here, and so here it was.

And my new acquaintance owned the place.

I stepped meekly but curiously to the large, wooden front door. Knocking would have seemed a natural thing to do, except that in a dwelling this large I doubted anyone would hear it. Without difficulty, though, I found a doorbell. As I pressed it I heard the muted sound of bells chiming from behind the door.

I had to wait for over a minute, and was beginning to doubt myself, but then Bastian answered, pulling the large door open easily. "Ah, Miss Maria. I should have known to expect you at this door." Today he wore a dark grey polo shirt with well-pressed slacks. "In the future please feel free to enter at your leisure from the side entrance." He leaned out to point toward the wing that stretched out to the east. "That's where anyone who frequents the castle usually enters."

I was curious about who else "frequented" the castle, but at the moment I was highly distracted. As he had leaned forward to gesture, he had brought himself close enough to me that I could smell the fragrance I'd noticed before. What was that? Not any cologne I knew of. It was pungent, but soft at the same time. I intentionally made sure not to dodge away when he came closer to me. I felt a minor thrill when he ever-so-slightly invaded my personal space for a few seconds before withdrawing again. Whether he thought anything of it I couldn't guess.

"Well," he continued, "I know you're here to learn about the book, but I'd like to show you around the castle a bit first. I'm happy to exhibit a bit of my home when I'm with someone who can appreciate the antique value of it, and the walk will give me a chance to bring you up to speed."

His tone just then and his use of the words "up to speed" threw me off. He was a puzzling sort of person, usually speaking with practiced refinement, almost the way my father spoke, but occasionally slipping into speech patterns I was more used to hearing elsewhere from day to day. It didn't bother me; I liked that he aspired to something elegant. He evidently had similar aspirations in tending to his home. "It looks like an amazing place," I offered.

He smiled and stepped back to make way for me. "I'm glad you like it."

As I followed him into the house, I smelled the fragrance again. It was lightly applied, but I had a good sense of smell, and this time I identified it: clove. I'd never smelled clove on anyone before, and I probably wouldn't have ever thought of it as suitable for cologne, but on Bastian it was almost troublingly attractive.

I tried to stay just a bit distant from him as I followed, just to be on the safe side. I could still smell his fragrance, though. I was suspicious that it would continue to grow on me.

His tour was quite brief, and confined to what must have been no more than a quarter of the structure. He mostly just took me through a simple path to the back of the castle, pointing out minor, unremarkable features along the way, and then brought me through a back door and into a walled courtyard with several potted trees. On the back wall, which sat at the exterior of the building, there was a wide arched window opening through which we could see the expanse of the orchard. He led me forward to the opening, where we paused to enjoy the view. I could see the boundaries, with regular residential areas beyond, but was impressed by the sprawling rows of trees.

"My family didn't build the castle," Bastian explained. "We came to live here about forty years ago." As he mentioned his family I waited, expecting him to explain more about them, but he changed the subject as if there was nothing to say. "It was built before 1920, I forget the exact year...the stone was taken from a quarry not far from here. The family who built it was quite successful with their orchards. These days I keep the orchard running but do little personally to manage it. The steward is perhaps too-well paid, but he gives me my privacy, and frankly, my interests lie elsewhere."

"Your interests," I parroted, "like...the mystic and mythical?"

"Yes, that too."

"I'm, um, quite eager to hear about it all. Right now I don't know anything more than anybody else. Most of what I know I get from movies."

He raised a skeptical eyebrow. "Really?"

I looked to either side and shrugged. "Well, yeah. Everyone figures they're just spooky stories, and I don't know any better."

He gave the slightest of lopsided smiles. "Well. You will. Come." He gestured toward the door that led back inside, and led as I followed. "The first thing I'd like to tell you is the story of a small fragment of a gemstone that I keep on display. Are you ready for a bit of a tale?"

I shrugged with a smile. "Sure."

He proceeded back through the house. "Some ancient legends tell of a star that fell from the sky and struck the top of a tall mountain, shattering into hundreds of pieces, most of them too small to ever find. But the pure of heart who searched the lengths of the earth sometimes did find a piece or two, and the finders never knew fear again."

I stayed reverently silent to appreciate the legend.

We walked through one room and then another, passing through a hallway in between. We came to a gallery of sorts, with various items on display throughout. "Another tale tells of one piece that was found: the Light Shard, as it was known. This piece was larger than the others, and it was said that those who were truly noble could cause the star's light to shine from it at will, with a brightness like that of the noonday sun."

He had stopped in front of a display case. On a small pedestal rested an elongated fragment of what must have once been a huge gemstone. It was a wide, translucent yellow-orange chunk with one smooth side and another that was much more rough and uneven.

He regarded me with folded arms and an inquisitive eyebrow. "Do you believe in tales like what I've just told you?"

I hesitated, feeling a sense of wonder. "Is that the Light Shard?"

"Answer my question first."

"Um, yeah, I guess I do." I didn't want to seem too enthusiastic, even though I was.

He smiled as he shook his head. "Those stories are not true. At least, the story of the falling star and the mountain isn't true. Sometimes people become very inventive in their efforts to explain the world around them."

I looked downward, frowning.

"However," he continued, "You are correct that yes, this is the Light Shard."

I looked back up, first at him, and then at the piece. "And it shines like a star and makes people fearless?"

"It doesn't seem to be shining right now."

"Oh, come on. You said people could make it shine. Let me try."

He shook his head. "You're too eager and too unprepared. Before you attempt to manipulate such things, let me tell you much more of what you do not already know." We walked again, arriving by a painting of robed figures. "Many, many years ago, *millennia* ago in fact, a group of alchemists worked to produce artifacts of great power."

The sense of import he probably intended was lost on me. "Um, alchemists? Like, people who try to turn lead into gold?"

He stopped walking and frowned. "I can see that you have no appreciation for the craft. I'll explain it for you. Alchemy is not about trying to create material wealth. At least, not for those who truly understand it and succeed in the study and usage of it. Alchemy is about seeking to know and feel and impel the forces that cause existence."

"Kind of like science?"

"Exactly like science, though perhaps more open-minded, and sometimes less precise." He continued walking down the hall, speaking as if lecturing in a classroom. "There are those who would call it science. Others would call it magic. Whatever the best name is for the craft, there have been those throughout the ages who have learned it, and some who have used it as practically as you use a light switch."

"And they made 'artifacts'."

"Yes; they crafted items that were imbued with a special nature of some sort or another, much as men these days craft automobiles or pistols or computers. Many of those items were simple and weak, and their effects were often attributed to luck." Bastian looked back at me with a gleam in his eye. "However, the true masters of alchemy, who lived those long millennia ago, focused all of their efforts and created jewels of incredible energy, unmatched by any power wielded previously or ever since."

"They created the jewels from nothing?"

His expression relaxed quickly. "Oh, no, hardly; creation never occurs from nothing, and a key part of true alchemy is having the right ingredients. No, they first sought out some of the finest jewels before dedicating years to instilling and permeating them with force."

"What kind of force?"

"It was different for each alchemist. Though they worked together, each had a distinct pursuit. One of the jewels was infused with the light of the sun, many years' worth."

"The Light Shard?" I glanced back at it, sitting in the display case.

"The Light Stone. It seems that somehow the Stone was damaged, crushed apparently, with only a single large piece remaining, which was then called the Light Shard. I'm fortunate enough to possess it, though it does me little good. It hasn't removed fear from *my* life."

His features became clouded as he spoke those last words, and I felt worry creeping up inside me. What was it that he feared? I wanted to avoid a heavy atmosphere, so I guided back the topic of conversation by indulging my other curiosity. "But it does make light?"

He brightened a bit, and smiled at me slyly. "I am glad that you're eager. Perhaps you will see it shine someday."

"Not if it just sits in a case." I leaned in to examine the gem more closely. "How does it even work?"

"It has to be actuated, or stimulated, you might say, for its energy to flow out. In principle, you would merely hold it in your hand and focus yourself mentally while exhaling."

I didn't know why he didn't just let me touch it and try to figure it out. Maybe I was too new. I'd be sure to ask about it again later. "How many other jewels did they make?"

"Hmmm. That much is uncertain, though ancient texts refer to at least seven others. Some are described in detail, while the exact nature of others is unknown. The artifacts' names are often indicative of the power the master alchemists desired. The bearer of the descriptively-named Sight Stone could essentially see anything he desired, as long as he knew what to look for, with the ability to look past walls, mountains, and distances of hundreds of miles. The name of the Dreadstone is, in fact, all that we know about it. I've only ever seen a handful of obscure references to it."

"It's lost, then?"

"They are all lost to the world, though most are likely in the possession of individuals who don't care to advertise their treasures."

"Or they were destroyed, like the Light Stone?"

"I'm sure it's possible, but I know of no other tales of these artifacts being destroyed. The alchemy itself that was used to empower the stones also gave them additional durability, and it was expected that some form of additional enchantment would be needed to undo what had been done before. Normal methods of destruction weren't expected to succeed, though it's doubtful that they were attempted often. Most people who came to possess them wouldn't want them destroyed."

"Hmm. Okay. What type of gemstones did they use to make those artifacts?"

A certain vigor animated his words. "The Sight Stone was made from an enormous pearl; the Dreadstone seems to be a black star sapphire. The stones' natural qualities were intended to enhance the effect of the alchemy, the pearl being useful in some way for augmenting vision, and the contrasting white star of the sapphire against its black background could have had symbolic value or perhaps it plays well for evoking an emotion of fear. Then again, maybe the alchemist just liked it for its uniqueness."

He turned past a small statue of a woman, whose origin I couldn't identify, and when he spoke he was more relaxed again. "The common names of other enchanted jewels are not so indicative of their natures. The Damsel Stone and Kamahra's Longing, made from rhodolite garnet and turquoise respectively, are believed to have been made by female alchemists, which is unusual. It seems they were even sisters, though apparently their desires were diametrically opposed. The Damsel Stone somehow granted its bearer great beauty, likely by casting an impression in the minds of those who witnessed her. It also had healing and restorative properties, which again served to preserve beauty. Among those who know the lore of the stones, it's a commonly held belief that the Damsel Stone has been passed on by one means or another through many generations, among key historical figures including Cleopatra."

"Really."

He nodded. "While the creator of that artifact surely wanted attention from those around her, her sister, who by ancient accounts already possessed great beauty, must have wanted the opposite: Kamahra's Longing allows the bearer to pass unnoticed among others while in plain visibility. Legend has it that Kamahra's Longing allowed her the privacy she desired, while others who possessed it later were able to pass through private or secure areas or observe enemies undetected."

"I can see the usefulness of either of those jewels, especially the one that healed people."

"A healing quality is actually not uncommon among enchanted gemstones, though usually the effect is so minimal that it's easy to dismiss as superstition. A *powerful* healing effect, however, like that of the Damsel Stone, is *not* so common, though even its power was limited. The fact that the Stone changed hands so many times is indicative that it cannot prevent all loss of life."

"What others are there?"

"The Gem of Heracles, or 'Hercules', if you prefer. Its possessor reportedly had great strength and was nearly impervious to harm, and assumedly it also had some healing qualities, or at least helped instill vim and vigor. It also presumably imparted self-confidence."

"So what type of gemstone was the Gem of Herac— Hercules?"

"A diamond. An unusually wide diamond that didn't shine like most, almost certainly because of the cut. The sparkle and shimmer of diamonds you normally see greatly depends on precise angles, but this gemstone had to have been cut differently. At one point it had also been set into a belt."

I pointed to the Light Shard. "And what type of stone is that?"

"A citrine. Which is a somewhat rare type of quartz. One old reference said that the Light Stone was topaz, but it was mistaken."

I looked back at him. "You know a lot about gemstones."

"I ought to. I'm a jeweler by profession."

"Are you serious?"

"Certainly. The trade was passed on to me by my father." His voice became strangely tight as he said that. "Of course, I'm relatively new to it, and not at all as experienced as he was."

I noticed his usage of the past tense when speaking of his father. It made me curious, but he wasn't explaining anything more and I felt it would be too awkward to ask about it. Jewelling was a remarkable topic by itself, though. "So you make rings, and bracelets, and such?"

"I do."

"That's kind of impressive."

He gave a single, closed-mouth laugh. "It's a useful hobby."

I reviewed the jewels he had mentioned already, counting them in my mind. "Wait; I thought you said there were at least eight enchanted gems, but you've only mentioned six."

"To be precise, there are eight known artifacts created by the master alchemists of a past age, and many, many more gemstones and other items with less-powerful alchemic qualities to them. But yes, there are two more jewels of power that I have not mentioned yet. I saved their explanation for last intentionally."

He walked from the room at this point, leaving me to follow.

After passing through a hallway we came to another room I hadn't yet seen. The walls of the room were mostly lined with bookshelves and closets, a pair of tall tables and a large, dark, sleek, and expensive-looking notebook computer on a desk in the corner. A window on one wall let in sunlight.

Bastian sat at the large, central table in front of *Demons and Dark Essences,* resting his elbows on the table as he began speaking again. "The remaining two powerful jewels are the Life Stone and the Demon Stone."

I waited for him to continue; he gestured at another chair near his, and I took it.

As I seated myself, he resumed speaking. "What the Life Stone does exactly is not clear. It is certain to bring health to the bearer, and must also have the power to engender life elsewhere, but like the Dreadstone, there are almost no available references to its powers."

Again, I waited.

"And the Demon Stone…well, I'll let you see for yourself." He opened the old book in front of him and flipped through several pages, scanning each. "Here."

3.1

He turned the book around and lifted it toward me so that I could see it. The script inside was handwritten, and one of the two visible pages was illustrated.

At the top of the page on the right were the words, "THE DEMON MASTERS". A lot of the wording on the left page was smudged and hard to make out, but the picture on the right was clear. An exceptionally tall, dark-skinned woman with a short cape and a jagged afro held out a staff with a jewel at the end, which cast rays out over a group of monsters that flanked her. They appeared to be waiting on her, as if she were their leader; those closest to her stood in protective stances. Her mouth was open in a snarl, as if she were chanting an incantation or issuing a command.

"Take a glance at the pictures," I heard Bastian say, "and I'm sure you'll get the idea."

Turning the page, I saw two more illustrations, each featuring a lone human figure among various devilish creatures. One of the "demon masters" wore a horned helmet and a breastplate with a gemstone set in the center—presumably the Demon Stone. In the third picture, a robed man, bald but with a long goatee, simply held the jewel in his hand. His other hand was outstretched; the beasts gawked in the direction of his gesture. In both pictures, the men with the Demon Stone seemed to be in no danger from the fiends around them, but instead they were clearly commanding the brutes.

"The Demon Stone is used for control," I surmised.

"Exactly. Demons must normally act with a will of their own, but the demon masters you see in those images were able to use the Demon Stone to override that will in favor of theirs."

"That could be dangerous...maybe for a lot of people."

"Extremely."

I flipped the page; the backside had several written paragraphs, but what was more noticeable was that the book had been damaged; only the top corner of the following page remained. "There's a page torn out."

He frowned. "Two pages, actually. It was in that condition when it came to me. It was very disappointing; I was particularly interested in those pages."

Almost no text was visible on the page fragment, but one word was clear at the top: "LUCTUS." The paragraph beneath began with what looked like "The Summo", but anything that had followed had been torn away.

"What's this word here?" I asked, pointing to the top.

Bastian leaned over to see. "Ah, yes. Luctus. It's a Latin word. I looked it up a while back. It means, 'grief.'"

"What was this page supposed to be about? What is the 'grief'?"

He shrugged. "I can't be sure, but it must refer to the usage of the Demon Stone. We'll never truly know unless there's another copy of this book out there somewhere and we can get our hands on it. I'm not holding my breath for that to happen."

I set the book down and moved to the window. This was a lot to absorb. I watched the trees and clouds outside, but my thoughts remained on the alchemy Bastian had described. These empowered gemstones were tools, and could surely be used for either good or bad. Maybe some would be fairly inconsequential to the world, but evidently at least one of them was capable of causing grief; the word "LUCTUS" struck me as ominous and troubling.

"You seem distracted," Bastian said.

I looked at him, then turned back to stare out the window again. "No, not really. I was just thinking, what would a person actually do with these enchanted artifacts, especially in our modern world? I mean, some of them would be handy just to have around…the Damsel Stone for some extra attention, the Gem of Hercules to help with physical labor…but anyone with real ambition would probably have some bigger goal in mind."

Bastian sat forward silently, leaning his elbows on the table and dropping his head to rest his mouth on his hands.

"I guess I'm not creative enough to come up with those goals, though," I went on. "Maybe if you're beautiful you can rule the world? Or even just a nation. Cleopatra did well enough with that. What do you do with superhuman strength? Professional wrestling? Sports? I guess I can't imagine that something like that would be satisfying enough. And what was that other one called…Kama…Karama's…"

"Kamahra's Longing."

"Yes, that one. Maybe you could be a good spy with it. But again, I can't help but think that it would be more useful in some other way. I think it should be, anyway."

He didn't say anything back.

"And the other two?" I continued. "What would a person do with them? Would someone with the Gem of Hercules go into law enforcement? Would someone with the influence of the Damsel Stone enter a beauty contest?"

He sat back. "I'd be very skeptical of that. I can't imagine that anyone who could obtain such powerful relics would have such trivial intentions for them."

"Well, right, that's kind of what I'm saying; maybe some people would seek them out just for the sake of having something valuable, but otherwise they'd have to have some larger purpose in mind."

"Well, that's actually the crux of the problem we're facing right now."

"What problem?"

Bastian folded his arms and grimaced. "Maria, there are people out there who *do* have a larger purpose in mind. If you'd kept reading you would have found that, although these artifacts have great power individually, there seems to be a way of combining their power."

"All of them together?"

"No, not necessarily. Probably never all together. The result of even two gemstones used together would likely be hard to predict, and with any more than two, the alchemy might well interfere counterproductively. But some of the text specifically mentions a ritual intended to combine the power of the Life Stone and the Demon Stone by fusing them together. I don't know if anyone ever completed the ritual; in fact, I doubt it. But one of those two missing pages describes in detail how to accomplish the ritual."

"So you think it can be done?"

"Oh, absolutely." He strode forward another step, placing himself right in front of me. "There's something you should know. A man named Grismur knows of this ritual and intends to conduct it."

Grismur…what kind of a name was that? It sounded sinister. "Who is he? Does he have the jewels?"

"Very few people know his name, and those who do know little more. As for the jewels, like I mentioned before, the whereabouts of the artifacts are generally unknown, but if he had both of them he would have completed the ritual already. That hasn't happened. He may have the Demon Stone, but not the Life Stone. He hasn't found it."

"Well, that's good." But did Grismur already have the Demon Stone, and had he been using it already? Had he sent that creature to attack me two days ago? And if so, *why?* I wasn't important to anything he was doing. Or was that attack unrelated, or coincidental? I couldn't help but feel that I would encounter this person named Grismur, and that I needed to stop him.

"However, he might yet find the Life Stone soon," Bastian continued. He leaned forward again, regarding me intently. "The only way we can be sure about the future of those gemstones is if we control them."

"So if the Life Stone hasn't been found, we need to find it."

"Yes. If Grismur obtains it, he will conduct the ritual and use the combined power of the artifacts to summon an army of demons. With such an army he'll be an unstoppable force."

So the incomplete word in the book was probably "Summoner", as in "summoner of demons". I shivered. "He could end up killing a lot of people."

"Or enslaving them. Most people relish having the power to tell someone else what to do, and they enjoy it even more when they can force that person to comply. But there are always those who are too independent, too free-spirited—those who will resist. Frankly, the people who do resist won't be a match for the demons, and some will be killed. Death will be unavoidable. That's probably the source of the 'grief' of Luctus."

"That's horrible."

"For Grismur, it will be worth it."

Worth it...did people genuinely think in terms of mass killing being somehow justifiable in view of some other goal? I'd had history lessons like anyone else, so I had to accept it, but that way of thinking clashed so fiercely with my own. I shook my head. "I guess I kind of have a hard time believing that anyone would want to do such terrible things."

He scoffed. "Oh, believe it. That's the nature of the average person."

That struck me as an unfair and pigeonholing sort of characterization. "The average person? Now you're speaking in generalities. I don't believe it at all. I think most people try to do what is right."

He eyed me almost with an expression of pity. "I think most people are far more concerned about what is convenient or gratifying than what is right. *'Right'...*" He over-pronounced the word. "The average person doesn't get an opportunity to do anything really depraved, but people take plenty of opportunity to wrong others in smaller ways, and more often they simply don't do what they actually think is *right*. For example, most people around here don't vote, and most who do don't educate themselves enough to make a vote worth something. Most people don't stop their car to help another motorist who is stranded on the side of the road. Most people won't intervene when a violent crime is committed right in front of them." He gave a short sigh. "Most people won't even go to their neighbor's house to help them out when they need a hand."

I didn't want to argue with him, but what he was saying just didn't match up with what I'd seen in life. "That's not true. People are good neighbors all the time. I don't know about car trouble, but I've been out with a church group quite a few times to do service projects for people in the neighborhood."

He laughed. "A church group? Service projects?" He grunted. I could feel myself blushing. The scorn bothered me, and I fumbled mentally for a moment as I struggled to produce a comeback. Normally, I would want to fire back quickly at someone who took a mocking attitude, but I was off balance from the way he affected my emotions. Then he breathed deeply, shook his head, and gave a small but genuine smile. "Well then, you, Miss Maria, are unusual. I don't want to argue about human nature right now. I'm sure if we want to, we can discuss it later. And we'll return to the topic of the gemstones soon enough, but I'd prefer to talk about a more pleasant subject now: you. Indeed, you are an uncommon marvel."

An uncommon marvel? Okay—points for him. I was not only disarmed by that statement but also pleasantly flustered, and the easy response for me was to give a brief denial. "Oh, hardly."

He touched his chin. "So...all people are different in their own way, but you're something else altogether. Tell me, Maria: what's unique about you?"

"About me?" I almost felt a bit of relief from the change of subject, but at the same time, my foremost unique quality was an uncomfortable topic. While I felt wary, I also wanted to be carefree with him in general. I wanted him to know me. "Well, let's see. The easy answer would be my hair, but that's shallow." I took just a few seconds to think. "No, I'd have to say it's my aloofness...the distance I keep from most people."

He raised an eyebrow. "*That's* what you think makes you different?"

"Yeah. I don't get close to most folks." Did that sound silly?

"And other people would agree that it's your most distinguishing feature?"

"Most distinguishing? No, no...actually, if people really knew me they'd definitely think of something else. Something that I don't think should be such a big deal."

"And what is that?"

I never liked keeping secrets, especially not now with Bastian, but I couldn't hope for a positive reaction to this particular secret. "It's a...I guess it's a surprise. I'll tell you someday."

I'd tried to say the word "surprise" as if to make a game out of it, but instead of feeling playful I was troubled. I'd just promised him something that I'd rarely promised to anyone else.

He showed no sign of being bothered by my discretion. "Well, they're probably right. It probably is what really makes you different from others."

"No!" Even if he didn't know what I was referring to I still had to insist. "No, it's not a big deal. Honestly, it isn't. People make a big deal out of things that shouldn't mean anything. I don't want to be defined by one aspect of my nature. There's a lot more to me than that."

I expected him to be curious, given the way I was hinting at something but not explaining at all what it was, but I was glad to find that he didn't ask anything more about it. "I suppose that's fair," he went on. "We don't like to be oversimplified, do we?"

"I know I don't. Especially not with something bad."

He again lifted a skeptical eyebrow. "Bad? Bad...that's mysterious, but I can wait for a surprise." He sighed and stood. "It's not *it*, though."

"It's not what?"

He stepped closer. "'Something bad'...that's not what I'm sensing."

"Sensing? What do you mean?" My curiosity wasn't quite edging out the cheer of being the center of attention for him.

"There's something about you." He stared straight into my eyes, as if trying to find something in them. "I don't know what it is, but there's something...good. Good for me, anyway."

And with that I was dizzy. I felt like I should respond, but I was feeling far too disoriented for the moment.

He went on, still searching my eyes with his. "I guess...you seem strangely and uniquely familiar."

My heart jumped, almost embarrassingly. "Like we've met before?"

He now gazed out the window, into the distance, as he replied, "Only in a dream."

My breath caught within my chest.

That was just too odd...odd in a good way. My dream of dancing with him came to mind, and in an almost wishful way I wondered if he'd dreamed of me also, but what made me pause was something else. The very words he'd spoken were also a line from a movie that had been my favorite since I was a child. They struck in my heart more deeply than he could have possibly expected, and more than I would have guessed also. The emotions he produced made me feel so stereotypically girly—but I liked it. I turned away abruptly, biting my lower lip, and letting my breathing resume as normal.

I could hear a worried tone in his voice. "Did I say something wrong?"

I glanced back at him, and then away again. "No, no. Far from it."

I thought of telling him that I also sensed something similar about him, as if we were already well-acquainted, but with that thought came a feeling that quieted me. It rose in my chest and made me fear to say the words, and yet it wasn't a fear of anything bad...it was more like a fear of things going too well for me, of somehow gaining a destiny so wonderful that I couldn't possibly have done anything to deserve it.

"Maria..."

I looked back at him, into his eyes. "Yes?"

"I think you should take some time to think about this before committing to it. Sleep on it, and we can discuss it more tomorrow."

I stopped breathing again, this time out of surprise.

This was a disappointing turn in the conversation. I'd wanted to keep sharing the mood, and the sweet mutual thought, and suddenly he was bringing it to a stop altogether. "What? Why? Do you think I'm not up to it? Do you not trust me?"

"Actually, I've already trusted you quite a bit, and I'm rather counting on you being capable in our pursuits. I just want you to be sure about this. These are serious matters, potentially fraught with danger. You'll need to steel your resolve, and put your trust in me."

"I can do that."

"Good." He smiled. "But still, sleep on it."

Well, drat. He was being insistent. "Oh, fine." I sighed, resigning myself to a break. "It's all fascinating, though. I want to learn it all."

"It'll be just as interesting tomorrow." He offered his hand. "Let me show you to the door."

I wasn't happy to be leaving, but as I took his hand I didn't mind so much. He nodded courteously before leading me from the room and back through the corridors of the castle. I paid little attention to the passages and the turns; I was preoccupied by the sensation of his hand under mine. I felt acutely every place where his flesh and mine touched. In passing I noticed that his skin was calloused but not overly rough; more important, though, was the mere contact. As he guided me his hand moved slightly this way and that, and I used the shifting to ease my grip more around his, hoping simultaneously that he would and wouldn't notice. I tried to savor at the same time both his grasp and the persistent scent of clove.

Presently we arrived at the front door—too quickly for my liking. He opened it, first releasing my hand, and was about to lead me outside, but I halted inside the door. I was amused at the momentary reversal, with me standing inside as if the resident and him standing outside as if the visitor. "I'm not dying to leave so soon," I said with a blush. "I've barely spent any time with you today. I did get to see your home a bit, but otherwise all we did was talk about jewels and serious stuff."

"And you wanted some lighthearted banter? Very well. I suppose I still have a few minutes."

I thrilled at the idea of staying longer. "Let's walk."

"Okay. There's a nice path around the orchard we can take."

I followed him, and quickly launched into a series of inquiries which were mundane but gave small details about him, and his likes and dislikes. We talked for an hour or maybe two, circling his orchard; time and again I asked a question and he gave an answer, and I sometimes shared my own corresponding thought, but mostly asked and listened. I avoided the topic of family. He was at ease; he spoke casually, without worrying much about sophisticated speech. I didn't worry about particular subjects, but rather kept noticing how natural it felt to be around him. Among other things he related, he spoke of having appendicitis and surgery several years before. He told of how feeling such "shocking weakness" during the illness made him intensely upset, even after he'd recovered. Beyond that, by the time we stopped I doubted I could recall everything he'd said, but each word had been a delight, and I felt that I knew him better, as if I'd been watching a form take shape at the hands of a sculptor.

We did indeed stop, eventually, back at the front of his castle, when Bastian suddenly said, "Goodness! I didn't pay attention to the time. I was supposed to meet some people at the airport. They might be waiting already. I need to leave."

"Oh. Well, then, I won't hold you up any longer."

He smiled with soft eyes. "It was my pleasure. Remember, as I said before, that you can use the side entrance next time."

"Okay. Thank you, Bastian."

"I hope to see you again tomorrow."

"You will." I stood for a moment longer, looking at him almost expectantly, then smiled and walked energetically back to my car. He remained near his front door, silently attendant. After starting the car, I waved once, then drove away. In my rear-view mirror I could see him waiting by his door until I was well away from the castle.

Within moments I was back in normal life again, among everyday residences and businesses. For as secluded as I had felt, it was jarring to be back in the city so soon, as if I'd been cheated out of privacy with my own thoughts and forced to contemplate the mundane practices of everyday life.

Still, my time with this captivating young man had been enthralling and I was certainly invited back, so regardless of the humdrum everythings I had to deal with for the moment, I kept myself cheery with patient anticipation.

3.2

"Look who decided to show up."

"I've never missed a week."

As I'd walked into the small diner a few blocks away from our houses I'd seen Hansen sitting at our regular table. The place must have been making enough to stay in business, but it was never busy, so we were always able to sit in the same spot. In other circumstances I liked to mix things up by sitting in different seats in a classroom, bus, or anywhere else, even to the point of forcing other people, indirectly, to break patterns by taking seats that were "theirs". For these get-togethers, though, each of us always took the exact same seats. Of course, more recently the third seat was empty.

"I know," Hansen replied as I sat down opposite him. He wore scuffed jeans and a Hawaiian shirt. "Not since Nova left; you're good about not breaking our tradition. You're still late, though, Maria." There was always something a little bit wrong with the way he said my name, almost as if he was calling me Murray (or maybe Marie). It didn't ever bother me, but I always noticed. It wasn't quite charming, either, but it was impossible to dislike Hansen and his warm grin. He called to a nearby server. "A warmed glass of whole milk and a Caesar salad for the lady, please."

I smiled. "You always know exactly what I want."

"Even if it sounds terrible." He shrugged happily. "I'm just good like that." He took a drink from his own glass, which was surely an ice-cold ginger ale, his favorite drink. "So what's the topic tonight?"

"I've got just the thing." We tended to choose particular topics for our gatherings at the diner, then toy around with ideas, just getting a feel for each other's thoughts on various subjects. Sometimes they were serious, and sometimes lighthearted. I had to make a good effort to focus myself after the day's earlier events, but I had chosen the night's diner topic for a specific purpose. I hoped that it would sound as natural as anything else we'd discussed in the past. "Someone was talking about it on the radio a while back. Nova would like it."

"So, what is it?"

"Superpowers."

"Superpowers," he echoed.

"Yeah, specifically, the superpower of your choice."

He smiled. "Oh, I get to pick, do I? Well, before we can talk about what superpower we get, don't we have to figure out how we got it?"

I shook my head. "*After* you decide your superpower, then you can decide how you got it."

"Okay. Hmmm...."

"Obviously there are options like flight, but that's kind of boring."

"Boring?"

"Well, too common. Uninventive. It also might be kind of cheating."

"Why's that?"

"Well, if you've got the ability to fly, you must also be at least partially impervious to harm. Maybe not completely, but think about it: you could kill yourself *waaaaay* too easily. Out in the open air you'd be fine, assuming you could breathe easily enough, and assuming you didn't hit a bird or bat or something, but if you were close to anything at all like a building or a tree, or, heaven forbid, an airplane or a power line, a bit of bad aim could kill you in a jiffy. Even just a bad landing would do the trick, and bam, you're done! I've thought this through."

"Okay, I guess I take your point. A little bit of imperviousness is fine, though, isn't it?"

"And those windmill electric generator things! Those things would be deadly!"

He raised one eyebrow above a half-smile.

"But yes, I suppose it'd be acceptable. That was just for clarification, though. You still have to answer the question."

"Well...being super-strong would be fun."

"Too common. Be imaginative."

"I'm brainstorming. Invisibility is another good one, but I'm sure it's way too normal for you, too."

"As is super speed."

"Sure," he conceded. "What would be a good one? Oh, I don't know...maybe something like huge, bulbous knees?"

I snorted in a failed attempt to keep myself from laughing. "How is that a superpower? What would you do with them?"

"Not a clue. What about you, though? You'd better have an answer to your own question."

"Naturally. My superpower would be the ability to either telekinetically or telepathically make anyone feel the repeated light sensation of a fly landing on their right ear."

He shook his head at me, showing the same smile I knew so well. "Okay, well, if you're going along those lines, I know what I'd want. My superpower would be that people's cars would run really well when they were around me, even if they had bad motor problems. Then I'd work in an auto shop."

I giggled at the thought of numerous perplexed customers, and the server returned to our table to drop off my salad and milk. I thanked him and said a brief prayer of gratitude, as was my custom, before lifting a bite of salad.

"The thing is," I began, pausing to take a bite of lettuce and crouton, "superpowers, real ones I mean, not like the fly-on-the-ear-sensation thing—I mean, not real ones, but you know what I mean—"

"Try saying that again without a mouthful of food. Boy, you must have been hungry."

I made a show of swallowing. "Anyway, I was saying that superpowers can also be a curse. Even normal abilities can."

His smile was easy, relaxed. That was the common descriptive term for Hansen: relaxed. He almost always did his best to be at ease with people, and he was good at showing interest. "What do you mean?"

"Well, even stuff like just competence and beauty. Those definitely aren't superpowers, but they have their drawbacks. Haven't you heard Mr. Carey say that competence is a curse? He says that the competent are cursed with more work. And beauty. Any pretty girl will tell you she gets more attention than she wants."

"Well, maybe you'll only have to worry about one of those."

"Yeah, and—" I cut myself short, giving him a disapproving scowl. He just grinned at me.

"But weren't we talking about superpowers specifically?" he asked. "Wasn't that the point?"

"Yes. Think about it. In any superhero story, they always end up getting more negative attention from the bad guys. They have to deal with the major headaches more *because* they're more able to deal with them."

"Okay…I'm not sure I'd call that a curse, though."

"What about the superheroes that drain people's energy when they touch them, so they can't ever have normal relationships? Or along similar lines, what about the Midas touch? That's a different sort of example, but the classic myth still makes the point well."

"Yeah, I can see those ones. But not all superpowers have drawbacks like that."

"No, maybe not all; but *some* superpowers either are a curse or come along with one."

"Sure."

The conversation was fun, as it always was, but this time I'd chosen the topic for an especially important reason. Partially, it was inspired by what I'd heard about enchanted gemstones, but there was something else, something lurking in my conscience. For as close a friend as Hansen was, there was something about me that I'd never told him, just as I hadn't told Bastian, and as I'd gotten older it had begun to make me feel more and more dishonest. I didn't have superpowers like those in a typical comic book, but my own abilities *were* superhuman in some ways, and they sure came with a curse.

I didn't intend to tell him my deeper secrets right now, though part of me yearned for the disclosure. I did feel like I could at least drop a hint, so that one day, when I did tell him more…I didn't know what would happen, but hopefully he would at least know that I'd had him in mind, and that I'd been readying myself. In the next moment he looked back at me, and as our eyes met the desire welled up in me with enough strength that I almost thought my vision faded around the edges. In a lower, voice, I asked him, "What if someday I told you that I did have some sort of power?"

He sat absolutely still for several seconds. His eyes had lost focus. Perplexed by his stillness, I glanced to the side, almost as if to make sure that the rest of the world was still moving along like normal. It was.

When I looked back at him, his head was tipped downward and he was blinking. "Whoa…um…what just…did you just say something?"

"Ugh. Pay attention, you scatterbrained boy. Yes, I did just say something. I asked you a question. I said, what if I told you someday that I *did* have some sort of power?"

"Oh." He shook his head gently, then smiled again. "Well, if you could fly you'd have to take me to the music store every once in a while."

"Seriously, Hansen. You wouldn't freak out if I was a bit different than most people?"

"Of course not. We're tight like that. Would you freak out if I was a freak?"

That was something else…though he didn't realize the implications of what I was saying or what he was saying in return, he was indirectly calling *me* a freak. "Of course not. But what if my power was a curse?"

"You sound like you're actually worried about this."

"Well, I don't want to sound like I doubt our friendship."

"Good. Because you could have any curse and you'd still be my Maria, and it wouldn't matter."

That was more reassuring than he could possibly realize.

He laughed. "The superpower you need is just the ability to be on time. What was it tonight, anyway; did you have a hot date or something?"

This was a nice thought. I couldn't do anything but try not to smile for a moment; it was kind of exciting to think of my time with Bastian as a date. "I wouldn't call it a *date*, not tonight so much, but I had met with someone."

Hansen's smile vanished. "That was supposed to be a joke."

I shrugged.

"Who was it?" he asked.

"Just a boy that I met in a bookstore. He had a book I wanted to see."

"You read a book with him."

"Well, yes, kind of." I didn't like his frown. "It was a study session."

"But you're not in school."

"I didn't say it was for school, silly. It was just a…personal interest."

"So you hung out at the library with a guy you didn't even know."

"No, not the library. His house."

He sat with his mouth partway open. "And you don't even know him."

"I can take care of myself, if that's what you're worried about."

"He didn't try anything funny, did he?"

"What? No! Of course not. Really, I was just fine. It was very normal." *Aside from the subject matter,* I supposed.

"Does he live in a good part of town?"

"Actually, he lives in a castle."

He was silent again.

He didn't look happy.

"Hansen, you're reacting like I've started selling drugs."

"No, I just don't know how I feel about you trusting a complete stranger like that."

"Well, aren't you quite the overprotective brother."

He grimaced. "Yeah, I guess so…"

It almost looked like he was even more bothered by that. "Honestly, thanks for the concern, but like I said, I can take care of myself."

He seemed preoccupied for a while after that, and we sat in silence for several minutes before speaking again. Meanwhile, I finished my meal. Silence at our table in the diner was not common, but whenever our conversation subsided for a while I was always determined not to let it bother me. My mother had once told me that the definition of love was when a husband and wife could sit comfortably together in silence; while my father talked more around her than anyone else, she'd also had to learn to appreciate frequent bouts of silence, and her love for him was enough to make her happy with it. While I didn't know this kind of romantic love personally, I trusted her, and the idea made sense to me. I figured that good friends should also be able to enjoy silence now and then, so while I didn't think of Hansen in a romantic way, I wanted to be content with the current lull.

Hansen didn't seem to be enjoying himself, though, at least not like he had a few minutes ago. He was staring out the window with a frown. "You seem suddenly pensive," I told him.

He looked back at me. "Yeah. I guess so."

"Does it really bug you that much that I spent a few minutes with him?"

He shifted. "Not really. I don't want anyone treating you wrong, but you're smart. I was thinking of something else."

"What's that?"

He waited a couple of seconds before speaking. "Oh, nothing. Nothing you need to worry about, anyway." He took another drink from his glass. "Hey, I'm going to head out now."

"Shall I walk you home?"

"Not today. I've got some thinking to do."

"Well, okay. This one's on me?"

Now he smiled a bit. "Not a chance, Maria. I'm paying. It wouldn't be good for me to order for you, then make you pay for it." He stood up.

I followed suit, stretching my arms high as I stood. "I suppose we'll have to finish the superpower discussion another time."

I wasn't sure if the expression I saw on his face was a grin or a grimace. "Take care, Maria."

I walked to the door of the diner and looked back; he waved from where he stood at the cash register. I waved back and then walked out.

Upon arriving at my father's house, I found my mother again in the greatroom. I let her know I was home, but she had been reading and I didn't want to interrupt, so I said little else before sitting in a nearby chair with a book of my own that I had nearby.

As I read, I couldn't help but notice that she frequently stopped reading to stare out the window. Her mind evidently wasn't on her book. Between Hansen and my mother, it must have just been a good day for thinking.

I also found my mind wandering. I was thinking about the scent of clove and mysterious jewels. After making slow progress in my book for a while, I set it down, walked to my mother, kissed her on the forehead, and then went to my room to go to bed for the night.

However, presently I found that I was still too preoccupied to go to sleep. After a few minutes I figured that I might be able to clear my head if I were to vent my thoughts. I didn't feel like telling my mother, but I could certainly tell Nova. I had waited long enough to write her back anyway; given the slow delivery speed of "snail mail", waiting too long to respond would make for a larger break in communication, which could break a good habit.

I went to my desk and grabbed my pad of paper and pen, and began to put words to the paper:

Nova,
  So it goes. I've met a boy, and he's gorgeous.

He's got long black hair that might look weird on someone else, but it works for him. His eyes are this amazing blue that I can't stop thinking about. He's not the sort that you'd see on a magazine cover, but I think somehow he's redefining my idea of handsomeness.

He's also intelligent and refined, and he likes the same things I do. It's more than that, though, in a very peculiar sort of way. When I see and hear him I feel like I already know him, like I've seen and heard those things before. As if I knew him before

Before what?

birth. Maybe that sounds crazy. Based on the idea that we did know other people before this life, well, statistically speaking, there are a lot of people in this world, and it's probably not very likely that we would encounter those we knew before, or if we do, it must not happen often at all, because I've never felt this before meeting him.

I probably shouldn't say any more now, but if anything develops you'll be the first to know.

Otherwise, there's not much new going on here. No job yet. Have so much fun over there for me! Tell Aline I love her!

Love,
Maria

The letter was short, like most were. We'd agreed beforehand that even a half-page would be enough. It was mostly important just to keep up the communication.

Now that I thought about it, she was probably due to return soon. When had she said she was coming back? We might not have many opportunities for letter-writing left. Oh, well.

I folded the letter and placed it in an envelope, which I addressed and stamped before setting it on a bare corner where it would catch my eye tomorrow when I could take it to a mailbox.

Before setting the pen in its case I took a short moment to examine it. It was an elegant, handmade, high-end fountain pen made of blue resin and big leaf maple burl wood, with a titanium nib. It was a gift from my father that must have cost a small fortune, and certainly far more than I would have ever spent on any writing instrument. He had said that the written word was of the greatest importance; it was notable, to me, to be given something "mightier than the sword" by someone who was so capable with swords.

Frankly, he was capable with a lot of things, but he'd had many years to gain and hone skills.

He'd been gone for another full day, and we'd had no word from him. I couldn't be sure how worried my mother was. I wasn't worried yet myself, and in truth I couldn't think of any circumstance in which I would be worried about him, but I didn't like not knowing where he was or why he had left. It must have been both important and urgent for him to leave the way he had. I had a hard time imagining that my father wasn't involved in some sort of significant work, but I didn't know much at all about the work he did. I was frustrated now for not having asked him more already, so that I might have some clue as to where he was.

I put the pen in its case and went to my bed.

Having set the pen aside, I found that my mind returned to Bastian. My attempt to set aside romantic notions had failed. The thoughts came back the same as before.

This time I also wondered about something he'd said—the comments about the nature of people. I didn't know why he had such a pessimistic outlook. I really didn't agree with him about that, but I supposed that everyone had disagreements. Maybe when we spoke about it again I could enlighten him a bit, or help him understand better.

It was early, but I was content to lie in bed with my meditations until I finally dozed off.

4

We all practice a certain amount of arrogance as we learn, in that we feel we can use knowledge to make judgments on the rest of the world around us. Because we deal with other people a lot, we make judgments about them—we assign motives, we assume capabilities or a lack thereof, we think we know what "type" of person someone is. We have a tendency to categorize and presuppose away individuality from others and then we like to think that we know what to expect from them. It's simply part of our nature to judge others, and we do it all the time.

This is particularly true with visual appearance. Part of our assessment of others comes from their speech and actions, but a disproportional piece comes from our first glimpse of them. We say "don't judge a book by its cover" to mean that we shouldn't assume things about people based on what we see at a glance; while this is partially true and can be useful, the fact is that we do judge people by what we see and hear from them, and most everyone chooses their appearance so that others will judge them a certain way. Business folks wear clothing and hairstyles that project professionalism. Hippies wear clothing and hairstyles that are supposed to reflect a freedom from restrictive social conventions. Girls often wear clothing—competitively, even—to emphasize and display their feminine curves because they want to be judged as a specimen of beauty and to be appreciated for it. Ignorant of the great irony, punk-type people give themselves a look that broadcasts their independence of thought, even though most are just copying other punks. Whatever façade people choose, most choose it because they know others will judge them accordingly. They want to be seen that way, and they know that a first impression is a lasting impression.

Despite what we say, we *want* to be judged by others, and unintentionally we follow the Golden Rule as we judge them right back.

I wouldn't acknowledge it openly, but I wanted Bastian to judge me, too. Though I was modestly dressed for this visit to Greywall Castle, my current appearance tended a bit toward displaying attractiveness.

So did that of the girl who answered Bastian's door.

She had glossy, straight black hair, mostly short but with sharply uneven bangs that fell stylishly over her left eye—mostly obscuring it—and down past the corner of her mouth. She wore a dark pink long-sleeved shirt with a black half-poncho over her right shoulder and arm, dark pink high-heeled shoes, and a pair of black capris that showed a trim figure to a careful eye. A round obsidian gem dangled at the end of a silvery earring on each ear. Her makeup had been carefully applied, with an apparent emphasis on dark mascara and eyeliner.

In comparison, my own outfit seemed a bit plain. My sun dress showed off my ankles and the little green flowers on it highlighted my green eyes, but next to this girl I couldn't imagine being the center of attention.

We stood in silence for a few seconds, each of us obviously surprised to see the other.

"Um, hi, I'm here to see Bastian."

She reacted with the sort of face she might make if I'd offered her a moldy sandwich. "No, sorry; that can't be right."

What? Who was she to say so? "I'm quite certain," I insisted. "We spoke the other day and he invited me here for a study of—well, a study session. He gave me a calling card." I pulled it from my small purse and held it in one hand, out of her reach but so she could see it. "I was here just yesterday."

She squinted at the card, grimacing, then responded, "He didn't say anything to me about it. Did he tell you what you were going to study?"

Why was I being interrogated? Without knowing her I wasn't sure how much I wanted to divulge. "It's something of an unusual topic. We're going to read some old books."

She sighed, frowning. "Well, all right. I guess we're part of the same study group. You may as well come on in." She walked back into the castle.

I was evidently an unwelcome surprise, but Bastian hadn't said anything to me about this girl either. I followed, trying not to let too much irritation enter my voice as I asked, "I don't mean to be rude, but who are you?"

She had stopped, and now gawked at me with surprise. "Oh." She frowned again. "I guess *I'm* the one being rude." She sighed. "I'm Amy."

I nodded. "Maria. It's nice to meet you."

"Nice to meet you, too."

We stood in silence after that; neither of our greetings had the sense of much real pleasure behind them. I had no idea what I'd done to ruin her day. "So, where's Bastian?"

"Oh. I'll take you to him. Shut the door."

I was a little taken aback, but complied, closing the large wooden door gently. *She could have at least used the word "please".*

"This way," she said without looking at me, while walking to a hallway I hadn't gone through before. She walked as if alone and in something of a hurry—not as if she were trying to lead anyone—with her clicking high heels definitely not slowing her down. Having used the side entrance of the building for the first time, I didn't know these passages at all and I worried that I could lose my way easily in this new wing of the castle. She got so far ahead of me that I lost sight of her, but fortunately our destination wasn't far.

The room had aged wooden paneling, arched wooden bookshelves set into the walls, and wooden flooring. It was elongated with a stone fireplace at one end. At the other end was a sturdy-looking desk, while in the middle of the room there were couches of leather in natural tones with burgundy pillows that matched the heavy rug in the center of the floor. On the end tables next to the couches there were brass lamps whose shades were also burgundy; the lamps were necessary to supplement the somewhat dim light coming from the chandelier. The chandelier itself, made of brass like the lamps, appeared at first glance to be modeled after antlers, but it was actually an intertwining set of multiple human arms. At the ends, cupped hands held small bulbs from which the inadequate light emanated. I was fairly astonished by this feature.

Bastian stood near the fireplace.

"Ah, Maria, you've returned," he said. "Wonderful. I see you've met Amy, also, but allow me to present a formal introduction." He approached and stood near us so we could face each other but still see him. "Amy, meet Maria. I just met her the other day. Maria, this is Amy Valentine. We recently became reacquainted, but we knew each other many years ago, when we were younger. Amy has always been fascinated by the supernatural, and while I can't say I appreciate the study of alien life like she does, we both are eager to find what truth lies behind the tales of demons and monsters."

Amy shrugged. "What can I say? I'm a believer."

A "believer", she had said. Interesting term. To me, that had always implied someone of religious faith. "So have you already found some of the 'truth behind the tales'?"

She leaned back. "Nothing to speak of, but don't you believe in anything you haven't seen?"

"Well, yes, without question, but…" I wasn't sure how to say what I was thinking without feeling like it would come out wrong. Sure, there were things unexplained by science that truly existed but that we, as humans, didn't know much about, but how would knowledge of real-life demons (or aliens, for that matter) truly enrich anyone's life? It just didn't seem to have real importance in a way that would change the way we lived with each other, or that it would have any lasting, important impact. Compared to some knowledge, it seemed hollow.

I had trailed off; Amy misjudged the conclusion I was getting to when she finished my sentence. "But you don't expect us to ever find that truth."

"No, that's not it. If I didn't, I wouldn't be here, right?"

Bastian had been watching, as if our exchange was entertaining him. "Anyway, Amy, Maria; Maria, Amy."

I tried to be sincere. "It's nice to meet you."

"Charmed, of course." Her tone was basically cordial, but I was quite certain she wasn't charmed; while her words clearly said it, her face didn't.

Bastian spoke again. "As she implied, Maria is here because she also takes an interest in the topics we're studying."

Amy scowled. "I didn't know we were looking for anyone else."

"And yet it will be a delight to have her with us." He grinned at me, not seeming to notice Amy's mild exasperation. "And this, Maria, is my study. I keep all of my interesting books here, including the book of which we spoke, along with various other records and assorted oddities."

"Oh," I burst out, "I have no idea why, but that reminded me of something." I pulled out my small bottle of iron pills and popped two into my mouth, chewing them contentedly and swallowing.

My sudden unrelated action must have surprised both Bastian and Amy; Bastian in particular regarded me with a curious expression.

Just then, I heard a door open, and a man I'd never seen before walked into the room. He was of average height and wore a black suit with a tie and white gloves. He was well-groomed with carefully-combed brown hair and slightly tanned skin, and almost had the air of a magazine model. He might have been as old as thirty, but maybe much younger. What struck me most was that he had a distinctly discontented expression that seemed somehow totally natural to him. Maybe it was just his downturned mouth.

Bastian glanced over at this new man as soon as he entered. "Ah! Abbott. I'm glad you came in. Maria, this is Broderick Abbott. You can call him 'Brody' for short, though we often refer to him by his last name. He was formerly the head of our household staff here, and currently is the entire household staff. He's also a reliable friend and has assisted us with our studies. He happens to be the one who helped me find *Demons and Dark Essences,* so he's really quite invaluable to me."

I stood to meet Abbott. "It's nice to meet you."

He regarded me for about two seconds, as if to do nothing more than acknowledge my presence. Then, without responding to me at all verbally, he looked at Bastian and said, "Sir, the task you charged me with earlier requires personal attention." Bastian grimaced, and was about to reply to him, when Abbott continued, "From you."

Bastian sighed. "If you will please excuse me, Amy, Maria." He looked at each of us in turn. "This shouldn't take long."

He walked from the room; Abbott followed without seeming to care about either of the rest of us.

I was familiar enough with what's called "awkward silence" to recognize it during the next couple of minutes.

Amy, frowning at the doorway, turned her attention to the nearest bookshelf. I wasn't sure what to do, myself; being such a recent arrival, I wasn't comfortable snooping around in this new place.

So I just stood there for a while, feeling overly self-conscious.

I kind of wished Amy would do something to help me feel at home.

Then, abruptly, she spoke. "Yeah, I think things are moving along nicely with Bastian."

I wasn't sure what she meant. "The research?"

She smirked. "No. Oh, the research is going fine, I'm sure, but that's not what I was talking about. I meant that things between *me* and Bastian are progressing nicely. In a personal sense."

What was she doing? Trying to claim Bastian as her territory? I looked away, generally toward the bookshelves on the other wall, then moved closer to them to pretend to inspect them.

She kept talking. "We really haven't known each other well for all that long, but sometimes two people just hit it off, you know?"

I wasn't at all sure I believed that she and Bastian were mutually interested in each other, but mostly I was irritated that she was trying so hard to convince me. It bothered me a little too much; for a moment all I could muster in response was, "Uhhh…"

"Or maybe you don't know," she continued. "Don't worry. Someday you'll meet someone that's just right for you."

I was getting angry now. I hardly knew her at all, and didn't feel like contradicting her about Bastian and kind of wanted to chew her out for patronizing me, but I didn't know what to say. So I didn't say anything. I just kept staring at the same book on the same shelf.

She must have tired of trying to convince me. I couldn't see her, but in any event, she stopped talking.

After a few minutes I also began to feel bored. How long was Bastian going to be gone?

When the discomfort and boredom grew too oppressive, I grabbed one of the books and let it fall open to a page somewhere in the middle. This book, or this part of it, contained scanned images of an old text on the right page and a typed transcript on the left. It was an account of some sort of battle. It didn't grab my attention much; in fact, my thoughts seemed to be anywhere but on the words right in front of me while I struggled in vain not to focus on the other girl in the room. I figured there must be something wrong with her; normally I didn't have trouble with people, but something about her was setting off alarms in the back of my head. I certainly wasn't keen on her trying to stake a hold on Bastian.

I almost didn't even notice when Bastian and Abbott came back into the room. "Oh, you've started already," Bastian said. "What are you studying?"

"Oh," I muttered, startled. "I don't..." I allowed my voice to trail off weakly; I was abruptly embarrassed by genuinely not being able to answer the question. With a pronounced blink, I decided to try to play it off casually. "Nothing, really. I was just flipping through pages."

He was unfazed. "Well, then, if there's nothing else to delay us, let's get right to the subject at hand." He held up another book so that I could once again read the title that had first captured my attention: *Demons and Dark Essences.*

4.1

"First let's open your mind a bit." Bastian sat down in the large chair, assuming a relaxed posture. "The subject of the book you saw before is creatures that most people place in the realm of fantasy. Goblins and gargoyles, and such, to start with some of the more well-known monsters."

"Goblins and gargoyles."

I'd repeated his words to prompt him to continue. I didn't mean to sound incredulous, but either I sounded that way to him or he must have anticipated such a reaction. "Oh, yes. Goblins used to be more numerous but were hunted almost to extinction. Even so, they are quite prolific, and have consequently survived in certain pockets of the world, often in caves. They tend to have green or grey skin, and—well, as for a visual description, this will suffice." He opened *Demons and Dark Essences* and turned it around to show me an illustration that made me start.

The wiry form depicted on the page was strikingly similar to the beast that had accosted me: gaping, toothy frown; misshapen face that couldn't be confused for human; three-point stance with a single claw raised as if to strike.

I must have displayed surprise; he drew back slightly. "Are you all right?"

"Fine!" I gave a little smile that I hoped was reassuring. "It's just an ugly thing. So goblins are real, and this is what they actually look like?"

"It's a fair depiction. They do tend to stay in dark places, massed in large tribes. As a generally weaker, less intelligent species they rely on the strength of numbers. Even the smallest imps and devels can be found alone at times, but goblins never are without a pressing need."

"Did you just say 'devils'?"

"'Devil' with an I is a religious idea I can't vouch for. 'Devel' with an E is a small, winged creature, like an imp. Both are smarter than goblins."

I wanted to change the subject. "What about the gargoyles?"

Bastian looked over at Abbott. "Would you care to explain the gargoyle to our new friend, Abbott?"

Abbott rapidly uttered, "No," without looking up.

Bastian smiled. "Well. All right." He set *Demons and Dark Essences* on a tall table nearby, still open. "The more well-known gargoyles are nothing more than statues, sometimes fearsome, sometimes comical, and often grotesque. Some of them are just statue heads projected away from walls or corners of buildings. But if you happened upon the right statue at the right time, you just might see it wake up, and move around, and display very clearly that it is in fact not a statue at all."

"Really."

He nodded. "They're probably lithovores and I'd guess they're related to dragons. Their key feature, though, is the ability to perform a near-perfect imitation of carved stone when resting. In a short period of time you'd never know the difference, but if you visited their roosts frequently you would notice that while the same supposed statues were there, they could be in different places and poses than what you'd seen before."

"That's wild. What's a 'lithovore'?"

"A creature that consumes stone for sustenance. If gargoyles ingest large quantities of minerals and incorporate them into their tissues, it could account at least in part for their stone-like appearance. I would expect them to be partially carnivorous as well, but nothing I've read describes their eating habits. Either way, lithovores of any variety are quite rare indeed; effective camouflage in animal life is not." He turned and adjusted a few items on a nearby shelf. "When it comes to imitations, though, the real master is the doppelganger, a demon that is horrifying in its own unique way."

"Why? What is it?"

"A doppelganger takes on the physical appearance of its target, mimicking it almost perfectly in voice and attitude, although to those with a sharp eye it ultimately can't hide its sinister disposition. It seems to always be in the service of some master; as it does so, its purpose is twofold: to deceive a target's associates and to eliminate the target itself. Doppelgangers often match or exceed their targets in physical strength, and have a great advantage in the sheer surprise and shock that the targets experience upon encountering beings who not only look identical to them but also desire to do them harm. People also tend to have psychological difficulty struggling against their mirror image, and it can prove to be fatal."

"And the doppelgangers take their place in society?"

"Only long enough to accomplish their purposes. What they do afterward, I don't know, but they care little for the damage they leave behind."

I was shuddering inwardly at the thought of meeting a monster that took my own appearance when Amy spoke up. "When a doppelganger kills the person it's going after, does it change again later and start to look like someone else?"

Bastian leaned back, looking upward as if to find the answer above him. "Hmmm. That's a good question. Everything I've read about them seems to indicate that a doppelganger is sort of a one-trick pony. Nothing I've read ever mentions them taking multiple forms. But I couldn't be sure."

I shook my head. "I'd be terrified to see a demon that looked like me."

Amy laughed. "Doppelgangers might not be so bad, depending on who they cloned. Some people are kinda nice to look at." She stared directly at Bastian as she spoke.

"Trust me, my dear," he answered, "regardless of how they appear to the eye, they wouldn't make good company. Their temperaments are less pleasant, and I believe they're quite incapable of mimicking human displays of affection."

She only smiled and kept her gaze steady in return.

"Well, Maria," Bastian said, turning back to me, "you say you'd be terrified to see the mirror image of yourself. Perhaps you might be even more frightened to see someone you knew who had died just days before?"

He seemed amused at my stunned silence. "Um. Yes," I muttered. "That would be frightening."

"Then you wouldn't care for an encounter with a revenant."

"Revenant." I hoped I wasn't parroting him too much.

He regarded me inquisitively. "I take it, then, that you don't speak French."

My revealing hesitation was just long enough for Amy to break in. "In French," she said, "it means, 'coming back'. Like, coming back from the dead." She was the picture of smugness.

In the next fraction of a second I spared a quick thought for her, feeling pretty sure of one thing: she also hadn't known what it meant until Bastian had explained it to her sometime before. "So you speak French, Amy?"

She pursed her lips. "Not really. I only know a couple words: *Au revoir.*"

Being men, Bastian and Abbott probably didn't pick up on the not-so-subtly implied suggestion. Of course, I wasn't sure Abbott was even listening.

Bastian started talking again before I could come up with a suitable retort. "As Amy explained, a revenant is said to be a person who has come back from the dead. They do not return to normal life, but instead haunt those they knew for a time, visible, audible, but distant, shadowlike, ever out of reach, bringing only false hope and pain. They end up being rather physically insubstantial, so it's unlikely that they possess the actual body of the deceased, but rather just its appearance. They could be said to be mischief-makers, except that the problems they cause tend to be more serious than simple mischief."

I wondered what kinds of problems those would be. A person's death brought a lot of changes, and confusion about death's finality would certainly be no light matter.

"And there are more like the revenant who are neither living nor dead. Amy?"

"The undead?" she piped up. "The really evil undead. Vampires."

Evil undead? "You're serious." This time I was careful not to simply repeat the last word she said.

She lowered her head and smiled. "Horrible creatures who eat nothing and drink only blood. Undying shapeshifters with unnatural strength."

I raised an eyebrow. "They're shapeshifters, too?"

"According to some accounts," answered Bastian, "vampires can turn into bats, dogs, even mist to accomplish their evil designs. That might be embellishment, though—false details added to legend over time."

"You call them evil. How are you so sure of that?"

Amy laughed aloud. "Are you serious? They kill to live. I'm pretty sure killing falls into the category of 'evil'."

I was taken aback. "Maybe they don't always kill. Maybe some of them drink something else…I don't know…cow's blood."

Amy laughed as loud as before.

"Oh, come now, Maria," Bastian said. "If you were a vampire, would *you* drink cow's blood?"

What a strange question to have to answer. "Well…no…"

"Hmmph." His satisfied smile bothered me. Why was he so insistent on making the point? He shook his head. "I'm sure that only human blood would be satisfying to the vampire—no other sacrifice would be sufficient."

I looked away. This was making me far too uncomfortable.

Amy spoke again. "They can also hypnotize people."

That was too much. "Now they're hypnotists."

"In fact, there actually are stories of mind control," Bastian offered, "though they might be exaggerated."

"Forgive me," I said, "but at some point this is getting a bit far-fetched."

"Well," he replied, "there are many different accounts, and sometimes it is difficult to tell which are more reliable. Old accounts of vampires disagree on even their basic form and appearance. Some state that a vampire is rather hideous and inhuman whereas others make them out to be human but inhumanly beautiful, while others relate an appearance just like normal people. Often they're said to be pale-skinned, but some stories depict them as ruddy or otherwise discolored. I suppose we'd have to meet one to be sure."

I diverted my eyes again. I suddenly became wary of myself for being overly defensive about the subject. It didn't seem like they were suspicious of me, but I didn't want to arouse any suspicion, especially when they already had a negative impression of vampires. I decided to keep the conversation going. "What makes a demon a demon, anyway? I take it that there's a long list of other types. But I mean, aside from those that kill people, what makes demons so generally evil?"

"Partly it's because they're dangerous," Bastian said, "though the same is accurately said of many very human people. But, also like some people, they're simply different. On one hand, they're humanoid but they look unusual, and, well, scary. On the other hand, because they're different they're not well understood. That makes them even more fearsome."

I reflected on this.

"And there's something else," he continued. "Their origin. In some cases they probably have no common origin with humans, but in others…they manifestly are corrupted humans. For example, the first vampire wasn't born a vampire; he *became* it. Vampires also are not known to reproduce in any way other than corrupting and transforming human subjects."

Not known to reproduce…a vampire isn't born, but has to "become" a vampire…that was something to ponder.

"Finally, through more than just their paranormal origins, demons all possess a quality of being *unnatural* in a way we can feel. The very existence of vampires and revenants is defined by a disobedience to the most fundamental law of life—the law that decrees an eventual end of that life. People, even those who make efforts to prolong their natural lives, have an instinctive sense that in due time death will arrive to us all, with a distinct finality. When they meet a being who defies death, they sense that something is wrong."

"You think people are always that astute?"

"Not always, no, but demons have a sort of aura that conveys their twisted nature to the rest of the world. It's just one more reason we think of them as 'evil', as Amy said. But if you meet any demons yourself, you can make a judgment call for yourself then. You'll have to let me know if you disagree with my assessment."

"You'll be the first to hear." Of course, just recently I'd encountered something that sure seemed to be a demon of the goblin variety, but I'd hardly had time to breathe, much less take notice of any "aura" it had.

"Good. But while I'm sure this has been interesting to you, I think I do you a disservice by telling you too much. The joy of discovery is often keenest when reading. I think now I'll let you peruse the book you've been waiting to study." He extended his hand toward the book he'd just placed on the table.

The conversation had been fascinating, but I was still eager to examine the book, so his prompting was welcome. "Okay." I moved to the table and sat.

"Bastian," Amy said from somewhere behind me, "can you show me where the sugar is?"

"Again?" he asked, seemingly amused.

"I figured I'd make some lemonade."

"That would be refreshing. Right this way."

I looked back; Bastian was already leaving the room, but before Amy left the room she gave me a smug smirk over her shoulder.

Only seconds after they'd left, Abbott stood and said, "If you'll excuse me," before also walking out.

Having been unexpectedly left by myself, I was annoyed. Who left a guest alone like that? I also wasn't sure what to do; I was still too new in the castle to feel comfortable going anywhere on my own. So I decided I could use the time to inspect the book that had brought me here.

It was lucky in a way that I would be able to read alone. A great part of my curiosity in the book came from wanting to better understand myself, and such personal exploration was probably best conducted while unaccompanied.

Bastian had set *Demons and Dark Essences* on a high table where I could examine its contents while still standing. I turned the page to find a section about the last type of paranormal creature he'd mentioned. The bold word stood out on the page: "VAMPIRE".

There were more illustrations here; they were peculiar, especially when I already had an idea of what a vampire should look like. Something struck me about each; in general, they seemed to be characterized more by the horrified reactions of the humans also shown in the images than by the depiction of the vampires themselves. The human onlookers were all either in open-mouthed terror or anger, or less commonly, were engaged in some sort of antagonistic gestures. Even in those cases the vampires never seemed to show fear, but rather annoyance.

Some of the vampires were less human-looking than others, and one in particular had an especially grotesque appearance: bald, gangly, gaunt, and with exaggerated fangs. While I supposed it was possible that the picture accurately portrayed some past individual, it made me begin to wonder about the accuracy of the book. Thus far I had simply accepted it as an authoritative source of knowledge, perhaps merely because it was old, but how was I to know that it was correct? I decided that even if this information about the supernatural world wasn't perfect, it was certainly more than anything else I'd ever seen.

That in itself was strange. While I still worried a little about what had happened to my father, I also began to wonder more and more why he'd never explained much about these things to me. For all his concern about my education in other areas, he seemed to have deliberately kept me ignorant about a significant aspect of my nature. I trusted him implicitly, but I almost felt betrayed by this ongoing omission.

I was far too interested in the book to keep worrying about my dad, though. I skimmed over the text, briefly searching one description after the next. Sure, vampires live on the blood of others. Sure, they're pale. But then I read some other "facts" that didn't match up with what I knew, like the classic can't-go-out-in-daylight myth. I scanned it a bit more carefully; after reviewing that passage again I saw that it was describing a particular individual who "didn't" go out in daylight, rather than "couldn't". I still had the uneasy feeling of uncertainty about the book, rather like having an itch that I couldn't reach to scratch.

My curiosity thus being insatiable, I kept searching. The book then highlighted a particularly noteworthy vampire: the famous Dracula. I'd never imagined him as a real person, but the book not only portrayed him as historic but also as heroic. The author, Drake, spared no words of praise: commanding, potent, gallant, regal, mighty, wise, stalwart, formidable, majestic, magnificent…there was a clear bias here. No matter how the author felt about vampires in general, Dracula was held in respect and even veneration throughout this text. But for the lack of a crown, the stately figure depicted in the full-length image that covered his introductory page could have been a king. Under it was inscribed the single-word caption: "DRACUL."

I couldn't see much detail of his face, though. That was almost disappointing. Not that I felt the same way about the "Prince of Wallachia" as the author did, but for some reason, perhaps because he was only newly real to me, I wanted to know more about him, including what he looked like.

The book didn't mention his origin, but mostly his accomplishments; whether he achieved them as a mortal or as a vampire was unclear. It almost felt like the author didn't care to consider his previous mortality at all, though I assumed that all real vampires were once human. What Drake did describe were events like the defense of nations and other displays of military prowess, and ruthless efficiency in administering from a governing seat.

Then the tone changed, and the actions described were clearly those of not only a vampire, but a being with great and unusual power. The ability to turn into mist, to commune with and even command certain animals, to bring dark weather, to conjure fire "from the depths of hell"…he was more than just a blood-drinking monster, but almost a sorcerer.

I closed the book while holding the page so that I could examine the cover, then turned to the title page. I noticed a symbol inscribed above the author's name. At first it appeared to be an eye, but when I looked at it directly I could see that is was, in fact, a dragon viewed from the side, but plainly shaped to look like an eye. The dragon's body was arced into a mostly ovoid shape with the tail curling sharply back underneath to form the general shape of the eye, and with a wing folded downward to form the pupil. The dragon's tail didn't quite reach all the way around to its mouth, but the shape was still definite. The icon was small, but detailed. I wondered why it was there. I flipped the book back open to the Dracula section.

"Finding what you're looking for?"

I snapped the large book shut at the sound of Bastian's voice and spun around. "Oh!" I laughed lightly. "Yes, I suppose. I don't know that I was looking for anything in particular, but it's very informative."

"I hope I didn't startle you."

"Hah! Well, you did, but it's okay. You came in quietly."

"My apologies. I had no intention of making a silent entrance. Perhaps it's habit for me. I actually came in a moment ago, but I was hesitant to interrupt. I was glad to see you engrossed in the text."

I smiled in return.

"Unfortunately," he went on, "something has come up, and I'm afraid that to take care of it I'll need to cut things short today. I know we've only just begun, and not even had a chance to delve into the matter together, but we'll have to adjourn until tomorrow."

"Wow," I said, not trying to hide my disappointment. "So do I need to leave already?"

"I apologize, but yes, temporarily."

"Could I at least borrow the book?"

"Oh. No, I tend to be extremely protective of that volume, especially given that it would be quite impossible to replace if damaged or lost."

I didn't know why I had to leave after spending so little time there, or how to feel about it.

"Don't worry," he said. "You'll have plenty of time tomorrow. You can come by again tomorrow, right?"

"Yes." I was quick to answer; perhaps too quick. It only took me about half a second to remember that today was Saturday, which meant that tomorrow was Sunday. Normally I reserved Sundays for different activities, but I could probably come back later in the day, well after my church services were over. He seemed bothered by having to make me leave, so I wanted to reassure him as well. "It's actually just fine; I have a few things to take care of at home today anyway."

"Good. Would you allow me again to escort you outside?"

"I think I can find my way back." Having said it, I was no longer sure, and I reminded myself that I wasn't in a rush to leave his company.

Fortunately, he insisted. "But it would be my pleasure." Again he offered his hand.

"Well then," I said, smiling as I took his hand. "Please."

The next half minute, not at all long enough for my preferences, was a pleasing recurrence of my departure from the castle the day before. I was almost certain that he was holding my hand more confidently this time, and it would have been with great disappointment that I would have let go, except that he added a surprising formality at the end. After leading me through the large exterior door and outside, he spun me gently, holding my hand up between us, and said, "Miss Maria, it has been a true pleasure, however brief. I am anxious for your return." And then he lowered his lips to my hand, leaving a light kiss on the top.

Wordlessly, I smiled and made my way to my car. This gorgeous young man had kissed my hand! As I walked I half felt like I was being carried above the ground. Once again he waited by his door as I drove away, but this time I didn't notice the abrupt change from castle and forest to city. Instead, my mind was focused on one small spot on the top of my hand.

4.2

There would be no more studying for me today at the castle, but on the bright side, I'd still have company. Saturday was when our housekeeper, Señora Catalina Moreno, and groundskeeper, Mr. Verner Freitag, made their regular appearance. Oh, and then there was Casey, Señora Moreno's helper. He was a newer hire, having replaced another young assistant who'd gone off to college a while back. They generally came over on Saturdays, though they also showed up at a moment's notice if a need arose on a weekday.

After getting back home I found Señora Moreno and Casey in a hallway outside one of the bathrooms. Small but stout, with dark hair that had been slowly greying for years, Señora Moreno had a perpetually worried face, as if she expected us young kids to start a fire somewhere any moment. At present she seemed more upset than usual and was shaking a finger at Casey while delivering a rapid tirade in Spanish. Casey, a blonde kid not quite my age, was shrinking in front of her, wincing at every wave of her hand.

After a few more short outbursts she was done, and hustled away to attend to something else. On her way out she passed by me, and with a cheerful smile said, "Hola, Señorita Maria."

"Hola, Señora Moreno," I answered before continuing over to the severely dressed-down Casey.

Casey sighed. "Between her and the old guy outside, I feel like Saturday is supposed to be foreign language day."

"Hah! I actually feel like that, too."

"Don't you guys hire anybody who speaks English?"

"They *both* speak English, and so do you. Señora Moreno just prefers Spanish and doesn't seem to mind it when other people around here don't speak it. What was she getting after you for?"

"I don't even know! I mean, at first she said something about not scrubbing the toilet right, and she got down and was showing me how to do it or something, but then she stood back up and started firing away in Spanish, and I didn't understand a thing."

"Yeah, she does that. Don't worry, though. It's kind of a sign that she likes you."

"Are you kidding?"

"Nope. You'll get to know her better."

Casey exhaled and walked back into the bathroom. I left him to his work. I was reminded, though, that I had my own bathroom to clean. My parents saw to it that our housekeepers didn't do *everything* for us.

So I grabbed a scrub brush and went to my bathroom, but I didn't stay there for long. I didn't want to spend a lot of time cleaning. Admittedly, I was feeling a little lazy, and I wanted to be around people right now rather than on my own.

I could easily track down Señora Moreno, but I knew she wouldn't be good for conversation while she had work to do. If I wanted to talk to her I'd have to wait until her various tasks were done. Mr. Freitag, however, was always happy to converse for a moment while he worked.

Freitag was German for "Friday". My mother had a tradition of greeting him every week by telling him that he was one day late, and at some point he had begun thinking each time of some imaginary excuse for this false offense of tardiness. They were both always entertained by it. For myself, I'd always thought it a humorous coincidence that I should have a good friend named after a month and a groundskeeper whose family was named after a day of the week, but irritatingly, no one else saw the humor in it. On a few occasions I'd brought it up with people, and the results were all exasperating. Hansen had shrugged, Nova just stared, my mother only said "oh" and went about her business, my father made a pithy comment about not finding it strange, and Señora Moreno replied in Spanish. So I stopped telling anyone how funny it was.

I had finally gotten comfortable pronouncing his name. I knew he appreciated it when others spoke his name with a proper German accent instead of Americanizing it. The V sound at the beginning of his given name and the long I sound and the "ah" in his family name were all natural to me now, or natural enough, anyway. I didn't think I had it spot on, but it was close enough to satisfy him.

I viewed Mr. Freitag as something of a wise man; he had lived in several different countries when younger and spoke each of the native languages—perhaps five or six in total. Most of the time he didn't have much lengthy conversation for me, but here and there he'd been unusually perceptive and had given highly sound advice. Though it was often a corrective sort of advice, he was always good-natured.

While I'd never asked either of them about it, I was under the distinct impression that both Señora Moreno and Mr. Freitag knew what my father was. I knew that he trusted them implicitly. That meant, in turn, that I also trusted them, in the sense that I knew they'd never try to harm me or my family in any way. I didn't necessarily trust them with my deepest secrets, though. My parents had been my only true confidants. But in an emergency, if my parents weren't available for some reason (like my father wasn't right now), Señora Moreno and Mr. Freitag were people I could turn to.

While Señora Moreno's realm was within the house, Mr. Freitag was almost never there. Instead, to find him I had to search outside. He wasn't hard to find. As I circled around the house, I saw him quite a distance away next to the hedges at the edge of my father's property, in front of my father's very small orchard area. I also noticed Hansen in his yard, picking up something off the grass. I called to him. "Hi, Hansen!"

He looked up and waved, then trotted over toward the gate between sections of hedge, evidently eager to see me. "Hi, Maria. How are things?"

"Fine."

"I talked to your mom earlier. She said your dad's gone right now."

"Yeah, he's travelling."

"That's what she said. If you need anything while he's gone, let us know. My family would be happy to help. You know we're always there for you."

"I know. Thank you."

"We should probably have you and your mom over for dinner sometime. It's been a while."

I thought about it. "Yes, it has."

Hansen smiled. "Hey, I've got a few things to do, so I'll talk to you later, okay?"

"Okay," I said, and he turned and walked away. "Bye, Hansen."

He gave another smile and a wave over his shoulder, and walked on.

I turned back toward Mr. Freitag, and moved toward him.

"Hallo, Herr Freitag!" I called out as I approached. "It's nice to see you."

"Ah, guten nachmittag, daughter of the master." He never called me by name. It almost irked me, but not quite. I knew that for him, this title of address was laced with implicit respect for my father. "You have been tending to the gardens." His white-grey beard was short but rough, especially under his cheeks, as if he hadn't trimmed it in a while. For being as old as he was, he looked like he'd been extremely fit in his younger years. His amber-colored eyes glinted as he regarded me.

I hoped he liked my work. "Yeah, I wanted to help out."

"It was carelessly done," he said. "I will correct it." He didn't seem seriously bothered by it, though I couldn't tell if somehow he was amused. Probably not.

"Maybe you could teach me to do it the right way sometime," I offered.

"The cultivation of life is a worthwhile skill." He clipped the end of a branch. "Perhaps you will make a good student. I will consider it," he said with a smile.

I watched him make a few more snips with the shears. "Mr. Freitag," I began, "my father is away. He's been gone for a couple of days, but he didn't tell us anything before he left."

Mr. Freitag stopped smiling. "You are worried for him?"

"Well, not really."

"That is good. You should know better. But it may be that concern is warranted...in recent days I feel something disquieting to my heart." He looked toward the sky, inhaling deeply as he examined it. "A dark wind passes...I do not know what it means, but I think that it does not mean nothing. I would advise that you be cautious for the time being, most especially with the master away."

"What do you mean? What's wrong?"

"As I said, I do not know, but a thing nearby is wrong." He took a heavy breath. "I can feel it seeping into my soul. I will take my own precautions, but you must also."

I don't even know what you mean! "Precautions against what?"

"Once again, I do not know, but you must watch. You must keep your eyes ready and your mind as keen as shears." His words weren't as warm as usual, but he appeared genuinely concerned.

I nodded to him. "I will."

"If I learn anything of your father, I will let you know."

"Thank you. I hope his absence doesn't keep you from getting paid."

"I received compensation for my services long ago," he replied. "My arrangement with your father is satisfactory to me, and requires little attention from him."

I had no idea what he meant. But even if I was confused, I was still appreciative. "Okay."

He returned to his clipping, seemingly with a more thoughtful bearing than before. I left him alone to his thoughts while I went back inside the house to try to sort out what he'd told me.

I'd been unsettled by my last conversation, but as the evening wore on, I felt less and less daunted by Mr. Freitag's warning. By the time I got into bed, the ubiquitous sense of security of my home had helped me feel very much at ease.

I was glad to think that even if a "dark wind" was blowing, I had a new ally. Bastian knew things that other people didn't know, and he was looking out for me. So while I did want to take Mr. Freitag's words to heart, I was largely reassured by my new acquaintance being not far away.

When night came, that assurance made me feel so at peace that I fell asleep earlier than usual.

4.3

Amy answered the door again.

This time she was wearing black leggings, black calf-length boots with pointed toes, a bright green sleeveless tunic, a thin silver arm cuff that spiraled around her upper right arm, and a black sash around her waist, tied at her right side. She had on the same obsidian earrings as before.

I mentally reviewed my own apparel, instantly feeling dissatisfied. I hadn't wanted to feel as if I was in any sort of contest with Amy, so after church I'd stayed in my white cowl-necked shirt and dark purple draped skirt with heels. It was nothing bad, but also not as showy as it could have been, and in hindsight I felt I should have dressed more competitively. Like it or not, the contest was on, and this was the second time I was going to be considerably outclassed in the arena of fashion.

"Maria. Good to see you again."

It was difficult to respond with any kind of sincerity after hearing the false—and weak—enthusiasm in her voice. "Of course. You, too."

She gave a disingenuous smile and held the door open for me.

"You're sure showing up late. Bastian's been gone for a little while; said he had something he needed to do. You can do some studying on your own though, to try to catch up to us."

"Okay." I didn't want to let her get to me, and I figured that simple politeness was the best reply to any taunt she might throw at me.

I followed her into the study; when I arrived, Abbott was there, in the same black suit he'd worn before. He handed me a small piece of paper, folded in half with my name written on the top. On the inside a short note was printed. It read:

> *I realized I needed to finish something today. It won't take me long. Please study more by yourself to catch up.*
> *- Bastian*

It was irritating that he and Amy had said something so similar, but it must have just been an unfortunate coincidence.

Neither Amy nor Abbott seemed like good company, so I followed the suggestion to do some studying on my own. I sat at a table and stayed there quietly, minute after minute. I kept my back toward the center of the room as often as possible. For some reason it was kind of hard to get into the spirit of the research today, and nothing I read or skimmed caught my interest enough to stay engaged.

Amy and Abbott left and re-entered the room at times. I eventually got any distracting thoughts out of my head, but as the time passed—I must have spent two hours just sitting here—I found myself impatient. So far I'd mostly had a lot of compelling information given to me, and that kind of "research" was easy to follow, but left to myself and having to pore through material without knowing where I would find pertinent facts proved to be not only unsatisfying, but boring as well.

While letting my mind wander I thought back to seeing Hansen in church earlier. He'd been a little stand-offish at first, or at least he seemed to pay less attention to me than usual, until I delivered a kick to his buttocks in the hallway (certainly not in the chapel). He'd spun around, clearly surprised, but any sign of anger had disappeared when he'd seen me. He'd asked me what it was for, and I'd said that he just looked like he needed a good kick in the pants. He'd warmed up after that.

If Hansen was concerned about me being alone with Bastian I could reassure him on that point, what with Amy and Abbott almost always being around, and at the moment Bastian was gone anyway. Resigning myself to having poor company, I tried again for a while to do some research.

Eventually I needed to use the toilet. I didn't bother to excuse myself. I just got up and left the room wordlessly like the others had done.

As I walked to the bathroom I became curious about the castle. There was much that I'd never seen, so I walked down a different hallway to explore just a bit. Casually glancing through an open door, I was startled to find a very untidy bedroom. Not only was it generally a mess, but several of the items strewn about were damaged, and the frame of the bed itself was broken. Surprised, I backed away and went back to the restroom.

When I came back to the study, I could hear Amy's and Abbott's voices raised in some sort of argument.

"If you're really worried about it, you can ask him when he returns," Abbott was saying as I walked in.

"You can bet I'll ask him. He owes us an answer!"

"Amy, just calm down!" It was the most energy I'd seen him display yet.

"I'll calm down when I feel like it!"

"What's wrong?" I asked, walking toward them cautiously.

"Grismur," Amy spat. "The name of the big, bad guy we're trying to stop. It's French. Funny coincidence. 'Gris' means grey, and 'mur' means wall."

My head spun. I had no idea what to make of this news.

Abbott said nothing to deny it.

I was stunned for a moment, but then I asked Amy, "How did you figure that out?"

"Listen," Abbott interjected before Amy could speak. "It doesn't matter."

"How could it not matter?" Amy almost shouted. "This whole time we've been studying and searching to try to stop some big bad guy named Grismur, and now it turns out that it's *Bastian's* name."

"It's true that 'Grismur' is a rough translation of my family name," Bastian admitted, stepping abruptly but coolly into the room, "but I'm not the only man who bears the name 'Greywall'." We all waited for him to continue speaking. "You may have noticed that my father is conspicuously absent from this home. We had certain...disagreements...particularly about how the Demon Stone should be used."

Amy put her hand to her mouth. "Grismur is your *dad?*" Her eyes were wide. "Bastian, I'm so sorry for accusing you!"

"It's not something I like to talk about a lot, though I suppose eventually you were all bound to learn the truth."

I probably felt as embarrassed as Amy. The whole quest took on a new aspect now; not only was Bastian trying to stop someone's evil ambitions, but that person was his own father. How difficult it must be for him.

If anything, the news made the quest all that much more important. Whatever else happened, sorting out this problem meant resolving a serious family matter for Bastian as well. If he had to contend against his father I wanted to be there to support him, and if somehow they could be reconciled to each other I wanted to help.

The thoughts occupied me entirely for a moment and before I could move into any sort of action, Amy shimmied over to Bastian and put her hands on his shoulders. "I'm so glad you're back, and I'm so sorry about your father. Are you going to be okay?"

"I'm fine," he said, smiling and gently removing her hands. He stepped closer to me. "You're not distressed, are you?"

"No, no."

He stared directly into my eyes for several seconds. "Let's take a break, shall we? I want to ask you something anyway."

Amy shot him a glance that almost seemed worried. He didn't show any sign of noticing it.

"Okay," I said, standing up from the table. Bastian walked to one of the doors; as I followed I tried not to pay attention to Amy, but I couldn't help seeing her out of the corner of my eye. Instead of looking jealous, she seemed almost hurt.

So be it.

I followed Bastian down a hallway and into a separate room that was furnished as if to be a lounge. I couldn't see any sound system, but from somewhere I heard what sounded like the end of a song. Then as Bastian moved to the window and adjusted the shades, I heard familiar recorded notes from a piano, followed by a woman singing. I had recognized the tune already, but hearing the first few lyrics of *Misty* solidified my surprise. "You like Ella Fitzgerald?"

He tried to avoid speaking while she was singing. "*The incomparable* Ella Fitzgerald. Yes, I do." He then remained silent for a while, not looking at me. I guessed that he was just listening to the music, but after a moment he broke in with somewhat muted speech. "I take it then that you also know her work?"

I also spoke quietly so as to not spoil the song. "Oh, yes. My father and mother both enjoy it, so I couldn't help but know it as I grew up."

"So, I didn't ask you this before, but you like older music?"

"I like some contemporary stuff also. The Flea Radicals, the Really Big Siege Machines, the Nuclear Third Rail…"

He smiled. "I've never heard of any of them."

I smiled back. "I guess most people haven't. They were obscure a few years ago, and never advanced a whole lot. They all have songs on LP, though."

He stared at me for a minute, making me wonder what he was thinking, and why he'd brought me here. Ella sang about her unnamed love interest leading her on, and it being just what she wanted. Bastian's voice cut in: "Maria, are you attached?"

"Attached? To what, music?"

"Heh. No. What I meant to ask is: are you seeing anyone currently?"

Blood flushed to my face. "Um. No, no, I'm not dating anyone."

He reached for a small box. "I don't mean to be too forward. I just hope not to offend a boyfriend by giving you this."

Opening the box, he withdrew an ornate layered necklace with a pendant on the lower chain that was encrusted with obsidian. With its intercrossing waves the pendant had an elongated, generally triangular shape with the edges curving inward and the largest of the gemstones dangling from the bottom.

He held it up for me to see while I tried to mentally process the fact that he was giving me something so beautiful. He lifted it a bit more as he asked simply, "May I?"

I nodded to give consent, and he reached around my neck to fasten the clasp behind it. As he came closer his eyes were all I could look at, and I again smelled the scent of clove. He gazed back at me, unblinking, until the necklace was secure and he stepped back again. We stood still for several seconds before he smiled again and gestured to a nearby mirror.

I hesitatingly turned away and walked to the mirror, positioning myself so that I could see my whole upper body. My outfit seemed inadequate as a backdrop for the elaborate jewelry, but when I saw the shimmer from the metalwork and gemstones I had to bite my lip because I could hardly believe the necklace was mine.

"Do you like it?" he asked from behind me.

I smiled and stepped just a bit to the side so that I could see him in the mirror. "Of course I like it!" I turned one way, and then another, pleased with the results. "My goodness! This must have cost a fortune!"

He laughed. "I suppose it would be expensive if it was for sale, but I made it. This is what has kept me occupied outside of the study recently. I just finished it. I told you I was a jeweler, right? I'm still relatively new to it, but it was a family profession."

There was that past tense again when he spoke of his family. He'd never said anything about them until the startling revelation just minutes ago, and he'd only mentioned his father. I would have been curious enough to ask about them, but he was obviously sensitive about the subject and it was no time to pry when he was bestowing me with a lavish gift.

"Of course, I've been working on other skills also," he continued. "My ability in alchemy is even more limited, but this necklace is enchanted. It'll help protect you—think of it as a talisman, or even just a good luck charm."

I looked back at the necklace. "Thank you, Bastian."

"You're very welcome, Maria." He stepped forward. "I'd prefer it if Amy didn't see it, though. She might feel jealous."

"Okay." I reached for the clasp, but he caught my hands. A little shock of thrill ran through me as our skin touched; surprised, I withdrew my hands.

"No, please leave it on," he said, stepping back again. "You can conceal it with your shirt. Always keep it on, for your own protection. You'll find that it's comfortable enough to sleep in."

"Are you that worried about me?"

"I'm worried enough, but I mostly like the idea of you keeping my gift with you all the time."

In fact, it was light and comfortable to wear. "All right. I'll keep it on."

"I'm glad." He looked me over and then gazed into my eyes. "You look lovely. Radiant. Stunning, even."

"It helps to have nice jewelry."

"Trinkets can only accent beauty, but that beauty is certainly already there."

Hopefully my blushing was also an accent; with as warm as it was making me I was sure it was visible. I felt like I was floating and simultaneously wanted to be closer to Bastian.

After speaking the words, "If I may," he obliged my unspoken desire. He stepped forward again with outstretched hands, taking my right in his left and reaching around to the small of my back with his other.

Before I realized what was happening, my left hand was on his arm and he was leading me gently in small arcs around the edge of the room to the time of the piano in another Ella Fitzgerald song. She began to sing again, this time about not having anyone, "until you".

Bastian kept his eyes locked on mine as we moved. I was glad that he was leading, certain that if it was up to me I would be crashing into furniture or walls repeatedly. It was all I could do to keep my head while stepping in coordination with him and not turning to jelly. Between Ella, the dancing, and the gaze of the handsome man, I was scarcely able to think.

Bastian spoke softly. "You're uncommonly graceful. You're also easily led. I like that...very much."

Ella repeated her last few lyrics as Bastian continued to spin me throughout the room, finally bringing me to a slow halt as the singer mentioned Cupid. Then I was stunned into complete immobility as, after releasing my raised hand, he placed his left hand lightly under my chin and moved his head forward, bringing his lips closer and closer to mine. The world around the two of us disappeared and a flurry of fleeting but potent thoughts flooded through my mind: clove—blue eyes—hands—lips—lips so near mine—

And I flinched, abruptly turning my head to the side.

The instant I had done so, I flushed with embarrassment.

It seemed that thousands of silent voices in my mind shouted at me all at the same time: *"Are you crazy?"* And I knew I must be.

But at the same time, another voice was present, one that had been there all the time, so quiet that I barely noticed it, but all the same I could hear it and I remembered how my mother had warned me about boys and kissing. She'd warned me more than once, almost as if a boy's kiss was something dangerous. That was what had made me dodge away, directly against my instincts.

Mother! I thought. *You've ruined my best chance for a romantic first kiss!*

Unaware of my inner conversation, Bastian drew back just a bit, a light laugh now on those same lips he would have used to kiss me.

"I'm sorry," I blurted out. "I'm just...not used to that."

He grimaced and cocked his head.

I frowned. "Maybe I'm not quite ready. I'm sorry."

He smiled, tilted my head back to the side, bent forward again, and softly kissed my cheek.

I closed my eyes as I felt his lips touch my skin—ever so delicately, resting for an electrifying and savored but suddenly concluded moment—and then lift away again.

The kiss was more than thrilling; it was reassuring. Another man might have let my rejection turn him away permanently, but he had let me know that it was okay—he wasn't closed off to me, and he still wanted to show affection. This kiss on the cheek was a prelude and a promise. It made me happy—even grateful.

I let my eyes stay shut while the scent of clove diminished; he also stepped back, letting go with his other arm. I relished the fresh sensual memory for several seconds while in the luxury of no visual distractions.

Then I opened my eyes again, letting my arms gradually lower to my sides again. A shiver ran the course of my body.

Bastian, a step farther away, extended one hand to the side, gesturing toward the door. "Shall we return to the others?"

In the background, Ella Fitzgerald had moved onto a different song I didn't know quite as well, and was singing about not having time for the waiting game with some love interest. I nodded to Bastian, and he led me from the room back through the hallway and into the study.

During the short walk I gently caressed the jewelry with one hand and let the other hang free; I hoped that he would reach back to take it in his, but we continued without further incident. Before we reached the study, I tucked the necklace under my shirt so that it wasn't visible.

When I caught sight of Amy again, I halted mid-step. Looking at her earrings, I could see that they partially matched the style of my new necklace—they seemed to be made of the same materials, and fashioned similarly. Did Bastian also make them for her? I felt a bit jealous, although as I considered them it was easy to convince myself that my necklace was much more ornate.

I must have displayed some shock; when she saw me she glowered. "Is something wrong, Maria?"

"Oh!" I cleared my throat, then smiled naturally. "No, no problem at all."

She only frowned in response.

Little else of interest happened in the castle that evening. Maybe I was too lost in thoughts of romance to notice much. Eventually, I decided it was time to wrap things up for the day and go home. As usual, Bastian saw me to the door, and as usual, Amy stayed after I left. I wondered, in passing, where she lived.

I uncovered Bastian's necklace while driving home, gently fingering it now and then, but I put it back underneath my shirt once I got back home. Perhaps I worried what my mother would think about a boy giving me jewelry.

I needn't have been anxious; she still seemed so preoccupied that she probably wouldn't have noticed it anyway. There was little I could do for her concerns at the moment, and I was still conflicted about missing that first kiss, so aside from letting her know I was back, I said nothing more and went on to my room.

It was already late, and I had little to do before going to bed other than cleaning up a bit. As I got ready to shower I was about to take off the necklace, when I remembered his request that I keep it on, even while sleeping. Surely he didn't mean when I showered as well, did he? He had asked me to keep it on "always"...and there was something sweet about the idea of never taking it off. I noticed again how surprisingly smooth it was, and as I placed my hand on it again I decided I could continue to wear it comfortably all the time—even in the shower.

By the time I got out of the shower I'd started to doubt that he wanted me to wear it quite so persistently. Maybe I'd taken him too literally and was being silly; but by then the point was moot, and it hadn't gotten in the way. I was sure that I really could wear it all the time without being bothered.

I wasn't normally one to be preoccupied, but as I lay in bed my mind moved back and forth around one place, or, more accurately, one person. Without any real pattern I drifted between recurring thoughts of his hair, his eyes, his speech, the dancing, and various charming things he'd done. One thought that lingered powerfully, bringing a sort of warmth that almost made it hard to lie still, was the memory of him, his face, so near to mine as he'd given me a beautiful piece of jewelry, and again as he'd moved close to kiss me. I wanted to get something scented with clove to keep nearby, to make the memories more vivid.

He had crafted the necklace and pendant by hand. It wouldn't hurt to be close to a jeweler; I'd never be short of ornamentation. Maybe I could get him to make me a circlet. I couldn't imagine that they were in fashion, but I'd always liked the look when I'd seen it on elves in fantasy books and movies. Really, though, circlets were probably only for royalty in past centuries. Maybe romance was making me goofy. Still, it would be nice for him to keep making things for me to wear.

Of course, this was assuming I kept a long-term relationship with him, but I was comfortable making that kind of assumption. He'd sent some very strong signals! So yes, even though I wasn't experienced with this sort of thing I expected that we would have a long-term relationship. That idea was certainly something to ponder...with possibilities like what to wear on a special day, the most special of days...possibilities that I was bashful to think of, even in the privacy of my own room. I let myself think about wedding colors, cakes, dresses, and then I thought again about the sweetness of a kiss...but presently I felt a soft heaviness on my eyes. For the short time left that I remained awake that night my thoughts never left this young man with dark hair and profoundly blue eyes.

4.4

Why did she always answer his door?

I could easily picture Abbott ignoring the doorbell without a moment's concern about any visitors, but why wasn't Bastian attending to the entrance of his own home? I couldn't imagine that Amy wanted to see me, but she wouldn't have expected anyone else. Her presence was irritating.

As was the fact that her sense of fashion surpassed mine. Whereas I had stepped up my style and thought I looked great in jeans that matched the form of my legs and a loose-hanging bright green tunic, I felt like I was outmatched again. Today Amy wore a grey, one-sleeved, pencil-skirt sheath, purple lace tights, grey Mary Jane shoes, a purple ribbon choker tied in the back, and a ring on her right ring finger with a large purple rose the same shade as the tights and choker.

I noticed that yet again she wore the same earrings. This now made me curious. Bastian must have made them for her, and he might have made a similar request to her to keep them on all the time. Did his gift to me mean that I was replacing her?

I hoped that I would be able to spend time alone with Bastian today. If I was able to manage that, and after yesterday's events I believed I could, it wouldn't matter how good she looked.

"Well, don't just stand there." She walked inside, leaving the door ajar.

Hello to you, too…

I made my way to the study, where I found Abbott and Bastian waiting. Abbott was again wearing the same black suit with white gloves.

"Maria!" Bastian said with a broad smile, crossing the room partway. He was wearing a classy jacket that seemed inappropriate for indoor usage. "Welcome once more to my home. Today's something of a special day for you. Now that you've gained all of the foundational knowledge, it's time for you to hear the next part." Bastian pursed his lips. "This is crucial for the next steps we'll take. We've learned about an old Chinook tale…no, not Chinook…anyway, an old tribal American tale that tells of a guardian who possessed a jewel said to make grass and trees grower greener and taller."

"The Life Stone."

He nodded. "That tale is the most recent record of the location of the gem." Now he frowned. "That being said, many years have passed and this information might not still be accurate even if it used to be. I have more confidence in our other records, but for the Stone's location this is all we have to go on. According to the legend, this guardian lived in a cave. Further description is somewhat cryptic; it's written that the guardian lives 'above the chief and beyond the waters'."

"In a cave?"

"Yes. Water in a cave is not uncommon, but the 'chief' is a mystery."

"Where is this cave supposed to be?"

"We think it's actually not far from here, but where exactly, we don't know yet. With any luck, a bit more research will divulge the location."

"What do you know about the guardian?"

"Very little. It must be old, but likely still alive, sustained by the Life Stone. It has had the Life Stone for decades, or perhaps centuries. It is also said to be able to sense the heart of those nearby."

"It can read minds?"

"Maybe, though I get the impression that the word 'heart' was chosen specifically in place of the word 'mind'."

"I didn't know mind reading was possible."

"It might not be. It's hard to know how reliable this information is."

I smiled. "I guess we'll find out, right?"

"That is my hope."

"That's all we know about it?"

"It may well also be the same creature known elsewhere as 'the Forlorn'. In a separate account, the Forlorn is described as a being of long life that was either much like a man or that had once been a man, who had killed its own friends and subsequently chose complete solitude. Solitude is definitely something that a cave-dweller would have."

"Well, we just need to find the cave, then."

"And take the Life Stone for ourselves. We have a transcript of the old tale. A copy is in that folder on the table for you to read." He pointed.

Amy stepped into the room.

"Hello, my dear," Bastian said with a smile. It bothered me, but I had little time to react before he turned back to me. "There's one more relic to show you. It may be vital in finding the Life Stone."

After moving across the room, Abbott opened a desk drawer and pulled out a four-inch shining metal rod with a small jewel embedded in the end.

"It was inherited, and slightly damaged before," Bastian went on, "but I repaired the guiding rod. When we eventually seek out the Life Stone and the Demon Stone, we'll use this."

I stepped closer to see the item better.

"We call it a Seeker. When one points it toward another artifact that has been imbued with power through alchemy, the Seeker will grow warmer. From too great a distance or if not held in the hand, it does nothing, but the closer you are and the nearer it points, the warmer it grows." Abbott gingerly held it out to me.

I took it. "It's heavy for being so small."

"'Cause it's made of lead," Amy offered.

"With a relatively thick silver plating," Bastian added. "When we found it the silver was not only tarnished, but mostly worn away. I re-coated it, and it conducts heat better than before."

For a moment it felt like it was getting warmer, as Bastian had described, but Abbott slipped it out of my hand again with surprising manual dexterity and walked back to the drawer with it, placing it back inside.

"I keep asking Bastian to let me try it," Amy said.

"Oh, don't pout," Bastian replied with a smile. "I'm guarded with it, but we'll use it soon enough. It's not quite time for seeking the Life Stone, not yet, but I think it shouldn't be long before we know where to start."

I suddenly thought of my irons pills; I'd let a lot of time pass without taking any. I took out the bottle and popped a pill in my mouth. Everyone else in the room looked curious as I chewed and replaced the bottle. Amy was just opening her mouth as if to say something, but I spoke first. "So does that thing get pretty hot when it's right next to something magical?"

Bastian answered. "'Magic' is a bad word, but yes, you'll want to put it away when you get close enough to no longer need it. I'm not sure it would burn your hand, but I wouldn't be surprised. Let's not find out."

"Well," I said, "let's get back to studying, and find that cave."

"Actually," Bastian said, "we'll have to leave the research to you and Abbot for a short time. I believe you can find the vital clue we're missing. Meanwhile, Amy and I are going to seek out a person we think can help us. Including travel time, we should be gone for at least five days."

The now-familiar smug expression was back on Amy's face.

"Abbott, help me with my things," Bastian said. "Maria, I'll be back in a moment."

Amy still had the self-assured smile on her face as she watched Bastian leave, followed by Abbot.

She then turned toward me. "By the way, I didn't want to say this in front of anyone else, but I think Brody likes you."

That was unexpected.

"You two would make a great couple."

Now I really didn't know what to say. Was she serious?

"Don't move too fast, though." Amy smiled in a way that somehow seemed utterly false, and then winked and turned her attention somewhere else.

I had to admit that Broderick Abbott wasn't bad-looking, but I definitely had no interest in him at all. From what I could tell, he also had no interest in me. Amy was up to something.

With disgust I realized what she was after. Or rather, *whom* she was after. It wasn't complicated. She'd somehow set this up specifically to get Bastian to herself. I'd been caught off guard by what she'd said just now, but it was obvious that she was trying to turn my focus toward the other guy. For now, it seemed that part of her scheme had worked, but if she thought I might take a romantic interest in Abbott she was off her rocker. "Amy, you can bet your last dollar that I won't move fast with Abbott."

"Okay. Take it slow!"

I didn't want to talk to her any more. Thankfully, Bastian returned. "Amy," he said, "You'd better put your things in the car. We're otherwise ready to leave, and there's no sense in delaying."

"Sure thing, sugar." She winked and walked out.

Bastian closed the door gently behind her. "Maria, I don't want you to worry about Amy. I won't do anything untoward. I just need someone with me for this task, but I need you to keep on the research to find what we've missed—to succeed where we haven't yet. Okay?"

I wasn't sure what to think, but I decided to trust him. I nodded.

"I look forward to returning to you," he said.

I felt a rush in my heart. "Yeah." It was too simple a response from me, but all I could come up with at the moment.

"Come and see me off," he said. He took my hand and led me to the back door. Before stepping out, he raised my hand and kissed the back of it lightly. Then he released me and opened the door to step outside. He strode to his car—a sporty and obviously well-maintained black Jaguar, if I wasn't mistaken—and then walked around and got in without looking back.

Amy sat in the passenger seat; she'd appeared concerned at first, but when she saw me she gave a knowing grin, which stayed with her as she turned her head forward and rode away.

She may feel like she's won some victory, but I know better.

I walked back to the study, where I found Abbott.

It struck me that my mother wouldn't want me to spend time alone with a man like this, although for some reason I had been willing to overlook that same concern with Bastian. I supposed I was just comfortable with Bastian, but Abbott seemed less trustworthy. He hadn't been any real problem before, though, so this would probably be fine.

"Mr. Greywall seems to think that you'll be able to discover something we haven't," Abbott said. "I don't know why he has such a hope."

Okay; he was already getting on my nerves. "Well, Brody, I don't know why you're always so full of 'nope'. Maybe he's right. Maybe I'll be able to find something that you guys missed. It's not going to hurt to try."

"Suit yourself."

He then just stood there. Feeling insulted by his persistent cynicism, I decided to get right to work. I moved to the table, sat down, and opened the folder Bastian had indicated.

The papers seemed strange; it was just a few pages. While I didn't necessarily want to read a whole book, I couldn't help but think that a bit more context would be nice to have. Maybe the stories weren't all that long, or maybe the other parts were unrelated. Either way, Bastian had decided that this was the part that was important enough to leave for me, so I read through the few pages he had left.

Most of it was as he'd already described, albeit in different and sometimes hard-to-understand wording, and then there was a bit of extra information that seemed irrelevant. But one line of text jumped out at me. *The cave lies north of the river near the great land bridge.* Bastian hadn't mentioned that, had he? It seemed like a rather large clue. If the cave was somewhere nearby, the river mentioned must be the Columbia. Bastian must have realized that as well, but the Columbia River ran for quite a distance from the north and hooked around to also run quite a distance to the west before eventually reaching the ocean, so it didn't narrow down the search area as much as I would like.

I wasn't sure what the "great land bridge" was, though. When I thought of a land bridge, Russia and Alaska came to mind. In school I'd been taught that ancient peoples had crossed from Asia to North America by walking, but that the land they traversed was now submerged. That kind of land bridge didn't make sense, though. If there was a place on the river where the land reached all the way across, it would have to mean that the river itself was no longer flowing. So it couldn't be a bridge in the river itself. Maybe the land bridge was at the mouth of the river, but that didn't seem likely either. While the western coastal area of Alaska wasn't all that far from Asia, the last 300 miles of the Columbia, including its mouth, lay between the states of Washington and Oregon. To the west of those states was nothing but thousands of miles of ocean.

I sighed.

"Something wrong?" asked Abbott.

"I'm thinking about this 'land bridge' I read about here. It talks about a river, which has to be the Columbia River because it's the only one nearby."

He narrowed his eyes and gestured with one hand for me to continue.

"Well, a land bridge is supposed to be a place where people could walk across at one point, but you can't have something like that in a river."

He appeared supremely annoyed. "Maybe there are stepping stones somewhere."

"Over the Columbia? Come on. I'm genuinely trying to figure this out."

"Maybe you can find a book about geography in Mr. Greywall's collection."

For as irritable as he was, I didn't know why he stayed here. Abbott wasn't doing any research himself. It almost seemed like he was just waiting for something.

Almost as if on cue, he sighed and said, "I need to attend to my duties. I'd suggest perusing the other books here." With that, he left, not waiting for me to respond.

I was glad to see him go; we seemed to have a knack for aggravating each other. I even found his perfectly sculpted hair irritating, not to mention his perma-frown. Sometime I'd need to find someone equally as vexing to Amy and then arrange a blind date for them.

I surveyed the bookshelves. There was potentially a lot to go through.

Then one book caught my eye.

It seemed a little out of place—newer, shinier—but the significant feature was the title, printed on the binding. It mentioned the "Bridge of the Gods".

I vaguely remembered this modern metal bridge. It was, in fact, not too far away on the Columbia River. I'd even been there once, a long time ago.

I didn't think it could be connected to the cave, but the word "bridge" was too intriguing, so I pulled the book from the shelf and started to flip through it.

To my surprise, I soon found that this book made little reference to the modern structure, though a couple of pictures refreshed my memory of it and confirmed that it was the same bridge I'd seen years before. Instead, it focused on earlier legend and geography. With fascination and growing excitement, I learned that the metal bridge completed in 1926 was named after a geologic feature of the same name.

My heart was racing as I hurriedly flipped through the pages.

The book said that according to a Klickitat legend, Tyhee Saghalie, chief of the gods, had created a vast stone bridge across the river for the families of his two sons, each of whom had settled down on either side of the river after some dispute. Later, the two sons fought over a woman, destroying much of the area in the process and causing the bridge to fall into the river, which created the Cascades Rapids. Their upset father put an end to the fight and to their lives, and turned them into mountains along with the girl they fought over, which, as the old story said, is how Mt. Adams, Mt. Hood, and Mt. Saint Helens came to be.

That was all just myth, of course, and certainly interesting but of doubtful credibility at best. But according to actual geologic history there had been several landslides, including the Bonneville Landslide, during which a large amount of debris slid down from Table Mountain and Greenleaf Peak into the Columbia Gorge. The Bonneville Landslide occurred perhaps sometime as early as about 1100 AD or maybe as late as 1750 but probably right between. A lake formed, and eventually, the river washed over again and carried much of the debris away, but for a time there actually *had* been a natural dam, or a *land bridge,* across the river.

This was it! I could scarcely contain myself. I wished Bastian hadn't left; I wanted to tell him right away.

"Brody!" I called. "Brody, I found it!"

For all I knew, if the ancient Bridge of the Gods, such a large structure, had collapsed right near the cave, the cave itself might have collapsed with it. But we had no other leads. This was where we would search.

Or…maybe it was where I would search on my own.

A new thought had occurred to me. If Bastian was going to be gone for several days, I didn't want to sit around waiting. Abbott and I might be able to find the Life Stone before Bastian even returned.

Abbott strolled back into the study, evidently not having been far away.

I was so excited that I almost had a hard time speaking clearly. "I know where to look for the Life Stone! We can go right away!"

"Really," he answered, with an almost tangible skepticism dripping from the word.

On second thought, it would be best for me to leave Abbott here. I didn't know if I could stand his company for much longer.

"Don't even think about it, Maria," cautioned Abbott. "It'll be dangerous. Besides, Amy wanted to find the Life Stone so she could give it to Bastian as a gift."

That pretty much sealed my basic plan of action. "Yeah? Well, she shouldn't have…" I held my tongue; with Abbott providing resistance it might be best for me to refrain from telling him what I intended to do. "Oh, fine." I tried to sound resigned. "You're right, it probably is too dangerous. And if Amy has her heart set on it, I shouldn't take that away from her."

I expected Abbott to show relief; instead he seemed puzzled and mildly annoyed. "Yes, well. I agree. And I approve."

He *approved?* That was enough to make me want to yell at him, or throw a book at him, or a candlestick or something. Anything. I gritted my teeth but tried to keep my lips shut and not reveal my anger.

"We can do some more research before they get back, though," he continued. "We should link up tomorrow at the same time. I'll review your findings for accuracy and decide what to do from there." He still seemed troubled about something, but then his eyes narrowed and I was unsure about what he was thinking. He abruptly eyed his wristwatch. "Oh, I forgot; I have something I need to get to tonight. You wouldn't mind putting things away here and locking up when you're done, would you? The key closet is just around the corner behind the portrait of Nikola Tesla."

It all felt abnormal, but this would work to my advantage. "Sure. I'm sure I can take care of things."

I was kind of fascinated by how unhappy he could appear without any obvious reason. "Okay, then," he finally said. "I'll not see you until tomorrow." He curtly walked out of the room.

As he walked to the front door I followed quietly. After hearing him step out and close the door behind him, I immediately moved to lock the door, then peered out of the closest window just in time to see him walking away. Confident that he wouldn't return tonight, I returned to the study.

With a bit of luck I could find out the location of the Life Stone and go to find it the next day. I might even be able to meet Abbott at the regular time and show it to him. If I didn't show up in time he'd be suspicious, but by then it would be too late. He'd be angry that I...had I lied? I realized that I had, though it didn't instinctively feel wrong to lie to Abbott about this. Maybe that was just because I was so irritated with him and Amy. Well, even if he was angry, I would still have the Stone, and he couldn't be too unhappy about that.

And if he *was* unhappy about it, I didn't care.

As late as it was, I wouldn't be able to start my search today. It would have to wait until tomorrow, but in the meanwhile I had preparations to make. Fortunately, being alone in Greywall Castle meant that I could gather a few useful supplies unhindered.

First, the Seeker was in the drawer exactly where it had been before. As I dropped it into a pocket, I kept faith in Bastian's remark about it only functioning while in someone's hand. It would be awkward—and painful—if I accidentally turned toward an enchanted artifact and my pocket lit on fire or something.

Next, I went to retrieve the Light Shard. If I was going into a cave I would want a good source of light. Sure, I had flashlights I could use, but I was fascinated by the small piece of quartz. I went through the house to the display case. It was locked.

Maybe this wasn't a problem, though. I went to where Abbott had said the "key closet" would be, and found a large painting of a man with confident eyes, a sharp nose, short hair parted in the middle, and a small mustache. This must be Tesla, whom I'd heard of but didn't know much about at all.

"Behind the portrait," I muttered to myself, repeating Abbot's earlier words. The frame around the painting was sturdy. I tried pulling one side, and then the other; the picture didn't move at first, but my hand brushed past a small latch, which, once opened, allowed the whole painting to swing away from the wall. Behind it there were several rows of key hooks, all labeled. I easily located a key marked for the Light Shard and took it with me, closing the picture-door afterward.

I returned to the display case and was pleased to open it with no trouble using the key. I took the Light Shard and held it to the light to appreciate it for just a moment.

It felt a little odd to be taking it without permission, especially when Bastian had been protective of it before, but maybe he only needed me to prove myself, and the ends would surely justify the means in this case. I didn't feel fully certain, but I had already gone to the trouble of obtaining it, so I quickly walked away to prevent any further mental dispute.

It occurred to me how nice it was just to be in the castle without the perpetually surly Broderick Abbott around. "Great couple" my foot. I wouldn't date Abbott if he took me to the ritziest place in town.

Bastian was the one who had won my heart. Now it was time for me to win a prize for him.

End of Part I

The Weapons Gallery
(six years earlier)

It was strange to me that I had never before wandered into this room in the back of my father's house. I was immediately fascinated by it when I entered; it was the sort of place that would captivate anyone. I wasn't quite surprised by what I found, but it did strike me as bizarre that my father would own quite so many weapons. The entire room, no small space to be sure, was devoted to storing them. Most were swords of varying sizes and styles, though here and there I saw a mace, nunchucks, and even a set of brass knuckles. They all looked old, but they seemed to be in very good condition. Of course he took good care of them.

He had neatly arranged them on wooden and metal racks that formed little aisles throughout the large room. Even more weapons hung on the walls. I kind of meandered about, peeking at this one or that, not daring yet to touch any until I came to a long leather whip, which was coiled several times and hung from a post. I wasn't sure why it drew my attention, but this one item I actually lifted off its hook to inspect.

As I grasped it a sensation went through me that I could only describe as an echo of physical pain that had been translated into deeper anguish. In less than a second I had half-visions of demons crying out and perishing, with howls screaming forth from jagged-toothed maws. I reflexively clenched my fist around the handle, and as quickly as I had felt the sensation everything became normal again, and I held only an old whip.

He must have already been in the room, but he only made his presence known at that moment. "Be careful with that one," he said. "You'll give me a scare."

I jumped when he spoke. He was impressively skillful at moving about silently. "Dad! I didn't hear you come in!"

"You left the door open."

"Sorry. What do you mean, I 'might give you a scare'? You know how to use it, right?"

"Yes, I do."

Like usual, he said little, and right now I was feeling impatient. "Show me."

He raised an eyebrow and stood still for a few seconds before moving to me and taking the whip. He strode to an open area at one side of the room and lit several candles that were positioned on the wall. Stepping back about four meters, he uncoiled the whip and cracked it with a quick, fluid motion. It looked as if he put as much effort into the movement as he would when brushing dust or lint off a sleeve, but the resounding smack was as loud as a gunshot. The flame of one of the candles disappeared, while the candle itself was undisturbed. "Like that," he said, turning back to me.

It was easily one of the coolest things I'd ever seen. "Wow."

He regarded the candles again and paused, and then, looking at one as ordinary as the others, he smiled. I loved his smile, partly because he had such great teeth, partly because it was so rare, and partly because he didn't show it around anyone but my mother and me (with the exception of one wedding photo—he smiled for that). Facing the candle, he did something curious to me. He gave this little smile and lashed out with the whip again; this time the candle all but evaporated with the loud crack. After taking a satisfied glance he coiled the whip again. He didn't smile after that, but the way his eyes glinted I felt like he was smiling. He held the whip in front of him. "It belonged to a good friend. He was a hunter of sorts, and in his dangerous quests this was his weapon of choice. Do not remove it from this post again." He replaced the whip on its hook and began to walk from the room.

I wanted to ask him more about the whip, but he'd probably explained as much as he ever intended to and I had other curiosities anyway. "Do you know how to use *all* of these?" I asked, gesturing to the other weapons.

He stopped and turned back to me. "Yes."

I indicated a nearby sword that hung horizontally, in a sheath. It looked to be about the same width at all points, and was slightly curved with the convex side facing upward. "What's this one?"

He stepped closer. "It is a type of katana, a Japanese sword. Only the top edge is a cutting edge. This one is particularly light, more than usual."

Underneath the katana were several other similar swords, but I didn't ask about them. Instead, I walked to a different large rack and pointed at a long, straight sword just next to me on it. "What about this one?"

He followed me over and stood in front of the weapon. "It is an estoc, meant to be thrust so that the point pierces an opponent's armor. You see it has no cutting edge. This type was common in Europe in the 16th century."

The sword next to the estoc was slender, with an elaborate hilt and hand guard. "This one looks like a rapier," I ventured.

He raised an eyebrow. "And it is. What can you tell me about it?"

I would have loved to have been able to say something intelligent. "Umm, it's French?"

The eyebrow lowered. "In fact, this sword is German-made. Hmm. It seems that I have neglected a portion of your education."

This was an opportunity. The rapier didn't look too heavy; with as much style as I could muster I pulled it from the rack and held it out in front of me. "So, educate me."

If he had been entertained at all by the rest of the conversation, he wasn't any more. "That's not what I meant."

"What good is the history of a weapon if I don't know how to use it?"

He drew a long, silent breath. I got the impression that he had known that this conversation was coming. "You must know that in today's world, skill in swordsmanship will not be of any advantage to you."

But I've always been daddy's little girl, and not five minutes later he was instructing me on proper form and basic strikes. We spent well over an hour in that first lesson. When we went to dinner, Mom was alarmed but she didn't make any real effort to dissuade us. Each time she said something about it, I gave a sincere compliment on the meal.

Over the next few weeks, I came to be very fond of that rapier.

Part II

The Artifact

5

I couldn't have expected this. A year ago, a month ago, or even a couple of days ago I couldn't have expected to find myself driving to some mountains by the Columbia River to search for a cave in hopes of finding an enchanted jewel. I supposed that life was just that way, that by nature we have events thrown at us that we couldn't have seen coming.

One of those events that I certainly didn't anticipate more than a week ago was that I would be so taken by a young man, so much that I would want to do something like this. It felt a little bit crazy, but I so wanted to please him. I wasn't the sort to fall for a guy—any guy—but for some reason it hadn't been the same with Bastian. I'd fallen for him fast…maybe too fast. That was also why it was so unexpected.

Regardless, the drive was beautiful here. I'd been driving south for a couple of hours already and had eventually reached the river, where I turned to follow it to the west. The forested mountains had begun to reach up on either side, naturally displaying a distinct majesty in the morning sunlight that felt to me like the Columbia River Gorge was a work created by some mighty being merely as a demonstration of power; in a way I supposed that was true.

I could almost sense myself getting nearer. The water flowed downstream with me, ever moving, spurring me on. Rivers were paradoxically enticing and terrifying to me; I relished the thought of their iciness but dreaded the idea of sinking in their depths. Any body of water more than a few feet deep wasn't shallow enough for me. I didn't think I'd be able to go near the all-but-eternal expanse and depths of an ocean, much less cross one. How my father had managed that feat I couldn't imagine.

Driving alongside the Columbia wasn't a problem, though. Certainly not today; today the water was my ally, encouraging me, almost pacing me like a running partner. No, it was better than that; I'd never been an avid runner. I could almost feel the energy of the river, and I found myself accelerating a bit too much a few times. After going too fast for comfort around a sharper curve, I relaxed and let the car slow down before hitting the gas pedal again.

The car wasn't too warm, but I decided I wanted some fresh air and lowered my window. The clean mountain air was a delight.

Just after reaching the river and turning west, I had passed an art museum that seemed bizarrely remote. Most man-made or natural features failed to hold my attention for long today, though. I was impatient to find specific locations that would confirm that I was in the right area. It wasn't long before my desires were fulfilled. I saw a peak ahead of me in the distance; that had to be Table Mountain. I was here! The Seeker must be close enough to use by now, or it would be soon. On the right side of the road I saw a sign for "Bridge of the Gods", "Toll Bridge", and "Cascade Locks".

Although I hadn't been here often, I remembered driving over the modern Bridge of the Gods once, many years ago. Mostly, I remembered that it was unimpressive—for having such a grand title, it was just a simple metal bridge, and not even particularly large. Once I'd gotten past the underwhelming ordinariness of it, however, there were parts of it that I had liked. First, there was the beautiful Gorge all around it. Second, the bridge's driving surface was a long steel grating, and it was possible, though difficult from inside a vehicle, to look straight through the bridge to the rushing water below. Today I might even have crossed the bridge for fun, if I hadn't been so enthusiastic to start my search for the Life Stone. Well, that, and I didn't want to pay the toll on the other side.

As I continued on, I looked for good places to start hiking. I took one detour that led me through several back roads with pleasant-sounding names—Blue Lake Road, Ash Lake Road— but decided that I wasn't close enough yet. After returning to Highway 14, next to the river, I soon passed a sign that welcomed me to Bonneville, and then another announcing the Bonneville trailhead. That was tempting, and I almost got out to explore, but wanting to see more I kept going even farther.

Feeling like I was about as close as I could get to Table Mountain from the highway, I took the nearest turn toward the mountain and proceeded through a small residential area, winding around a path that I hoped would lead me up the mountain. Eventually I was rewarded with a dirt road that became steeper and rockier. When I found a small cluster of other vehicles, I parked just below them and got out.

And so began my adventure. I put my hair in a ponytail and slipped on a baseball cap. Then I put several large water bottles and bags of protein shake powder mixed with extra powdered milk in my backpack, strapped it on my back, and started walking.

After making a sharp turn, the road soon turned into more of an uneven trail, and I was glad I'd left the car behind. I also presently found myself among trees on either side of the trail. The air around me was luscious and I could hear nothing more than the soft sounds of nature.

The first trees had been fairly short, and back toward the river behind me they were easy to see over, but as I'd progressed, most had become taller. Grasses along the side of the path had been replaced by low, leafy bushes that I couldn't hope to identify. Their leaves fanned out in clusters on short branches that reached up from the ground through other leaf clusters. The foliage was quite thick to either side, generally showing no branching track off the main trail. The path itself showed parts of dark, buried rocks but was otherwise strewn with small pieces of branch and bark atop the brown soil; as I walked, sometimes the path became quite rocky but not difficult to traverse. Sunlight fell unevenly on the bushes and tree trunks through the treetops overhead, illuminating some spots but not others as if according to whim.

There must have been other people up on the mountain, given the other parked cars near mine, but I could see no sign of them at the moment. I followed the trail for ten or so minutes as it generally marked a straight line across the mountain, here and there passing a minor landmark such as a small stream that crossed the path, or a clearing off to the side.

Eventually the trail started to curve more to the right, away from the mountain peak, and I started to wonder if it was going to lead me the right way. I came across a small bridge with uneven wooden slats and stopped to try to get my bearings.

I wasn't going to be able to go any farther without the Seeker. Thinking of it reminded me of my iron pills. I took iron daily, and though it was early, I figured it was best to take some now so as to not worry about it later. I pulled off my backpack to retrieve the bottle of pills, thinking that I might also mix some protein powder and water and have a drink, but I wasn't thirsty, so I settled on grabbing a granola bar, which I put in a pocket.

Just then, a young man came strolling along the trail. He had brown, close-cropped hair and a light beard of only a few days' growth. He seemed light-skinned from a distance, but as he got closer I could see that he had spent some time in the sun. He was wearing a backpack whose shoulder straps and waistband, at least, were in a camouflage pattern.

"Good morning!" he offered brightly, as I chewed a pill.

"Hello!" I answered back after swallowing.

"Nice day for a hike, isn't it?" He had hazel eyes, like the color of autumn.

"Yes, I suppose so." I put the iron bottle back in my backpack and slung the pack over my shoulders again.

"I'd be out here even in the rain, but I like it better like this."

"Sure. Do you hike often?"

"Yeah. It's a hobby of mine. I've been on a lot of mountainsides like this. What about you?"

"It's my first time."

"First time on the Pacific Crest Trail?"

"Um, I guess so. I actually never go hiking like this anywhere."

"And you're out here alone?"

"Yep. Getting some me time."

"Oh. Well, you shouldn't be."

"Shouldn't be getting time for myself? That's intruding into my personal decisions quite a bit, don't you think?"

"No, I mean you shouldn't be out here alone."

"Why not? You are."

"Yes, well, no offense, but you seem a little unprepared."

"What do you mean, 'I seem unprepared'? I have everything I need. I've got snacks, water, and boots."

"What about a compass and map? Your phone might not always have a signal out here and you should have a backup."

"I don't have a phone."

"You...but you have a compass and map, right?"

I hadn't thought of getting a map, but... "I have a compass...of sorts."

"Of sorts? I don't know what that means, but you need these things if you're going to be walking around the mountains. Otherwise you could get lost. It's dangerous. Most people use phone apps but if you don't have that you need a paper map at the very least."

"I'll be fine."

"Maybe, but with me around, you sure won't get lost."

This guy was irksomely sure of himself. "I'll be fine."

"What's more, you're a girl."

I put my hands on my hips. This was too much. "And helpless, I'm sure," I said through my teeth. "I suppose only boys can be out here alone?"

"Kind of. You probably won't run into many people out here, but when you do it just might be a bad sort of person, and you won't have the general public available to help if they try to hurt you. As a girl you're, uh...you're a more attractive target, so to speak. As for me, if someone out here tried to assault me, I'd punch them in the face. What would you do?"

"Punch them in the face."

He opened his mouth as if to say something, then glanced to either side as if figuring out how to respond. "Well," he finally said, "offhand, I'm not sure your punch would be as effective as mine, and you're still a more likely target than I am." For a moment he had a sort of patronizing smile, but then it faded as he seemed to understand the peeved look I was giving him. "But anyway, where are you going?"

I didn't particularly want to answer him, but I also didn't want to be rude. He seemed basically nice, if overly concerned. "I'm looking for a cave."

"Any cave in particular?"

"Yes."

"You've been there before?"

I hesitated. "I know how to get there."

He also waited. "Okay, well I could use some company. Do you mind if I go along?"

"What? I don't even know your name."

"Easily solved. I'm Grant." He held out his hand.

Maybe I was getting too relaxed with strangers, but I shook his hand anyway. "It's nice to meet you. I'm Maria."

"Maria?" He paused mid-shake. "You don't look Hispanic."

"Right. I'm *not* Hispanic."

"Oh. I just...never mind." He waited another moment, looked down at our hands, smiled, pumped the handshake two more times, and released me. "Well, it's nice to meet you, too. Now you know my name."

"Okay..."

"So, where's this cave of yours?"

I sighed. "I really am comfortable finding it on my own."

"And then finding your way back again?"

I had to pause to think. I was pretty sure that my "compass", the Seeker, would get me to the Life Stone, but now that I thought about it, I couldn't see how it would guide me once I *had* the Life Stone.

He didn't look relieved at all by my hesitancy. "I'm telling you, people get lost in woods like these."

"I really don't think I'm going to get lost."

"Okay, then, I've got a bit of a test for you."

Was he serious?

He went on. "The ground is level enough here. Walk about 40 paces off this trail, close your eyes, spin around ten times, then find your way back."

"Are you kidding?"

"Not at all. Do you think you can do it?"

"Easy."

"I'll bet you can't."

"Will you leave me alone if I do?"

He hesitated only a second. "Sure."

"All right," I said, turning and stepping off the path. "I'll be right back."

I counted my steps as I walked off the path, weaving around trees and ferns. I considered just leaving, but figured it would be too impolite, and I wanted to prove myself. At around 12 steps I suddenly wondered if a "pace" counted as one step or two. Unsure, I decided to go somewhere between 40 single and double steps. Along the way I identified a few trees that seemed distinct enough to guide me back. When I decided I'd gone far enough, I closed my eyes and called over my shoulder, "Okay, I'm going to spin now."

I heard a somewhat distant "okay" in return.

After about three turns my foot caught something and I stumbled. Picking myself back up, I wasn't sure if I'd completed a turn, but I took my best guess and kept spinning around. Well before I'd counted to ten I became entirely unsure if I was completing a full circle each time.

Then I opened my eyes again.

And I had no idea which way was which.

I scanned one way and then the next, trying to identify trees that looked familiar on my way in, but failed at every attempt. There were trees and shrubs on my left, trees and shrubs on my right, and trees and shrubs in front of and behind me. I couldn't identify any of the trees I'd spotted before. The greenery was so thick that I couldn't see a gap anywhere close that could be the trail. Neither could I see any of my footprints on the ground.

Being lost was uncomfortable, but I was mostly annoyed that this guy...what was his name?...Grant, I remembered...I was mostly annoyed that he was right.

"Okay, fine," I called out. "I admit it. I don't know which way I'm going."

No response.

"Hey! Grant! Where are you?!?"

"Over here," I heard from my left.

I tramped back through the undergrowth toward him. When I got back he was holding up an item in each hand; he identified each in turn: "Compass," he said, holding up one, and then, "map," holding up the other. "The map is essential. These days most people use hiking applications on their phones, but I prefer printed copies. The compass is especially handy when in the middle of a bunch of trees, like you were, but otherwise I usually rely on terrain association."

"What's terrain association?"

"I identify mountain peaks and other obvious features to get a sense of where I am, though it's harder when surrounded by trees. I also rely on marked roads or trails a lot. I end up not actually using the compass much."

"Okay, well, if you really want to tag along with me, go ahead, though I can't imagine why you'd want to."

"Why? Just general concern, and you're also...never mind."

"What?" His little smile was aggravating.

"Nothing, nothing; I just don't want to see you get lost out here."

"Well, fine. Where'd you learn about all of this stuff anyway?"

"Army ROTC. We do a lot of dismounted land navigation."

"Dismounted?"

"Walking, as opposed to being in a vehicle."

"Oh. So you're in the Army?"

"No, actually, I just take college classes. I need to decide if I'm going to keep up with it. If I do, then I'll go ahead and join the Army, and take on a four-year service obligation."

"It sounds like a big decision."

"Yeah. I'll figure it out. Anyway, I've spent a lot of time hiking around mountains. I'm new to this area, though."

"Well, so am I."

"But you're looking for a cave. Can you find it on a map?"

"No, I just know what direction it's in."

He looked at me with an arched eyebrow. Was it truly so hard to believe?

"Okay," he said, "what direction?"

I turned away from him before withdrawing the Seeker. Holding it one way, then the other, I felt for a change in temperature. Then...there it was. The warmth was mild, but present. At the same time, I thought I could see a tiny spark of light within the jewel at the end, though it wasn't very dark around me despite the shade of the trees. I held up my arm and pointed. "That way."

"I am *quite* curious about your compass now."

"Get used to it. That's the way to go, though."

"Huh. You don't know how far it is?"

"It's not too far."

"Okay, you don't know how far it is. Okay." He squinted his eyes shut for a second. "Well, if I knew the distance, I could plan the best path, but as it is...." He held up his map to review it. "It looks like we can follow this trail for about two or three hundred meters, then take a branching path for quite a while before cutting through the woods for...a while."

I sighed again. "Okay. Let's go. But don't give me any trouble, or I'll punch *you* in the face." I caught another smile from him, which was irritating. "I'm serious," I said. "Right in the mouth." I started along the path again.

I didn't like inviting him along, but I supposed I had to resign myself to his company. I was sure he wasn't an awful sort of person, and in fact he seemed to genuinely want to be helpful, but I was normally very comfortable on my own. After a minute I conceded to myself that a bit of company wouldn't be bad. I remembered the granola bar and ate it, jamming the wrapper back in my pocket when I was done.

I walked down the trail, lost in my own thoughts, wondering what it would be like when I found the Life Stone, and how Bastian would react when I brought it back. The fresh mountain air was invigorating, and it seemed to heighten my anticipation. What would Bastian say? What would he do? At first I imagined him just smiling and saying something to congratulate me, somewhat blandly, but then the more exciting idea came to me that he might hold my arms and take the kiss that I had denied him before.

I stumbled on an exposed root, mentally slipping back to Earth with the mishap.

Did I really want Bastian to kiss me? A strongly emotional part of me certainly did, but another part was full of memory and different emotion. My mother had given definite instruction to me about kissing, a lot like what she'd told me the other day with her pearls-before-swine analogy. She said that physical intimacy, even starting with a simple kiss, was unavoidably cheapened when shared with more and more people. She told me that my father was a better example than she'd been, but she hadn't done anything that would have brought her real regret, and she had great hope for me. She said that my kisses and anything else that followed were a treasure she expected me to only ever give to a man once I was engaged to marry him.

At some point, I'd told her it sounded weird and old-fashioned. I'd argued that it was normal for people to kiss while dating, but she'd countered by saying that what was normal wasn't always what was best. She'd also said she knew people personally who had never kissed until they were engaged or sometimes even until they were married, and who had exceptionally happy and fulfilling marriages. While I appreciated her counsel and recognized its merit, it ended up being something I never decided on.

I shook my head. This subject was getting too heavy again for an eighteen-year-old. I preferred more fun ruminations. I gave my mother a lot of credit, but when I considered Bastian's possible reactions, without looking past them, it was still hard not to be excited.

It was rather fast, though, to be thinking about kissing Bastian when I'd known him for such a short time and I was so reserved about kissing. It was remarkable that my liking of him had led me to trust him so immediately.

Evidently, I was also fast to trust Grant for some reason. This made me think that maybe I was just becoming too trusting in general, but that didn't seem right. A quick glance at the young man by me revealed nothing. I wasn't sure I should rely on just intuition, but maybe I could just sense in some undefinable way that he was a good person. He certainly wasn't showing any signs of being dangerous.

After a short hike, we came to a fork in the trail, though the branching path was barely recognizable. My thoughts were just returning to Bastian and his book when Grant interrupted them. "Go left here."

I spryly stepped down the next trail.

After about another ten seconds, I heard his voice again. "Are you always this quiet?"

I halted and looked at him. "No."

I kept walking.

From behind me I heard a single sharp laugh, as if it had swelled up so rapidly that he couldn't quite contain it. I looked over my shoulder to see him grinning widely. "I guess you're *almost* always quiet."

"I was thinking about something."

"Oh?" I was walking on but could still hear the smile in his voice. "And what were you thinking about?"

It was just occurring to me that if goblins lived in caves, for all I knew there could be some in the cave I was searching out. I gave Grant a one-word reply. "Demons."

He went silent behind me, and then I heard another burst of laughter. I kept walking but peered over my shoulder again to see him where he had stopped; he hurried to catch up.

I called back, "Is something funny?"

He arrived next to me again and kept pace. "Well, yeah."

I supposed that without context my answer probably was funny. "Fine. I'll try to be less weird. If you're so chatty, tell me this: if you could have any superpower, what would you choose?"

He was quiet again, this time for long enough that I felt the need to looked over to make sure he was okay. Finally, he spoke. "I'd want to be able to communicate an idea perfectly to others, directly to their mind, without the limitations of language or skewed perspective."

"Oh." I hadn't been expecting a serious answer.

"Does that sound silly?"

"No, that would probably be really useful." Inwardly, I wondered if I was immature for only thinking of inane answers. Even if my jokes were puerile, though, they were harmless.

"I guess there are just important truths that I wish more people knew," he said. "I mean, I'm pretty young, but it seems like a lot of people lack some basic principles that even I understand, and I think the world would just be a better place if we learned from each other more."

"Communication works both ways, though. Wouldn't you want to be able to understand other people perfectly also?"

"Well, yes, and also kind of no, sort of. Honestly, yes, but facing truth can be a daunting task."

"But what other people think isn't necessarily truth."

"No, but their sincere thoughts can still be pretty hurtful."

"Yeah, sometimes. It might also be really nice to know when someone truly loves us. To understand that perfectly—that would be…'nice' really isn't the right word, but it would be nice."

"Hmmm. True. What about you?"

"Um, what about me?"

"What superpower would you choose? I assume from the way you asked it that you've thought about the question before."

"Well, yeah, but my answers stink compared to yours."

"I don't mind. Try me."

"No, let me think about it." I was kind of surprised to realize that I hadn't given it any serious thought. What kind of power would I truly want? In a way I almost thought I'd rather be as normal and power-less as I pretended to be, but I certainly couldn't explain that to this boy.

He spoke again. "You look like you've got something in mind, but you're not telling me."

"Well…you're right, but there are some things that I just don't tell other people, and you're going to have to live with it."

Grant shrugged his shoulders. "I'm patient." After a moment, he stepped forward and reached one hand up toward me. "There's a cobweb on the brim of your—"

Abruptly, a swarm of huge bats converged on him and pulled him away from me.

5.1

With a second glance, I saw that the flying creatures were much too large to be bats, but their more distinguishing features were developed arms and legs in addition to their wings, and oversized heads. Their skin tones varied in similar shades of green, brown, purple, or red, but their eyes all had a red glint to them.

Grant was being swiftly pulled backward into the forest; it looked as if the things were trying to fly away with him, but unable to achieve enough lift to get him off the ground. I hastily stepped off the trail after him, taking little time to wonder what they were.

He'd screamed when they first appeared, and now he repeated the words, "Help! Help!" He was unable to twist free of the grasp of the winged things, and clearly frightened. While I was strangely not shocked just by seeing these flying things— perhaps I was now too accustomed to the supernatural—I was scared for Grant, who was unable to resist his attackers and was being carried away.

I ran after him, rapidly gaining ground on the struggling victim. I then could have sworn that I heard the scratchy voice of one of the things as it uttered the words, "Kill it!" To my horror I saw a cliff not far behind him; they must have intended to throw him off.

"Get away from him!" I yelled at the flying things, as I lunged and swung at them with my hands. I succeeded in striking two of them in rapid succession. They fluttered away, hovering nearby in the air with what somehow seemed like confused expressions on their distorted faces for a second. Focused by the greatest urgency, I repeated my command to the other creatures holding Grant, who was now dangerously close to the edge. "Leave him alone!"

Almost instantly, they looked at me and released him. I sensed that they didn't intend to harm me at all. They hovered slightly closer to me after letting him go, and he simultaneously backpedaled a few steps, eyes wide with shock.

I rushed toward him, brushing the flying creatures aside, and yelled, "Grant, don't—"

But it was too late; his left foot slid back just too far, and he was suddenly off-balance, teetering off the edge. He slipped downward, hitting his leg on a large rock on the edge as he twisted, but managing to catch himself with one arm and then swing his other forward to brace himself. His grasp was tenuous, though; he seemed to be using every effort just to hang on.

I hurried forward to him; as I did so, the winged things followed, flapping small wings all around me. "Leave us alone!" I yelled, swatting at them again.

Surprisingly, they did. In seconds they were all gone.

I reached down and grabbed one of Grant's arms, then, reaching underneath his armpit, lifted him up and back above the ledge, where he hurriedly shuffled to a comfortable distance from it, eyes still wide.

He sat forward on the ground, clutching at it as if glad to be on something solid and wide, breathing heavily for a moment and looking around a couple of times. I watched him to make sure he was okay. After a moment he must have felt some pain in his leg; he began to rub it, gritting his teeth as he did. Finally he looked up at me with bewilderment and some remaining fear. But he didn't say anything, so I leaned over slightly to peer over the edge where he had nearly fallen.

There was a small stream not too far below, and after a short distance the ground sloped sharply upward again. I tried to be reassuring. "It's actually not that far of a drop. I don't think falling that far would kill a person. Maybe break a leg or two, but probably not kill."

"What were those things?"

I looked at him, then down at the stream. "I have no idea."

I could hear his breathing, still heavy but seeming to lighten up with time. "How did you do that?"

"Do what?"

"Lift me up like that, on the edge there, with only one arm."

Had I? I shrugged. "Adrenaline, I guess."

"You don't seem excited enough for adrenaline. You're completely calm."

As a matter of fact, I *was* strangely calm. Shouldn't those monsters have frightened me more? Was I already getting used to dealing with demons, or whatever strange creatures these things were that I'd seen recently?

I didn't answer him.

I started to wonder about myself. That other part of me had usually seemed so distant, so unreal even, but with these recent paranormal appearances I had to re-evaluate my self-perception. Doing so made me think of my iron pills, and I felt an odd desire to take another, as if doing so would make that other part of me go away more, and make me more normal. I knew that logically, it didn't make sense, but I still wanted to. So I pulled my backpack off and got the bottle out, opening it and popping a chewable pill in my mouth.

"What's that?"

"Just iron. I take it every day, just like my dad." I held the prescription medicine bottle aloft after chewing and swallowing the small pill. I looked at him, and for some reason a family story came to mind just then. He was becoming too inquisitive, so I decided to mention it to help distract him. "It's funny; if it wasn't for these pills, my parents might never have gotten together."

He squinted and furrowed his brow at me for a few seconds, then gruffly took his backpack off and set it down. "Okay, listen, that sounds interesting, but there is obviously something unnatural going on here, and you haven't been open with me about it, and I'm not going anywhere until you tell me what's going on."

"You mean those flying things? I told you, I don't know what those were. Honest."

"Well, yes, those things also, but I'm talking about *you*."

"What do you mean?"

"You are different. You're exceptionally strong—I don't believe the 'adrenaline' excuse—and you're take iron pills casually after seeing little flying monsters, and after just taking some pills earlier for that matter. But even stranger than just seeing those flying things, which was without a doubt enough to make anyone doubt their sanity, was seeing the way they responded to you, almost as if you *outranked* them."

"I'm not in the Army and I doubt they are either."

"But they followed your orders."

"No, they didn't! We scared them off. That's all."

"I don't buy that for a second. They didn't attack *us*—they attacked *me*. There's something strange about you."

"You're a little weird yourself."

"No." He gave a bleak laugh. "Oh, no. Not like that."

I hesitated to provoke any further conversation.

He continued anyway. "You're out in the woods claiming to be looking for something with a 'compass' that points toward a cave instead of just pointing north like a compass does. But hey, no crime there. Then, I'm no weakling, but I think you're actually a lot stronger than I am, and you don't have anywhere near enough bulk to explain it. That's kind of hard to accept mentally—I don't know how that's even possible. But then you have flying monsters following you and taking orders from you, and that's plain crazy, but really I think that I'm still sane. So what's going on?"

"I told you before that I just don't tell people some things. Deal with it."

"No."

"Fine, then. I'll go on without you."

"And you'll get lost in the woods."

"I'll manage. Like you said, I'm strange. I'll figure it out. But stop saying that those things were taking orders from me. I honestly have no idea what they are. I've never seen them before."

"So seeing monsters isn't normal for you?"

"No, it's not normal…" I averted my eyes. "Not until recently, I suppose."

"You've had other trouble like this?"

"Just once. A few days ago. I was attacked by something bigger. Without wings."

"I take it you ran away."

"No, I fought it. Then *it* ran away."

He massaged his leg. "I've never believed in monsters. Not since I was a kid. But I'm inclined to believe my own eyes. Earlier you said you were thinking about demons. Well, those things…they spoke—I heard at least one of them speak—but they weren't human."

"No, they weren't."

"Are you human?"

I hid my gaze. This was the question above all that I hated. I didn't want to be something else. I hated being different. I wanted to be accepted by other people, and not through their great personal efforts but just naturally, easily accepted like anyone else, like Grant had accepted me until now.

He made a simple conclusion based on my evasiveness. "You're not human."

"Oh, stop it! What do I look like? Do I have wings? Do I have claws?" I waved my arm at unseen creatures in the distance. "They're the monsters. Those things out there. Not me." I pulled off my hat and hairband, then shook my hair out and ran my fingers through it.

"I didn't say you were a monster."

"Well, maybe I am after all! You don't have any idea."

"How can I? You're not explaining anything!"

"This is why I hardly associate with anyone. Can't you just treat me like everyone else? Can't I be normal?"

He considered my words. I didn't honestly expect him to make sense of them. "Okay, fine. I didn't want to upset you. I'm just still freaked out." He sighed heavily. "But maybe you could at least explain something else. Are these monster attacks connected to why you're out here?"

I exhaled upward against my hair. "Maybe. Probably."

"What is it you're looking for?"

"I don't think you'd believe me if I told you."

He grunted. "Is it a personal concern, too?"

"No, just far-fetched."

He threw a rock forcefully into the forest. "I don't get it. Why are you so secretive? Obviously, you don't want me to know something important about you. Don't you trust me?"

"How can I? How do I even know when I *can* trust someone?"

He stood up, wincing as he put weight on his hurt leg. "I think the only way to be sure you can trust someone is to trust them. I only just met you, but don't I seem trustworthy? If I don't, that'll bother me anyway, but have I done anything to lose your trust?"

I had to think it over. He waited, showing a perfect example of patience. The silence must have lasted for four or five minutes while I deliberated, with him doing little more than stare expectantly, but eventually I decided to give at least a small bit of information. "Maybe this will be easiest if I start with the iron pills." I ran one hand through my hair and let it rest on the back of my neck. "Iron is the key component in hemoglobin, and hemoglobin is a big part of blood." I let my hand fall and then wrapped my arms around myself. "I'm in a group of beings that normally need extra blood to survive."

He kept waiting as if wanting me to complete the thought. I hesitated out of habit—strong, oft-reinforced habit—but I was also driven by an underlying desire that had lasted as long as the secret itself.

"I'm part vampire. Because my dad is part vampire."

5.2

I had wanted to tell someone all along. In that moment the desire blossomed within me, sprouting a peaceful but encompassing sense of relief. The words brought with them a muted excitement. The two powerful yet subdued emotions flushed through me more than I would have thought possible in a few brief seconds. However, immediately afterward, the old, familiar worry reemerged and quickly took over. I hadn't said anything about this to anyone for many, many years, partially because it was a matter that concerned my family but largely because I didn't know how people would react. They might be horrified, disgusted, hateful, malicious, sarcastic, antagonistic...in any case, positive reactions seemed unlikely.

For his part, Grant seemed skeptical. When he finally spoke I could hear it in the tone of his voice. "So, you turn into a bat and kill people?"

And with that dumb response the worry transformed instantly into irritation. "What? No, of course not."

"Then how can you be a vampire?"

I rolled my eyes. "I said we're *part* vampire, and killing is wrong, and we don't drink blood. That's gross. And I've definitely never turned into a bat."

"I don't know if I believe you. How do I know you're not taking me somewhere far away just so you can kill me without drawing attention?"

"If I was going to kill you, I would have already, especially with you asking all of these questions. Besides, I'm happy for now with the granola bar. And I never asked you to come with me, anyway—that was your idea."

"Well then, how do I know you're not taking me to some other vampire in this cave we're looking for, so he can kill me?"

"How could I be taking you somewhere? I don't even know where anything is out here! That's why you're here! If I was getting food for some creepy vampire I could grab anybody."

"Oh." This must have made sense to him. "Huh."

I glanced around. "So, time's a-wasting. Can we start walking again?"

He shrugged. "Yeah, I guess so." He rubbing his injured leg again, then took a few steps to test it out.

While he did so, I hastily checked the Seeker and put it away again. "We should be done with the trail. Let's go this way."

He nodded, seemingly satisfied with his leg, and we began walking again. We then went for a short while without actually saying anything, which was fine with me. I was more concerned about walking than talking right now. He must have felt differently, though. "So, were you born, like a regular person is?"

"Yep." I stepped over a large fallen branch. "My dad was, too. I don't know where most vampires come from, but part-vampires come from the womb like any regular human. We did, anyway."

"And those pills…how did your parents 'get together', as you said?"

I sighed. "It was my mother. My mother fell in love with a vampire. She said it was his hair. But he'd also saved her from her possessed boyfriend. Not truly possessed; just a weirdo. So he wasn't that bad of a person in the first place—my father, that is. Technically, he was only half-vampire, so that makes me one-quarter vampire, but I'm not into blood sucking. I drank my own blood once, when I was a kid—just to try it out—but it wasn't that great. Low on iron. My mom says that vampires are anemic, not that she's an expert or anything, but when I was old enough to know what I was craving she started making me take a daily iron supplement. That helped the taste of my blood, but I still don't crave it."

"You've never drunk anyone else's blood?"

"Nope. I've never really wanted to. I mean, it's kind of a gross thought, but I imagine it's also because of the iron supplement. But I was talking about my mom and my dad. Sometimes with my mom I just call him 'the vampire', just to pester her, but she gets mad at me—says he never killed anyone for their blood. He takes his daily iron supplement too. Actually, he takes five a day—one with each meal and two at night, so he won't get night cravings. It's prescription-strength, too. The doctors he sees are supportive of his desire not to drink blood, so they give him all the prescriptions he wants. This would be expensive—not that he has any shortage of funds—but the pharmacy he gets his refills at gives him a frequent-buyer's discount. Personally, I think they're afraid he'll come after them and drink their blood, but nobody in town ever treats my dad poorly to his face."

"So, people know what he is?"

"Actually it's just a few people, and probably only a few more even suspect anything close to the truth. He keeps to himself a lot, and people do strange things when they're afraid, so he tries not to arouse suspicion when in public. It's hard to believe anyway, and hard to gossip about. Tell someone that your neighbor is an adulterer, and they'll pass the word on, but tell someone that he's a vampire and they'll just think you're crazy."

"Yeah, I guess so."

"They don't know about me, but I only take two pills a day, so I don't drain my dad's supply much." I leaped over a small hole. "So, back to my mom and 'the vampire'. They met while my mom was dating that possessed boyfriend of hers. She was nineteen or something. Anyway, this crazy boyfriend of hers tramped around shouting political slogans. He was convinced for some reason that this one man would save the world and just had to be elected. One day, he runs into my dad while he's running down a street, telling people that the world is gonna burn if they don't vote for this guy, and trying to use matches to illustrate the point. Laura—that's my mom—was running after him, trying to calm him down, but he just turns around and starts throwing matches at her. He lit them, too, before he threw them at her. She didn't get hurt though; the force of his throw blew out the flame. Well, Lucard—my dad—stepped out of a rug shop just when the boyfriend was about to throw the whole box of matches at her. So the vampire walks up behind him and catches the guy's fist in his hand. The guy screamed and thrashed, but Lucard simply twisted until he gave up."

"What did your mom see in the other guy?"

"I don't know. She doesn't like to talk about it. She says women make stupid choices and settle too easily for guys that aren't good enough. She says we're tricked easily. She says we're superficial. Which is funny, because even though my dad is a wonderful man (or half-vampire) it was something superficial that got her interested. While Lucard was overpowering the boyfriend, my mom was spellbound by his hair. My dad's hair, I mean. It was the only thing she noticed. Luckily, I gathered what happened from my dad because my mom told me, 'It was the brilliance of your father's hair that frightened my boyfriend into submission.'"

Grant laughed.

"And that's how my parents met. How they got married is a different story. The vampire—being half vampire—is relatively emotionless. He has quite a voice. It's seductively deep (don't think I'm weird for saying that—it's the way my mom describes it, and I think she's right), but it's flat. So while he is a thoughtful and sometimes expressive man, I never really knew if he felt a lot. He's never spoken much—only in bursts. Luckily, my mom dramatically makes up for these things. Not that she's wildly emotional, but she does feel a lot, inside, including love towards a vampire."

"He doesn't talk much to her, either?"

"Oh, I think he talks to her more than anyone else. It's just that I feel like we have to distract him from something to get him to open up, like there's something he constantly remembers or something he intentionally reminds himself of that keeps him somber most of the time. I've asked him about it before, but he just tells me he's glad I'm mostly human."

"Hmmm."

"Well, after Lucard defeated the boyfriend, my mom couldn't stop following him around. She said his hair was mesmerizing, and she told me 'the desire to have silver-haired babies was overwhelming.' She said that—those exact words. When my mom wasn't at work, styling hair, she was investigating Lucard from afar. He didn't care much when she 'accidentally' but frequently crossed his path. He just went about his business. Then she ran into him at the pharmacy as he was filling one of his big iron prescriptions." I mimicked their voices subtly as I related their conversation to Grant.

"'My word, Lucard, are you ill?' she said.

"'I am cursed,' came his flat reply.

"'Really? Do you need help?'

"'Perhaps, but no one can help me.'

"'Maybe I can.'

"'My mother could not help my father.'

"'You can't be as hopeless as your father was, if your mother wasn't. Let me try to help you.' He didn't know what to say, and he normally wouldn't want to discuss it anyway, but he also didn't want to leave her, and my mom kept talking. She asked him, 'Have I ever seen you smile?'

"'I don't smile.'

"'Why?' she asks, and this is the great part. For some reason, he blurts out the truth, and she totally isn't shocked at all.

"'Because I'm a vampire.'

"'Is that a reason not to smile?' And that's all she says. At first he just looks at her, but she keeps staring at him with her inquisitive stare. Finally, he gave up and forced a smile, and she was completely charmed. Later, my father told me that she treats him as if she never notices his fangs. Unless they cut her lips, which has happened a couple of times, and then he has to take extra iron, though my mother says that he actually has excellent self-control and could do just fine even without the pills if he needed to. She has always had such faith in him. Anyway, it was her unabashedness that eventually won him over. After the smile, he explained that he was actually only half-vampire, and they spent the next fifteen minutes arguing over which half was dominant. He wasn't sure why he wanted to talk to her, but it was with that small conversation that Lucard began to feel something for my mom."

"You remember the story well," Grant said, looking at me sideways.

"My mom loves to tell it. She cries sometimes because she's so happy to be with him. He's happy, too, though he doesn't show it in the same way. But I can tell. Still, there's always something else that still haunts him and comes back to take away the smile from even his eyes. I've never been able to figure that out. Mostly, though, I'm just glad he has her. He's lived for a long time, and has known a lot of people, but from the way he speaks about it, on rare occasion, I get the impression that he just didn't care about any other women. Mostly. I also get the impression that a long time ago he knew and cared for someone else." I took a moment to try to picture her in my mind as I had done many times before. "I think her name was Maria."

Grant didn't respond but just kept walking with me.

"He's never said much at all about her, and neither has my mom, but he's the one who chose my name, and no one has ever told me why. Anyway, I think he'd been very lonely for a long time, not just because he didn't care about most women, but because he's so different from other people in so many ways, including some that make them fear him. For good reason. So thinking about my parents being together makes me happy."

"And it was just 'happily ever after' from there?"

"No, not exactly; they have their own problems to work out, but my father is very mature, and very selfless. My mom says that's key to making a marriage work. They're pretty good at it, too; I've never seen them fight or yell at each other. Not once since I was born." I took a moment to search through my memories and verify what I'd just said. "Of course, when I *was* born, my mother saw she got her wish: I had silver hair just like my father. As I grew up, my mom would threaten me: 'Maria, if you ever cut or dye your hair, I will send you to your grandfather!'"

"The real vampire? Or, rather, *full* vampire?"

"I think so. They never talk about him. That kind of remark is the most either of them has ever said about him. He must have done something bad, or a lot of bad things, which wouldn't be surprising seeing as he was a vampire. Or is a vampire. If he's still around."

That created a lull in the conversation. We continued making our way through the forest, staying generally true to the course we had set initially. I lost myself in thoughts of my parents until Grant spoke again. "So," he said, stepping over a large rock, "are pure-bred vampires invisible in mirrors?"

I stopped walking, paused, and looked at him. "I guess I don't know what they're like, but I don't think so. I don't know how that kind of thing could happen." I'd never considered the question before. "I doubt it. I know I have a reflection. I spend *pleeenty* of time in front of a mirror." To accent my words, I brought my hair up to the sides with both hands and let it fall freely back.

"Well," he said with a sheepish grin, "it's time well spent."

I glanced at him again, and in that moment he suddenly looked different to me. It confused me, and unconsciously I gaped for a moment, but somehow right then he seemed more...more something. When I realized I was staring I shook my head, said, "Thank you," and kept walking.

"So you haven't spent much time with pure-bred vampires?" he called from behind.

"Actually, no, none at all. I've never known any." I pulled my hair back into a pony tail, secured the band, and replaced my hat. "I'm sure they have reflections, though. If they didn't...that would just be weird."

"Oh, that's the only weird part, huh?" He laughed.

I kept walking, but took a few glances back, unsuccessful in figuring out what had changed. "No, that's not the only weird part. You've already seen how I'm different; from what my dad can tell, vampires metabolize iron in a way normal people don't. The metal works its way into our tissues in large amounts, making us heavier and more durable. Also, either because we have to work harder just to move around or due to some other effect, it makes us physically stronger as well. When we're not able to ingest the necessary iron, we become weaker, until we get more."

"Iron. And that's the only reason you drink blood? Or, excuse me, the only reason vampires drink blood?"

"No, I think there's something else in it, too, something that makes the taste sweeter to them, but the iron is what mostly causes the cravings. That's what my dad thinks, and he's smart, though we're not sure about it all because there's only so much credible research that has been done on the subject, and it's hard to find. And I'm not sure exactly why, but senescence occurs at a much, much slower rate."

"Senescence?"

"Aging. Like I said, my father has lived for a long time."

"How long? A hundred fifty years? Two hundred?"

"A few more hundred than that."

"Wow. Anything else?"

"Water. We don't do well with water. On one hand, we're not quite as buoyant, and on the other, we can't drink the stuff. Not by itself, anyway. I mean, we still need water to live, or at least my dad and I do, but for some reason we can hardly swallow the stuff if it's not mixed with something—that's why I have all of these flavor packets with me for this trip. Milk is good, especially whole, juices can work well enough, Kool-Aid is almost bearable, and I particularly like hot chocolate, as long as it's creamy enough, but it's almost impossible for me to drink plain water. And soda, too, for some reason—terrible stuff. I don't know why. I also don't usually like to drink anything cold, no matter what it is. That probably has something to do with blood being warm when it comes straight out of the body. Who knows? But eating cold Jello is okay, though."

He shook his head at me as he walked. "So I was right. You are really, really weird."

I scowled. "What? I'm just telling you how it is." He looked at me again, and yet again something seemed different about him, but I just couldn't figure it out.

"Do you heal faster than regular people? Vampires heal a lot faster in movies."

"I don't think I do. I don't know. Nothing I've ever noticed."

"Have you always known you were part vampire?"

"Since I was a kid. At first my mother didn't want me to know. My father felt just the opposite. When I was young they were both concerned about me saying too much, but then my father changed his mind. He assumed that if I said something no one would believe me anyway. He was mostly right. I did say something to another kid once, and people made fun of me for it until middle school. For some reason that died out, though, maybe because people became more mature, or maybe because they started to believe it. When I got to high school I was pretty comfortable with it but smart enough not to tell anyone, and because of school boundaries I didn't ever see most of the people I'd known in grade school."

"Is it hard to keep it a secret?"

"No, not really. My mom says that everyone has their secrets, whether it's bad stuff they want to hide or just things that are so personal that they shouldn't be shared much. I blend in well, and again, people wouldn't believe me if I told them, at least not without seeing things like you have."

I tend to build up verbal momentum quite easily sometimes, but while I'd been sharing my parents' story I'd been inwardly reminded that one of them was missing. When I paused for a minute, I had time to wonder again when I would see my father. Somehow I had a feeling that it wouldn't be soon. I wasn't really worried, but I didn't like him being gone.

When Grant broke the invading hush again I didn't know if he sensed my uneasiness or was simply curious. "So," he began, "if your dad lives so long, will..." He trailed off, scrunching his eyebrows as if he was seeing something he didn't like, though he didn't seem to be focusing his eyes on anything in particular.

"Will what?" I prompted.

"Are you serious about that? I mean, a lot of what you're saying is far-fetched, but to not age..."

"I didn't say he doesn't age. He says he does. It just happens slowly. That's not unheard of in the natural world. Some turtles display negligible senescence, and there's a tiny organism called a hydra that appears to live indefinitely."

"Are you kidding? A 'hydra'? It sounded like legitimate science until you said that."

"What? No, I'm not kidding. Look it up yourself."

"Okay, sorry."

But he'd left something unsaid before. "Weren't you about to ask something?"

"Well, yeah, but it seems kind of personal and intrusive."

"Hah! In the last hour I've told more personal stuff to you than anyone outside my family, which is really strange, actually. I don't know what you could ask now that would be too intrusive."

"Well, I was going to ask...if your dad doesn't age, doesn't that mean that he will outlive your mom?"

I didn't miss a beat on this one; we had discussed it openly in the family many times. "Yes. Given how slowly he's aging, it's basically certain. Unless something goes terribly wrong he'll live for a long time after her."

He seemed to give some thought before offering up his next brief words. "That's sad."

"No, not at all! I mean, it seems that way at first, but what's he supposed to do? Mope around all lonely for years and years and years? Isn't it better that he should love someone and share her life and have a child with her?"

"Well, yeah, sure, but won't he be lonely again afterward?"

"Of course he'll miss her, but it'll still be better for him than it was before. One big difference is that I'll be around. I'll be glad to keep my father company when we're both missing Mom. Who knows which of us will outlast the other...we think that could go either way. I'd like to think that he's better off with me than alone, and that he's better off with her while he's got her."

"Well, sure. Of course."

"More than that, my mom has told me that he's changed a bit since knowing her. She wants him to feel good about himself. It's a real goal of hers to change him in that way, and she's done a good job of it. It means everything to her. She has always been happy, in a way that makes her even cry a little bit sometimes, to make mention that my father accepts his human side more and more, and that he's okay with it."

He walked several steps before muttering, "Huh."

"What?"

"Oh, nothing."

"No, really, what are you thinking?"

He laughed. "My life is boring."

"It can't be, if you do a lot of hiking. These mountains are beautiful."

"Okay. The hiking isn't bad."

We didn't say anything else for a short while. It gave me an opportunity to look around and enjoy the beauty I'd just mentioned. I figured I should make time for this sort of thing more often.

Grant spoke up again. "Has your dad considered turning your mom into a vampire so she would live longer?"

I stopped walking.

"I mean," he went on, "could he do that?"

"I...I don't know. Neither of them has ever said anything like that." He had caught me off guard with that question. I did my best to remember and was quite certain that neither my father nor mother had ever suggested such a thing. "I don't know if he can turn anyone else into a vampire."

"I guess it's just something I've seen on TV."

"Yeah, me too." I thought on it more. "He's just never mentioned it. So I don't know. But even if he could, or can, I'm sure he would never want to. He would never want to put that kind of curse on anyone else if they had a choice. *Especially* not my mom. And one of them will outlive the other no matter what happens."

Maybe Grant noticed my discomfort. "Lucard...is that French?" he asked.

This was a fair question, and one I could answer much more easily. I was glad to change the subject. I walked as I answered. "Hmm. It sounds French, but he says that our family, on his side, anyway, is from Romania."

"Romania? Interesting. I don't even think I know exactly where that is."

"Eastern Europe. By the Black Sea."

"Have you ever been there?"

"No. I've never been much farther from home than I am right now."

"Really? I'm not a big traveler myself, but I've been through several states. Don't you feel like you're missing out on a lot?"

"Not so far. Not exactly like that. I like my home. Sometimes I feel like I want to see the world, though, like my father, but I'll probably have plenty of time for that later. I think I've felt like travelling was a more adult thing to do, and I'm barely an adult now."

"You're only eighteen?"

"Mm-hmm."

"Wow. You seem older. That's fine, though."

"What? How old are you?"

"Twenty-two."

I scoffed, then feigned astonishment. "Oh, my, you aged senior citizen! You must need some help getting along! Let me find a branch that you can use for a walking stick."

"Oh, come on, now."

"Well, you act as if I'm so young."

"You kind of are."

"Four years' difference isn't much."

"I guess not. And that's a good thing."

"What does that mean?"

"Nothing." He was smiling again.

I sighed. For as much as I had appreciated the relief of sharing my secret, it also felt almost too good to be true. "Grant," I asked, "how are you so calm about all of this? About being with a part-vampire?"

He looked down, as if thinking, but didn't take long to respond. "I don't know. It's not as hard to accept as I would have thought. I don't want to see those other little things again, but you, well, you're fine. You're nice, actually. Everything you've explained makes sense and you really do seem normal most of the time. I don't feel like it's hard to accept you as you are."

That hit my heart. "Thank you."

As I was looking at him, to the side of my field of vision I thought I saw a flapping of small wings perhaps a hundred feet away. They were not the wings of a bird. I stopped walking and stared directly at the spot where I thought I saw them. Nothing unusual was visible. Trees swayed in the wind; clouds above them drifted slowly.

"What's wrong?" Grant asked.

"Um, nothing." Truthfully, I was worried that I'd seen one of the flying creatures, but if I had, it was staying out of sight pretty well. Nothing worth making Grant uneasy. I would just need to keep a sharp eye on the forest as we continued. But for now it was time to keep walking. It was getting later in the day; this was taking longer than I'd expected. "You getting hungry?"

"I was just about to ask you that. You said you have snacks?"

"A few."

"Well, I brought some old Army rations. Do you like minestrone stew?"

"I don't know."

"Well, you can try it out. Hang on a second."

He loosened the shoulder straps from his backpack, then took it off and set it on the ground. "Did the Army give you that?" I asked.

He looked up. "The rucksack? No. I use a different one for training with the ROTC, but I bought this one from an Army surplus store. I could have spent a lot of money to get something nicer and newer, but this works for me. For now." He opened the top and reached inside, then pulled out a boxy brown plastic bag with black lettering on one side that labeled it as a Meal Ready-To-Eat, Individual. "Have you ever had an MRE?"

"No," I responded.

He pulled the top of the container open. "This is left over from a training exercise a few months ago."

I drew back. "Is it still good?"

He laughed once. "I don't know if they're ever good, but it's still edible, if that's what you mean. These things last for years." He retrieved a long box from within the larger container, which he then opened to remove a thin packet. "So, a question: how long do you want to take to eat? Are we going to sit down for a while, or eat on the move?"

"I'd rather move along, but we can take just a few minutes to eat first."

"Okay. MREs come with heaters, but they take a while to work, and most all of the food can be eaten cold. Except maybe the rice. And the omelet, but don't ever eat that anyway." He tore off one edge of the packet, holding it open like an envelope, and handed it to me. "I've got a spoon, too..." He withdrew a plastic spoon from the original brown container, pulled off the thin plastic covering, and handed it to me. "Bon appetit."

"What about you? What are you eating?"

He pulled out a couple of other items as he spoke. "A dense approximation of wheat bread with some cheese spread."

I tasted the minestrone stew. "It's not the best stew I've ever had."

"It would be a lot better warm, but like I said, this is faster. I think most MRE food is pretty decent, but I hear they're not as good after eating them for three weeks straight."

"How often do you eat them?"

"Normally only on special occasions."

Neither of us took long to finish. When I was done he extended his hand for the empty packet and spoon, which he stuck back in the box, which in turn he placed back in the original brown bag. "I pack it in, I pack it out."

We each got a good drink from our own water (mine with a large amount of protein powder mixed in) and then he hefted the rucksack onto his shoulders again. "Do you like the Army?"

"So far, but I'm still pretty new to it." He adjusted the shoulder straps. "Well, let's go." He resumed walking, this time in the lead.

I caught up and kept pace with him, moving around vegetation but staying roughly within his field of vision.

"So," he said, "is there anything else weird about vampires?"

"Um, just bruising. I think I've mentioned pretty much everything else."

"Bruising?"

"Yeah. Bruises stand out more, because we're pale, but they also don't last long. We seem to re-absorb the blood much faster than most people. But in a weird way there are times when we have spontaneous subdermal hematoma—a surprise bruise— around the eyes that just lingers for quite a while. We don't know what causes it or why it doesn't clear up quickly. My mom calls it 'contusion confusion'."

Grant laughed.

"It hasn't happened to me in quite a while, but I used to have to be careful with it because it looked like someone had been beating me. It's really creepy; it happened once just before Halloween, and we worked it into a zombie costume."

"But it hasn't happened recently?"

"Not for a few years."

"That's funny, though. A vampire dressed up as a zombie for Halloween."

"I'm not a vampire! That's only part of me, and it doesn't ever play into things much. Seriously. I'm sensitive about it."

"Okay, okay. Sorry. But it's still funny." He grunted. "It's also funny that you say you're not a vampire but it's what you call your dad."

I'd never thought about that.

"Boy, speaking of bruising," he continued, "I'm not old, but right now I probably could use that walking stick you mentioned. What about siblings?"

"Excuse me?"

"Are you an only child?"

"I think so." I was still pondering the word "vampire".

He looked incredulous. "Isn't that something you should know?"

"I grew up without any brothers or sisters, but over there years there have been a couple of times, just twice, when I've heard my parents say something that made me think I almost had a brother. Maybe my mom had a miscarriage or something. It seems a painful subject—they talk about it even less than they talk about my grandfather. I've learned to not ask about it."

The forest abruptly thinned, and I saw a rock wall behind the trees. With a few steps we reached a point where we could no longer advance forward. A quick glance upward revealed no obvious vertical path or destination.

Grant looked up also, and then to either side. "Okay, where to now?"

I frowned at the impasse and once again pulled out the Seeker, aiming it until I found the orientation that produced the greatest heat. With the kind of warmth it was producing, I had to wonder if at some point it would run out of energy, but maybe it was more like a magnet than a battery. I let my hand fall again. "Well, it's that way," I said pointing slightly to my right and just a bit upward with my other hand.

"Maria, you're pointing at the face of the mountain."

"There's supposed to be a cave."

"What is that thing, anyway? It doesn't look like a compass. And what cave are you trying to find, anyway?"

"The cave is where the Life Stone is. It's a jewel."

"So we're treasure hunting."

"Eh. Sort of." I held up my "compass". "This is the Seeker. When I point it in the right direction, it gets warm."

"Are you kidding?"

"Not at all. Try it."

He took it from me and pointed it toward the mountain as I had, moving it to aim it in different directions. His eyebrows shot up and he stepped back. He lifted the Seeker so he could inspect it. "Well, it's not the strangest thing I've seen today." He handed it back to me; I placed it in my right pocket. "So this jewel you're searching for is buried in the mountain, and there's a cave entrance somewhere. It's obviously not right in front of us, but if there's some sort of natural tunnel leading inward it won't follow a straight line anyway."

"So it might be further along?"

"Maybe. Which way do you want to try?"

"Ummm…" I pointed to our right. "That way."

We marched along the cliff face, following the horizontal and vertical contours, and finding no openings into the mountain.

"It just occurred to me," Grant said, "that we'll want to look upward every so often. Your cave might be above us."

This was a good point. Even so, I was discouraged; this was not the simple task I had dreamed up yesterday. The world was a big place, and my search here seemed harder than that for the proverbial needle-in-a-haystack.

After some time, we reached a steep incline. "We might be able to climb this…" I said.

Grant stepped forward. "Honestly, Maria, I'm up for a bit of climbing, but I'm really doubting that we'll—"

I was waiting for him to complete the sentence, but he was just staring up at something behind me. "What's wrong?"

"Nothing," he said. "That might be it." He pointed upward.

I turned, and, raising my eyes just a bit, saw a hole in the side of the mountain just overhead. It was nestled behind an outcropping and wasn't visible to anyone farther away. It wasn't large; an overweight person would probably have difficulty fitting through. Fortunately we were both pretty thin, because if that was the entrance to the cave, we'd each have to fit. "I think you're right. It's worth a shot." I took off my backpack and cap and set them down. "Hand this to me once I get inside."

He exhaled heavily. "Hmmm. I don't know if I actually expected us to find something like this. Caves can be dangerous."

"You are such a pansy!" I said with an exasperated smile as I reached for a handhold, perhaps wanting him to prove me wrong. "You're the one who wanted to come along." I stepped up onto the rock wall. "If you don't want to go any farther, that's up to you. But do me a favor and once I'm inside, hand me my backpack. I don't think I'll want to wear it in there, but I don't want to leave it out in the open either." He watched as I made my way up to the hole and peered in. Not much light got in through the small opening, so I couldn't see far, but the gradual downward slope that was visible appeared negotiable. There was just a slight ledge in front of the hole; it looked like it would be easier to sit on it and slide in or swing my legs sideways, rather than trying to crawl in headfirst. The handholds on one side allowed me to lean against them while swinging each of my legs over the edge and into the opening. After some awkward squirming, I could see Grant again, just below me. "Okay, give it to me."

After he handed the backpack to me, I was about to move further into the cave when I heard him say, "Take mine now, too." I shoved my backpack aside to an open space, not too far away from the entrance, and then reached back up to peek out of the cave again. He was holding up his pack now as well.

With a smile I took it and pulled it inside, setting it next to mine. I slid further into the cave to make room as Grant pulled himself in after me.

5.3

The cave opened up gradually and soon formed a large room. We slid and then walked inward; at least for now, there was only one way to proceed. The top of the cave was mostly smooth-ish with a large jagged edge off to the right side that ran along as we progressed further in.

We immediately found the need to use flashlights; some few rays of light entered the cave and reached downward, but after a short distance the open space and the walls beyond grew dim. The flashlights, which each of us had brought, provided helpful but limited lighting. "Grant, how's your leg?"

"It still hurts, but it's fine."

"Good. Stop for a second."

He did. "What's wrong?"

"Nothing." I pulled out the Light Shard. "I want to try something out."

I turned off my own flashlight and set it down, then held the Light Shard up to see it easily in the beam of Grant's flashlight.

I spoke to Grant. "I'm new to this stuff, but while some of these kinds of things work just by holding them, some need to be activated."

I breathed out, intentionally emphasizing the exhalation.

At once the Light Shard began to glow, emitting a light that reached farther into the depths of the cave than the flashlights, and which shone out in all directions except those particularly blocked by my own fingers. I was almost surprised that it worked. Why did I need to exhale? Was it something in the air, like carbon dioxide or water vapor? Those were in the air already. Maybe it was just necessary to have a distinct signal, and breathing out was the signal the ancient alchemists chose.

"Amazing." Grant gave a low whistle after turning off his flashlight. "I'm not going to be able to tell anyone about any of this, am I?"

"I'd rather you didn't." As I held the jewel aloft, I realized why it was rumored to dispel fear. Light in a dark place always tended to drive away fear as it pushed back the darkness. Light and darkness had made for excellent metaphors for many years; fear of darkness was nothing more than fear of uncertainty, and light or truth could cast them out just by being present.

But enough philosophizing.

I continued onward. The downward slope was about to level off when I heard Grant slide and fall with a grunt behind me. "Are you all right?"

"I'm fine." He lifted himself up and kept walking, but I thought I could see him limping.

The cave had opened up enough that we could stand upright, and now the roof gradually got higher and higher overhead while the floor had ceased to drop. We had entered a large room with a generally rounded ceiling, and blob-like rock formations on the sides. White veins of some mineral appeared in patches here and there on the ceiling, and sometimes bits of green glimmered in the reflection of the light coming from the object in my hand. Otherwise the stone was sort of grey or tan, and not as noteworthy. The floor remained even enough to walk on comfortably, though it was covered with broad dips and bumps. We kicked a few small clouds of dust as we walked, but the cave seemed mostly clean.

I glanced back toward the entrance, which was still bright enough to see easily. I was sure that it wouldn't be hard to get back out.

"Have you done a lot of spelunking before?" Grant asked.

"No."

"I haven't either. I always preferred being out in the open." I laughed. "Are you scared?"

"What? No, I'm not, but I don't like the idea of wandering through unknown caverns when nobody could help us if something goes wrong, especially since no one even knows we're here."

"It sounds like you're a little scared."

"It's a practical consideration."

I tried for my most patronizing tone. "It's okay to be a little afraid."

He sighed, and in the sound I could hear that he wasn't really bothered with me for teasing him. I liked that.

"How long will that last?" he asked, nodding at the Light Shard.

"I don't know," I said. "Maybe forever. If it stops working we still have our flashlights, though."

"I know."

We reached the end of the large, ovoid room, and there we found an arched opening to a second chamber. After crouching and stepping through the hole, I saw that this room was similar to the first but much smaller. It seemed to be less dusty, also.

Along the left side of the room there was a huge chunk of rock that appeared to have fallen from the ceiling, but the significant feature of this room was a cluster of several rock formations at the end, just to our right. There were three of them, each shaped not quite like a snowman, but as if they'd had balls of dough or clay dropped in layers on top of each other, partially smashed each time in the process, and then hardened. The center formation was the largest; it looked to be about five or six feet tall. Above them ran what resembled a stone ribbon. "Look up there!" I said to Grant.

"It kind of looks like bacon."

I stopped; he was right. "Thinking with your stomach, huh?"

"Hey, what can I say? I like bacon. It really does look like that, though."

I nodded, and having almost reached the lower formations, stopped to scan the room. "I don't see anywhere else to go."

"Hold the light up higher."

I complied, allowing the light to shine on all of the walls without being blocked by my own body. His silence as he also looked around confirmed my own concern. The only exit from the room was the hole we'd used to enter.

"Was there a different way to go back in the big room?" he asked.

"I didn't see any. And I think it was too plain to be hiding anything."

"Maybe there's something behind this big rock over here." We tried to see around the big fallen chunk, but neither of us found anything that looked like it could possibly be another passage. On one side I did see some small things that might have been pebbles. "I think that's bat guano," he said. "But I don't see any bats. There might not have been any here for a while."

I huffed. There had to be a way onward. I wasn't willing to accept the possibility that we were in the wrong cave, or that the passageway had been blocked by this huge rock.

Again I checked the three rock formations at the end of the room. They almost looked like people, sitting still and just waiting for others to attend to them. Almost like...

That was it. My heart sped up.

"Grant," I began to ask, "if those boulders over there were royalty, which one would be the king?"

He shrugged. "The one in the middle."

"Yeah. If I had to call this place something, I'd call it the 'throne room'." I started walking toward the formations.

"I think I've heard of things like this in some other cave, somewhere. A throne room, I mean. It sounds familiar."

"Maybe it's just something that naturally comes to mind."

He followed after me. "Why do you ask?"

I looked at the wall behind the boulders. It was sloped, rather than being perfectly vertical. "An old legend says the Life Stone was 'above the chief', or something like that. Where I see a king, someone else might see a chief. It's worth checking, anyway." The ceiling above sloped upward with the wall, and it looked like it ended in what might be a shelf with a wide enough hole in front for a person to slip through.

The wall itself was uneven, with several small ledges that appeared to be good handholds and footholds.

Grant had moved up next to me now. "Look at this," I told him, pointing to one of the handholds. "Is it just me, or is this one cut out of the rock?"

He squinted. "I think you're right."

I reached up and began to climb, but found that it was difficult while holding the Light Shard. I called over my shoulder to Grant. "Turn on your flashlight, please."

I heard a click as he did.

As I put the Light Shard back into my pocket, it went dark. The cave seemed distinctly dimmer when lit only from the beam of Grant's flashlight, but I could see enough to climb. I made my way carefully so as to keep from falling to the 'chief' below.

The climb was precarious, but the slope of the wall helped, and eventually I reached the hole. Sure enough, the ceiling behind me made a sort of shelf. I pulled myself up onto it, and for a frightening moment I worried that it might not hold my weight, but not even the edge chipped or cracked.

I could see almost nothing, so I pulled out the Light Shard again. I found that it illuminated again as easily as before. The ledge led upward on one side to another room above me that looked smaller than the others.

I held the Light Shard down for Grant. "Come on."

He climbed up after me. As he got closer I moved further up on the ledge, still trying to shine enough light for him to see.

The next room was indeed smaller and rather unremarkable, but what mattered was that it went on. We'd followed the clue.

"Is your Life Stone here?" Grant asked. "I don't see much. I thought you said it was 'above the chief.'"

"And past some sort of water. It's further on."

He raised an eyebrow.

"I guess I didn't mention that. But don't worry! We're on the right track."

Beyond the small room was an open space with an uneven floor. A massive stalactite hung from a lower portion of the ceiling. Higher up on either side, the light reached only faintly. I was walking forward, still looking upward, when Grant's hand landed on my shoulder, restraining me.

"Hey!" I exclaimed.

His grip didn't soften. "Maria, take a big step back and then look down."

I shot a glance downward before stepping back, and immediately regretted it. Just in front of me the ground dropped away into a pit with no visible bottom. I wavered, and then felt Grant pulling me forcibly backward.

"You're going to want to watch your step here."

The uneven floor had initially concealed the hole; I realized that normally I would expect to see a stalagmite under the stalactite. I'd just been careless. I breathed heavily. "Thank you." I looked back at Grant; he nodded once humbly.

I leaned forward cautiously, peering down into the pit. Even holding out the light as far as possible, I could see no bottom.

"If you die by falling down a bottomless pit, can you really consider yourself buried?" I asked to myself.

"That's too deep for me," Grant said, lifting his flashlight and stepping forward, around the pit.

Was that a joke? I wondered.

I followed him. Fortunately, a walkable path led around one side of the room that we could cross if we were careful.

A tunnel led further into the mountain and then abruptly we reached another open space, but here the ceiling quickly rose until it was no longer visible, and the walls wrapped distantly and unevenly around the largest compartment we'd yet seen inside the cave. The lowered floor was dark and as smooth as glass.

It was too smooth, in fact; natural stone didn't look like that. I advanced suspiciously; as I moved closer I found that, sure enough, the "floor" I'd first seen was a different type of surface, and the rock floor was underneath that surface.

"Past the water, right?" Grant stood next to me, surveying the chamber. "Here's your water. How do we get past?"

I tried to visually gauge the depth of the water. "We might be able to just walk through."

"Are your boots waterproof?"

"No."

"Neither are mine. I hate walking in wet boots."

"The other question," I said, "is where do we go?"

Scanning the vast room was intimidating; in the relatively dim light it just seemed like a broad dead end.

"Can you make that thing any brighter?" Grant asked.

"I can try," I answered. I repeated my actions from before, exhaling and focusing mentally on the Light Shard, pleased to find that it did shine brighter than before. The expansive water-filled room, however, was just as daunting as before. I looked one way and then another, not seeing any potential destination.

Next to me, Grant clicked off his flashlight, then pointed. "I think there's a wall there, and the water goes behind."

I looked where he was indicating, and I could see what he was talking about—a place where the far wall looked abruptly more distant to one side of an uneven but more-or-less vertical line. "Yeah. That could be it. I don't see any way to go around the edges of the room. Let's go right through the middle."

I stepped forward into the water. It licked up against my ankles and seeped into my boots, surprisingly cold. The air in the cave had gotten cooler as we'd made our way further in, but not uncomfortably so; now I noticed it more against my lower legs. Grant must have noticed too, but he was apparently good at not complaining. I tried not to get too far ahead of him, but I wanted to get out of the water as soon as possible.

By the light of the gem in my hand I could see that the true floor under the surface of the water dropped away on either side, and it looked particularly deep off to our right. The higher portion mostly stayed about six to ten inches below the water's surface. The walkway became thin and it steadily twisted back and forth in long arcs to either side as we progressed, but so far we were making good progress across the small lake.

The glow from the Light Shard seemed to have dimmed again to its former, lesser brightness, but it was still more than sufficient for us as we sloshed our way toward the opposite side of the room.

"I'm glad it isn't muddy," Grant murmured behind me.

He was right; the floor was solid, and as we passed through we didn't kick up clouds within the water. Here and there I saw loose rocks under the water, but the path we followed was mostly clear and it continued all the way across, briefly rising to break the surface of the water at one point farther on. Soon I reached the jutting wall Grant had seen. Just behind it, an incline led upward, out of and away from the water.

I was stepping up when I heard a sloshing behind me and a grunt. I turned around to see Grant with one knee in the water. "Are you all right?"

"Ouch," he answered. "Yeah, I think so. You let the light fall for a second, and I stepped on a rock in the water. It was slick."

"Oh...I'm sorry..."

He lifted himself back up, holding his leg with one hand.

I reached out to him. "Here," I said, extending the hand that didn't hold the Light Shard.

"I'm fine," he said, and he limped past me.

Ahead of our small alcove, beyond the water, there was a passage, above which the ceiling was still too far up to see. The passage seemed to be a great fissure within the mountain, splitting it entirely in half except for the uneven floor, where material from above had filled the lower part of the gap.

To the side of the recess we were in, there were several fallen boulders. Grant slowed to a halt next to one that was large enough for him to sit on. "Okay, Maria," he said with a rough edge to his voice, "I don't mean to be a wimp, but I'm going to need to sit down for a minute. My leg is really starting to hurt. That last slip sure didn't help." He moved to the side and leaned against the boulder. "That jewel of yours should be close now though, right?"

Abruptly a new voice sounded crisply in the darkness, quiet and raspy but also deep and clear as it echoed in the cave from somewhere ahead of us. "I go to such efforts to be alone, and still, despite the difficulty, the curiosity of man drives him to intrude into my home."

The sudden words, combined with the irritation in them and the mystery of their source, caught me off guard, and I had no immediate response. The words were clearly English, but I didn't recognize the accent. Grant remained seated but looked alert. "Turn on your flashlight," I whispered to him, reaching for my own and holding the Light Shard in a closed fist. He complied.

The low voice rang out again. "It never ends well for the intruder."

5.4

I could only assume that the voice belonged to the guardian of the Life Stone. I wasn't sure how close the person was. "I can't see you."

"Neither can I see you. If seeing me is what you desire, you will have to advance further. I would not recommend that course of action."

"I'll come closer."

"At your own peril."

Grant spoke in a whisper. "Maria, who is that?"

I whispered back. "A guardian. I guess I didn't mention that part either."

"Ugh." Grant shook his head. "Is it another monster?"

I bit my lip and shrugged. "I don't know."

Grant gave me an exasperated look, and then called out to the voice. "Are you really all that dangerous?"

"Yes," it responded. "Though I have no desire to feast upon innocent beings, I do require sustenance, and it has been so long since I have dined on fittingly fleshy fare."

I placed my hand on Grant's shoulder to try to reassure him; in the ambient glow of the flashlight he probably looked more afraid than he really was, but I forced myself to remember that I was putting him at risk in a foreign environment and he definitely had reason to fear. I turned back toward the sound of the voice. "We've come to see you and we'd like to be able to leave in peace once we're done."

"You have strange notions to enter the abode of another with the intent to set the terms of the visit, particularly as we are not acquainted."

"It's a request; I ask that you promise to allow my friend and me to enter and leave unharmed."

"I will make no pretense of giving you such an assurance. If either of you choose to come closer you place your life at great risk, but if you are not fearful, and if your journey is of great consequence, then come forward."

I began to stride forward at a measured, careful pace.

The voice didn't wait long to speak again. "You ought to be fearful."

I looked back at Grant one more time. "I think you should stay here," I told him. He began to speak but I interrupted him before he could. "You need to rest your leg, but also, this is my task. It's something I need to do, but there's no need to put you in danger for it."

He frowned. "I don't like the idea of you going in there alone."

I smiled back. "I'll be fine. I'm a tough gal, remember? If I think I'm getting into trouble I'll call for you."

"My leg's not so hurt. I can come along."

"But you don't need to! You need to take a break. I'll be okay. I'm sure it won't be anything to worry about."

He put some weight on the injured leg and grimaced. "Fine." He looked up again and caught my wrist, holding it tightly. "Don't be in there for long."

"I'll hurry." I turned back. Calling toward the voice, I asked, "Will my friend be safe staying here?"

"He will be safer than you."

I looked at Grant one more time, who seemed not at all reassured by the voice's last words, and then I gently withdrew my hand and began to walk onward into the passage. I kept the Light Shard in my left hand while holding the flashlight in my right. After weaving through several zig-zags between the rock walls, I called out, "Are you the one who is known as the Forlorn?"

The voice was silent for a brief moment before responding. "I am. Why do you seek me?"

"I'm looking for something, and I understand that you have it."

"Advance no farther."

I stopped walking, unsure of whether I should speak again yet. Where I was now the passage opened on my right into something like an irregular room. The voice sounded close, but despite my good vision I saw no sign of the speaker.

The room itself was different from the rest of the cave. Whereas most of the rock wall, floor, and ceiling were previously all in normal earth tones and had a form that seemed normal enough to me, in this area everything was an odd mottled blue color, with hints of cobalt and turquoise. It was all bulbous, also, though further back there were what appeared to be many gouges in the strange surface.

The voice now continued. "You do me a disservice by disrupting my solitude. What is it that you seek?" The speaker was certainly nearby.

"An artifact—a jewel of power."

"Your description is inadequate."

I frowned. "The Life Stone. I seek the Life Stone from you."

A man came forward from behind a section of rock wall. He was tall and muscled, deathly pale, bald, and dressed only in tatters around his torso and pelvis. His eyes were a dull yellow color, with pupils that were faded and hard to discern. His startling grimace revealed large, jagged teeth that caught gleams from my flashlight. The light made him squint and turn just a bit to the side.

"Lower your light."

I turned my flashlight back toward the tunnel, feeling apologetic. The reflected light, while dim, was more than enough for me. "'The Forlorn' sounds so formal; don't you have another name?"

"I have had many names that I do not wish to take up again, and I rarely have need for a name." He looked closer at me, as if he was seeing something he hadn't before. "You are...unusual."

That struck me as almost humorously ironic. "Yes, I am." I assumed that somehow he could tell I was part vampire. "My father is 'unusual' also."

"You are not quite human...you have a touch of the enchanted in you."

"Or cursed, as some would say."

"Yes...yes, we are cursed, all of us..." He continued to stare at me for several seconds, but then his attention shifted.

He stepped to the side and reached for a nearby pillar. Scratching one of his claw-like hands down its surface, he removed a glob of the bluish stuff, which was evidently not rock at all but something covering it. He lifted the stuff, which seemed to be neither quite powdery nor slimy, to his mouth, and a long tongue scooped at it a few times until he'd eaten most of it. With a sigh he whipped his hand away, casting off a few small bits of blue.

He then turned back to me, and his grimace seemed sharper than before. "Few are aware that I am the keeper of the Stone."

"How can I be sure that you have it?"

He held his other hand forward and opened it face-up. On his palm rested what looked like a large, rounded emerald. "I have possessed this for a very long time. I am exceedingly doubtful that you can provide me with sufficient cause to give up my greatest treasure."

Though he surely knew the relic's nature better than I did, I figured I knew enough to make an important point. "From what I see here," I said, gesturing around me with my arms, "you don't seem to be using it much. Why is it worth so much to you?"

He closed his fist. "The Life Stone provides my sustenance, thus allowing me to remain in the seclusion I require." So the blue substance wasn't natural; I supposed that made sense enough. He went on, with some vexation in his raspy voice. "But while you have failed to see my use for it, you also grossly misunderstand. I do not keep the Life Stone solely because of its value to me. I keep it to prevent others from possessing it."

"Why?"

"Because of the harm it could cause."

That didn't make sense to me, but maybe I could convince him that I wasn't a bad guy. "I don't want to do anyone any harm."

"I am certain of that. I know so well the hearts of dark men and demons. I have heard in my mind full conversations of villains who passed by my dwelling far above the surface of the earth. I have spoken back to all of them so often, even though they cannot hear me. I hear them, I hear them…"

After that, I didn't know whether to think he was crazy or psychic, or maybe both…

His voice came back into focus. "If you had borne any malicious intent when you entered I would have known. You would not have survived long enough to converse."

I didn't doubt him. "Then why shouldn't I have the Life Stone?"

"I gather that you think the Stone is only useful for righteous purposes. Perhaps you will yet learn that almost any power, regardless of the reason for which it is bestowed, can be used for evil goals."

"I don't get it. You trust yourself with the Life Stone, but you're threatening to kill me; that sure sounds evil."

"Do not be unappreciative for being permitted to live."

The prospect of death solidified uncomfortably in my mind. "Well, fine, I guess, but you already said you know I'm not here to do anything bad."

"I said you had no malicious intent." He was breathing slightly through his teeth, making a soft sound as he did so.

"Right," I said back, confused.

"Nevertheless," he continued, "I have no assurance that you will cause no harm. Additionally, I am not confident that you would desire or be able to retain it for yourself—most assuredly, at some time you would lose possession of it to a party unknown to me. But this can be of no great concern, as you have done nothing to convince me to part with the Stone, and you have offered me no reason to bestow it to you over any other prospective guardian."

He made a valid point.

"I grow weary. It is obvious that your intrusion here is to be fruitless for both of us."

I suddenly felt like my plan was woefully incomplete, and I had little justification I could give him for wanting the Life Stone. *I want to get it for a cute guy and I was thinking that you might just give it to me.* In my overzealousness I hadn't considered what I might encounter once I found the stone. But maybe I had options. "Maybe I could trade it for something." I held the flashlight slightly forward to show it to him, flicking it off and then on again a couple of times to demonstrate its utility. "Maybe this."

"You are sorely misjudging the value of either the Life Stone or your trinket, and causing my patience to wear thin." His breathing was louder; his sharp canines glistened in the dim light. "As my patience grows thinner, so my *hunger* grows keener."

The way he hissed when he said the word "patience" was extremely unsettling; the low growl from him as he said the word "hunger" was downright bloodcurdling. I felt a thick coldness wash over me as he took a couple of slow steps forward. He scratched another chunk of his food from the wall, looked at it, then cast it down to the floor.

I felt stupid for assuming that he might be impressed by the flashlight. I had to try something else. I clutched the Light Shard in my fist, wondering if it might be acceptable, but I felt doubtful, and it wasn't actually mine to give anyway—it was borrowed, without permission. In a practical sense, though, it probably wasn't worth anything more to him than the flashlight.

I had another option, though. "Well," I said, pulling out my unique jeweled necklace so that it sat on top of my shirt, "what about this?"

If the flashlight had been unimpressive to the Forlorn, for some reason my necklace certainly wasn't.

It halted him completely for a moment. He first held his breath, then breathed in heavily through his teeth, then growled. "Whom do you serve?"

I leaned back, unsure about what he was asking. He breathed in and out heavily. My voice quivered as I responded, "I don't know what you mean."

He spoke louder. "WHOM DO YOU SERVE?"

I didn't know what to tell him; I had no idea why he was suddenly so upset. After seeing that I had no response he started lumbering toward me, slowly but steadily. He was changed; whereas before he had been a stranger with a ghastly appearance, now he was a monster. Rage fumed from his eyes and dripped from his teeth.

I took a step back, but as I retreated he moved forward faster. I attempted to backpedal farther but roughly bumped into the rock wall behind me and dropped my flashlight. In the darkness I dimly saw the horrific Forlorn lunge at me, and I had nowhere to dodge. Seeing no other way to defend myself, I thrust the Light Shard forward and caused it to illuminate itself by breathing out a powerful *"Ha!!!!"*

My act of desperation had a result I couldn't have guessed.

Whether driven by my urgency or my fear, the Light Shard shone out much brighter than before; it became brighter than anything I had ever seen. The outpouring of light made everything around me white beyond precedent, and then as quickly as the flash had appeared it vanished again, leaving only dim illumination from the flashlight on the ground.

I should have guessed that the brightness would be too much for the Forlorn with his eyes being accustomed to pitch darkness. He reared back, screaming out and clutching at his eyes; simultaneously, the emerald he'd held clattered to the rock floor. I leaped forward and snatched it up, staying low to the ground as the grotesque man flailed his arms this way and that, seemingly trying to strike me. Without another glance at him I ran from the chamber, calling out Grant's name as I dashed through the sharp turns of the narrow passage.

I jammed the Life Stone into my left pocket along the way, and with another concentrated breath, the Light Shard again glowed enough for me to see my way. I could hear the Forlorn following after me and roaring out unintelligible curses, but based on the changes in the sound of his calls I seemed to be swiftly putting distance between us. "Grant, get up!" I called. At the mouth of the narrow passage I almost ran into him. "I've got it! Let's get out of here! Hurry!" I grabbed his hand and kept moving as speedily as possible, though his shuffling gait was nowhere near as fast as would have made me comfortable.

We hurried back through the water, splashing so much that I worried about being able to see the safe path through it. I looked behind us just in time to see the Forlorn appear from the passageway; he proceeded hastily through the water. Turning to run away, I tripped on a rock and stumbled before falling sideways onto the dry ground just beyond the water. The cave went dark as I fell; the Light Shard slipped out of my hand, dimming completely before it even landed.

I rolled to my back. I heard wet feet slapping against the stone floor and in a trace amount of ambient light I could see the Forlorn stepping forward, looming directly over me. Strangely, his eyes were closed, but I still saw the glint of many sharp and terrifying teeth. Panic shot through me and I froze, not entirely unable to scramble backward but certain that it would do no good. The Forlorn reached down toward me. Suddenly the beam of Grant's flashlight was waving unsteadily and he sprung forward, ramming his shoulder into the Forlorn. The brute, caught entirely by surprise, stumbled backward and then fell into the water, dropping to the side into a deeper area and splashing wildly as he floundered.

Grant turned and reached his hand down to me. I took it and stood as he lifted to help me to my feet. As soon as I was steady Grant pushed me from the room, limping along with me, away from the Forlorn.

With the Forlorn's howls behind us, we hurried through the tunnel and into the pit room. Here we moved as quickly as we dared while keeping our distance from the hole. I hesitated a couple of times when the beam of Grant's flashlight moved away from the walkway edge. It was hard to see by the meager glow, and I realized with a shock that I'd left the Light Shard back farther in the cave. There would be no going back for it.

"That thing is coming to kill us," Grant said beside me.

"Yeah," I agreed. "Keep moving."

On the other side of the pit room, we took turns sliding onto the ledge, and then down into the throne room. I failed to move out of the way before Grant rolled down onto me and we both bumped against the 'chief' formation. The flashlight clattered to the ground nearby, blinking off for a terrifying instant as it hit.

"Sorry!" Grant said through gritted teeth.

"My fault," I said, rubbing my side. "We need to keep moving." I picked up the flashlight. "I'm really glad this didn't go out."

I got up and helped him to his feet, and with our arms over each other's shoulders again we shuffled forward a few steps. The room looked different on the way out, especially in the comparatively dim beam from the flashlight. I swept it back and forth quickly, and was relieved to locate the low arched opening. We hurried to it and individually crouched to get through.

Arriving in the large entrance area gave me a bit of hope, but I knew the Forlorn was still behind us and we didn't have a moment to spare.

We made decent time while moving toward the entrance of the cave, the natural light from it becoming brighter as we got closer. When we reached the slope and the ceiling came low to us again, I glanced back and saw the ghastly figure of the Forlorn coming from the throne room. "Climb!" I shouted.

We scrambled up the incline; after seeing our pursuer I moved with renewed urgency. Grant was still struggling.

"Pull yourself up with your arms!" I shouted.

"Already on it!"

I reached the cave entrance first. Before pulling myself out, I looked back at Grant. He was right behind me but panting with fatigue. Reaching down, I grabbed his extended arm and pulled him up to the mouth of the cave. With a cry of exertion he pulled himself through. I hurriedly grabbed our backpacks and shoved them out after him, and then I followed, trying to ignore the proximity of the Forlorn's enraged screams.

Outside the cave, I saw Grant holding to the side of the mountain and I realized that he wouldn't be able to climb down easily. Without hesitating, I jumped. I tried to roll but hit more forcefully than I expected. Hurriedly getting to my feet, I held out my arms and yelled, "Jump!"

Grant let go of the wall and fell toward me. I wanted to get under him to catch him but wasn't able to get ahold of him properly in time and he landed right on top of me, knocking me to the ground again.

"Ouch!" I cried out.

"Are you all right?" he said, rolling over.

"Don't worry about it. We need to get away."

He nodded and we both got up, grabbed our backpacks, and again moved together, donning our packs while shambling away from the cave along the mountainside where we'd been before.

Behind us I heard the Forlorn cry out again, long and loud, without the sound of the echoing cave walls. This was a cry of desperate rage; he had reached the opening and knew we were already out.

"Is it going to keep chasing us?" Grant asked.

"I don't know." I tried to move back along the same route we'd taken before, though it was difficult to recognize anything.

"We can start moving south through the forest as soon as it looks convenient. Even if we don't hit the trail, as long as we move south we'll eventually hit a road. The highway is our backstop."

South was easy to determine; the sun was lowering and casting shadows to the east. I didn't know what a backstop was, but Grant's general idea made sense. "Here," I said, pointing to a clearing in the forest.

I looked behind us but saw no sign of the Forlorn. Maybe he couldn't follow us any farther in the open outdoors. Then again, maybe he had a good sense of smell and could track us, or maybe he could even see signs we left behind in our hurried tramping through the forest.

Eventually, my heart rate slowed. "I think we're safe."

5.5

"You actually broke my fall pretty well back there." Grant sounded more at ease also. "Sorry for falling on you."

"Don't worry about it. It worked."

"Are you all right?"

"I'm in better condition than you are. I'm just glad we moved fast enough to get away from that thing."

"Yeah. Most girls don't move so fast with me."

That's another joke. "You see a lot of girls, then?"

"Actually, no. I don't date much at all."

"So, your leg isn't broken, or you couldn't walk, right?"

"No, it's not broken. Just bruised, I think. It hurts a lot, but I'll be fine. It's probably good to keep walking on it. Don't get me wrong, I'd love to stop and take a break, but I want to get as far away from that cave and that…thing…as possible."

"Yeah."

"What was that thing, anyway?"

"I don't know. It was like a person—it talked to me—but it wasn't human. Wasn't fully human, anyway. Maybe it was kind of like me. I don't even know. All I know is that it had big teeth and claws and was angry, and I'm glad we got away."

"You said you got the jewel, though, right?"

"Mmm-hmm." I pulled away and stopped walking, and reached into my pocket where the large emerald was. I withdrew it and held it for him to see. "I dropped my flashlight back there, though. It looks like I ended up trading for it after all."

"Wow," he said, regarding the gem. "That must be worth a fortune."

"Probably. That's not why I wanted it, though."

"Then why?"

"It has…some sort of power. It helps things to grow…I think."

He laughed. "Would it help with a hurt leg?"

I paused. "It might." I held it out to him.

He looked surprised, but reached for it and took it in his hand. As he held it he gazed into it, and his eyes narrowed. "That's weird…it…feels kind of good."

I observed it to see if anything was happening within.

"It's subtle," he continued, "but it feels like...like something is being set right." He took a single step with his injured leg, grimacing. "My leg still hurts, but not as much. I think this does have some power. It's helping."

I was glad. "Hold onto it for now. Let's keep walking."

I reached to put my arm around his shoulder again, but it seemed as we walked that he leaned on me less than before.

It occurred to me that someone else might be reluctant to later return a precious emerald like the Life Stone, but I trusted Grant. It was odd that I felt so much confidence in him when I'd only known him for, what, maybe six hours? In that time we'd been through some rather dramatic experiences, though. Trust could be born in a short time in some cases, especially when extreme circumstances provide opportunity to demonstrate it.

With the danger from the Forlorn no longer being imminent, I remembered the flying creatures we'd seen before. I looked around the forest but never saw any of them.

In the thick of the forest it was impossible to know how far we were going, but the terrain tended to steer us, and I was surprised when eventually we came to a trail that looked like the same trail we'd used on our way out. When we stepped onto it, Grant said, "I think I can walk on my own, now."

"Are you sure? I don't mind helping."

"No, it's okay. It gets awkward after a point, like a three-legged race. I mean, it was nice, too, but I don't want to lean on you too much."

"Okay." I realized something. "I left my hat back there!"

"Well, I don't think we should go back to get it."

"Ugh. I really liked that hat."

"Where'd you get the necklace?"

I'd left my necklace out after showing it to the Forlorn. "Oh. It was a gift from Bastian."

"Who's he?"

"A recent friend. He's got amazing eyes."

Grant leaned back, and it looked like he pressed his tongue to his upper teeth on one side. "Huh. It's kind of a strange thing to wear on a hike."

"I guess I could take it off." I reached up to the clasp, but suddenly felt light-headed, and swayed on my feet. I shook my head to clear it.

He reached behind my neck. "Let me get it."

I was about to refuse and push his hands away, when the lightheadedness returned, and I nearly fell over. "Whoa. Maybe I'm tired."

"Sit down," Grant said, and he helped me to do so. "The adrenaline rush is over. I'm not surprised if that whole adventure took a lot out of you."

I focused on just sitting still. "I guess so."

He blinked and then held out the Life Stone. "Here. Maybe this'll help."

I took the Life Stone, and as he'd suspected, I started to feel better. "Don't worry about the necklace. It's actually quite comfortable." My head cleared, and I stood up again. I tucked the necklace away again.

"You must like the guy if you want to keep it on while in the mountains."

"Yeah." I wasn't afraid to admit it. Grant turned and began walking down the trail. "Hey, wait up!" I put the Life Stone back in my pocket and hustled after him until I caught up. He didn't say anything for a while; to break the silence I spoke up again. "You said that this trail had a name?"

He looked at me, and then forward again. "Well, I don't know if this exact trail we're on is part of it, but the Pacific Crest Trail passes through here. It's over twenty-six hundred miles long, from somewhere up in Canada all the way down through California."

"Boy. Do people walk the whole way?"

"Sometimes, I think. You'd have to be a real hardcore hiker to do something like that. I sure haven't, but I know it passes through here."

The casual conversation felt nice; it was strange to think that we'd been fleeing for our lives just earlier. Grant seemed to be feeling much better also.

We came out of the forest, passed the first rough patch of trail, and were back where all of the cars had been parked earlier. Now, aside from my car, only one other remained; Grant stopped next to it. "And we're done," he said.

"Yep. What a long day."

He loosened his pack and let it fall off. "Do you need a ride anywhere?"

"No. My car's right there."

He hesitated. "So, you're off, then?"

"Yep. I got what I came for. I'm sure you got a lot more than you were looking for."

"Yes," he said with a funny sort of expression. "A lot more."

What was he hinting at?

"Maria, I have to say, you've opened up my eyes to a whole new world."

Oh, of course. "Yeah, all the monsters and everything are weird even for me, and I'm one of 'em."

Something I said surprised him. "Oh; yes. It *is* all new and strange, but that's not really what I...well, I had something else in mind."

I didn't know what he was getting at, but I was tired, and my confusion was vexing and I didn't want to linger. "Okay, well, thanks for the help with everything, and I'm sorry about all the trouble, but I should be on my way now."

"Wait." He lifted his hand, gesturing for me to stop. "I enjoyed our trip. More than I do with most people. You know, aside from the crazy stuff. I'm...glad to have spent the time with you. Can I call you sometime?"

Call me? "Oh, like, to hang out?"

"Yeah, something like that."

I shrugged. "Do you make it up to the Yakima area often?"

"Well, yeah, when I have good reason to."

"Do you often have good reason?"

He smiled. "I can."

I definitely was missing something, but didn't want to seem silly by asking anything more to figure out what he meant. "Okay." I wrote down my phone number on a scrap I tore from a paper in my backpack and handed it to him. "That's my home number."

"You don't have a cell phone?"

I shook my head. "I never get good reception; mobile phones tend to never work well for me. It's a curse. Actually, my dad would say that he truly is cursed, literally, though he has greater hope for me than he does for himself. I could probably get text messages to work, but they seem like the supreme social...what's the opposite of apex? Anyway, they strike me as the low point of social interaction."

He laughed. "Okay, well, I find text messages useful, but I'm happy with this," he said, holding the bit of paper.

And then I understood, though I didn't know what to make of it. I didn't know why I hadn't recognized it before. The way he was smiling and looking at me…

I kind of liked him, in a way, and the trust I'd given him wasn't something to set aside lightly, but I wasn't actually looking forward to having him call me. I could see it in Grant's eyes now, that he was beginning to care for me, that he wanted something more with me, and I was flattered…and then, as the shine left his eyes and his smile dulled, I could also see his realization that I didn't feel the same desire. My heart and mind were elsewhere; I was simply hoping that Bastian would be pleased with me for retrieving the Life Stone. That was probably why I hadn't made sense of Grant's evident interest in me before. I was already aiming my own affection in another direction, and similar interest from someone else almost seemed a nuisance. But now, I felt guilty for allowing my feelings for Grant, or lack thereof, to be visible to him. I didn't want the discomfort to last, for either of our sakes, so I tried to smile and make it sincere as I said, "Good. Give me a call sometime."

I now saw uncertainty; not quite hope, but not quite disappointment, either. "I will." He smiled again.

I didn't say anything more but just waved and left, hoping that I wouldn't encourage or disappoint him further.

As I walked away I wrestled with continued uncertainty. I couldn't avoid a feeling of disquiet, as if I was leaving something unsettled—as if I had done Grant some wrong, and maybe even somehow betrayed myself—and I almost wanted to turn back but I kept walking. I walked swiftly, and as I got farther away I distanced myself mentally from Grant also. I remembered the jewel I carried with me and my thoughts went back to Bastian. I was eager to show him what I had done. I was eager for him to be proud of me and express approval. I had made real efforts to please him and had succeeded despite unforeseen difficulties. I wanted him to know what I had done for him.

And, I just wanted to see him again. I wanted to see his eyes, and his hair. I wanted to smell the scent of clove that lingered with him. I wanted to talk to him and hear him say that I was capable enough to help him more—I wanted his praise and his trust. I wanted him to be surprised and delighted by my initiative and resourcefulness.

I stopped to think after tossing my pack into my car. What I really wanted was for Bastian to like me. In fact, I wanted him to like me more than Amy. That Amy—she was going to be so jealous. It served her right; she must have thought I was so much less able than she was, but she wouldn't have anything to say when I came back with the first of the two treasures Bastian was seeking. And she wouldn't have anything to say when he turned his attention to me, because I deserved it.

I so much wanted his attention. Little fantasies began to bring a satisfied smile to my face. Once again I thought about his lips...

My, oh my. Too much for me right now. I shook myself lightly to clear my head, and turned again to take a last glance behind me.

Grant was there, next to his car, looking in my direction. Even as far away as I was, I could see that he had a strange look on his face—something like concern, maybe, or uneasiness, or...disappointment?

I didn't want to have to see it any longer, so I quickly turned and got into my car. I started the engine, and as I drove away I looked back through the rear-view mirror to see if he was still there. He was; no longer able to see his expression, I pressed down further on the accelerator and soon wasn't able to see him at all.

It didn't take long to refocus myself. I had a gift to deliver to someone whom I was anxious to see. It no longer felt like a long day. The anticipation drove me on just like I drove the car; it was a test of patience to obey the speed limit as I returned to my hometown. The patience was easier to muster, though, knowing that I was victorious in one venture and that it would bring me closer to a victory of the heart.

The world passed along beside me. The sun fell slowly down, with rays of light recoiling one by one into other realms. Shadow came forth in long lances like prisoners creeping out from unguarded confines to seize the world, leading the way for the long night that was to come. I drove on into the evening and silent shade.

5.6

I debated between either going straight home or stopping first at the castle. With Bastian being away, my first impulse was to go home and get some rest, but Abbott may well have discovered the missing items. To avoid trouble I'd want to reassure him as soon as possible. Mostly, though, I was impatient to see Bastian and show him the Life Stone. I decided to go to the castle first, only stopping at a service station along the way. Abbott must have had Bastian's phone number, and could call him to have him return early. Somehow I would convince him that we didn't need any extra help, while saving the surprise to tell him in person. I sure wouldn't tell Abbott first.

When I knocked on the door of Greywall Castle, Abbott opened, raising an eyebrow when he saw me. "Maria…you've returned."

I couldn't help but feel smug, and I let it show in my smile. "Yes, I am, and I've brought a surprise with me."

"Mmm-hmm." He looked me over once as if to locate something on my person. "All right. Come on in." I stepped inside and he closed the door behind me. "I assume you want to see Bastian. He's in the study."

"He's…back already? I thought you'd need to call him."

He only nodded in response, with an expression on his face that I didn't understand. I followed his hand gesture and moved toward the study.

While making my way there I wondered why Bastian was back so soon. I'd thought he wouldn't be back for at least several more days—it had sounded like he was traveling some distance. He was reading from *Demons and Dark Essences* when I entered the study. He looked up from the book as I came in and gave a contented smile. "Maria. Good evening."

He was being cordial, but in a subtle way he didn't seem quite as warm as I would expect. "Hi, Bastian. I didn't know you'd be back quite so soon."

"It didn't take long to do what needed to be done." He said nothing more, and I wasn't immediately sure how to respond.

Abbott spoke up. "She says she has a surprise for you."

Bastian regarded me inquisitively, still with a satisfied smile.

"Um, yes, yes I do." For some reason I was apprehensive. "I made progress while you were away. We found a clue about the Life Stone and I..." I glanced at Abbott, worried that he might be upset with me for acting without his knowledge, but he seemed mostly emotionless. "I went ahead and got it."

"The Life Stone is with you, right now?" Bastian asked.

I had expected him to be shocked, but he wasn't. "Yes."

He stood, and his smile opened up. "May I see it?"

I reached into my pocket and pulled out the round emerald. He held his hand out, palm up, so I placed the Life Stone in it. I said nothing, waiting instead for his words of approval and appreciation.

"Well, well." He held the Life Stone up, examining it. "Surprise, surprise." Something about the way he spoke made it seem like the appearance of the Stone was no surprise at all. My uneasiness grew within me as I watched him rotate it with wide eyes and a strange smile. He spoke without looking at me. "How did you get it from the guardian?"

"I caught him off guard with the Light Shard and he dropped it. I think I might have hurt him."

He again grinned a bit wider. "Good."

Abbott watched from a distance, but gave a "hmph" at this.

I clasped my hands helplessly. "I...lost the Light Shard in the cave."

Bastian shrugged. "An acceptable loss." He tucked the Life Stone away. "Excuse me." He walked swiftly from the room before I could question him. Abbott made no attempt at conversation but stared at me with an expression I almost didn't dare to interpret. Somehow his underlying perpetual discontent was greatly intensified—almost palpable. I averted my gaze, unable to focus on any one object, while trying to make sense of what was happening.

Bastian walked back into the room, folded his arms, and gave Abbott a matter-of-fact look. "I told you she could do it."

Abbott said nothing in return.

I was awfully confused by that statement. "I could do what?"

Bastian looked back at me with a raised eyebrow, as if I had asked a stupid question. "Retrieve the Life Stone, of course. It would have been an excessively difficult task for most people to face the Forlorn."

Abbott sneered. "But as he's said before, you're *different*."

A low dread began welling up in me. They must have known more about me than they were letting on. "What...what do you mean?"

Abbot frowned. "Maria, there's no use in keeping up pretenses now. It's only fair to be clear that we know who, and what, you are."

I shot a quick glance at him and Bastian in turn.

"Really, Maria," Bastian said, gesturing at the book he had been reading. "Do you think we could study up so much on this sort of thing and *not* recognize a vampire when we see one?"

I drew in a quick breath. Among friends, this kind of knowledge shouldn't be a problem, but they had concealed that knowledge from me, and the atmosphere in the room was so strange. I glanced at the book and then back and forth between the two men. "I'm not a vampire."

Bastian raised one eyebrow again.

"I'm more human than anything else."

He rolled his eyes. "Come now. Really. I knew from the first time I saw you, back in that little bookstore. I thought it a strange coincidence initially, that I should encounter someone like you at such a pivotal time, but then I began to see you as an opportunity."

That word stung. My mind jumped from thought to thought as I tried to remember events from recent days and make sense of them in a new light. Bastian had been so refined, so romantic...was it all just to manipulate me?

He continued. "With a bit of research, I was able to find you again, and with your father out of the way..."

My heart raced. "What do you know about my father?!"

He raised his eyebrows in surprise at this sudden question. "Actually, not much at all, my dear, other than that he's unable to interfere...and that it's because of him that you're a vampire."

"Stop calling me that!" I wasn't used to hearing myself referred to that way, and it felt both inaccurate and unflattering. It felt like a pejorative, as good as an outright insult. "Why did you lie to me? If you wanted me to help, why weren't you upfront about it all with me in the first place?"

Bastian laughed once. "Well, my dark beauty, I just didn't know if you'd go along with it if you knew what we truly intended to do."

"Do? What do you mean?"

He grimaced. "Maria. Take the first 2 and the second 2 and work some magic with them. I honestly am astonished that you haven't come to the right conclusion yet. The reason I know so much about the combining ritual is that I'm the one who intends to conduct it!"

I suddenly wasn't sure I could remain standing. *Bastian* was the dark alchemist himself, and Abbott was evidently in on the plan as well. The full force of horrible realization washed through me as I remembered what Bastian had told me before about the Demon Stone and the Life Stone.

I'd been so fully duped that I had given a powerful enchanted jewel to the very man from whom I should have kept it.

Bastian retained his smile. "So I thank you for helping me."

As I struggled to come up with a response I heard a cry from a distant room. Abbott perked up at this, and said, "I knew he'd soften up eventually."

Bastian looked at him. "So it seems." He again began to walk from the room. "Excuse me, Maria. I have something to attend to." As he left, Abbott collected himself with a frown and exited as well, through the main entrance instead, leaving me alone in the study.

I was partly stunned by the revelation but wondered why they still expected me to accept everything. It was clear now that they were the bad guys. Did they really think I might help them when *not* ignorant of their intentions? They obviously weren't worried about me now, or they wouldn't have left me alone in the castle. Just minutes ago I had held the Life Stone, but now Bastian had hidden it away, and must have been confident that I couldn't get it back. As I stood alone in the room I knew I wouldn't help them in any way but I lacked a sense of what I should do next.

Until I brought my mind back to the ritual. If Bastian intended to conduct it, I would have to prevent him from doing so, and I knew how. He still needed the Demon Stone. If I could find it first…I wasn't sure what to do exactly, but in the end all I needed was to keep it from him.

I started to walk toward an exit, but I subconsciously raised my hand to my neck, where it brushed against Bastian's necklace. I felt some revulsion and sadness, and wanted to take it off. I reached behind my neck for the clasp. After pulling it around to my front I tried to undo it but suddenly felt lightheaded and had to reach for the wall to keep myself from falling over.

As I steadied myself, the voice I'd heard before screamed out again. I was so baffled when I'd heard it the first time that I hadn't taken any thought to wonder who it was or why they seemed to be in pain, but now the strangeness of it struck me. Aside from that of Bastian and Abbott, I had never heard another male voice in the castle. I had no idea who it might be. Given the recent turn of events and the new light cast on Bastian, I grew concerned for the welfare of this unknown person. Ignoring the necklace, I followed through the door that Bastian had taken.

Just down the hall, another door was open. As I walked inside, I was startled to see Bastian standing in front of a crumpled man who hung by the arms between two monsters that looked much like the beast that had attacked me a few days ago on the street. I let out a cry of fright and halted just inside the doorway.

The man who hung by his arms raised his head, with a clearly strained effort, upon hearing my yelp. His eyes grew wide as he tried to look at me. When he spoke, his voice was weak. "Maria, what are you doing here?"

My jaw dropped. "Art, is that you?" Though his voice was ragged, I recognized it as that of Artemis Brown. Years before, he had visited my father in his home and had been introduced as a sort of noble adventurer, and a good friend—one of few people who brought happiness into my father's life. Lucard had given him a rare endorsement, and though I hardly knew him I had looked up to him at the time. Now he was clearly in such pain that he wasn't able to stand under his own strength. His hair was mussed, his clothing was torn, and dark marks were visible on exposed skin.

Art's eyes gained focus, and he looked at me, or almost at me, but not quite at eye level, and his expression changed from pain to horror. "No, Maria, you've got to get out of here! Take off that—"

Bastian silenced Art with a backhand strike to the face. He followed it with a punch to Art's solar plexus, and then a vicious swing that rocked Art's head backward. I cried out and moved toward him, but Bastian intercepted me. "Stop!" he commanded.

"Bastian, what are you doing?" I cried as I tried to move past him to reach Artemis.

"I said, *STOP!*" Instead of blocking my way, Bastian pulled a dark object from his vest pocket. As he held it up I very suddenly felt a great weight on my body. The weight seemed to come over all of me, though it was distinctly concentrated on the necklace I wore. In spite of my natural strength I found myself unable to remain upright. I could do nothing but sink first to my knees, and then to all fours. It seemed that the more I struggled against the weight, the more it pulled me downward. After finding that I had no power against the force pressing on me, I ceased resisting and simply held myself up as well as I could.

"Now, was that necessary?" Bastian asked, looking down at me. "I suppose it was; it seems I was justified in taking this precaution." I could scarcely lift my head to see him. He turned to address the monsters. "I'm no longer entertained by this wretch. Take him away."

The beasts moved away, carrying Art limply between them. Moaning with effort, I tried to lurch toward him but found myself being pressed to the floor with such force that my vision went black. Again, when I ceased to resist, I felt the pressure lessen.

"I'd recommend lying still for now."

I was breathing heavily, but the urgency of the moment made me feel a need to speak. "What is that? What are you doing?" was all I could get out.

"This?" he said, holding up the object in his hand. It was a chunk of glassy obsidian, like the gems on my necklace, but much larger and misshapen. "This is the Demon Stone. I'm sorry to have lied to you, but I've had it for quite some time. The necklace you're wearing, the Slave Necklace, has been bound to it with alchemy. You can't take it off, and let me assure you, if you need any more assurance, that you won't be able to resist me or escape from here as long as I have the Demon Stone and you're wearing that necklace. I'm sorry to say that your demon nature is a disadvantage to you in this case."

I made a quick movement to reach for the clasp behind my neck. As my fingers touched it, pain shot into my body. I flopped down, stunned.

"Oh, I wouldn't try that. As long as I want it on, you'll find it quite impossible to remove."

I didn't reach for the clasp again.

I rested on the floor, trying to grasp what was happening. Part of me wanted to say something back to Bastian, to question him, to reprimand him, to plead with him, but I was too stunned and too fatigued to speak. I could scarcely keep my eyes open. I thought I heard him sit in a chair; he said nothing for the moment.

I heard the sound of the door opening, and others entering the room. Bastian spoke again. "Maria, I still want you to help me."

On the verge of unconsciousness I struggled to answer back. "You've got to be joking. I don't know what you're doing here, Bastian, but this is wrong and I can't support it."

He didn't respond immediately. "I'm sure you're a bit confused by the surprises we had here, but I'll expect you to come around and devote your efforts to my cause."

I let my head rest on the floor. "Whatever you're doing, it's wrong. I won't be a part of it."

Again he waited before speaking. "Your lack of vision disappoints me. Perhaps you can yet gain some perspective and change your mind." He addressed the others who had entered. "Take her to the dungeon. She'll have plenty of time to think it over there."

I felt rough hands lift me and start to carry me. I made one final attempt to move away, but once again felt the weight of the Slave Necklace sapping my strength. If it was making me a heavier burden for whoever it was that was conveying me, they showed no sign of letting it trouble them. I, however, barely avoided losing consciousness. We seemed to move through hallways, and then through my disorientation I became aware that we were on stairs.

My vision faded again and I fell into blackness.

5.7

My one luxury—just one—right now was that I had some time to think. That was essentially all I could do for the moment: think. Think about Bastian's treachery. About my own stupidity. About what might be going on here.

I could do nothing more than think for a while because I was chained to a wall in a dungeon.

Yes, I was in a real, genuine dungeon. That won the prize for unexpected events. I definitely hadn't seen that one coming.

It was dark and I couldn't see much in the room, but the essential components were obvious to me. Old-style metal chains and shackles held me to a stone wall. My wrists and ankles hurt from the rough iron wrapped around them; my wrists were particularly sore because the clasps had chafed them while I hung unconsciously, suspended by the metal links. Having woken up again, alone now, I had hurried to stand in order to relieve the pressure and pain; it quickly became irritating that neither hand could quite reach across to rub the opposite wrist.

The pain from the hard clasps wasn't on my mind for long, though. As I stared across a mostly empty room, for a time I was too stunned to bring my thoughts to a head, but the conclusions, however hard to bring myself to reach, were inevitable. As the shock diminished I moved repeatedly between thoughts.

Bastian was bad. He was hurting people, lying, and associating with goblins. I tried to think of other descriptions that would be more correct, but a general thought of "bad" was all I could come up with.

I was a dupe. I had been oblivious to a crucial reality while letting myself fall for a guy.

Bastian had taken advantage of me. He had tricked me into getting the Life Stone for him while he had the Demon Stone all along, and now he had both of the artifacts we'd wanted to keep from Grismur. I didn't know what to make of his stated intention to perform the ritual.

I wasn't sure about much of anything right now.

In such a short time everything had changed. I didn't know what to think of my recent friends and study companions. I didn't know what to make of my own feelings, or what I should be feeling toward a person who was doing such awful things.

The way he had struck Artemis, viciously, and not just once but three times, when Art was obviously already wounded and unable to defend himself…how could Bastian do that? And the way he had used this Slave Necklace to force me into submission, all while having led me on, having led me to believe that he liked me and might want to be with me…what else was he going to do? How could all of this be?

And how could I have fallen for it so completely? I should have seen it earlier, but I had been blind; I had been either unable or unwilling to see through a deception that had existed from the beginning.

More awake now, the staggering realization about Bastian sent a flash of rage through me. The sentiment was wordless in my mind, but violently potent. Without immediate external provocation, however, the intensity of my anger died down and I began again to question myself, and how I could have allowed myself to be so deceived.

Eventually I could accept my own foolishness without difficulty, and I didn't want to dwell on it. My thoughts, however, were still consumed with the other realization, which I struggled to believe despite having seen what I'd seen. This one thought led to another, and I was still left to think and wonder about many things, but two facts were paramount.

First, Bastian was a villain, and had been performing truly villainous acts.

Second, he was going to go further. Thanks to me he would be able to reach the pinnacle of some evil he had pursued.

I made use of my one luxury in an attempt to also find a comforting thought—some notion that might help me avoid breaking down in tears. The attempt was futile.

End of Part II

The Joyful Adventurer
(nine years earlier)

I stopped in my tracks, just inside the front door, as I heard the hearty laughter. It was a man's laugh, and it was rich and mirthful—a rare, foreign sound in my father's house. We had a visitor.

I had just returned home after playing at Hansen's house. It was close to dinnertime. I heard my father's voice, and then that of the other man. I couldn't hear distinct words, but both sounded like they were at ease. I hadn't made much noise as I had come inside, and I stayed quiet as I shut the door and walked in toward the sound of my father's voice.

He was in the greatroom. As I stepped into the entryway I saw my father and the other man both standing with their backs to me. Somehow, even seen from behind, my father was as regal as ever.

The other man was just as tall as my father, but was not dressed at all as richly. He wore a dusty and worn brown leather jacket, worn light canvas pants and some sort of leather boots with square-ish toes. A large knife in a leather sheath was attached to his belt and in his left hand he held a pair of gloves, also made of brown leather. He was bald on top, but the hair he had was thick and straight, and it matched the color of his clothing quite well. His skin definitely showed signs of having been in the sun a bit. He'd be able to blend in easily with a desert landscape; he also probably wouldn't look any different after having rolled around in a bunch of dirt. I stood silently several paces behind them, wondering who this dusty-looking person was.

"Maria," my father said.

I should have known that his hearing was too good for me to escape detection. The other man, surprised at my father's simple announcement, turned to regard me. His creased face made him look about forty years old but he seemed quite healthy, and he wore an expression that was both kind and curious.

My father also turned to face me. He had that brightness in his eyes that most people never saw, but he said nothing more for the moment.

"Good evening, Father," I said with a small, polite curtsey. I looked at the visitor and then back at my father, waiting for him to speak.

He addressed the other man. "This is my daughter."

The man smiled and stepped forward, placing his gloves in his pocket and extending a hand toward me. "I'm very pleased to meet you." As I offered my hand he leaned forward to shake it energetically with both of his. They were strong and rough on the surface, but his grip wasn't uncomfortable. "My name is Artemis Brown. I'm a friend of your father." He released my hands and crouched to meet me at eye level; when he spoke next I could tell that his words were no longer directed at me. "Yeah. She looks essentially human, but I can definitely tell there's something else there. I'd see it even if I didn't notice the family resemblance."

Family resemblance? Did I look like my father, aside from my hair? I couldn't remember anyone ever saying so before. And what did he know about me not being fully human?

The visitor inspected me from different angles, peering as if to find something hidden. I would have felt quite uncomfortable under such scrutiny, especially from a stranger, except that my father stood nearby, watching. If this Artemis had tried to do me any harm, my father would have prevented him. Gesturing at my mouth with his hand, the man asked, "Do you mind?"

I wasn't sure what he meant at first, but then I opened my mouth to show my teeth.

He seemed quite satisfied. "It's subtle, but there's no mistaking it." He spoke to me once more. "Your father says that you never drink blood. Is that a hard thing for you?"

He apparently knew much more about my family than most people. "It's not bad at all, really. I take iron pills, just like my dad."

He smiled as if contented but cautious. "I'm glad. I've not had to worry about that sort of thing myself, but I hear that it can be very, very difficult. If it ever is hard for you, just remember your dad. Try to be like him."

I didn't think the whole blood thing would be a problem, but he seemed like a caring sort of man, so I nodded silently.

My mother stepped in just then. "Maria, you're home! Good. I see you've met Art Brown."

"I think his name should be Artemis Tan."

My mother looked surprised; Art glanced down at himself and then broke out into laughter again. My father smiled silently.

"What a funny thing to say, Maria," my mother said, giving me a half-stern look and shaking her head. "Go wash your hands and join us at the table."

I curtsied again and skipped off to obey my mother. Having done so, I went to the dining room and sat down with the others.

We never wanted for good food, but the table was set for our guest just a bit more elaborately than usual. My father understood refinement but tended toward simplicity; my mother always wanted to show extra effort when we had company, not for the sake of appearances but rather out of a desire to serve. In any case, she had gone to no small effort this time. A large roast turkey was surrounded on the table by salads, vegetables, breads, and other foods.

My father invited our guest to pray; after the man had finished with his words of thanks, my mother was quick (as usual) to start up conversation.

"Art is a good family friend, Maria," my mother explained. "You've never met him before because he's away so often; he's quite an adventurer. He's done a lot of traveling, gotten himself into quite a bit of trouble, and done a lot of good things for other people as well."

"Ahh, you speak too highly of me," Art responded with a humble smile.

"Oh," my mother answered with mock embarrassment, "well then, Maria, just remember that he gets into a lot of trouble."

Art grinned as he answered, "That's true enough. I do like to do a good turn for someone here and there, but I mostly get out so much because the rest of life is just so boring! Sometimes that lands me in a bit of a fix."

He made me smile with his cheery manner. I was still curious, though. I set down my fork and put my hands in my lap. "You don't seem like a bad man, so if you get into trouble a lot, does that mean what you do is dangerous?" I asked.

Art gave an uncertain look to each of my parents in turn, then took a drink from his water glass. "Well, honey, yes, it's quite dangerous sometimes. There's always something to do to get out of danger, though. There's always something to do to handle any trouble."

"How do you know the right thing to do?"

He set his glass down and folded his arms. "Ah. That's a good question. A very good one. Well, little Maria, I can't say that I always *do* know what the right thing is. Let me tell you a secret, though." He leaned closer to me from the other side of the table. "This is something a lot of people miss. It's one of the more obvious rules of life if you're really paying attention, but somehow people usually don't get it. As you get older, you're going to have to solve a lot of problems—big, complicated problems sometimes. Smart living helps you avoid some of them, but you can't ever dodge all of 'em. When they come around, though, the real way to succeed is to not have to spend a lot of time and effort figuring out the right thing to do on the spot, all from scratch. No, the real way to succeed is to live well day by day, all the time for a long time, so that doing the right thing comes naturally to you. In high times, in low times, you have a sense of where you're going and what you need to do to get there because you've had your eye on the target the whole time. Some people would say you can get away with doing the wrong thing if it's something small, or if you can hide it, but you never can completely make up for it, or if you can it's sure not easy. So don't let yourself get lazy—keep on doing what you know is right."

My father slightly inclined his head and then also tipped the drinking glass he was holding just a bit to indicate approval of Art's words.

Art continued. "Your father knows what I'm talking about. Your mother, too. Even if it was possible I can't say that I hope you'll never face big problems, because those are important for us. It's important to face those big problems and solve them." He gave a big smile. "So, keep doing the right thing every day. From what your dad says, you've got a great start. Keep up the good work."

Part III

The Grief

6

I wasn't the first girl to be wrong about a guy, but despite the common precedent I was dumbfounded at my own variation on the theme. How could I have missed this? He wasn't even all that cute any more—what had seemed attractive before was just evil now. And he'd put me in a dungeon!

But before he'd put me here, he had been so charming. He sincerely seemed to be trying to be a good man…or at least an elegant man. Evidently refinement wasn't enough to make someone good. I thought back to the time I had first seen him; those blue eyes were all that mattered at first.

Now they didn't matter much at all. At the moment, I couldn't feel what I had before. I could hardly remember that feeling.

But then the door opened and he walked into the room and turned on a cheap ceiling light, and as I saw him and those same blue eyes, I did remember my feelings and I was beleaguered with confusion. I still felt the same way *for* him, but just not the same way *about* him. The once warm feeling and the new sting of betrayal seemed to be pulling my heart in separate directions within my chest. The inner plunging sting grew more painful with each repeating echo in my mind of *"Why?"* and *"How could you?"* The twisting pain of my inner conflict rapidly turned to resentment, and I wanted to hate him. I couldn't, though. I was unable to make sense of what I was feeling.

When he looked up at me he paused, with a seemingly startled expression on his face—almost as if he hadn't expected me to be here. He leaned backward, almost bumping into Abbott, who was also just stepping into the room. Abbott put his hands up to prevent the collision, resting them on Bastian's shoulders. Bastian looked over his shoulder and then back to me. He turned to brush off Abbott's hands, and when he turned back he had a strange look on his face.

"Ah, Maria," he began with a small laugh. "I'm sorry to have been so inattentive. We've been so busy making preparations and dealing with nuisances that I quite forgot for a while that we had you here."

His ostensible carelessness was insulting, but I said nothing to him in return. I owed him nothing.

"I'm sorry for the poor accommodations," he continued. "With our recent troubles from outsiders I'm perhaps a bit overcautious. And your reaction to the intruder was perplexing enough that I felt I had to be cautious with you."

I glared.

"I'm sure you'll understand why I've been taking these steps and pursuing my goals, once they've been properly explained."

He clearly expected me to converse; I took the slightest satisfaction in being able to disappoint him in a small way.

"Not very talkative, I see. I don't blame you, really, but I do want you to understand me and be my ally."

I couldn't help but scoff. "Do you normally put your allies in chains?"

He smiled. "Ah! She speaks," he said to Abbott, who said nothing in return. He looked back at me, speaking more assertively now. "As I said, I want you to be my ally. I just need to be sure of you. So, I'll tell you all about what we're doing."

"And you expect me to believe it? You *lied* to me."

"Yes, I did, but you'll believe what I'm telling you now. Unfortunately, when we first met I had to deceive you to get you to comply. You needn't make yourself look so affronted. Lies are a fundamental part of every human relationship; you're fooling yourself if you don't accept that. But as I said, with you it really was necessary. The best way to deceive, my dear, is to start by telling the truth. And people are so willing to accept lies when they feel good about them. What motivated *you* to accept my lies was enthusiasm."

Abbott finally spoke. "And, perhaps, a crush."

I felt small, and my face grew hot with embarrassment when he spoke that last word. "That's funny," I told Bastian, "I thought you actually liked me."

"Oh, I do. The lies were nothing personal, I assure you. It wasn't about you at all, but rather about me. It's vital for me to be skilled in deception if I want to gain and maintain power, and practice makes perfect. I have to have a good sense of what people will believe."

"Then you *do* like me. Huh." I raised my arms to display the chains.

"Of course. And I'm sure we'll get those off of you soon enough, but security before pleasure."

I curled my lip at that.

"But even right now it's important to set boundaries. I know how to handle people. In fact, one of the most important skills for a man who wants to have an effect on the world is knowing how to influence people."

"To manipulate them."

"You say it as if it was a bad thing, as opposed to being natural."

That made me think for a second. "Maybe it is natural. That doesn't mean it isn't wrong."

He smirked. "It's not only natural but necessary. If you believe it's evil, then it's a necessary evil."

"There's no such thing."

"Then it's not evil, or wrong, or bad."

"Keep telling yourself that."

He smiled again. "I don't need any convincing. Incidentally, part of that skill in mani—influencing others—okay, fine, have it your way," he said, glancing sideways with an annoyed grimace, "*manipulating* them—part of that skill is the ability to pit them against each other. In simple terms, it's the 'divide and conquer' strategy, but more than that, when you make enemies of two people or groups you can play on that enmity to achieve a particular effect. That's why I encouraged the hostility between you and Amy. It served to make each of you more ardent in assisting me."

When I realized that my mouth was hanging open I quickly looked away.

"You didn't pick up on that," he said.

I wondered how he could have ended up being so devious. "No, I didn't."

"It's a common technique. For example, political leaders thrive on the great division within a country—it's how they get things done. What other use could political parties have? For myself, I want to be able to control large groups but I feel it's important to master individuals first." He waited while I digested what he'd said, walking away and taking a deliberate breath.

I glared at him out of the corner of my eyes. "And you were quite certain that I would go after the Life Stone."

"Really, Maria, why *wouldn't* an impetuous and capable young woman such as you take on an adventure like that? Of course I was certain. You would have done it even without jealousy driving you."

"I suppose I should be flattered."

"Flattered?"

"That you'd have such confidence in me to get it."

Abbott broke in. "Don't read too much into that. I practically had to spoon feed you the cave's location."

Bastian continued. "We had an idea about that already, but we were actually more certain that you would make the endeavor than that you would succeed. Even if you failed, I intended to not only verify the precise location of the Stone but also to ascertain the real nature of its guardian."

As these pieces of an ugly puzzle dropped into place, I had no response.

"That's why the imps followed you. To my surprise and dismay, most of them didn't stay the course. I would have been sorely disappointed if you had failed and I hadn't learned what I needed. And I'd have been upset if you...hadn't returned."

He'd started looking directly at me and while he spoke something in his tone had changed; I didn't detect the same arrogance he'd displayed a moment ago. But while I was noticing this I also made a connection I hadn't before. "Imps. And those other monsters here. Those things obey you."

"The goblins? Yes, as I explained a few days ago, that's the purpose of the Demon Stone. The imps and goblins are quite content to recognize my authority as long as I carry it with me. The imps were instructed to protect you from anything that attempted to interfere with your efforts. They must have misunderstood my instructions—I'm still not sure how that happened—but they were certainly compelled to obey according to what they understood. And earlier, Gansak—the goblin who attacked you on the night we first spoke—only sought you out because I instructed him to do so."

I gasped. "You sent him to kill me?"

"Oh, no. No, no. To *attack* you. I put low odds on the possibility of you dying. Very low. I'm sure that no mere goblin has ever killed a vampire. I would have been so much more than disappointed if you'd been even seriously hurt, but I knew better. The Demon Stone grants me a great deal of insight, and as I said before, from the moment I saw you I was certain what you were. I knew you could handle yourself. I honestly didn't expect you to succeed quite as handily as you did, but I was also watching from a distance, and Gansak was instructed to leave if I intervened."

"Oh." I wanted to respond sarcastically but I didn't feel I had the energy for it, and my words came out quietly as I gazed downward. "Well. Thank you for being so concerned."

"My pleasure." His kept a large grin; I couldn't tell if my weak attempt at sarcasm was lost on him or if he was toying with me. He moved to the nearby table. From it he lifted the dagger I normally kept in my boot. "I was surprised; most girls aren't skilled at knife-fighting. This is a nice piece, by the way. Quality work." After rotating the knife to observe it, he laid it back down and stepped back toward me. "In general, even though I wasn't entirely sure about your ability at first, I've been quite impressed with you. Quite..." his voice trailed off, and I couldn't understand why he sometimes sounded haughty, but sometimes sounded very unsure.

I didn't want to accept his compliments at the moment, though. I didn't want to answer him at all. But part of the situation didn't make sense, and my curiosity was enough to prompt a question. "Wait...after the fight, why did you want me to talk to the police about it? That would have brought you unwanted attention."

"Oh, I didn't want you to talk to them." Here came the arrogant tone again. "I wanted you to feel that I was concerned about you, and that you could trust me. I had no reason to worry. You would have difficulty reporting such an unusual attack to the police, and they couldn't have done anything about it anyway. I'm sure they have no standard procedures for handling boogeymen."

I was sure he was right but with everything else he'd revealed I couldn't feel too bad about being tricked on that one point. His tone of voice was also really bothering me. "You're such scum."

"Oho!" He leaned back, and Abbott gave a single closed-mouth laugh without smiling. "Sticks and stones, my dear," Bastian continued, "sticks and stones. I'd suggest, though, that it's probably not wise to anger a man who holds you imprisoned."

"You're still crazy if you think that chaining me up will win me over."

"I told you, I hope to remove those chains soon, though honestly, they're basically superfluous while you've got the Slave Necklace on."

"Oh, yes, the gift. How romantic it all seemed."

He winced, and his voice went softer again. "That's just it, though. I truly wanted to give you nice jewelry. I put effort and craftsmanship into it. I did like giving you something beautiful to wear, and you do look dazzling with it." He glanced sideways as if overly conscious of the third person in the room. "It just happens to serve the dual function of letting me keep control of you. You may as well know the rest. Producing a strong sensation of weight or pain is not all the Slave Necklace does; when you wore it I was certain to always be able to find you. My minions used it to follow you, and with them assailing you and bringing their influence into the situation, the Forlorn was unable to discern what was truly happening. That was the idea, anyway. It seems to have worked."

"Well, as soon as I get my hands free I'll tear the thing off and throw it away, jewels and all."

"You're welcome to try, though I'm sure that a single attempt will be enough to convince you to stop."

I remembered what had happened when I tried to remove it before, and I almost wondered if I could convince him to take off either the necklace or chains, but if he could be persuaded to do so he probably wouldn't have left both of them on me in the first place.

It bothered me all the more that he'd gone to such lengths to deceive me. "So another of your lies," I said, "was the story about that fake villain Grismur. Just another trick to make it all seem urgent."

He smiled, looking supremely pleased, and gave Abbott a look as if to say, *I told you so.* "No, actually that story was true in almost every respect. You thought Grismur was my father, but *I* am Grismur. As you noticed before, it's merely a translation of my own family name. I'm not even sure it's a good translation— I think it's backwards—but it sounds good. Don't you think it sounds sinister? This was one of the more entertaining parts of the whole game; if you'd figured it out, it could have fouled up my strategy quite a bit. The risk was a genuine delight. You're right that I intended to create a sense of urgency. I didn't want anyone thinking about it for long enough to escape the larger deception. But everything I told you about Grismur was true. For me, it was merely a matter of using a nickname and speaking in the third person, rather than the first."

I was already tired of the conversation, and the more I heard the more I wanted it all to stop. I didn't want to see him, and the burn of embarrassment was all the more intense for him being there in the room. "Leave me alone, Bastian."

He crossed his arms. He seemed troubled, but I couldn't guess as to what he was thinking. "As you wish. I have things to attend to anyway. I'll return later. I still have much more to explain, but perhaps I can find better motivation for you to help me willingly." At this his eyes narrowed, but I had little time to wonder any longer about his thoughts before he strode away toward the door. "Try to get some rest," he said over his shoulder as he left the room.

Abbott lingered only for a moment, saying nothing, and then he turned off the light and walked out also.

First things first: if I could get the necklace off I would. I was doubtful, but I leaned to one side and reached a hand up to touch the clasp. As soon as my fingers touched it, I felt faint again just as I had before. I quickly withdrew my hand.

Try to get some rest, he'd said. It must be very late. I had no idea how I'd be able to sleep while hanging from chains, but I had no other options. Time passed, and I grew more and more drowsy. Eventually the weariness overtook me.

6.1

I awoke feeling almost completely unrested, and stood without delay in order to relieve the pain on my wrists. Had I actually slept at all? Bastian came to mind; how different it was now for him to be first in my thoughts.

It didn't take long for my thoughts to turn to others, though. By this time my mother would be worried about me being away from home for so long. I'd always been responsible enough to let her know if I was going to be gone for a while and I'd basically never spent a night away from home. It was bad timing for such an unprecedented absence with my father also being away, when my mother would have no one immediately to turn to for comfort and counsel.

And of course I still had no idea where my father even was. I didn't think Bastian was going to harm me seriously, but without knowing where my father had gone or why he'd left, I couldn't even be sure I'd ever see him again. I doubted that the situation could be truly so dire but I also didn't know at all what I should expect at this point.

My mother would probably ask Hansen if he'd seen me. She likely wouldn't ask his parents because she would want to avoid worrying them, but we all trusted Hansen in a way that we couldn't trust most people. So Hansen would be worried as well.

I wanted to think of myself rushing into a room full of my friends and family and reassuring them, talking of my current situation as something trivial in the past. I'd have to get out to make that scenario real, but the shackles were too tight to slip out of and there was no way I could break them or even damage them in any way. My best hope lay in Bastian deciding that his feelings for me were more important than everything else and coming to set me free himself.

Yeah. Fat chance of that.

Evidently he was to be the first person I would see today; while I was contemplating my family and friends he came into the room with a slight creaking of the heavy door. "Good morning, Miss Maria." He illuminated the room. "For some reason I've not been able to sleep well or for very long, but I hope your night isn't passing too poorly."

"I'm not sure how it could be worse."

"Fine. I'll grant that your current situation is undesirable—I'm busy and short on sleep myself right now—but it will soon change, much for the better, and you'll get over it. Soon we'll be chumming it up again, working together like before, and I'm sure that later we'll be able to look back on this little incident and laugh."

"Let's just say I doubt that. It's bizarre that you would even think I could find what you're doing acceptable."

"Maria, for being part vampire, you just don't appreciate the weight of what's going on, and you really are stuck too much in your black-and-white view of right and wrong. You deserve more perspective." He took my dagger from the table. "I'm going to help you out here; I'm going to open your eyes a bit." He brought his hands together and with a short motion he ran the blade across the lower part of one of his palms, making a small cut. It bled lightly; I instantly smelled the blood and my eyes locked on the trickle. He held his hand toward me. "Taste."

"No!" I whispered fiercely, more to myself than to him, as I turned my head to the side and averted my gaze. I could still smell his gently seeping blood, and had to control my breathing and clench my eyes shut.

"I'm not accustomed to being refused," he declared. I risked a glance toward him; with his unwounded hand he reached into his pocket and retrieved the Demon Stone, and though I opened my mouth to petition him I had no time to speak before the imposing weight of the necklace rushed down on me again. As I drooped he brought his cut hand to my mouth, and the liquid touched my lips.

I could no longer react with rational thought; the taste reached my tongue, and I knew nothing but rage and desire.

I seemed to be distant, as if I was watching everything happening from elsewhere, with blurred vision and muted hearing, almost as if in a dream.

I screamed with a haunting, raspy shriek like nothing I had ever heard before as I jumped and strained against my chains. Bastian pulled his hand away just in time to avoid the snap and clash of my teeth from my first attempt to bite at him. Finding myself restrained, I fell back and rushed forward again and again.

"My, oh, my. Still have some spirit in you, eh?" He seemed mildly startled, but amused.

I pushed away from the wall with all of my strength, straining toward him.

He stayed safely out of reach. "You begin to understand, don't you?"

I had no words for him, only hissing in response. I knew nothing but rage and hunger. I saw nothing but a bleeding animal.

"You're understandably distressed. I've just the thing for it."

He walked from the room, and when he and his blood were out of sight—and smell—the haze around my head began to lift.

And I saw clearly again.

I'd never truly felt the hunger before. Granted, I'd never gone long on an empty stomach, but that was always a given for me and my real underlying concern was with the vampire hunger my father had warned me of. It was much worse that I could have anticipated. I'd always had a supply of iron pills, and presumably they warded off cravings adequately because even when I had gotten lazy with the pills I'd never strongly felt the urge. I certainly felt it now. It was doubly troublesome; in the first place, it made me feel a desire to do something depraved, and secondly, even if I decided to give in to the temptation, I had no opportunity right now to fulfill the desire.

The hunger eating at me was of a kind that could drive someone to insanity; it created a drive to use other people as food, even when normal food was available. It made men into monsters, very literally.

In addition to the hunger, I was torn over the taste itself. Knowing what it was, I loathed the tang of blood, but at the same time, I now wanted it. I wanted to relish the vile and gratifying flavor. I wanted it on my tongue and in my throat, and I detested that desire. My yearning was interwoven with rage and indignation.

It was clear that I had never before truly known the hunger for human blood until I had tasted it—until *now*. I vaguely wondered if it was worse for "full-blood" vampires, if that term can be used accurately. As for myself, I knew that I had never before understood the sharp extent of temptation.

But at the moment, the man and his small wound were not there to draw my attention, and after not long my thoughts began to be lucid again and regain focus. With even a short respite from the harshly enticing pull, I could think again and recognize it for what it was.

It was wrong.

I relaxed physically as I struggled inwardly. The simple, brief taste I'd had, and which still lingered faintly on my lips, had made the hunger for blood real to me—had defined it. But I was able to reject that hunger. I breathed more slowly, stood up straight, and did my best to wipe away the final remnants of the blood from my lips with my arm.

My wrists and ankles really hurt.

I thought back to my father's words when he'd told me to never yield to the demon within me. I thought of his example, and made a promise to myself to never taste blood again.

Then Bastian returned, holding a wide goblet filled with aromatic red blood, and my promise seemed hastily made.

"Now that you've an idea of what you've been missing out on, here's a more ample serving." He held it out. "Drink up."

As the scent reached me I began to feel myself slipping away again, but I closed my eyes and clenched my teeth; I had regained myself enough after he had left to be able to think again. I exerted every bit of willpower to turn my head and lean back toward the wall. "Never," I said quietly.

He raised an eyebrow. "Really? I must say I'm surprised."

I scrambled for an excuse. "I don't even know whose blood that is."

He shrugged, then gestured to it. "Well, you can be sure all of that isn't mine, but it really doesn't matter whose it is. What matters is that you be honest with yourself and indulge yourself."

"Never," I said again, still in a whisper but more forcefully.

"I acknowledge that you're only part vampire, but I'm not blind. I can see that there's nothing you want more right now than to drink this. So don't delay any longer. Satisfy that desire. It's who you are."

Again I remembered my father's words to me in years past. "You must never give in. Never let it conquer you. Never let it tantalize you. Never let it win you over." He had taught it to me hundreds of times, no less frequently than once every week, and I had been weary of it to the point of apathy. But now it was different; now I heard those words again, resonating and echoing within me, and giving me a foundation. I wished that I felt more strength, but the teachings of my father gave me something to stand on. And I stood up against the evil facing me.

He held the cup even closer, but I lanced the word at him one more time with a quick shout: "Never!!"

He drew back a step, thoughtfully furrowing one eyebrow. "Strange."

I felt some relief when he set the goblet on the floor several feet away. He moved to the opposite side of the nearby table and began to push it closer to me. Once it was sufficiently close, he lifted the cup and set it on the corner of the table closest to me. With the table as close as it was, the cup was within arm's reach.

"Your efforts to resist might be admirable, if not for their futility. I know as well as you do that they won't last long. But I don't want you to feel like you need to resist just to scorn me, so I will depart. I'll leave you alone to enjoy your meal. When you're not so thirsty, I trust you'll be able to see everything more clearly." He walked back to the door, pausing before stepping out. "Until we meet again." He gave a short bow, and left.

I was glad for my victory of willpower over desire, but worried by the continued presence of that desire even after the victory. As I regarded the tempting liquid I began to wonder if Bastian was right. How long could I resist? The scent of the blood filled my nose and my mouth watered.

The hunger wasn't all I felt, though. Bastian's arrogance bothered me. It grated against my own pride, and the hunger I felt translated into anger at him, and at Amy and Abbot for also betraying me. I let the anger build until with a rapid strike I knocked the cup away from me, spilling its contents over the table and onto the floor. With my foot I pushed the table as far away as I could before leaning back against the wall to rest.

It was over. I could still smell the blood, and still wanted it, but I had won. I had made the right choice until I no longer had a choice. I knew that the smell and the sight would likely remain in the room at least as long as I did, but it was no longer a threat to me. I was sure that the physical pain and irritation I felt was preferable to the pain of guilt.

Or at least I thought so. I hoped I wouldn't have to be here long enough to doubt that thought.

As I calmed down, I again felt fatigue from the restless night. It made every irritation worse than they would have been by themselves.

6.2

With time I was able to start concentrating on other things. The blood, being out of reach, was no longer preoccupying me.

After surveying the room, wondering what I could use to escape, I found myself with few options. The room itself seemed not to have been originally designed as a dungeon, being mostly bare, though the metal chains bolted to the wall seemed old. While scanning the room, I noticed the light of morning coming in through the window and I wondered what time it was.

I was still trying, unsuccessfully, to envision an escape plan when the door opened slowly. I was filled with disgust as I saw Amy peek in, calling my name in a whisper, before stepping into the room and reaching behind her to close the door. "Oh, my goodness, Maria. I can't believe they've locked you up here. This is all so horrible." She glanced down at the floor. "Is that *blood?* Are you okay?" She eyed me as if trying to find open wounds, then looked back at the blood. She seemed unusually shabby and tired.

I spoke through gritted teeth. "Peachy. What do you want, Amy?"

She turned back to me. She looked uncomfortable, even worried. "I don't think I'm supposed to be here, but I had to see if you were okay."

The answer to the implied question seemed too obvious for me to oblige her with a response.

She shifted her weight and wrung her hands. "Maria, I'm scared. I don't know what Bastian is going to do with me. He thinks I'm not good enough for him, and with everything I've seen I think I'm in danger. You being locked up like this doesn't make me feel any better."

This was curious. Did she expect me to feel bad for her?

"Maria, you just can't imagine the evil things he's doing..."

I still didn't have anything to say; if anything, I was confused.

"I don't know what to make of all of this anymore. It used to be a game. I used to think I was getting a boyfriend. I thought you were an enemy. And now I don't know what to think. I'm worried. I'm...I'm lost..."

"Why don't you just leave?"

"I don't have anywhere else to go."

I remembered that I'd never known where she lived. Did she not have family nearby? I had taken her for an enemy as well, although now I was having a hard time justifying my attitude toward her. "Well, at least you're not chained up."

"Good point."

I'd expected her to argue in some way. I shook my head to try to clear it, particularly of any potentially incorrect notions.

"I'd let you out if I had the key," she said. "Why did he do this to you?"

"I guess it keeps things simpler for him."

"Boy, I guess." She shook her head. "I don't understand any of this."

I felt awkward just standing there, chained to the wall with almost nothing I wanted to say to her. I couldn't be entirely unappreciative for the visit, though, especially if she wanted to help me get free.

Suddenly a fairly urgent need presented itself. I didn't want to feel like I needed to ask Amy for help, but at the moment that was my situation. "Amy," I said, closing my eyes and mustering some humility, "I need to use a toilet."

She blinked. "Oh!"

"I guess I was kind of distracted for a while, but it's starting to get uncomfortable. Can you…I don't know…tell Bastian for me? I really don't want to pee in my pants."

"Yeah. Gosh. I can try."

"Thanks." I didn't know of anything more I could say. Then I remembered someone else; if Amy wasn't able to help me escape, she might be able to help him. "Amy, where's Art?"

"The man who came here?" She waited before speaking again as if unsure that she wanted to provide me with the answer. "I…I need to give you his message first, so I don't forget to tell you. That's partly why I came here now. He said that somebody named Luke wanted you to read the letter. I don't know what letter he was talking about. That's all he said."

I perked up when she mentioned my father. "Luc…I know that letter."

She seemed on the verge of tears as she continued speaking. "The man said he saw this Luke person just a couple of days ago or something, and was coming to investigate something here at the castle and then meet you, but he was surprised and captured by Bastian's goblins. That was yesterday."

"Is he okay? You didn't answer me—where is he??"

A tear rolled down her cheek. "I'm sorry, Maria. I don't know who he was, but if you knew him I'm really sorry, because he's dead."

Caught between sudden shock and anger, I was unable to respond.

Amy stumbled over her words. "He was chained up like you, somewhere else, and was really weak when I saw him, but when he saw me he gave me that message. I had to hurry away because someone was coming, and when I came back, he—oh, I can't even talk about it." Her voice faltered as she failed to contain sobs.

Sadness also crept into me now, and simultaneously, as I watched Amy crying over the death of a man she didn't know I began to see her differently. Out of habit I wanted to find fault with her, but at the moment I couldn't. It felt wrong. She meant to mourn with me. It was the act of an ally, a friend. I wasn't used to anything like that from her, and I had to look away for a while to try to collect my thoughts.

Amy sniffed and wiped tears from her cheeks. "I don't know what I can do to help." She exhaled deliberately. "Maybe if I can find the key and unlock you, we might be able to sneak out of here together."

I felt peculiarly numb, as if in just a few minutes the world around me had ceased to be real. I spoke without any sense of vitality. "Check behind Tesla. But it won't work. I won't make it far with this Slave Necklace on me."

Amy's breath caught in her throat. She stared intensely at the necklace, evidently noticing it for the first time. "What is that?"

"Bastian gave it to me a few days ago," I muttered. "He said he made it. It's enchanted. I thought it was supposed to help."

Amy's eyes went wide in surprise.

"He can make it feel incredibly heavy on me," I continued softly. "It just drains me. I can't fight it."

Amy's mouth quivered. She was raising her hands to her cheeks and had opened her mouth to speak again when an animal-like sound came from somewhere distant, beyond the door. She turned her head toward it quickly, then to me again. "I have to go, Maria." She walked away briskly, shaking her head with her hands to her face. "I'm sorry, I'm sorry..." At the door she took one quick, pained glance back at me, then disappeared.

And I was left to myself again, with a bit of time to try to figure out what to make of Amy and to make some sense of Art's death. Art's death! I was sickened to think that the blood Bastian had brought was probably Art's, and I was that much more relieved that I'd drunk none of it.

Death...it was hard to conceive of it. I had just seen Art, alive if not well. He had long been a part of my life in the background, rarely seen but possessing the extremely rare status of being one of my father's friends. Could he truly be dead? Amy had given no indication of being insincere or uncertain. Her tears couldn't have implied anything but real emotion over an actual event—my father's good friend Art must have truly been killed in some dark corner of this horrible castle.

I waited, but the idea never felt real to me. I'd never experienced the death of anyone close to me. Maybe my vampire nature affected the way I felt about death; on one hand, vampires existed to cheat death, and on the other, they did so by causing the death of others. Presumably. In principle, for a being like me death was supposed to be both trivial and necessary to sustain life. That ought to impact the way I felt about it.

And yet I didn't think that was really it. I could only think that if I actually saw Art's dead body I would be horrified. Partly I knew that I wanted to deny the monster within me, to think that I wasn't a remorseless killer, and I could be justified in that thought based on my own history. But otherwise I figured that I mentally rejected his death because I just couldn't conceive of it. It was too much to think that my father's friend was dead. Of course Art didn't deserve to be murdered, but Lucard—not just my father but the best, most worthy man I knew or could imagine—didn't deserve to lose a friend, either.

And yet he had. Wherever he was, he was probably alone right now, and with the loss of a dear friend he was more alone in the world. Suddenly, in the silence of the room and in my own aloneness, death became real to me. Death of self was just another step, but the death of friends...it was to be *alone*.

In my mind I pictured myself alone in this dungeon, and I saw my father, distant, alone, with no family or friends to support him. But I couldn't picture Art.

That's when the tears came again.

6.3

A short while later, I heard muffled grunting sounds and the door opened again. A brutish-looking goblin, maybe one that had held Art, walked into the room and straight to me. It lifted its feet while walking almost as if there were small, invisible springs attached to its lower legs. The goblin sneered at me and growled as it lifted a key to the clasp on my left wrist. It seemed like it was trying to say something antagonistic in some primitive language.

It fumbled at the lock, growling as it took longer to work the mechanism, but eventually there was a click and the clasp came off. It was almost relieving to have the shackle removed, but the pain didn't completely go away. The goblin moved over to my right wrist and began working the next clasp with the key.

Either using locks wasn't an easy task for goblins, or the claps themselves might have merely been old, but it seemed to take a long time for the goblin with the key to completely unlock me. While the goblin was working the second lock, I grew tense with anticipation of being free of the shackles. I wondered if I might escape despite still wearing the Slave Necklace, but I decided not to try. If Bastian used the enchantment on me again, I might lose bladder control. I wouldn't risk that, and it would be for nothing anyway. If Bastian wasn't sure that the necklace would stop me, he would have sent more than a single goblin here.

But then I saw I wouldn't have the chance anyway. After unlocking only my wrists the goblin backed away and barked toward the door, and a second goblin came in carrying a deep metal pan in one hand and a roll of toilet paper in the other.

I'd started gently rubbing my sore wrists, but was motionless as the thing approached and dropped the two items at my feet.

Was this really happening?

"I am not doing this," I told them, unsure if they understood the words.

The second goblin left the room again, but the first stood in front of me, waiting, as if it expected me to take care of business right in front of it. Maybe these creatures didn't have the same sense of privacy about toilet time, but there was no way I would do this with the goblin standing there watching me.

"Leave me alone!" I told the thing, but it did nothing in response.

The second goblin came back, carrying a bucket with water and a towel. It set them next to me also, and I could see a bar of soap in the water.

They both stood for a moment, one now empty-handed, the other holding the key that was too awkwardly small and fine for its inept claws. Then the second goblin made a grumbling noise and walked out again.

The first still waited, but I was determined to be more patient. Then I heard another barking sound from outside. The first goblin turned, glanced back at me, and then ambled from the room.

I waited until I felt sure that they weren't returning, and with much less humiliation than I had feared I made use of the items they'd provided, setting them aside afterward. I'd felt clumsy trying to handle things while my ankles were still shackled, but overall I felt that, to whatever extent had been possible, I'd maintained a shred of grace.

Ten or so minutes passed before the goblins returned. One of them attended to the items it had brought, while the other began to return the shackles to my wrists. "Bastian!" I called. "Please don't do this!"

No answer came back. The goblin fumbled with the locks and key for even longer than it had before, but to my dismay I eventually had the metal securely around my wrists again. When the goblin was finally satisfied it grunted at the other and they both left, each casting a malicious glare at me before walking out.

Boy, was I glad to have that little episode over, though it was frustrating to have the wrist shackles on again.

At least I had one basic need settled. Now I was just hungry—not just for blood, but for regular food also.

I really needed to get out of here.

6.4

At least a couple of hours passed.

As the time went on I found it easier to collect my thoughts. Once I had sorted out my emotions enough, escape was foremost in my mind for a while, but only a short while because I simply failed to come up with much of a plan.

It was easy to identify the only possible exits from the room. First, there was the door through which I had entered. The path from there to freedom was uncertain, and was likely guarded or patrolled.

Second, there was the window. The window made me curious. I had thought I was underground, that I had been carried down a winding staircase in my earlier stupor into a dungeon below ground level, but if that was the case, why would there be a window in the room? If I hadn't been carried down, I must have been taken up. From my angle I couldn't see well out of it, but it seemed to open into blank sky, and it was brighter now outside than it was inside. The tall window was open and neither barred nor blocked in any way, but if I went out through it, I might not have any way to get down to the ground safely.

That being the case, I still couldn't get to either the window or the door. I couldn't get out of the metal clasps around my wrists and ankles, and if I tried to escape under Bastian's notice he could debilitate me instantly by using the slave necklace I wore around my neck.

The futility was frustrating, and the frustration escalated into rage as I smelled the scent of blood around me. The anger bled over into other thoughts, though I didn't know how to define my feelings about Art's death. Anyone's death in such circumstances would be a tragedy, but Art was one of my father's friends, one of his very few friends! Bastian said he was dangerous—I had no idea what that meant, but I knew I would have given him the same trust my father did. He had looked so strong while held by those brutes, even though he had certainly been beaten until he could no longer stand. His eyes had showed it. His voice, as he tried to warn me, had showed it. That strength of character had been a threat to Bastian, and Bastian had eliminated that threat. He would have to answer for that.

I looked again toward the window, then tested the chains that held me, again finding them all too securely attached to the wall.

My thoughts were looping back repetitively without a needed epiphany when, with a sound that was oddly familiar by now, the door opened. Bastian walked in with a smug grin, but it instantly vanished as he looked and saw the blood spilled on the floor. "You reject my gift? I'm surprised, and very disappointed. You really need to cast aside your pretense." He came closer, first regarding the spilled cup and then me. "Your self-control is unnecessary, albeit impressive in a small way. No matter, though. Even if you haven't satisfied yourself properly it's time I explained a bit more about the ritual, as described in the one of those two missing pages that I actually possess."

I said nothing in return, only staring back with anger.

"I want you to understand. I want you to know what we're getting into. Yes, 'we'. I honestly do expect that you'll see the wisdom in contributing to our cause."

I remained silent.

He laughed and shook his head; it only irritated me more to see that he found my anger amusing. "My goodness, though," he said, suddenly more subdued. "I suppose this is cliché, but you are positively stunning when you're angry. Your cheeks glow, and the green of your eyes is frankly entrancing. They gleam. The whole effect is almost...breathtaking."

He very much caught me off guard with those words and the sincere gaze that accompanied them.

He lifted an object into view. It was a simple, oval disk with two holes next to each other in the center. It had a long, thick chain attached at the top. "This is another piece of jewelry I made. It's a pendant." He paused, observed my continued silence, and went on. "The chain itself is unusually long, almost absurdly long. I don't know why, but, I wanted to make an accurate reproduction, so, here it is." The chain itself was indeed long, and it was joined in several places above the pendant by short lengths of cord forming small loops that each passed through separate chain links on either side. This would certainly make the pendant hang low on Bastian, below his waist. It was odd, but he didn't explain it. "That's not the important part, though. Look here. You can see that it has two slots. See?"

Of course I see. Maybe he expected me to guess at their significance, but I knew I wouldn't humor him.

He went on. "Notice that the hole on this side"—he pointed to one opening—"is the same size and shape as the Demon Stone, which I possess. Similarly, I have adjusted the hole on *this* side"—he indicated the opposite side—"to hold the Life Stone, which I also now possess. I was quite close with my initial estimate; I'm pleased that I didn't have to make extensive alterations after obtaining the Stone."

I was curious about what he was saying, but angry enough to stay quiet.

"After I set the jewels in this pendant they will be ready for a combining ritual that will make them more powerful than either of them could be alone. The ancient text is clear that the ritual must be conducted in a place of power; while I could travel to ancient sites that surely would suffice, I've got a better place in mind, a place of modern alchemy and great power that's basically just around the corner. I'd have to start out in the yard, though."

Modern alchemy? I'd never heard of any sort of real alchemy until meeting him. While I didn't want to indulge him, I couldn't help but wonder what place he was talking about.

While speaking he had begun to look away, as if into a distance, but now brought his gaze back to me. He seemed to have noticed curiosity in my expression but to have mistaken the subject of it. "Yes, in the yard, outside, just for the beginning. As you know, I'm always interested in the science of this sort of thing, and there's a part of it that just fascinates me. While the process doubtless takes some time to complete, the conditions for the initial reaction are mentioned in specifics. They must somehow require light emitted by stars, but not by the star closest to us. I think I know what it is. I think that certain spectra possibly either facilitate the process or prevent it from happening. Spectra are like signatures or fingerprints of a star; each star's spectrum depends on its elemental composition, and each is unique. The sun's spectrum must contain something wrong. I don't know why that would matter, but the text is clear that only starlight will suffice, while the light from our own sun or even from the moon will prevent the effect. Thus, I can only do this during the night of a new moon. It seems like I'm always hearing about some story, in fiction, where people have to wait a few hundred or a thousand years for some mystical event, but happily, I won't have to try my patience like that. New moons occur quite frequently."

I already felt stupid for enabling him, but it was unsettling to hear him speak to some of the particulars of the ritual. It wasn't just wishful thinking, but a real plan. Despite everything I'd seen recently, I had a hard time wrapping my mind around bizarre ideas like needing starlight for an alchemic ritual, but it was also impossible not to take Bastian and his plan seriously. I had to concentrate in order not to be distracted by humiliation, anger, and worry. I knew I needed to keep my head.

He exhaled. "I'm sure the most interesting facets of all of this are lost on you. The ritual's details really aren't important, though. What is important are the results. The ancient master alchemists never actually carried it out, but they were certain that when the two gemstones are properly combined, they will grant the bearer power to summon forth an army of demons."

I finally felt like piping up. "This is complete lunacy. Why do you want anything to do with demons?" I gave a single, disgusted laugh. "I hadn't thought you were the bad guy."

"I'm *not* a bad guy. I don't intend to let the demons I summon run amok and cause indiscriminate harm."

"Oh, I'm sure you'll discriminate when you cause harm, just as how you chose to harm Art. You *killed* him, Bastian."

"The man you saw before? Maria, you don't even know who he was. You don't know how dangerous he was."

The way he spoke about Art in the past tense so easily was sickening, but I shuddered my way through it. "Unlike you, I suppose. You won't be dangerous at all, now, will you?"

"Not to those who have the correct intentions."

I only scoffed in response.

"I have greater discipline and wisdom than you give me credit for. The writings speak of a need for someone to bear the Stones. Maybe the ancient alchemists never conducted the ritual because they doubted themselves. I do not share such a doubt. I will have the power to summon life or to take it away, and while that *is* enormous power, I'll be able to control it."

"You have quite an opinion of yourself."

"It's warranted."

"This is all silly anyway." I mustered up some false self-assurance. "Do you actually think a couple of rocks and a bit of theatrics will give you that kind of power?"

"I am confident."

"You are crazy."

Bastian gritted his teeth and I thought he would yell, but then he apparently thought better of it. "I know you don't really mean that. I know you believe this can be done. You've seen too much of the supernatural. You are a supernatural creature yourself!" He chuckled. "You're too smart to believe that it's not possible."

"Well, you don't need me for it. Let me go. Carry on your science project without me."

"I can't risk your interference. And yet," he said without the lighthearted tone, "...it is right and fitting that I have a consort."

I scoffed. "Flowers and chocolate work better than chains. Besides, why would you need me when you have Amy?"

"You're different. You're...special. I can't deceive you any longer because I respect you too much for that now. But it's far more than that. There aren't many people I see as equals, but you...you're more than the average person. Beyond that, you have so many attractive traits. Of course you're beautiful to look at, but even the way you speak is delightful. And the way you move...I could watch you for hours."

At the moment his flattery failed to pierce my heart. I couldn't take any pleasure in the compliments.

"Amy." His tone changed; he spoke faster and less precisely. "Boy, did I miss the target there. I don't know why I didn't see before how weak she is. She's worthless. A waste. Pretty faces are a dime a dozen, but I wouldn't pay a penny for her thoughts. I can't believe I ever saw anything in that cheap trash."

I didn't like Amy much myself, but something about his insults bothered me, and the way he spoke made him seem petty and immature. "Listen to yourself." I put as much disgust as possible into my voice. "I knew all that fancy speech of yours was an act. Not so high now, are we?"

He gritted his teeth and struck the table with his fist. "My way of speaking is not an act. It's a decision!" He recomposed himself but retained a frown. "Most people these days have no class whatsoever."

"So what you just said about Amy was 'class'?"

He furrowed his brow. "Some of us are destined for greater things. I'm destined for greater things. For that matter, you're destined for greater things as well. In fact, I believe it was Fate that brought us together. Only Fate could have made us cross paths in the bookstore at a key moment."

"Fate's an excuse." I wanted to spit the words. "I already know that you set everything up."

"Not our initial meeting. No, I truly believe that the two of us are meant to make this journey together."

I wanted to sink my fingernails into him; unable, I wanted to throw some verbal retort back, but none came to mind.

He also didn't speak again right away; the pause in conversation broke the rhythm of our encounter. His face changed. Something different in his eyes made me unsure. What did I see there? Sorrow? Was that possible?

Then he spoke with more feeling, far less imperious drama, and a hint of vulnerability. "Maria, I want to be with you." We stood motionless for a moment; I was confused by the incongruity of the situation. I tried to read his face, but I wasn't sure what I saw there—maybe conflict, if anything. "Frankly, I can't make sense of it...the last week has been strange, and sometimes there was nothing I wanted more than your companionship...but with you it's harder for me to be the strong person I have to be..." He trailed off, frowning and turning away, but then a moment later seemed to catch himself, and he spoke again, almost smugly. "You can't escape destiny."

His sincerity had thrown me off; it had distracted me from my anger enough that a new thought occurred to me—a risky thought. Mustering all the willpower I could find within myself, I breathed once and addressed him again. "Do you think that there is some other force driving this?"

He faced me again. "Yes. Yes I do. The position I'm in right now serves to reinforce that belief. I've so perfectly succeeded, and I am now approaching the pinnacle of that success. And, although you fail to understand, here you are at my side. Destiny has had a hand in that."

At his side? Could he really have such a twisted view? I closed my eyes to hide the disgust I felt. "Maybe...maybe I could understand. Maybe I could come around."

He said nothing in return, though when I opened my eyes he stared back at me with intensity, as if he couldn't believe that I was changing my mind, but sincerely wanted it.

I concentrated, trying to block out the world. "Maybe I could follow your cause if I was really certain that you believe in it. Come to me."

He shifted, then approached several steps.

"Let me see if that belief is truly in you." The edges of my vision went dark as I focused. "Let me see it in your eyes. That's the only thing that can convince me to join with you. I have to see it in your eyes."

He advanced more, an arm's reach away.

"Closer."

He hesitated.

"Let me see it, and breathe it in."

He moved nearer until his face was directly in front of mine, and his lips parted. I could feel his breath. My eyes closed and then opened again, and seeing him, I knew that he was about to put his lips on mine with every bit of tenderness he possessed.

For a moment I was confused again, with those deep blue eyes right in front of me, with the fragrance of clove that had gained such a powerful emotional association, and with the scent of his blood in his body reaching into my nose and mouth and lungs. It was so much more enticing than the drying splash that still marked the floor, especially because I had already tasted its sweetness. That enticement confused my emotions more. Somehow it felt morally wrong to know the taste of his blood when we weren't married, and I resented him for sharing something that should be so intimate. That thought struck me simultaneously as both important and crazy. But even while I felt that peculiar caution, I also wanted intimacy. When he was this close, part of me wanted companionship, wanted to forget the ugliness I had seen and to try to change him, to convince him to turn away from dark pursuits...I wanted to believe that he really cared for me, enough to let go of everything else...

For a moment I was confused...but only for a moment.

With the speed of a diving eagle I thrust my hand toward the pocket that I knew held the Demon Stone. He had no time to react, no time to move away—but my wrist jolted against the chain that held it and my grasping fingers only brushed past the fabric of his vest. His eyes went wide and he took a hasty step back, shielding the pocket with both hands.

"You think me so easily fooled?!? You—you deceptive swine! You traitorous filth!" His eyes remained wide with surprise, and possibly hurt. "How dare you mock me with your trickery! How dare you!" His voice quivered, and as I watched him he was visibly shaken. Then he clenched his fists and repeated himself more loudly. "How dare you!!"

With that he reached out and slapped me with the backside of one hand. Whether it was the weakness I had been feeling or the power of the jewel in his vest, as his hand struck me it came with much more shock and pain than I expected, and I cried out and reeled with the blow. As I turned my face back he struck me again the same way, and the force of it would have caused me to drop to the floor had I not been chained to the wall.

I hung, broken and weak and panting.

He leaned toward me, seemingly wanting to yell but lacking enough strength. "You deny the gift Fate has given you! Bah! You're not worthy of it. No matter; I have no need of you. I will complete my task alone; I'll have plenty of time later to find a worthy consort." He strode toward the door.

I felt so stricken that I didn't lift my head as I responded. "Please, Bastian, don't do this. It'll only bring regret."

"Regret?" He spoke to me one last time, voice shaking again with humiliation or rage. "Before I leave I'll instruct my servants that they have free reign with you. It's a shame to abandon such a pretty thing to them, but no, my dear, by the time they're done with you, you're the one who'll be acquainted with regret."

My head had lowered even further as he spoke; I watched the floor and only heard him as he left through the door.

I felt too tired now to hate him. But I still hated myself for wanting him to love me, and for somehow still loving him even when he turned out to be so cruel and mistaken in his view of things. I hated myself for being so weak, for being chained to a wall, for not seeing everything sooner as it really was.

My mute anger couldn't last long here, though. I had no release for it. My bitterness shifted toward despair. Before Bastian's last visit I'd had no idea how long I would be imprisoned here, no idea when I would see family or friends again, but now I doubted I'd even make it out alive.

A flickering fantasy of rescue came futilely through my mind. First, I daydreamed that Bastian himself might come to apologize and release me—that his feelings for me were real and important enough that he would abandon his crazy quest and the darkness he was courting. That train of thought was cut short, though, by my own conflicting emotions and a very practical realization that the probability of such a thing was all but nonexistent. Inwardly, I knew that any chance that he would voluntarily release me was gone, and now he was going to sick his pet monsters on me.

Next, I thought of Hansen. I was sure he'd come to help if he could. Would he rush in by himself, heedless of the danger, or would he rally help, like the police? That was ever so slightly interesting to wonder, but I spent less time entertaining the thought than the idea of Bastian changing his mind. Hansen didn't know I was here. At some point he would discover that I was gone, but he wouldn't have any notion of where to look to find me.

No one did. I hadn't said anything to anyone about where I'd gone. Maybe my mother...maybe she would think to inquire at the castle, as she knew I'd visited it recently, but it would be easy for Bastian to deny that I was here, or that he even knew me. She had the greatest chance of anyone of being able to find me, but regardless, she wouldn't be able to help.

Of course there was my father; maybe somehow he would return. He always knew what to do; he would track me down one way or another. But no, the timing would be too perfect. I had no clue as to where he'd gone, and no reason to believe that he would conveniently return just in my time of need like a deus ex machina. More than anyone he would be capable of reaching me, impervious to harm from creatures like simple goblins and smart enough to deal with any trouble Bastian or Abbott could provide; I could easily picture him dispatching the monsters with nothing more than a blade and a quick flick of his wrist, letting nothing stop him from advancing through the castle. But ever since he'd first gone missing I'd sensed that he was far away—I'd felt it inside—and I still felt it now. As much as I wanted to see my father, I wasn't going to.

And then, curiously, I thought of Grant. I had a sudden yearning for him to come to my aid. It didn't make any sense either, because he had no idea what was happening, but I wanted him to be there. Somehow, a day ago, he had found me out of the blue and had turned aside from his own pursuits to help me with mine. He had continued after being injured. He had risked his life for me. He knew what I was, and in a way he knew *who* I was better than most people. In a short period of time he had managed to gain my trust and had been true to it. I'd been too caught up before with the anticipation of pleasing Bastian, and hadn't realized what a significant figure Grant had become in my life in a matter of hours.

I looked up, not seeing the wall in front of me but thinking back to my last sight of Grant, shrinking in the distance as I left. I had been rushing away to please a villain and I'd left someone who wanted my company with perhaps greater sincerity, and who was drastically more trustworthy. I also thought of the odd way he'd looked at me after complimenting my hair…and for some reason it hurt to remember. What a dumb little girl I was not to see these men as they really were, and to so quickly abandon Grant after what he had demonstrated. With this hindsight I knew what he would do for me if he could. I knew that he would come to help me if he simply knew where I was.

But he didn't know.

He wasn't coming.

No one was coming.

The dirty, bloodstained floor, the barren room, the stone walls…were these, and the attack of hideous goblins, going to be the last things I saw in this life?

I felt sure of it. And again, I could only blame myself. It would have been so easy to have avoided it all if I just hadn't been so thoughtless. In a way it seemed right that no one could solve this problem that I had created.

But then again, after I was dead, the problem would grow larger…much larger…and others would be forced to try to solve it. How would the world even react to the sudden appearance of supernatural demons? Would people even be able to handle it all? My mistakes might not only bring about my own death, but potentially many others' as well…

No way out. No one coming to help. No one who could share the blame for my foolishness.

I let my head loll back, and I hung against the wall. I felt the pain in my wrists from the clasps but didn't care enough to try to relieve the pressure.

I was exhausted, and despite the pain and the daylight coming through the window I wanted to sleep. For hours I tried, fitfully, buried in thoughts of failure and humiliation, as my hope faded along with the daylight.

6.5

My eyes flashed open as I heard the creaking of door hinges.

Horrifying visions of demons victimizing me rushed through my mind until I saw Amy enter, checking behind her uneasily before closing the door again.

"I'm so sorry, Maria. I just have to say it again. I'm so sorry for being jealous and petty, and I'm sorry for allowing you to be taken like this. I'm sorry I was so stupid."

I didn't know what to say. I didn't know what emotion to feel. Rancor born from habit was mixed in my heart with a desire to accept her apology and a yearning for an ally. While I knew I would enjoy drinking from her arteries, I didn't want to harm her—I still felt the blood hunger, but sadness dulled it until it didn't matter.

She held out her hands; in them I saw a familiar bottle. "I brought you your pills. I'm sure it's hard for you without them." She gaped downward at the nearby stain of spilled blood. "I'm...glad you didn't drink what he gave you."

If she knew what Bastian had tried, then she must have realized more. "Then you know that I'm..."

"Yes."

I tried to measure the look in her eyes. It wasn't wary or fearful; it wasn't angry or mean, or negative at all. If anything, it was sad.

She went on. "Yeah, when Bastian decided that I wasn't good enough to be his girl he pointed out all my 'deficiencies'. He compared everything good about you to everything he didn't like about me." She gave a single, pitiful laugh. "I didn't feel too bad, really; by now I can see him for what he is, and his opinion doesn't mean much to me. But, he did say that you were something more than human. When I said I didn't know what he was talking about, he explained. He laughed at me for not knowing, as if I should have known. That's when he really started laying the insults on thick. It was stupid, and it hurt. I don't know why I never saw that petty side of him before. Anyway, I left and came to try to help you; I had found these things and I figured I knew why you were always taking them." She opened the bottle and poured a couple of pills into her hand. "How many?"

I looked at them, almost feeling a yearning, but not at all like I had for the blood. "Three. Four!" I closed my eyes against the hunger I felt. "Four."

She shook out two more, then capped the bottle and set it on the table. "I don't have anything for you to drink with them." She reached toward me with the pills in her hand.

"That's okay; they're chewable, remember?"

"Oh, right."

I opened my mouth and took them as she awkwardly offered them, chewing them all together once she had finished. My mouth felt dry with the powder of the crushed pills.

"Feel any better?"

I closed my eyes and grimaced, and swallowed. "No, not yet. I don't think they work the same as blood would. I'm sure I'll feel better soon. I hope." It didn't actually feel like they were doing any good, at least not immediately, but I couldn't imagine any ulterior motive for her in bringing them to me. She must have genuinely wanted to make things easier for me. "Thank you."

"I'm looking out for my own interests, too, you know." She pulled a key from her pocket and brought it toward one of my wrists. "After I let you out, I don't want you to come after me." She began working the lock on the shackle at my wrist. I was silent as she undid the lock. She suddenly paused. "You're...not going to come after me, are you?"

"No, no. Of course not," I said, looking directly at her. She stared back, not blinking an eye. "I could never do that. Ever."

She evidently didn't need much reassurance, and hurriedly began working the lock again. I heard a satisfying click. "We've got to get out of here, Maria," she said as she let the clasp fall and swing down against the wall. "We've got to get as far away from him as we can. Bastian told me to leave, and believe me I was okay with that, but I knew I couldn't leave without you. I snuck back in and took the key. Now I think we should take him up on his offer." She moved to my other wrist and turned the metal shackle.

With my free hand I reached toward my necklace, attempting in vain to unsecure it. As my hand found the clasp my fingers stung with a sharp pain, and I cried out. Amy took a step back, startled.

I reached for the necklace itself and pulled in a brief attempt to break it, but as soon as I applied any pressure the all-too familiar weight pulled me down, nearly making me lose consciousness. My hand fell, and as the sensation lifted I did my best to keep my head clear. "Amy, please," I struggled to say. "Help me get this necklace off first."

She examined it, set the key on the table, grasped two sections of the necklace and pulled against them, then frowned despairingly. The action still produced a weight on me, and I instinctively pulled away. "This is a lot harder than taking off my earrings," she said. "Mine came right off. Of course, the Demon Stone wouldn't work the same way against me, because I'm not..." She trailed off as if she'd said something embarrassing.

"Your earrings?" I echoed, only now seeing that she wasn't wearing them.

"Yeah. Bastian gave them to me, just like he gave you a necklace, but he did something to them first. I just asked him about them and he admitted it." She drew back with her eyes closed and her hands in tight fists at her sides. "He used them to spy on me. They..." She breathed twice before continuing. "They let him hear everything that I could hear. Even our last conversation—he heard every word of it."

I felt a certain shock as I realized that my privacy had been so invaded, but almost immediately it also occurred to me that Amy had always worn the earrings before, whenever I'd seen her, and that if Bastian could listen through them she'd had essentially no privacy at all. Bastian had used alchemy on her earrings like he had with my necklace, though in her case she hadn't been subjugated with the enchantment like I was. After Bastian gave them to her, he must have fooled her into keeping them on as often as was possible, just as he had encouraged me, though it was evident now that I would have been unable to remove the necklace anyway.

Amy began to tremble and a tear appeared in one eye. "He heard everything. He heard my deepest secrets; he heard when I spoke about *him*. I'm so embarrassed. Maria, you can't imagine how stupid I feel! I hate him."

She wasn't the only one who felt stupid. "You know this is my fault."

She glanced up. "What? No, no, it's not."

"I let Bastian fool me. I let him make me think he cared for me. I gave him the Life Stone and he's going to use it to bring monsters into the world."

"Hey! Hey!" She snapped her fingers with each repetition of the word. "Listen! You're talking about things he's doing, not you. This is *not* your fault. He lied to us and tricked us."

I wasn't sure I could absolve myself of responsibility. "Hmmm. But you got your earrings off."

"Yes!" Her eyes focused back on my neck. "And we need to get that off of you!" She reached behind my neck for the clasp; I turned my head to try to give her better access. She twisted her face in concentration, struggling in vain to undo the clasp. As she pulled at it, the pain returned, and I gasped, shrinking away.

"Maria! Are you all right?"

"I will be. Don't worry about that. Just get it off."

"I can't turn the clasp. It just won't move."

I began to sob without tears, doing my best to keep some composure but not feeling as if I had much success.

Amy spoke with an underlying strength. "Maria, I'm not gonna let him do this to us. I'm sorry if this hurts, but I can't let this go on any longer."

She gripped the necklace with both hands and pulled in opposite directions. The crushing sensation returned, and it was all I could do not to collapse. The sensation continued, and Amy grunted but then released me. Without waiting, she gripped the necklace again, this time with one hand on either side of the pendant. Despite my exhaustion I was about to speak again when she pulled once more, and I could say nothing at all.

The pain was unbearable. I couldn't tell how much time passed, nor was I aware of anything happening around me other than a searing and pounding feeling about my neck. My vision was blank. I couldn't tell which way was up or down. I felt as if I was screaming but couldn't hear anything. I felt as if my whole body was screaming, but utterly muted.

And then: release.

Abruptly, it all ended with a gasp from Amy and a tinkling sound at the floor. Within seconds my vision returned, I regained my feet, and I began breathing again—I must have stopped before. My weariness began to fade surprisingly quickly. Amy clenched her hands in front of her, and then she shook and flexed them, breathing hard through gritted teeth.

"There," she said, weary relief showing in her eyes, "now we can go."

"Thank you so much. Oh, thank you so much." It was wonderful not to have the weight pulling down on me. Even when I wasn't struggling against it, there had been an ever-present heaviness since Bastian had first used it, but with the necklace off, I felt a lightness I hadn't enjoyed in what seemed like a long time. Pieces of the now-broken necklace, including the bejeweled pendant, lay scattered on the floor around me. I gazed back up at Amy, who was gently rubbing her hands. "It looks like that hurt you a lot."

"Trust me," she said, "it hurt you worse." She shook her hands one last time. "Now let's get the rest of those chains off you and leave."

"But Amy, we can't just leave. We've got to stop Bastian before he uses those jewels."

She flinched backward. "Stop him? I don't want to be anywhere near him. I just want to get away, and we'd better go before—"

The door opened, and a grey goblin entered. It had an open gash across its chest that was partially scabbed over. It glared evilly at us.

"Gansak!" I cried, recognizing it.

It seemed surprised that I called its name, but it hunched its shoulders and began to take birdlike steps toward us. "Gansak AAARRRRAAAAAHHH!!"

Amy picked up the key from the table and threw it to me as she ran toward Gansak. "Maria, get free and save yourself!"

I caught the key as Amy and Gansak ran toward each other. When they were close enough, I could only watch as Gansak reached and struck her. Amy wasn't heavy or muscled; she pitched to the side and stumbled to the floor. Feeling helpless, all I could do was muster a yell of, "No!!"

The goblin moved toward her again as she began to lift herself to her knees. I hurriedly took the key to the shackle on my other hand. With an appalling smack sound, the beast struck her again before she could stand, spinning her and knocking her down. She fell between the goblin and me. As I turned the key in the lock, my other hand came free.

"Why don't you come get me, you monster!" I yelled. "I'm the one you're here for!"

It looked at me and crept closer with light strides. Frantically, I reached for the clasp at one of my ankles.

With a grunt, Amy reached out her foot to trip the goblin. Though obviously weak, she managed to entangle her leg with its legs and it fell. Screaming out, it picked itself up again and turned back to her. I pulled one ankle lock away and moved the key to my other ankle.

Gansak was moving faster than Amy; before she was upright it grabbed her by the shoulders, then turned and threw her sideways. Her cry abruptly went quiet as she disappeared out the window.

I didn't have time to deal with my shock as Gansak turned back toward me. With a half-exultant gasp I pulled the last lock away and shot a glance back toward my attacker. It charged me, and just before it reached me I jumped to the side. It tried to turn but didn't react quickly enough and rammed the wall with its shoulder.

I cursed inwardly and felt some fear as I realized that I was still feeling weak. Gansak spun toward me and charged again with its arms forward. Mustering what strength I could, I reached in past its arms to pull down on its head while I jumped upward, bringing one knee up into Gansak's chin.

I flopped sideways to the floor, but Gansak stumbled backward with its eyes closed and fell, landing on its back.

I had difficulty lifting myself, but stood and faced the thing again. It also was standing up, slower now, and it held its chin with one claw and leaned on the table with the other.

An instinct awoke in me and I gritted my teeth toward the beast, showing them as a threat. I raised up my hands as I would if I had sharp claws, ready to strike.

The monster stepped backward now and eyed the doorway as if contemplating retreat.

"Come on! Kill me!" I yelled at it, crouching toward it and readying myself to strike at it with my bare hands. I caught sight of my dagger resting at the edge of the table and picked it up with a quick movement.

It now saw the dagger as well, and it screeched at me. I lunged toward it, but it took a quick step behind the table and pulled upward on the underside, overturning it and blocking my path. As I jumped back away from the table, Gansak fled from the room without a backward glance.

I realized I had no time to rest when I heard the growl of other beasts coming from beyond the door. I slipped the dagger back into my boot and rushed to the window. Darkness lay beyond, not only up toward the sky but particularly down toward the distant ground below. It was an unusually dark night, which made it hard to see outside even with my good vision, but I could perceive a ledge beneath me from a lower window. I guessed that I was on the back corner of the castle, in the taller tower I had seen before. I climbed out the window, hanging on with my arms and then my hands. An inhuman cry came from the room's doorway; I looked up briefly enough to see several goblins walking in, and then I let myself drop to the ledge below. My feet caught it, but I jolted unsteadily, and I fell backward. I dropped through the darkness, not knowing what lay beneath, and hit the ground back-first. My head struck earth only an instant later.

I was dizzied from the fall and unable to breathe. After several seconds of struggling almost motionlessly, I turned to my left side and rolled to my belly. I felt pain across my entire body now, and though I pulled myself to my knees, for a moment I couldn't lift myself any further. I coughed a few brief coughs, trying to start breathing regularly again. As the breaths began coming in and out again with more and more regularity, I found that I could see a bit better than before.

A limp form lay almost directly in front of me.

I moved toward it, comprehending at once that it was Amy. She lay face up. I reached my hand under her head, and my fingers felt a warm wetness. At the same time I smelled it, and the sensation of hunger welled up in me. I immediately stood and staggered away, trying to brush the blood off of my hands, wiping them on dirt and rocks and anything else nearby.

No! I thought, hating myself for retreating. *No, don't leave her here with these monsters! Take her with you!*

With tears in my eyes I began running away. Somehow I didn't think I was too weak to carry her small frame, but I felt too weak to keep myself from doing something foul. The hunger was still too much—just too much!

I kept running, running, running, not sure exactly when I had gone far enough to be safe. I ran to keep terrible thoughts of reality out of my mind.

But with every step, I wished I could go back.

I wished I could go back and bring Amy's body away from that horrible place, away from those fiends, without feeling the desire to drink the blood that would soon grow cold.

Even more, I wished I could go back to each moment in time when I had misjudged her, when I had seen motives in her that weren't there, when I had been jealous and petty just as she had said that she was. I wished I could go back and truly befriend her, and work with her to stop Bastian's plans. I wished I could go back and apologize, and embrace her, and know that she forgave me.

But, no matter how much I desired it, I couldn't go back.

I had sorely misjudged Amy and now had sore guilt because of it. There would be no way to pay that price quickly. I needed no artificially-imposed consequence for my flawed estimation of her. A far greater punishment came with the severe pain of discovering my own arrogance and the regret of knowing that any opportunity to make things better with her was now lost.

As I continued on foot I was aware of one more thing.

I had misjudged someone else, too, and the sting of my own exposed conceit was sore on this count also, but in this case I might have a chance to make things right. Bastian was evil—it was as simple as that—and I was embarrassed and hurt, but I knew that I would have to move against him. I had to oppose him. I had to resist him and fight him and prevent him from causing any more pain and grief.

But I was weak, and tired, and alone in the dark, and mostly right now I just wanted to get away. I wanted to get away from the blood, and the death, and the pain, and the guilt, and from anything that would remind me of my own foolishness.

I ran on through the night, fleeing from the results of my own decisions. I ran, and I ran.

7

As I approached my father's house I felt that the bloodthirst had lessened. The iron pills Amy had brought me had served their purpose.

Amy...in my head I could see her, dead, lying in the dirt, and her blood was quite literally on my hands despite my efforts to scrub it off. I didn't know what to do for her now. I didn't think I should notify the police; I wasn't sure what would happen if they went to Greywall Castle and found goblins there, but it just seemed like the wrong thing to do. And yet, I didn't know what the right thing was. While I didn't want to leave her there, I didn't feel like there was anything left I could do for her.

I had run from Greywall Castle until I was too tired to run, and then I had kept walking until I was able to run again. I'd been tired far beyond anything I'd ever been accustomed to, but equally impelled to get away from the castle. I'd slowed down eventually, but kept moving, wary of any possible pursuit and entirely heedless of the banal aspects of normal night life in the world around me. While walking on a main road, a kindly older woman stopped to offer me a ride. I accepted, making an excuse about car trouble when asked. I kept quiet afterward except to thank her. Finally, on the walkway to my father's house, guarded by the familiar stone warriors, I was able to relax a bit.

As I passed by one of the statues, a strange, dark mark on one of the spearheads caught my attention. It was a liquid, evidently; it looked as if several drops had fallen from it to the walkway below. I'd never seen any such marking before and couldn't imagine who or what would have left it, but I took little time to wonder as I made my way onward to the front door of the house, where I found something startling.

The door was locked.

That was highly unusual; to my memory, this door had never failed to yield to me. Had my mother gone out somewhere, at this time of night? I rapped the knocker against the plate, then pulled the cord on the side of the door and listened for the bell that rang inside the house. Gratefully, I didn't have to wait long before the door opened.

"Maria!" my mother said. "Come inside, quickly."

I complied, and my mother shut the door behind me and locked it again. Then she turned back and embraced me, squeezing me tighter than I would normally think was necessary, though at the moment I cherished the sense of security from just being with my mother. She sighed before speaking. "Maria, I'm so relieved to see you." She held me a bit longer before drawing back enough to look at me. "Are you all right? You look like a mess! Where have you been?" I saw something in her eyes that I wasn't sure I'd ever seen before. It didn't make me any more comfortable.

"I'm sorry, Mom. I'm so sorry for making you worry. I don't know how to answer you, either; I'm not sure how I can tell you. Something is happening right now that isn't...normal."

"I know, Maria. I've known since your father disappeared. I've seen strange things in the shadows outside, heard strange sounds in the night...don't think I don't remember who your father really is, and what he is, and what else is really out there that we don't normally talk about. I tend to not ever think about all that, but I know better."

"I still...I still don't know what to say, Mom. I don't want you to worry about me. I don't want you to be afraid."

"Tell me the truth, Maria. I'm already worried and afraid. Tell me what you know about what's going on so that maybe I can do something about it instead of *only* worrying." She noticed my hands, and held one of them to get a better look. "Is that *blood?* What happened to your wrists?"

I lifted my hands up so I could see them again, now in the lamplight of my own home, and as I saw the general reddish tint and the few darker blotches I had difficulty giving an explanation. I ultimately couldn't speak anything more than a few words. "Amy is dead, Mom."

Her eyes went wide. "Tell me you didn't do this."

I tried to blink away tears. "Of course not, Mom. She fell. I mean, she was thrown, and she fell. She was attacked. I was, too. I—I got away, and I found her, and I wanted to drink her blood. But I didn't. I ran away. I couldn't help her. I couldn't help her, Mom."

She put her arm around my shoulders and began leading me away quickly. "Let's get this washed off." She brought me to the bathroom sink, where she used a bar of soap to scrub the dirt and blood from my hands.

Everything around me was shattered. Bastian, and evidently Abbott also, were villains, and all of my efforts, which had been driven by jealousy, had only helped them. I had taken a powerful artifact—in fact, if I was being honest with myself I would have to admit that I had *stolen* it—from someone I didn't even know. I had wronged Amy and now she was beyond reconciliation. My father was missing. My mother was frightened.

I felt like my entire body was about to crumble. I tried to keep myself from shaking, though I was sure my mother noticed it despite my efforts.

Thankfully, she seemed as strong as ever despite her fear, and she was steadfast in her task. I was glad to see the blood go, glad to see the normal pale shade return to my skin. My mother left me for a moment and returned with gauze and bandages, which she wrapped over my wrists.

"I left her there, Mom. I had to get away. I didn't have much iron in me, and I thought I was going to drink her blood even after she had just died. I almost couldn't help myself and I had to get away."

"I'm proud of you for resisting the temptation," she said back. "I don't know what that's like, but from what your father says, sometimes resisting that can be harder than anything else he has had to do."

I didn't have anything to say back. When she was done bandaging me I sank to the floor, leaning against the wall, and my mother sat beside me. When she put a hand on my shoulder I clasped it with both of mine.

"Who attacked you? And where have you been, and why haven't you come home sooner? It's not like you to be gone for so long, especially without letting me know anything."

"I was held against my will, Mother. I was chained to a wall."

"What?"

"Yes. He—" I hesitated, unsure if I would cause my mother too much stress and concern by speaking further. "I don't know if I should tell you this. I'm okay now, so don't worry any more about me. I'm okay, but while I was there, he struck me, and he tormented me with a cupful of blood. I didn't drink that either. He killed someone else he had imprisoned—he killed Artemis Brown." My mother put her free hand over her mouth at this news. "I don't know why Art was there, but he's dead now. I didn't even know until after. There was nothing I could do."

My mother's voice was barely a whisper. "Oh, my…"

I swallowed before continuing. "Amy told me about him. She was just someone we'd been studying with. Then I had to fight a monster. It was a goblin or something. It killed her…threw her out a window…and I had to fight it to get away. There are more goblins, and Bastian controls them. And Bastian has enchanted artifacts, jewels, and is going to use them to perform an evil ritual and bring more demons into the world, and I was the one who gave him one of the jewels. I didn't know what he was going to do yet when I gave it to him. He tricked me. Before that, just to get the jewel I put myself in danger in a cave with some other monster, who was really freaky, but I got away without being hurt. Sorry; this is all sort of out of order." I sighed. "To top it off I've done all of this when Dad isn't around to help."

My mother was silent as she absorbed the news of these horrors.

"I'm sorry, Mother. I lied to you before and got involved in something bad and risked my life and made you worry, and I've helped a very bad person, and I'm really sorry. I'm sorry."

She had kept a constant gaze at me while I had been speaking, and still held it as she now spoke. "Your father told me, before, that someday you would face danger, real danger, from things I wouldn't understand right away. It wasn't that I didn't believe him. No, I trusted him and I believed him, like I trust him about everything, and it terrified me to think of what might happen to you. Oh, Maria, the dreadful stories he has told me…I think I would rather live in ignorance of the horror out there. I believed him, but as the years passed and you grew from a small girl to a beautiful young woman it never seemed possible that you could be part of that dark world. It never seemed that what he said would come to pass." Now she let her eyes fall and sighed. "And yet here you are, not just adventuring like your father, but meeting with terrors that would take you away from me forever. I don't know if I can handle it, Maria."

"I don't know if I can either, Mom." A tear escaped one eye and rolled down my cheek, not quite reaching my chin.

It was one tear, wet and coolly evaporating from my face.

Something changed.

Something bothered me about that tear.

I held still, feeling the increased sensitivity on my skin where the tear had run. *That boy has made me cry in front of my mother when she's worried. He's made me feel weak at the time when she needs my help.* It was the least of many negative consequences I had experienced recently, but it seized me, and seemed to hold me firmly in place. That small tear, vanishing into the air even as I sat, confined me in a lucid stillness and pushed back the panic and weakness from me. What a proud girl I was, to only find resolve after having my self-respect offended, but all the same, as I despised that little, fading drop of water and the man who had caused it to appear, I found myself growing more intent.

Amid the shattered bits and pieces of my life, I found a truth. In a key moment I knew something, and it set a clear course for me. "And yet," I continued, "I have to handle it." I stood up. "I'm the only one who can."

My mother's brow furrowed as she contemplated me, unable to know what I was thinking.

"I need to confront those terrors." With my hand I wiped the last bit of moisture from my cheek. "I need to confront the person who is doing all of this. I'll probably have to fight him and the monsters that are guarding him."

My mother closed her eyes and lowered her head, and breathed deeply.

"I won't just be taken by them, Mother. I'll be able to fight. Dad trained me for this, remember? He couldn't have known what was going to happen, but he prepared me for it."

"Oh, Maria, if I lose you…"

"You won't, Mom." I crouched near her where she still sat. "But I've got to do it. I can't let Bastian go through with his ritual, especially when I'm the one who enabled him."

"Are you going to kill him?"

A quick answer came to my lips, but I held it in. I hadn't thought I would need to kill him, but I really couldn't be sure. "No," I said, weighing the possibility in my mind, "no, I don't want to kill him. Maybe I can't. Mother, I loved him, or I thought I did, or…or maybe I still do…and even though he's done awful things to me I don't think I could kill anyone. Any *person*, that is, though I may have to kill his…minions."

"Take your sword."

The quick response shocked me into stillness again. "What?"

"Your sword. You're really very good with it. I've watched you, and even though I don't like the idea of you having to use weapons, you handle yourself well with it and I want you to be protected."

Oh.

"And take armor."

What had come over my mother? "Mom, any armor we own is sized and fitted for Dad. It wouldn't work at all for me."

"What about your fencing gear?"

"My—oh, Mom, really, that's for practicing. For sport. I doubt my jacket and plastron and breeches are going to help me against these creatures."

"I want you to take them anyway."

"No, Mother, really! And that sword is for practice, too, and I don't think it'll be enough."

"I was thinking of your other sword, the older one."

"The rapier dad gave me?"

"Yes, that's the one! I want you to take that one."

"Mom, I can't believe you're talking this way."

"Believe it. I may not know how to use any of the stuff myself, but you do and you'll need it. Don't think for a minute that I'm going to let you run off into danger poorly-equipped. I'm serious when I say I want you taking all of that with you. I'm getting up now."

I helped her to her feet.

7.1

I wasn't leaving immediately. I couldn't set off until I had a good plan, and I needed rest anyway, and more food, even though I'd already wolfed down some leftover meatloaf from the fridge.

I was also insatiably intrigued by what Amy had said. Art had spoken of "the letter" from my father. This could mean only one thing.

A week after my father had given me my first lesson in swordsmanship, he solemnly handed me a sealed envelope, which, he said, held a letter that I was not to read then. The right time would be later in my life; when I asked what time, he said he couldn't give any more specific answer. He said the important thing was that when I did read it, I'd know that he'd had these thoughts all along, and that I shouldn't ever think that he'd neglected to tell me something so important. I used to wonder if it had to do with how babies are made, but my parents had already gone over the basics with me before then, and later had given additional details on occasion when necessary; he'd never mentioned the letter then, so it had to be on a different subject.

Wherever he was now, he'd sent word to me that it was time to read it. The letter seemed to have contributed indirectly to Art's death. Well, maybe Art had meant to come here anyway, but regardless, a time of seriousness had come that merited my opening of the letter.

From recent events that I'd seen for myself, I knew that this point in time was momentous, but did my father also know about Bastian and his plot? If so, why was he gone?

I figured that he must not know about it. Even if something else was going on elsewhere, if he'd known that I was in danger he would have either stayed or returned to help me.

But he was gone, and it was now imperative that I read The Letter.

I had told my mother about Art's reference to it, and she had put one hand to her mouth, perhaps wondering what it meant for her husband. She told me I'd better not wait to read it, and I agreed, even though I was exhausted. She also asked that I share it with her when I finished, if the contents were not so personal as to forbid that. I assured her that I would.

In my room I had a special box hidden away with a few old treasures. I hadn't even looked at it for at least three years, but had never forgotten it. It was in a secret compartment in my closet. I extracted it delicately and blew off a bit of dust, then set it on my desk.

It was locked with a special key. I'd also hidden this key for many years, though I doubted that the lock would hold up to much force—it was mostly a simple child's trinket. I lifted a corner floorboard and removed the hidden key from underneath.

I used the key, opened the box, and found the letter still there. The paper was a shade yellower than I recalled. It was odd to hold it again after having set it out of my mind for so long. I tore the top with a letter opener and withdrew the paper inside, recognizing my father's handwriting instantly.

My Dear Daughter Maria,

You and I are unique in the world that you know. You have already been aware that our cursed bloodline comes from another dominion, a kingdom of shadow. I have kept that realm of dusk far from your life and endeavored to raise you in continual dawn while you were yet young, but you must know that the shadows beyond your sight have never faded.

I have never held expertise in family matters, but I believe that any loving parent will shield their children from the dangers of the world, whether physical, chemical, or ideological, while the children are young, knowing that those children must also grow stronger and more independent so that they can one day face those dangers without falling. My two greatest joys in life, if "life" is the appropriate term for my existence, have been my shared love with your mother and the privilege of watching and helping you as you've grown from an infant.

Like any father regarding his child, I rejoiced with every painful lesson you learned and was even amused by your mischief. With the responsibility of providing for your needs, I gained a purpose that surpassed any I had ever known before. I came to know a superlative pride as you became a smarter and more capable person, and as you developed so many talents and skills. I took immense delight in who you are.

The most important part of your upbringing, however, was and is the development of character and integrity. This will be a lifelong effort, even if you live as long as I have, for personal character is a treasure that must be maintained. It is an ornament of fine silver that must be polished or tarnished, with daily effort given to the polishing. This task ever remains for you to accomplish, but know that I have no doubt that you have been true to what I've taught you, and that you continue to honor me by obeying the counsel I've given over your several years.

If you've found reason to read this letter, I am not with you, and it is most probable that the shadows have crept close enough for you to feel their cold touch. If so, you will need all of the knowledge, skill, and strength of character that you've gained. Take the greatest sense of earnestness now in continuing to learn. And now you must also learn about the many forms and courses that those shadows take.

My home is a safe haven for you and your mother; I hope that it ever will be. The heart of this home is my personal library. In the back room, in the first bookcase, on the third shelf up, you will find a set of timeworn books, the first letters of the titles of which will spell M - A - R - I - A. These volumes will be of little consequence to you other than to designate a location. Next to those books you will find several tomes which you may use to learn about many dark and unnatural things.

This means that you will learn more about yourself. You will be advantaged over most people in this world by having particular insight into your own nature, and yet you are disadvantaged by having a challenge that will never relent and that none around you can understand. Some day you will know your nature, and you will learn the depths of that trial. Embrace your strengths. Reject temptation. Eschew the evil that resides inescapably in your nature. Be the woman you know I want you to be.

Know also that while your individual ordeals will be severe, it is also human nature to have weakness to overcome, and that all women and men must make the same basic choices in order to forge their destinies. Many have gone before you and pressed forward nobly and uprightly. Take courage.

It is with apprehension that I think of you entering this dark world, but I know that you will be strong. I know also that, having that strength, you must necessarily be called upon to use it. Never shrink.

While I am writing this my memories are fresh of you discovering my collected weapons. I never desired for you to learn the art of combat but I felt I would be remiss by not teaching it. Concern for your safety leads me to wish that you will never need it, but practicality demands that I expect otherwise. I hope you do not seek out violence, but sooner or later it will find you. Make yourself ready in mind and body.

Such weighty matters. Alas, that I must address them. I look forward to many more years of lightheartedness before you must read this.

If my mortal course is ended, remember that I love you and believe in you. Never turn from what you know to be right. But even death will not keep us apart eternally.

Until we are reunited in family bliss, remember my love and faith.

--Your Father, Lucard

I wiped a tear from my eye, but this tear was okay.

7.2

I let myself go to sleep and didn't rise until morning was gone. I felt that I'd gotten sorely needed rest, but I couldn't shake off the grogginess for some time. I got myself a late breakfast (a late lunch, really), and did a few simple exercises to try to wake myself up. They didn't help enough.

I took the letter to my mother. She read it and cried also. "He isn't dead, though," I said to her. "Art had just seen him."

"I know in my heart he's not dead," she replied. "I suppose some people wouldn't think that was enough proof, but it is for me. I miss him more than I ever have, though. He must have expected not to return soon. At least you're here with me; it's so much better than being alone."

I felt the same, though while our company was mutually comforting I knew that at least for me there was a lingering uneasiness over the unresolved problem of Bastian's ritual. That was a problem that wouldn't just go away with time, and I couldn't be fully at ease until it was solved.

I hugged her. "Mom," I said, "I need to get into Dad's library but I don't have the key. Do you know where he kept it?"

"Well, yes. I never go in there, but I can get you the key."

I followed her to her room. In more recent years I'd thought it was respectful to leave that space to her and my father, so I waited outside, but she returned promptly with an old, large, brass key. "Here it is. I can't say that I want to join you; that part of your father's life is just more than I can handle sometimes."

"It's okay, Mom." I took the key. "Do whatever you need to do."

I followed the hallways to my father's library. For as much as I liked books, like my mother did, I never spent much time there. His selection had never appealed to me greatly, but it also felt like something mostly private for my father—I usually felt like using his library would be intrusive. I wasn't sure if coming in here while he was away made it better or worse.

The main room looked as it always did; shelves, books, a few chairs and a couple of small tables and a desk. Nothing terribly unusual.

The door at the back was solid and heavy. I'd only seen it opened a couple of times. The large key turned without difficulty in the lock and the thick wooden door gave little resistance as I pulled it open.

The small chamber beyond was unfamiliar. I'd caught a glimpse through the doorway once, but I'd never been inside. Bookshelves lined the left wall and wrapped around to the rear of the room; some of the shelves were nearly empty and some held other objects including an antique pair of glasses, a corroded metal teapot, a mask that appeared to be made of stone, a few leather pouches, and an engraved animal horn with a cord attached at each end. On the right wall were a few small tables and additional shelves that held vials of several shapes and which held liquids of varying colors; hanging next to them was a rack holding a black cloak with a red lining.

I took all this in only at a glance; curiosity welled up within me as I approached the bookshelves on the left. In the first bookcase, on the third shelf up, just as my father had written, five books were arrayed so that the first letters of their titles did indeed spell my first name. I wondered how long they'd sat in that arrangement. Six years, at least.

When I looked at the books next to them, one caught my eye instantly. *Demons and Dark Essences.* I pulled it from the shelf to inspect it. While the title was the same, the book itself seemed much, much older than Bastian's copy. The title page also bore a symbol of a dragon curled into the shape of an eye, and even though this copy seemed more ancient (maybe by a century or several), the author was still listed as Drake. Maybe production of the manuscript was a task passed between generations of the same family? I pictured some wizard-bearded fellow handing the book to his son and charging him with the duty of updating it; for some reason the Drake or Drakes came to mind as males.

I flipped through several pages, carefully in case the paper had become fragile with time, and I immediately noticed something worrisome. It was clear that Bastian's version of the book was different. I certainly hadn't memorized that version, but I was positive that the wording was different here. The language used was older, and a bit harder to read, like something from Shakespeare. I looked again at the outside of the book; while it was also leather-bound and was generally the same size as Bastian's copy, it otherwise didn't appear greatly similar.

As I scanned the pages within I found that while this book was not identical to Bastian's, page for page and word for word, it still contained much of the same content. The images and description of Dracula, for example, were about the same as far as I could remember. I also easily found the section on the Demon Masters that was either mostly or exactly similar to the corresponding section in Bastian's book, and I hurriedly flipped to the pages that followed.

My purpose in looking through these books my father had mentioned was twofold. As he had written, I still had much to learn about "unnatural" things and about myself, but more immediately, I hoped to find something that would give me a way to prevent Bastian from performing his ritual. The section about Luctus would surely give me some clue.

Except that it wasn't there.

Evidently, that portion had been added in a later version of the book, because there was no trace of it here—not even any remains of torn pages. I flipped from page to page, thinking that maybe the Luctus section might have been part of the original text but that the later version had been re-ordered, but I didn't find it. With frustration I had to acknowledge that this book contained no reference to the ritual Bastian had described.

I did notice a different section I'd never seen while in Greywall Castle, though. Where I'd expected to find the pages for Luctus, there was a description of "Rakades". It was another "world", ostensibly some sort of other planet or dimension that was home to demons. It seemed to be the place where all demons had originated, much like how Earth was the home of humanity. The existence of such a place was a bit of a shock to me, but I took no time to contemplate it. I scanned through the passage, searching for any mention of methods for summoning demons from Rakades or preventing them from being summoned but found neither. Maybe this demon realm was where Bastian would get his demon army, and maybe not, but either way nothing in this book could help me.

Bastian...thinking of him again sent a tormenting jumble of feelings through me. It was nothing I hadn't felt or thought already, but my mind revisited the pain of betrayal and longing that had plagued me while I was in his dungeon.

I had to get that out of my head.

I exchanged the book for one of the others on the shelf, and after several minutes, yet another. Some other time I would review it all more closely, but at present I was desperate about finding a way to prevent the ritual.

More time passed, and my exasperation was mounting, exacerbated by a persistent bleariness from a lack of sufficient and proper sleep, when I finally found something on some loose sheets of paper that stirred me.

A Disenchanter.

The ink on these pages was faded and sometimes impossible to read, but they detailed another type of artifact, manifestly not unique but with several reproductions having been made, that could undo or eliminate some alchemic creations, by expending its own power in the process.

The other few intelligible words gave me a burst of hope. The Disenchanter was made by affixing a certain jewel (probably described more in the faded text) to the end of a leaden rod coated with gold or silver. The rod grew warm when directed at an enchanted artifact.

I laughed aloud with the realization that the Disenchanter was almost certainly the same "compass" I had with me.

Of course, it might not be the same thing; there could easily be separate Seeker and Disenchanter relics with similar function but differing end purposes. I doubted it though. Even if only by a desire to believe that I'd found a way to stop Bastian's plan, I accepted the Seeker and the Disenchanter as the same alchemic tool.

It was likely that Bastian didn't know that the Seeker had the power to disenchant; I didn't think he'd be so free with something that could disrupt his plans. Then again, maybe he did know, but he also knew that the "Seeker" wasn't powerful enough to stop the Demon Stone, which by his account was one of the most potent enchanted artifacts ever made.

I didn't like the uncertainty that came with that thought.

Still, it was something to go on. I could take some more time later to figure out other ways of stopping Bastian, but the other problem that remained was finding him. He wasn't going to conduct the ritual at his castle; he may potentially have gone anywhere in the world, and easily far enough away that the Seeker couldn't help me locate him.

So my next step was to look at a few maps. Fortunately, my father had an atlas in his library, back in the main room. I stepped out into that room and found the oversize atlas on the corner of the desk.

I opened it and scrutinized a world map, feeling a bit hopeless as I did. Nothing whatsoever came to mind, which wasn't surprising because I didn't know the world well at all. I'd spent most of my life close to home.

Maybe he hadn't gone quite so far, though. Still feeling discouraged, I flipped to a map of the United States, which was less intimidating but no more helpful. But maybe the site of the ritual would be even closer, like the Life Stone had been. On one hand it seemed like it would be too much of a coincidence, but on the other, why would he need to go very far? He'd made it sound like the location was useful, but not the critical element of the ritual. I flipped more pages until I came to a map of Washington State.

My first reaction was more pessimism, but after studying the state map for only a few seconds, a location jumped out at me.

Of course!

Bastian had said little about the site of the ritual, but his few words gave obvious clues if taken in the right context—in this case, a literal context. Most people in the world probably wouldn't be able to figure it out, but other locals might. While I didn't know the world well, I did know a bit of eastern Washington, and there was a particular chunk of land nearby that I'd seen once, years before, that held a building that matched the expressions Bastian had used. Fortunately, I wouldn't have to travel far after all to reach the site.

With this realization, my plan was essentially complete. I felt a sort of imperfect sense of relief, knowing that the largest task lay ahead, but also that I now knew enough to accomplish it— assuming that the Seeker was, in fact, the Disenchanter, and would, in fact, render the Demon Stone powerless. For my own sake I had to make that assumption at this point; I had no more patience for doubt.

I wanted something to help me relax, so I went to my room and grabbed a hair brush. In comparison with everything else going on it might have been a petty and girlish concern, but my hair was in awful condition and that was at least one thing I could control and set in order, right now, and feel better about.

My mother walked in as I brushed, holding a tray with sandwiches on it. "Dinner time. I kept it simple tonight."

"They look great," I said. "I didn't realize it was so late."

"That happens when you sleep past noon." She set the tray on one of the small tables and sat down next to it.

"I think I have a plan now," I told her. "I found something in some of Dad's stuff. I think it'll work. I'm glad, because I probably don't have much time left to stop Bastian."

"Much time? What do you mean?"

"He was going to conduct his ritual during the next new moon—said something about needing only starlight for it." My mother was motionless for long enough to make me wonder, and when I looked directly at her, I saw that her mouth was hanging open. "What's wrong?"

"Maria…the new moon was last night."

I froze with my brush just over my hair.

I knew better than to ask her if she was joking, but it was hard to accept. If the new moon was last night, then I could no longer prevent Bastian from conducting the ritual; he would have completed it hours ago.

By now, demons were already being summoned. A calamity of unknown proportion was already underway. At this moment, Bastian must be marshalling forces and preparing to take some action that, even if only by publicly introducing supernatural demons to the world, would introduce a measure of chaos for which the world had no prepared response.

I'd already lost.

"Then I was wrong," I said back. "I have no time."

7.3

I began to pull on my fencing gear. Truthfully, I could do a lot worse where armor was concerned. The protective clothing was made with Dyneema, a fabric constructed using ultra-high-molecular-weight polyethylene. Stronger than Kevlar, so they said. Sturdy stuff.

My father had spent good money to get the best equipment available. It fit me well. Having put on the breeches, jacket, plastron, and plastic chest protector, I opted for my hiking boots instead of my regular flat-soled fencing shoes, which wouldn't give me a good grip on uneven ground. It felt awkward, but I could think of nothing better. As long as no fencing partners saw my combination of gear (and they wouldn't), I'd be fine. Lastly, I strapped the dagger boot sheath outside the leg of my breeches.

Before putting on the mask I took a look in a full-length mirror. I felt terribly uneasy, looking at myself mostly in an outfit that I used for sporting competitions. I would have to remember that the rules of those contests wouldn't apply where I was headed. Another difference tonight was my sword, which was not a competition sword; it was distinctly heavier and sharper than the saber I had often used in sport. I had practiced at home with the old rapier, though. I looked goofy with my mismatched boots and blade, and I was glad no one was taking pictures. To increase my confidence, I donned my sword-hand glove, lifted and drew the sword itself, and gave several cuts and thrusts in the air between me and the mirror. It worked a little bit.

My mother stood in the doorway. "Are you sure you can't wait until tomorrow? It's already late in the day."

"No, Mom, I can't wait. If I have any chance of stopping this, I need to do it now."

She watched me as I made a final sword move. "Be careful."

"I will." I sheathed the sword and buckled the sword belt around my waist, over my breeches. I walked to my mother and hugged her tightly. "Say a little prayer for me, okay?"

She didn't say anything more but nodded.

I held her hand as I walked to the front door of my father's house, carrying my fencing mask in my other hand. At the door I faced her once more. I could see that she was doing her best to keep herself from crying.

"I have faith in you," she said. "I do. I wish you weren't going out to these strange things, but I have faith in you. You have so much of your father in you. I wish he was here to guide you."

I didn't want to shed tears myself; at the mention of my father I had difficulty keeping myself from feeling the disquiet that had been lurking around us. "I'll be okay, Mom. I wish he was here, too," I said, feeling a bit stronger just by acting that way for her sake, "but I'll be okay. Dad's been guiding me for my whole life."

She nodded and wiped her eyes.

I hugged her one more time, briefly, and stepped out the door.

I took my mother's car; mine was still back at Greywall Castle. At first I'd just been hurried to get away; it didn't take long for me to remember my car, but I hadn't felt safe enough to retrieve it with it being parked just outside the castle where goblins would likely be on guard. Once all of this this was resolved I would worry about getting it back. So my mother's car was the natural choice. She didn't plan on going anywhere right now anyway.

In my brief return to my home I'd gained a bit of hidden knowledge, and now I had to leave again. What I'd learned about my father would give me inner strength. What I'd learned about a small artifact...well, I hoped it would be enough to stop a villain.

As I went to the car, I noticed that the night seemed especially black. I knew that was partially due to the new moon, but it felt like there was something more blocking any source of light around me.

8

The Hanford Site. The nation had rushed to build multiple facilities across the expansive site, at a cost of millions of dollars, in order to produce a weapon powerful enough to end a world war. In 1944, at the height of World War II, scientists had synthesized a previously unknown element—plutonium—though it was only created in miniscule amounts. This new element could be used in a nuclear bomb, but in order to produce sufficient quantities, a large reactor was required: the B Reactor. Inside, uranium was bombarded by neutrons in a chain reaction of atomic fission, changing some of the uranium into plutonium for the bomb that destroyed Nagasaki, Japan. The reactor was indeed a "place of power" for "modern alchemists", as Bastian had put it.

It seemed a strange thing for Bastian to mix recent technology and ancient alchemy, but perhaps there was some lingering essence, some sort of aura in the reactor that added to the effect of his ritual.

I had taken a public tour of the site two years ago and knew exactly how to find it. I drove past Rattlesnake Mountain, and past the Rattlesnake and Yakima Barricades (which were much less impressive than their names suggest and are nothing more than security gates that had at one time been manned during the day). I had been driving a bit faster than would be appropriate, and when the bridge over the Columbia River came into view I hit my brakes harder than I should have, coming to a halt a short distance away from a small bluish shack on the side of the road.

That should put me right by... I thought, and then, looking to my right, I saw the other gate. It was just a couple of concrete blocks with a swinging gate between them, but the notable feature about the gate right now was that it was wide open. I drove forward, closer to the shack, and got out.

The land of the site was rather barren. It could be and once had been useful for farming, though farmland required irrigation from the nearby river. Now only desert plants grew across the face of the land. No one lived nearby, and anyone who worked in the site, perhaps as part of the long-lasting cleanup effort, would only be in the area at all during the day. Bastian and Abbott were the only people I would see here tonight.

I re-buckled my sheathed sword at my waist, but I left my fencing mask in the car. I didn't expect to have to protect my face from an opponent's blade and even though I had good visibility through the mask I didn't want to worry about it, especially at night.

I took a few steps along the reservation boundary, which was guarded by only a single strand of barbed wire hung across thin metal posts laid a few meters apart. While security fences at other places broadcast a message more like, "YOU ARE NOT AUTHORIZED TO ENTER," this single strand gave off a weak vibe more like, "Hey, come on, guys, don't come in here. Really, guys. Come on, please don't." Presumably there was neither a large group of intruders into the nuclear site nor much reason to intrude in the first place.

I could see myself easily compared to my surroundings. That was disappointing; it would make a stealthy approach more difficult. Maybe it was just my good night vision, but my fencing gear was plainly visible, even though it was grey instead of the more common white, and even though the night was dark. There was nothing to do about it, though. There was no time to come up with anything else, so I had to press on. I gave a short, silent prayer for help as I stepped forward.

I reached the open gate and paused before walking down the straight road ahead of me. Just a few miles away I would find the old B Reactor, the only building in the vicinity still standing even though it had been shut down decades before. Having only been a historical site for years, it was now being used by Bastian for his ritual.

But had he completed the ritual? Did he already have an army of demons at his command? What lay down the road ahead of me, and in the reactor building itself?

Nothing was going to get any easier if I hesitated, so now was the time to find out.

8.1

There was no one around to hear me speak, but I didn't want to talk anyway. I felt the seriousness around me, the danger...I felt like the joy of youth had been stolen from me. I didn't know if people were supposed to age mentally in rapid bursts, but I felt that I was a different person than I had been just days before. I felt older, and more somber—perhaps more like my father. And for as much as I would have wanted someone there with me for support, I had nothing to say to anyone. It was not a time to say, but to do.

The sky, thankfully clear of clouds, allowed the starlight to fall down on me, the road, and the surrounding sagebrush. I was glad for that; even though I could see well in the dark, it was surprisingly uncomfortable to be alone and in danger without the moon to guide me and sustain me. It had never occurred to me before then how much I was comforted by the moon, but now without it I felt especially lonely. Even though I knew it wasn't visible I took a wistful glance upward, taking time during several steps to lament its absence.

I listened to the night as I walked along the road, peering to the side from time to time but mostly looking down the path itself. There wasn't much to see. There was a bit of wind whipping by with a rustling sort of sound. It seemed like it was a cool night, but I was insulated pretty well from it inside my fencing gear.

I expected one or more of either Bastian's goblins or some other type of demon to be right outside the reactor building as guards, but they might be out further away also; I would need to be watchful. I imagined a group of goblins suddenly appearing and overwhelming me, or a swarm of imps descending on me. I felt crazy coming here, looking for a fight, when I actually had no idea how I would handle myself.

Off to my left I saw an old, small stone building. It had once belonged to a farmer, if my memory served me well from tour information I'd heard a couple of years before. Tonight, though, it was just another landmark. In the darkness I could see the outline of the B Reactor, still a short distance away ahead of me and to the right.

The road had fallen into disrepair, but was still solid in most places. It was straight but rose and fell in a few small waves over the uneven landscape. I felt vulnerable and uneasy at the troughs, but I was also nervous as I approached another apex, where a new stretch of road was just coming into view.

And then I saw an inhuman-looking sentry, maybe five meters away on the far side of a small hill. It happened to be looking away from me; my silent approach was rewarded with acute fright as I realized how close I was to it.

It had been crouching, but stood up just as I came close enough to see. It was much larger than the goblins I'd seen before. The great black ogre—I couldn't think of anything else to call it—stood a full foot taller than I did and had bulky, muscled arms and legs instead of the wiry limbs of the goblins. Its rough flesh was dark enough to blend with shadow. As it turned its head I saw stubby grey horns protruding from its brow, and great black eyes that were even darker than its skin. Large, sharp-looking teeth curved toward each other from its jaws. Somehow the teeth were dark also, with a brownish-grey color. One raised hand showed a pointed claw at the end of each finger.

I'd been startled into stillness upon first seeing it. I had expected to see Bastian's summoned minions, but this pitch-colored creature was more intimidating than anything I had envisioned. Even though the sword in my hand was familiar, and I knew it was sharp and strong, I was suddenly unsure.

I stepped to the top of the hill, keeping low and doing my best to make no noise. I could hear the ogre's raspy breathing now, as if it were sucking air through its teeth when it inhaled and growling a little when it exhaled.

I gripped my rapier's hilt, trying to mentally prepare myself for combat. I couldn't feel bad about striking the thing down, but the act of killing was foreign to me. Beyond that, as I took in the sight of the hulking monster, I wasn't sure the sword would be enough.

It would have to be, though. Trusting in my father's words from years before, when he explained that this sword was "imbued with more than merely a sharp edge", I drew it from the sheath.

And I made a faint noise by doing so.

The black ogre turned its head, and suddenly lurched toward me, faster than I expected for a creature of its size.

I had almost no time to react; I drew the blade back slightly, then thrust it straight forward, aiming for the heart.

The ogre fell toward me and I felt its weight as the handle of my rapier seemed to be stuck against it. In horrific but almost thrilling surprise I realized that my blade had found its mark and gone through the ogre's body cleanly. I had to swiftly step back and turn to the side to let the ogre's momentum carry its body past me to the ground. As it fell I held firmly to my sword and withdrew it.

The black ogre lay still.

I stood frozen in place for a little while; again, the combat had happened so fast, and I'd succeeded to an unexpected degree. The dark thing on the ground was surely dead. I'd had no chance to avoid fighting, but the moment the fight had started I had killed the ogre, without hesitating.

So that's how this was going to be...

I turned forward and continued down the road.

Fortunately, the black ogre hadn't cried out either when it saw me or when it died; such a sound could have attracted attention from any others that might have been nearby. I didn't know how many of these things Bastian had summoned, but given that fighting seemed inevitable, I didn't want to encounter any more than I needed to, especially all at once.

I also wondered again if I would see more goblins. Did the goblins and these coal-black monstrosities get along together? Did they fight each other? Did they eat each other?

One thing of which I was certain was that I had more lethal combat ahead of me. Despite the victory with my sword a moment ago I was uncertain about my technique; my father had spent a lot of time training me, but we were generally both either armed or sometimes both unarmed; he didn't teach me to attack an unarmed rival with my sword. My father had never trained me to fight demons; maybe he never expected me to encounter them, and he might have only intended my skills as a swordswoman to be used for sport. I acknowledged that the monsters weren't completely unarmed, but was I supposed to treat their claws like they were swords, or like daggers? Remembering a line from a movie I enjoyed, I reassured myself that as long as my weapon's pointy end went into the other person—or monster in this case—I would be all right.

I felt no remorse at having killed it—the *monster*. I doubted that I could strike at a person with the intent to do them much harm, but it was as Bastian had said before: these demons were unnatural and didn't belong here. When I had seen the black ogre's eyes it seemed wholly devoid of any sort of goodness; I wasn't sure it lacked intelligence, but I could feel it, all through myself, that it hadn't been something that should live and exist— not in this world, anyway, and maybe not at all. Something was just wrong about it.

Then again, I wasn't something that should exist in this world, either. The vampire side of me was no more natural than the ogre I'd killed, or the goblins or imps I'd seen in recent days. Did I deserve to be destroyed?

In any case, I had acted in self-defense. I did my best to use that fact to mentally brush aside any worries about guilt. Never mind that I was encroaching on what they considered their territory now; they shouldn't be here anyway. I couldn't afford to struggle with internal uncertainty right now, and I knew that my task was necessary for...well, for my home at least, but even, I supposed, for the world.

The cold wind brushed past me, more noticeable this time. I started walking again.

8.2

I was wary as I advanced farther. I made every effort to tread softly, but I also stopped occasionally to listen. With time, I became less patient and began to walk steadily again and then to hurry forward, trotting lightly with my blade still drawn but held to the side. I kept a measured pace that allowed me to cover ground swiftly without producing any great fatigue.

A few minutes later the blocky shape of the B Reactor building loomed ahead of me. I approached the fenced enclosure, walking cautiously past a few portable buildings. The gate of the fence was open just as the gate by the outer road had been. As I came closer to the building I wished there was more illumination; the angular outline of the top of the building showed against the night sky like a small geometric mountain, though I could see ventilation shafts breaking up the harsh angles on the right side and the tall steam stack rising up behind them. To my left, about fifty feet away from the building, a couple of engines from an old train lay on a short segment of track—just a historical display of no importance to me tonight. Just in front of the building I saw Bastian's black Jaguar, somewhat dwarfed by everything around it.

When I had first visited, I had been underwhelmed by the building's simplicity and age. I expected nuclear reactors to have a high-tech sort of look, but this building had an ordinary sort of industrial appearance. Tonight that appearance was ominous in the still night.

The main entrance of the building, the one I had entered during my tour years before, was right in front of me. The heavy steel outer doors had been pushed aside along their tracks, allowing access to swinging double glass doors. So far, I was alone as I drew near to it.

When I was only about twenty feet away, a person became visible through the doors; the person pushed one door open to step outside, and I realized that it was Abbott, without his regular suit jacket and gloves, and looking somewhat disheveled.

He saw me almost as soon as I saw him. His eyes went wide at the sight of my raised and dirtied sword, and he reeled back. "Get her!!!" he called out to unseen parties, stumbling backward and almost falling, "Intruder! Kill her! Kill her!!"

I hurried forward to pursue him, but as he backpedaled into the building another great black horned ogre came rushing toward me from the side, roaring as it loped.

I spun toward it, raising my weapon high above and behind me with the point toward the demon. It seemed to see the blade and slowed before it reached me, but failed to stop outside of the reach of my sword. Stepping forward with my rear foot I lunged with a flèche attack and was relieved to see the tip of my blade strike the chest of the beast. It screamed out and retreated several steps, but stayed on its feet. Looking back at me again it appeared ready to attack me in return, but I swung across, slashing its chest, then lunged again, piercing it once and then again more deeply. It let forth a low, breathy sound that was less a growl than a grunt. I pulled the sword away again and struck across once more at it, knocking it down, though the last strike was unnecessary.

Although Abbott had stopped fleeing at first to see the beast attack me, he must have also seen it fall and had run away within the reactor building to hide. I followed after him as fast as I felt I could safely run with my sword still drawn; it seemed wisest to keep it unsheathed.

I pushed one of the glass doors open and stepped inside. I tried to remember the layout of the building. A narrow hall lay to my left; the control room was beyond. A room was open to my right; but Abbott didn't seem to be inside. The large hall I was in extended further ahead of me with several doorways on either side. The paint on the walls was familiar; through much of the building it was green from the floor to a line about four feet high, and white above that. Doors were painted the same dull green. Directly in front of me, at the end, closed double doors with illuminated signs above them marked one of the entrances to the reactor room. A couple of display cases in the hall had been knocked over.

I heard Abbott's voice from some hidden place. "Is that you, Maria?" His voice echoed along the walls. "Have you come to court the demon master?" He laughed aloud. "Are you looking for a kiss?"

I gritted my teeth; I had no desire to respond to his petty taunts. He must not have been near the control room next to me; I continued walking forward, glancing to my left and right, seeking him out.

A low rumble sounded from somewhere ahead of me, perhaps in the reactor room itself. It was an animal sound; it might have been a subdued roar or a groan, but whatever it was, it must have been made by something large. Was it one of the black ogres, or some other kind of monstrosity that Bastian had summoned? I had paused upon hearing the roar, but as it died down I continued walking.

Abbott's voice rang out. "I hope you brought a good rock to impress him. Something shiny. That seems to win him over, right?"

At that he laughed again. It was a loud, arrogant laugh. I hated that he found himself so entertaining. I kept moving forward; while he was still in mid-laugh, he came into view on my right, just inside the entrance to the valve pit room. We caught sight of each other at the same time; he abruptly stopped laughing and dashed away without giving me a second glance. I ran after him, careful to hold my unsheathed sword to the side and behind me to avoid accidentally injuring myself or striking nearby objects.

I passed through the doorway into the valve pit room. The floor under my feet became metal grating, which I knew only ran along the sides of the room; my vision had been mostly obstructed upon entering, but memory flashed through my mind and I recalled the room generally. Because the old atomic reactor had generated such intense heat during its past operation, a coolant was required. Water from the Columbia River had been pumped through the reactor at high speeds and volumes in order to absorb the heat before the water was released again into the river. In the more open part of the room, at the lower level, were many large pipes. They were opened conspicuously for the sake of inspectors from foreign powers, who ostensibly wanted to ensure that the United States was keeping its part of a nuclear non-proliferation agreement.

There were also many exits from the room, including another door to the reactor itself, though it was clear that he had not moved toward that way. He instead ran toward the outer edge of the building.

He was fast; I was always fleet-footed myself, but I had difficulty catching up to him as he dodged behind various objects and rounded corners in this place I didn't know well.

As I followed him down a hallway, I had only a brief warning from the sound of heavy footsteps approaching before two more black ogres came running down the corridor at us. Abbott twisted and ran around them; they seemed to ignore him and continued toward me.

I slowed in an attempt to stop, but before I gained solid footing or brought my sword to bear on the new aggressors I found myself too close to them. One of them lashed out with a claw, striking my left shoulder and spinning me to the ground as I grunted in pain. The other ogre leaped at me but I rolled away, coming back to my feet. I had held onto my sword as I fell and rolled, and I was able to bring it forward as I stood again.

The second ogre partially blocked the one that had struck me, and as they jostled each other I had a few seconds to backpedal and regroup. I cried out softly against the ache in my shoulder; while the monster's claws hadn't penetrated my jacket, its swipe at me had been fierce. I could still move my left arm well enough, so my injury couldn't have been as bad as a broken bone, but it hurt and I was glad that the monster hadn't struck my sword arm. In a passing moment I almost wished I had brought a shield from my father's armory, or even a small buckler, to absorb the force of attacks, but I'd never trained much with shields, so they would only be marginally helpful anyway.

I was retreating into a more open space, a room with World-War-II-era objects strewn about in disarray, as the black ogres advanced toward me. I realized my mistake when the two creatures used the space to move to either side, attempting to put me between them. I wasn't sure I should back up any further. In an effort to keep them at bay I swung my sword widely first at one, then the other in tall arcs. After several slashes I saw one shifting to move toward me once my sword had moved past it. It pounced, but I continued a turning movement while dropping to a knee and bringing the point of my rapier back toward it just in time to thrust it forward into the ogre. Again the blade went deep, and the weight of the monster pushed me down. I moved to the side just barely enough to avoid having the ogre's body pin me to the floor, but while dodging I lost my grip on my sword.

I turned and repositioned my feet so as to stand back up, but before I could lift my head to locate the other monster again I felt its claw swipe against my chest and I fell backwards.

I attempted to roll backwards over one shoulder, but succeeded only in flopping to my side, landing awkwardly on the sword sheath at my hip. My hand bumped against some smallish, hard object; without knowing what it was, I grabbed it and hurled it at the ogre. I was rewarded in seeing the object strike the monster in the face and bounce off. With a yell of surprised pain it stepped back once, putting its hands over a wounded eye.

Without waiting I stood and hurried toward it. I dropped low and delivered a partially ineffectual kick to the inside of its right knee with my right leg, followed by a mostly ineffectual left palm strike to its gut, after which I fell off balance and stumbled back a few steps. I had only a moment before it turned its attention back to me, but in that moment I grabbed my dagger from my exposed boot sheath and rushed forward, driving the dagger up and into the ogre's chest. I kept pressing forward as the ogre weakly retreated before backing into a wall; with a gurgling release of its last breath it slumped forward to the ground and I had to step backward to stay out of its way.

And for a moment I could slow down and breathe.

I glanced around to make sure that no other ogres were near, and then tried to lift the fallen brute enough to retrieve my dagger, but the weapon was now at a difficult angle and with the pain in my left shoulder I was unable to pull it free. With a frustrated sigh I let go of the ogre and looked for the other one I had impaled with my sword. It wasn't far away, and thankfully I found that my rapier was still accessible from the way the monster had collapsed. With some effort I withdrew it from the ogre's body, trying to ignore the sound it made against the ogre's rough skin as it came out.

Having retrieved my sword I sat on the ground and gave myself a few seconds to rest. My once-spotless-grey fencing gear now had many stains of dark ogre blood. I felt great relief that I could see none of my own. The reality of my fighting began to strike me, and I felt shock. I started to worry that I might be overcome by the horror of the situation, but then I again thought of Abbott and of Bastian. Remembering my purpose, I rose to my feet, shrugging off the aching shoulder. The sword sheath had proved to be a bit awkward; I undid it and the dagger sheath and set them on the floor against a wall. I wouldn't want to sheathe my sword until it had been cleaned, and assuming things went well I'd need to come back here for my dagger anyway.

"Maybe these were the last of them," I wishfully muttered to myself to break the silence a bit, taking a last glance at the remains of the two ogres as I walked into the next room.

Heavier steps sounded ahead of me. I halted, leaned forward, and raised my rapier to the level of my eyes, with the point directed upward at pair of ogre eyes.

This black ogre was larger than any I'd seen yet. It also stopped walking forward, seeming to take the extended sword into account, but it didn't seem daunted. Beyond reason, it almost seemed to be smiling, as if amused. Maybe it thought I was foolish to challenge such a large opponent.

Even if it was entertained, I was unquestionably not in a light mood. I began to raise my left arm behind me for balance, but feeling the ache again I instead held it much lower than I would have preferred. I wasted no time and took steady strides forward, bringing up my rear foot several inches at a time and then stepping in turn with my forward foot, making the movement smooth and keeping my weapon trained on the hulk in front of me.

It also stepped toward me, and without warning swung a massive claw down. I brought the point of my rapier up and drove it into the fat forearm, and then withdrew it swiftly as the ogre also drew back. The ogre began a low growl, as if preparing to attack again, but I gave it no opportunity. I rushed forward before it could react and with all the speed I could muster stabbed into its chest as high as I could reasonably reach. I immediately backed off again to judge the effectiveness of my attack.

The huge black ogre stepped back, and its grin was now definitely a great, toothy grimace. Then it moved forward again with claws extended at me. I struck at each of its arms in turn, and using the resulting opening I thrust my sword again into the body of the ogre. This time I struck lower, into the beast's belly, not just once, but twice. Again I retreated after striking.

The ogre took one short, stumbling step forward with one leg, and dropped to the other knee. I debated internally about whether I should strike again. The demon heaved a great sigh, then a growl, and then a nearly silent gasp as it fell sideways. Thudding on the floor, its frown still showed clearly. I could hear its soft but labored breathing; the sound wasn't quite right, and I figured that I must have pierced one of its lungs.

I let my sword point drop. So far I'd taken these ogres to be nothing more than monsters, but this thing, lying on the floor and dying, seemed to be in pain. Somehow when I could see it in pain I could no longer be so sure about it. No matter how evil it was, no matter how unnatural, I didn't want it to be in agony.

I only wanted to end it—to end the creature's pain, and its existence.

Its labored breathing again became a growl, a feral sound. It rapidly cleared away my hesitation, my feelings that had almost turned to something like sympathy. I came close enough to pierce its chest one more time, aiming for its heart. Whether or not I found that exact target I wasn't sure, but the final attack had the desired effect. One claw reach toward me again and then dropped, and the ogre became still.

I wasn't sure how much more of this I could take. It still felt, with each ogre that I killed, that I was righting a wrong, that I was putting an end to things that should never have started. But the violence of it all was something I'd never known, and it was something I was sure I still didn't want to know. I didn't like it. I didn't like ending a life—even that of a demon—and I hated feeling that it was necessary to do something so brutal. It was nauseating.

As it was, this particular bit of violence was over. My undertaking tonight wasn't. "Brody!" I called. "Where are you?" I wasn't sure which way to go now; I'd already passed through much of the building, and it wasn't a labyrinth, but I didn't know it well. I took a side passage and after another turn I saw another entrance to the reactor room just ahead of me, beyond a concrete archway.

"Poor Maria!" he called back. "Whatever it is that you're here for, you should turn back! You're only in for disappointment." While he spoke those last words, his voice grew louder. Suddenly, as I rounded a corner, he was right in front of me and we collided. He must have tried to double back and slip past me, but he had guessed the wrong route for my approach. He bounced off to my right, stumbling while trying to regain his step. Before he could run again I had my sword point at his throat; he leaned backward against large machinery behind him to try to avoid it. His eyes went wide as he felt it, but then his expression went dark, and his lips curled into a sneer. "Are you going to kill me, Maria?"

"I'm here to stop this. I don't want to kill anyone, but I'm not going to let you go on with it."

"The really amusing part is that you actually think you *can* stop it. What's not amusing is that you don't understand the need for a horde of monsters to roam again on the earth."

"Need? Are you totally nuts? What kind of need could we possibly have for demons?"

"First, get that away from my throat. If you slipped you could kill me."

I was sure I wouldn't "slip", and I was quite satisfied to be in a dominant position with him, but his words gave me just a moment of pause; perhaps using the sword point really was too threatening for him to speak. I pulled back only slightly and then angled my blade to the side and brought the base of it close to his neck, forcing him again to lean back. "With one movement I *could* kill you. Now what are you talking about? What could be good about demons running amok?"

His eyes and sneer belied clear dissatisfaction with the presence of the sword, but he spoke. "I didn't say it was good. I said it was *needed*. Don't tell me you're so blind to what the world is. Don't tell me you can't see the decadence and corruption that grow worse in society with every day. Indeed, 'the love of man waxes cold'. Callousness, hatred, and greed are now the norm. Our modern cultures are revolting." He paused, intensity in his eyes. "The people of our day need to be punished, and humbled, and purged of the filth they choose to absorb at an ever-increasing pace. Then they need to be governed by rulers who won't allow them to ruin themselves. They need to live in enough fear and pain that they won't have reason to inflict fear and pain on others. They need to be controlled, and you know what? They often secretly crave it. Freedom can be such a burden, and they abuse it. They won't abuse it for much longer, though. If I understand the ancient writings correctly, they won't have a chance of defying Bastian. Humans are making advances in the technology of war all the time, but with an endless army of the Terrors of Hell even the fanciest rifles and bombs would only be cheap insulation against the cleansing fires he'll unleash."

I was stunned by what he said. Part of it didn't make any sense, though. "He never said anything about that. He didn't want to destroy anything."

"He didn't know what the stones would do to him, either. There were portions of the old writings that he never saw, because I kept them from him, and not even I had a full appreciation for what would happen. The idiot. He always wanted to explain everything away so scientifically, but he understood little more than his own trivial alchemy. Hah. He doesn't have to worry about that anymore."

"What do you mean?"

Abbott smiled a pleasure-less smile. "If you go to see Bastian now, you'll find that he's very different from when you saw him last. He is changed. You won't recognize him, and I doubt that he will recognize you. He won't talk to you. He'll probably try to kill you." He sounded pleased by that idea.

"…I don't believe it. Why wouldn't he recognize me?"

His wicked smile formed into a sharp grimace. "Maria, I'm telling you, the Stones have changed him! He's not even human anymore. What he told you before about gaining the power to summon demons was true, in a way, but it's much more than that. He all but gives *birth* to them. He's not the same person you knew. He's not even a person anymore!"

"You're lying."

"Hah. I have no reason to lie. Not any longer, not now that my purposes are accomplished. Don't you see, Maria? I've already won! And I don't mind gloating about if even if you are threatening to kill me. I tricked Bastian into becoming the monster I needed him to become, just like I tricked you and Amy into helping me. And here you are now, coming to try and stop him from using the Stones, but the ritual is already done. It's over. You can't stop it now or undo what has already happened. Even if you can dispatch a handful of demons, you can't prevent the coming destruction."

I didn't restrain myself any longer; I let the blade come away from him as I crouched slightly, then threw him to the side into a wall. He hit it and caught himself on his feet.

He grunted. "I suppose you feel that hurting me might do some good, but my part is done here. Nothing you do to me will change anything. I'm leaving now while this place isn't overrun by bloodthirsty creatures. I've got to find out how to gain full control of Bastian's army."

"Brody, I'll make you pay for what you've done."

"Oh, no, you won't. Come, now. You'll let me walk away in innocence. You didn't come here to see me. You're here to see Bastian." He laughed with rage. "Well. Go to him!" He gestured toward the large sliding door as he took several steps away. "Seek him, if you like. All you'll find is despair!"

I stared at the door as Abbott fled. I expended no further thought on him. All I could think of was Bastian and the terrible notion that the man for whom I had felt such powerful feelings was no longer a man. Without even being sure how much I could trust Abbott, somehow I sensed an inevitable horror and anguish.

To punctuate the growing dread inside me, another roar emanated from the reactor room, like what I'd heard after entering the building. It was louder than what I'd heard before, and was accented by a couple of rough barks at the end. It was surely no black ogre making such a large noise. A dull thud followed and the building shook a bit—as if something large had fallen to the ground or struck a wall—and then the building grew quiet.

Staring at the door and unable to picture what might lie beyond, I only knew that I wished I could somehow undo everything that had occurred. I wished I could become a little girl again, innocent and free from the cares I'd come to know. I even wished that I had never met Bastian, and never known the wonderfully sweet emotion that I'd had for him—that I *still* had for him despite my knowledge of his pettiness and his brutal treachery.

Yet, the stillness around me demanded my action. There was nothing to distract me from my purpose; I had no options but to retreat, delay, or go ahead. One of those was my clear choice.

I reached for the door, slid it open, and walked forward.

9

From memory, I knew what the reactor room looked like.

The ceiling was very high, maybe forty feet, to accommodate the reactor. The back wall and two side walls were plain, with the same green and white paint scheme, though the white stretched high up to the distant ceiling. The walls had little more on them than a few pipes and rails. Lower were several displays with historical items and explanations of both the process of controlled nuclear fission and the original site layout. These were all now in a state of considerable disarray. One wall ahead of me was in fact not a wall at all but the reactor itself, built from thousands of graphite blocks laid row upon row in a vast grid. Most of the blocks, aside from some at the corners and edges, had holes drilled through them to accommodate the uranium fuel rods, which, years ago, were inserted using the mechanical "METAL LOADER", as it was labeled off to the right; they later dropped out behind the reactor. The thousands of squarely-aligned holes on the face of the reactor had extending tubes that were covered with blunt caps. The uranium loader itself was on a horizontal rack that spanned the width of the reactor, and which, during its operational years, could move up and down as needed. The top of the loader was currently about twelve feet above the floor, higher than I remembered it.

With a quick glance I took in quite a bit of the mostly familiar room, but as I stepped inside, memory gave way to reflex and I leaped forward, away from a huge fist that came crashing down onto the floor behind me.

I whirled about, and then backpedaled in wide-eyed stupor as I witnessed the most horrific sight I'd ever seen.

An immense demon crouched in the corner of the room. Much larger than the ogres I'd fought, it might have been twenty feet tall. Its skin was dark and mottled, in colors I couldn't quite call black, brown, or purple. The skin was loose and wrinkled, but didn't hide the muscles of the enormous body. The face was twisted, lumpy, and dark, though not completely inhuman. Its eyes seemed to be all pupil. A mess of long, matted black hair grew from its head and reached in shorter lengths down its shoulders and chest.

The creature heaved with each breath, as if it were exhausted. It was turned slightly, probably as a result of trying to reach for me when I'd entered, though now it stayed still with its fist in the same place it had struck a moment ago. From the way it was twisted I could see its back, which was unevenly covered in large, smooth, bulbous areas.

On the walls and the floor around it there were splotches and layers of some sort of filth. I could scarcely guess at what it was. Excrement? Secretions? Some of it looked slimy, as if recently dropped or thrown.

Then I noticed the smell. Whether it was the filth around the huge monster, or the monster itself, or probably both, something was giving off a terrible odor, like rot and disease.

The demon slowly withdrew its arm, still bent over as if too weak to stand upright. There was no other noise in the vast room other than the monster's laborious breathing. It gradually stood and turned toward me.

What I saw next brought a shiver through my whole body.

The enormous beast wore a pendant around its neck, suspended by a chain that was far too tight and pressed into the skin underneath. The pendant was simple and oval-shaped, with a large green emerald and a misshapen chunk of obsidian embedded next to each other in the center.

No.

No, that couldn't be Bastian.

Abbott's words came back to me: Bastian was "not human anymore"; he had become "a monster". This vile behemoth before me wore the same pendant that Bastian had shown me in his dungeon.

The combined power of the Demon Stone and the Life Stone had hideously mutated and enlarged Bastian's body. I was mute with shock; it was hard to conceive of such a transformation, and even worse, such a transformation happening to *Bastian*.

The ties across links of the chain hung, broken, on either side. They must have snapped as Bastian's body grew larger and larger, turning into this thing in front of me.

Was he still himself, in his mind? As his body changed, did the alchemy leave his essence inside the shell, or was he altogether gone? Did he still know the world, the people in it? Did he still know me?

I had to find out.

"Bastian, it's me, Maria!"

He looked back and forth, seeming to scan the room, but gave no indication of recognizing me or even caring much that I was there.

"Bastian!" He stood still. "Don't you know me?"

His black eyes looked at me but only glistened stupidly.

I began to walk toward him—or it—still stunned but wanting to see him better, but before I took a third step one of its great arms swiped out at me, then swiped back again. It was too far away now to quite reach me, but it seemed to have the intention of either harming me or shooing me away.

It was definitely an "it" now. Bastian had *become* Luctus, the demon summoner, an embodiment of grief. *He* was no more; there was only *it*.

It lifted itself slightly but before bringing itself fully upright it fell forward again with a loud grunt. Its breathing began to be labored. I couldn't see any injury, but it seemed to be hurt.

Then the monster heaved and lurched to the side, falling to one knee, with arms outstretched to brace itself against the horizontal frame of the uranium loader. It let out a sort of bark, deep and rough, then reached high and clawed downward against the reactor, popping off several of the caps that covered the reactor's fuel insertion tubes. The uranium loader rack shuddered under Luctus' weight, and seemed to bend slightly. As the fallen caps clattered to the floor I wondered if there might be some danger from radiation, but immediately dismissed the thought. The reactor had been inert for decades, and was even a public tour spot.

Luctus growled again, low, almost hissing. One of the largest of the mounds on its back began to quiver, changing shape as if something was moving within. It looked as if it were about to erupt, and then it suddenly burst as first a clawed hand, then arm, and then an entire, hideous body spewed out onto the ground with a wet slap.

The newly born creature was a dark ash color and covered with grey slime. It writhed on the ground, lashing out with limbs as if grasping for something. Though not as dark as the monsters I'd fought earlier, I could see that the basic features were the same.

Then I understood. This was one of the black ogres at the beginning of its life; this was how they came into being. This was the purpose of the ceremony for "summoning" demons.

As the parent sat back on its haunches to rest, the new ogre stumbled to its feet, attempting to scrub or swipe away the slime from its face. If it wasn't actually summoned or transported from somewhere else, but instead created, it must have had instinct; it was already upright and aware of its surroundings.

As I stared in horror, the colossal and grotesque monster that once was Bastian turned its head to look back at me with a hollow gaze, still showing no sign of recognition. Almost immediately, though, it began a low, guttural growl that built up into a roar. The newly born ogre, as if in response to a command, locked its eyes on me and began to walk forward with its claws outstretched.

It walked slowly and unsteadily, though. I was unsure of what to make of Luctus, but I knew what had to be done with these black ogres. I felt no hesitation as I strode several steps forward to meet it, then lunged forward with a full-voiced cry, piercing the ogre through the chest with my rapier. It halted silently, the surprise evident on its grotesque face, but then its features began to droop.

Face to face with this ogre that had just been born, I'd become rapidly uncertain that I'd needed to kill it; while it had surely been moving to attack, it obviously was no match for me. There was no use in letting it live, but it struck me as unfair that it should be created in the first place, with death as its only destiny. I held my sword in place for several seconds, and as the ogre faltered I withdrew my blade, sobbing once and withdrawing a couple of steps as I did so. I looked down on its crumpled form, and its pained visage, as its blood dripped from the tip of my lowered sword. Even though I knew I needed to kill this ogre, its death so soon after its birth struck me as terribly tragic, as was its very existence.

It was good that I had kept a bit of distance from Luctus; I found myself needing to dodge one of Luctus' massive arms as it lashed out at me again. I could tell that the abomination was exhausted, though; it remained resting on one knee and, after the unrepeated swipe braced itself with both arms and paid me no more attention.

I stood, appalled and noiseless, unsure of what to do in the face of this monstrosity. There was slight motion within several other large, bulbous humps, like a sort of churning. It looked like another of them was almost ready to erupt. There were more ogres growing there, right on the larger monster's back, waiting to be developed enough to burst out. I then saw that there were many smaller bumps, seemingly only waiting their turn to swell and house a new fiendish creation.

Bastian had meant to "summon" a demonic army, but no portal to another world was needed. This was how it would be done.

How often did Luctus birth them? How long would it continue? I couldn't know how long his transformation had taken, but he must have been this way for only a matter of hours; certainly less than a day. How many had I killed? Six? Seven? I couldn't remember. Perhaps he would spawn another ogre in as little as an hour or so. Maybe less. I doubted that there were any others on the premises; I hoped I'd killed all of them. I was confident that I could kill the next if I lingered long enough for it to be born, but there was no reason to wait that long to solve the larger problem. The monster that was or had been Bastian was certainly going to keep on producing these atrocities, for an indefinite period of time. If I was going to prevent the arrival of more black ogres, I had to stop the parent.

Certainly if I were to kill Luctus it would stop, but I wasn't sure my rapier was enough to do the job, and though Luctus paid me no heed for the moment it would surely defend itself if attacked. As large as it was, I was unlikely to kill it with a single stab, even if placed well, and if it focused its strength on killing me I'd be finished with one hit from its huge fists.

More importantly, even if it were possible for me to put it to death, I wasn't sure I could bring myself to do it. This thing had been the young man I cared for. It didn't even recognize me now, but maybe there was a way to undo what had been done. Maybe I could find some way to bring him back to humanity…or maybe not. There was no way I could know what was left of the Bastian I'd loved or if it was possible to see him again as a normal human. Was he lost forever to the form of this monster? I'd come here doubting that I could kill Bastian even to stop him from unleashing demons upon the world, and faced with the titanic brute he'd become…

Part of me *wanted* to kill it. I hated Luctus not just for being a monster, but for having been the man for whom I'd felt so much. I hated Bastian for allowing himself to become this…thing. But again I knew I could not go through with it.

And anyway, it was huge, and all I had was a thin sword.

But maybe…maybe it wasn't all I had after all. Bastian had said that it was the Stones, combined in a pendant, which gave the power to summon the demons. The enchanted jewels had always been the enablers, and even now Luctus wore them. The pendant must have been providing the force by which these things were created, as there was no visible source of food here in the reactor room, and thus no source of body mass. Well, perhaps there had been food before; maybe that was partly why there was muck encrusted on the walls and floor around the creature. Either way, the pendant was what had made this possible, and I might be able to stop it all by destroying it. Then again, maybe the process was irreversible, and the pendant's job was already done, but I guessed that the monster was still relying on the enchantment's power. I had to try to destroy the pendant, just as I had intended before I knew that the Stones had already been used. Fortunately, I had the tool I needed. Hopefully.

I reached for the Seeker in my pocket and withdrew it. As I held it toward the jeweled pendant, it grew uncomfortably warm. I quickly replaced it.

But how to get to the pendant? I needed to get close enough to put the Seeker directly in contact with it, or if the Seeker didn't work, close enough to try to rip the pendant off. On the gargantuan creature's neck, it was far too high for me to reach while standing on the ground.

But Luctus was still leaning against the reactor. Perhaps the reactor wall itself…the surface appeared to be scalable. If I were to climb up on the protruding ends of the tubes, I could get on top of the uranium loader rack. I couldn't be sure, but I guessed they would hold my weight and would provide good hand- and footholds; how solidly attached were the caps? High above me on either side of the reactor were small platforms with rails obviously intended to prevent a person's fall, but I could see no ladder from here that would provide easy access to those heights. Scaling the face of the reactor and moving across the uranium loader rack was the only clear way for me to get to the pendant.

Circling around the room in a half crouch, never letting my eyes off of Luctus, I approached the reactor. I kept as far away from Luctus as possible. As it looked in my general direction I couldn't tell if it was really seeing me.

When I reached the metal railing in front of the reactor, I realized I would need to lay my sword on the ground in order to climb. I placed the blade next to the wall, with Luctus' empty stare on me constantly, then vaulted the railing and stepped next to the reactor.

I was glad the rack of the uranium loader was at a fairly low position; it was going to be tricky climbing the reactor. I gripped the caps over the fuel holes with one arm and then the other, then lifted my feet up on them as well. I was able to move slowly upward, stepping on other caps, keeping my legs a bit wide to push against the side of the small round caps for a better grip. As I neared the rack I looked up to see how close I was, and I reached simultaneously for my next handhold. Suddenly the cap under my left hand slipped off, and my heart lurched in my chest and skipped a beat as I nearly fell, but I quickly caught on again and just held still for several seconds. I reassured myself that I wasn't all that far off the floor, so I had little reason to fear personal injury, but all the same I was eager to finish the precarious climb.

I heard a shifting noise from Luctus and I began to worry that the monster might move away before I could get to the top of the rack. Glancing over at it, I saw that it had closed its eyes, as if it was asleep. Its breathing seemed steady. I continued my awkward climb upward.

The gap between the rack and the reactor was only barely wide enough to fit through. As soon as I could reach the top of the rack I got a handhold and used it to pull myself up on top, relying mostly on my uninjured right arm. I was grateful to be off the troublesome caps. Looking at Luctus again, I saw it as it was before, unmoving apart from its huge torso rising and falling evenly with its breathing.

I pulled the Seeker out and waved it toward Luctus. As it passed by the pendant it again warmed almost instantly; the heat reached me easily through my glove. It struck me as a foolish move; if it had burned my hand I might have dropped it to the floor below.

I took several steps toward the monster. As I neared it, I was practically assaulted by the stench, now much sharper up close. Luctus reeked with an odor worse than anything I could imagine the earth producing naturally. I wavered in my step and had to brace myself with both hands to avoid falling over. I tried to only breathe through my mouth; after half a minute or so I found that I could stand and walk again.

Having mostly overcome the smell, the grotesqueness and size of the thing also struck me more than when I had seen it from a distance. Had that malformed face truly been Bastian's?

The way its head was bowed would make the pendant hard to reach, but first I needed to get over the arm it was using to rest on the rack. Its elbow was right in front of me, preventing me from walking any further on the rack itself. This was going to be trickier than I had expected, and I was suddenly unsure that I would be able to reach the pendant at all…but I had to try.

Holding the Seeker carefully, and making sure it didn't point toward the pendant, I reached and pulled myself up onto the wrinkled elbow.

Luctus' eyes opened. It looked up at me and stopped breathing.

It was still for a half-second, with me only a few feet away from its head.

Then its head lifted and I could feel and smell its foul breath as it first exhaled lowly, then roared with a volume that pained my ears. I had no time to spare in hesitation, though; I sensed its arm moving beneath me. When it raised its head it opened up the space in front of the pendant. Against the onrush of rank air, I leaped forward, reaching out with my free hand for the thing's matted hair near its chin.

My hand found purchase, just in time; I held on with all my strength as Luctus began to stand up, roaring all the while. I dangled precariously, far above the floor, but soon came to rest against the repugnant chest and shoulder of the fiend.

Now was the time.

I swung the Seeker up and over, reaching for the pendant and driving the rod in my hand toward the embedded jewels. I drove into the pendant as hard as I could, feeling the Seeker beginning to burn in my hand. Almost like the peal of a bell, a shrill tone from the Seeker rang out and then grew louder and louder as the rod itself grew hotter.

In the briefest of moments I sensed movement behind me before a massive hand gripped my body. I heard a deafening crack and a burst of light blinded me at the same time as I felt myself lifted away by the huge claw. It flung me and I felt a fleeting weightlessness before crashing into a wall, taking the brunt of the impact on my head and injured shoulder. I slumped to the floor, partially blinded, in desperate pain, and completely dazed.

Lying on the floor, I heard a great, low groan of pain that seemed to come from all around me. I was deaf to my own grunts in the face of such a sound. I had rolled forward after falling, and had to lift myself on one arm to view the results of my effort. Opening my eyes, I found myself surprisingly far from Luctus. The monstrosity ahead of me slowly lurched and sunk to its knees. The pendant was simply gone, as if it had melted, leaving only a single large piece hanging from the length of chain on the monster's left side.

Luctus shuddered, once, twice, and then a third time; pieces of dark grey flesh began to fall in dry clumps to the ground, clapping dustily as they struck. Its breathing became labored and loud, and it held out its arms as if trying to grasp something that wasn't there. It quivered again; as the pieces of skin and other tissue fell off, the thing began to be smaller. Though in stunning pain, and almost unable to keep my head up, I could see his transformation occurring in reverse, and as I saw some change take place I expected to see the thing turn back into the boy I had known. As I watched I forgot my pain as hope in Bastian's return ignited. Riveted, I watched as layers of flesh fell to the ground in shapeless globs, and the form underneath grew more humanlike. Was that shadow his dark, glossy hair? Was that Bastian's mouth? Were those the hands that had touched me? It seemed that even his cry was becoming more human.

The strange hope grew within me. Maybe things would be fine after all. The pendant was destroyed, and with it the summoner of demons.

Maybe Bastian was returning.

And yet I didn't know how to handle that hope. On one hand, although Bastian had committed evil, I abhorred the literal monster he'd become and I wouldn't want even a villain to be condemned to such a form. But still, while I had loved him, he had betrayed me. What did hope even mean now?

The pieces of his monster body that fell to the ground seemed to immediately begin a rapid decomposition, each breaking down quickly into a chunky goo. The humps on the abomination's back had also sloughed off in turn, showing the outline of partially-formed ogres underneath the outer tissue. The largest of these unborn monsters writhed inside its fleshy shell for several seconds before becoming still and also starting the quick decomposition.

The monster's groan ended; it abruptly brought its arms tight to its chest, clenched them there for several sickening seconds, and then as it let loose with a terrible, agonized scream it punched one fist downward into the floor, snapping its own bones in the process with horrific cracking sounds. Still falling apart, and seeming to shrink at the same time, it stumbled forward, reaching with its one good arm, and collapsed in front of me, forcing me to sit back against the wall to avoid it.

The echoes of its scream reverberated and died away.

With the silence, my hope, however confused it had been, now melted into that familiar ache of loss that had overcome me after his betrayal.

I could now see a more humanlike body lying mostly face-down in front of me. The flesh was still grey, severely oversized, and misshapen, the hands and feet were still claw-like, and the bony spine still bespoke an inhuman nature, but I recognized features in his face—wrinkled and rough, and not quite returned to his former self, but distantly familiar to me again. One difference was sadly obvious, though. There was nothing left of the once-beautiful black hair.

And its eyes, or his eyes, were dull, without a hint of the lustrous blue they once held, and without a hint of life. Dark liquid trickled from his open frown onto the floor.

He lay still.

Death.

This was death before me, in greater ugliness than I would ever expect to see again.

It made me feel detached from the world as I viewed the carcass on the floor before me. In death Bastian became constant: forever broken and corrupt. It was utterly clear that a return to his former appearance—or in any meaningful way, his former essence of self—was not meant to be.

After passing an unknown time in aching stupor, I began to reach toward him, maybe to close his hollow eyes, or to try to be of help *somehow*, but I then stopped myself as I came to my senses again. Even if it were possible to interfere with the consequences he had brought upon himself, I had no desire to try, and no desire to sully myself in the attempt.

An array of thunderously loud sounds had echoed through the vast reactor room only minutes before, but now it was absolutely silent except for the soft noise of my own breathing, still rough and tortured.

I glanced around, still finding myself alone with the remains of monsters. I wasn't sure right away what to do next. My task was complete. The Demon Stone was destroyed, with the Life Stone. Bastian was…no longer a danger. There wasn't anyone around to fight, or to address. I became vaguely aware that tears had run down my cheeks, and there was a new pain in the palm and fingers of my right hand.

The smell of the dead monster flesh around me abruptly hit me, and I brought the back of my left hand to my nose to ward off the stench. I backpedaled also, and bumped gently into the wall behind me again. Off to my left I saw my discarded rapier on the floor, and I moved to pick it up. Realizing that I had nothing left to do here, I turned and walked out through the double doors, with barely enough presence of mind not to let my sword clatter on the ground or in the doorway.

I encountered no resistance as I made my way home.

9.1

My mind was dull as I travelled.

There just wasn't anything that I wanted to think about. Memory brought the unpleasantness of blighted love, betrayal, shame, filth, and death, while wonderings about the future provided ample amounts of uncertainty and lost hope. So I restricted myself to recognizing my current state and several trivial details of the world around me, but even thoughts of the present mostly came to my messy outfit and the physical pain I was in. Rather than deal with any of that, I tried not to think about anything at all. It didn't work well, but I ultimately just didn't know what to make of everything that had happened in the last few days, so I ended up stumbling back to my car in a pained stupor, then driving home slowly but carefully enough not to get in an accident.

I'd had enough presence of mind to take care of at least a few necessities. Fortunately, on my way out of the building (undoubtedly forever) I'd managed to push aside the rapidly rotting remains of a black ogre and retrieve my dagger, as well as my weapon sheaths nearby. I'd even closed the gate at the edge of the site, near where I'd parked. It seemed almost senseless to add that tiny amount of order to the area after leaving such messy carnage behind, but maybe it helped me feel better somehow. While driving, I used my turn signals even though for most of the drive there were no other cars around to see it.

Sometimes I accidentally let myself decelerate to under half the speed limit and puttered on slowly for a while before I caught myself. Otherwise, I continued without further incident until I was nearly home.

And then in an odd surge of chance or fate, the car stopped. The engine suddenly sputtered and then turned off. The vehicle coasted gradually to a halt a few blocks away from my house. I had to crank the steering wheel to get it to the side of the road, but I eventually parked roughly against a curb. I sat in the car for perhaps several minutes as if I expected it to start up again. I couldn't fathom what the problem might be, and I had no energy to investigate and figure it out. Then, in a mild flash of inspiration, I checked the gas gauge, which was on empty.

Simultaneously, I found that my composure was drained. Tears welled up rapidly in my eyes and then flowed freely. It seemed silly for me to have let this happen, especially when I was sure I had passed several gas stations, and even sillier that I would be so close to home when the car gave out. I leaned forward against the steering wheel and let myself weep. But between sweat, grit, and extra layers of clothing, I began to feel coarsely warm and itchy.

Eventually I staggered out of the car and started walking the rest of the way home.

The last time I'd passed by the sentry statues in front of my father's house I'd been hurried to get home to safety. They had always, in general, provided that feeling of security, but this time they didn't strike me quite the same way. There was simply no further danger, nothing from which they would protect me. The lack of feeling was only a smaller part of the pervasive numbness that was lingering with me after leaving the reactor site. Passing the maidens again gave me a sense of welcome, but it was muted. Finding the front door locked again also failed to produce an emotional response within me. Mechanically, I struck the knocker several times.

Then I stood in silence—impatiently. After all I'd gone through tonight I just wanted to go inside, and waiting for my mother to answer was just slightly maddening. Fortunately, she didn't take long to reach and open the door.

"Maria!"

As soon as she opened the front door and saw me she pulled me inside, shut the door again and re-locked it, and then quickly embraced me by holding my head to her shoulder.

"Maria, you don't know how I've worried for you."

I kept my arms out to the side as she held me, with my now-sheathed sword in one hand and my mask and dagger in the other, trying to avoid sharing the mess I had on my clothes. I could hear her breathing in large gasps and then holding her breath as she failed to prevent herself from crying.

"I didn't stop praying for you." She sniffed and I felt a tear gently splash on my neck. "Not once while you were gone. Not for a minute. I didn't stop praying for you."

I waited; she held me like that long enough that I became too uncomfortable. "…I want to take off my gear, Mom."

She stepped back and regarded me. "Oh, my…" She took my sword, dagger, and mask from me and set them on a nearby table while I stood there doing nothing, and then she helped me to pull off my chest protector, plastron, and fencing jacket, tossing each carelessly into a corner. Pain shot through my shoulder with every tug on the equipment, but I was glad to get it off. I still had my breeches and boots on but felt unburdened enough that I could relax, and in a rush I felt my weakness and fatigue. I collapsed into my mother's arms. The weight might have been a bit much for her, or maybe she was just being considerate, but she said, "Here," and pulled me gently to the floor by a wall where she could rest against it while holding me.

Neither of us spoke. Thoughts danced joltingly through my mind; normally I would probably feel the need to speak them in order to deal with them, but I didn't want to say anything. Then I didn't want to think anything again. I didn't want to do anything but forget.

I didn't want to remember Abbott's disgusting deceit and exposed pursuit of evil, the nightmarish black ogres, or the gruesome and horrifying violence I had conducted with them. I didn't want to remember ancient books and gemstones and rituals. I didn't want to remember blood and pain and death. Among the things I didn't want to remember, I knew I'd never forget the corruption that had taken the place of what could have been thrilling, deep, and lasting love, and I'd never forget that in ending that corruption I had also put an end to the last remnant of the boy who had inspired such love.

But in my home, with my mother, I was now able to find respite from those thoughts. My severe fatigue dropped a gray curtain in front of them, and they were no more.

I thought only of the shoulder and arms where I rested. I was comfortable. I felt blessedly heavy and blank.

My mother held me until I fell asleep, and then she held me through the night.

9.2

Throughout the next day I didn't leave the house and stayed mostly in my room. I took to standing or sitting by my window and just staring outside. My mother was unmistakably happy for me to be nearby, in our home, and was content to leave me to myself for as long as I wanted.

There seemed to no longer be any danger; whatever threat my mother had previously sensed outside was now gone. It felt like a time to rest. Sure, Abbott was still out there, somewhere, and was doubtless up to no good, but he was no longer any concern of mine. He wasn't going to be able to fool me again.

So I could return to normal life, without goblins and imps and black ogres and enchanted jewels. Without fighting and killing. Sometimes it seemed, in a way, as if it had never happened. If, just over a week ago, I'd never visited that bookstore, I would be roughly in the same place I was now; the time in between simply would have been more normal.

My shoulder was still sore. My mother had looked me over and decided that I didn't have any wounds serious enough to seek medical attention, but I'd need time to heal. I hoped she was right; the pain seemed worse today than it had last night, but I was pretty sure nothing was broken.

My rapier was now positioned on my dresser. It wasn't that I felt it necessary to keep it ready. But now, after having used it for its intended purpose, I felt like it was really *mine* more than I ever had before, and I liked having it nearby. Of course my father had given it to me years ago, but it had always been a decorative piece or a training aid. Now it was indisputably my weapon. I even felt like I should name it, though I didn't know if that was a normal practice.

It was also clean again. I'd had to wipe it down well to get all of the ogre blood off. My mother had helped with that; I think it reassured her, even though I'd obviously made it safely home, to have evidence of my victory over the dangerous fiends who had tried to harm me. I think it also somehow helped her cope with the uncertainty of my father's absence. But it was also comforting to remove the filth, to rid our lives of those remains of foulness.

I was afraid that my fencing gear was permanently stained, though. For all we did to scrub it and soak it in hydrogen peroxide, dark marks remained; though somewhat faded, they still stood out against the solid grey of the unspotted portions. The gear was no longer fit for use in a competition; while no one would ever guess at the source of the discoloration, it simply wasn't presentable. I wasn't worried about the financial burden of buying new gear, but I didn't know what to do with these pieces I still had. They were still strong, still intact, and while at the moment I had no mind for the future, I couldn't ignore the possibility that I would need to use them again for demonic combat. So we put them in my closet, carefully set out of the way. Perhaps they were something of a metaphor for me. Just as they sat there, continually bearing the dark blots, I would also permanently bear in mind the potential for facing evil again. It was unquestionably a part of my new world.

We cleaned my dagger, also. The ogre I'd killed with it had begun accelerated decomposition kind of like Luctus' flesh had, and I'd made more of a mess while getting the short blade away. It was disgusting work, both the retrieval and the cleaning, but the blood and muck came off of my dagger as well as the rapier, so all was well that ended well, I supposed.

That adage held true concerning my weapons, if not elsewhere; I couldn't feel that my relationship with Bastian had ended well at all. That relationship itself was a mystery. Why had I come to feel so strongly for him? I knew, basically, that people my age sometimes "fell in love" with someone only to find later that it wasn't truly love, or at least I'd heard about it all the time when I was in school, but this wasn't the same. I didn't think so, anyway. A young woman naturally has romantic tendencies, but wasn't it terribly strange to feel something so powerful for a person I'd only known for a few days?

There had been some kind of immediate bond. I felt foolish trying to explain it to myself, and it was surely tainted from the beginning, but it was there. And it was potent.

But why him? Why not someone else? Why not someone with genuinely good intentions? I'd known plenty of boys in school, some of whom seemed quite pleasant and attractive, at least from a distance. I'd come across plenty of strangers who didn't catch my attention no matter how good-looking they were. Why Bastian?

There was nothing more for me to learn; this mystery would remain unsolved, probably for as long as I lived.

And in the meantime, it would still wrench at my heart.

I'd heard that it could help to write down troubling thoughts, so I once again went to my desk to vent my emotions in the form of a letter. Maybe it was a silly idea, but I wasn't busy with anything else at the moment. Taking up my pen and paper, I began an address to the young man who had entered my life so abruptly and then left forever:

Dear Bastian,

Part of me says that this letter will never reach you, but another part hopes that wherever you are now you can read it. That same part of me has a certain hope for you even now that your mortal life has ended.

If you can read this,

I paused in my writing, thought for a moment, and sat back in my chair. When it came down to it, I wasn't entirely sure what to say. I breathed deeply a few times, then put my pen to the paper again.

know that I have no illusions about how wrong you were. I have to say that up front. I never would have supported you in the evil you were undertaking. No matter what I felt for you, it wouldn't be enough to make me want to do such awful things.

But I did feel something for you. It was surprisingly, amazingly powerful. It was something I've never really felt before. I still feel it, even if I don't understand it. I almost hate that I ever did feel it. Almost. Because this obviously hasn't worked out for us. It seems so strange that I should feel something so strong and then have it come to nothing. It makes me angry.

It was something so wonderful, and exciting, and even overwhelming at times, that I would have thought that I could only feel it for someone who was my soul mate, if such a thing existed. I can't think that way, though. I know I still want to be with someone—that I don't want to be alone throughout my life. I don't know who it will be, and I don't know how I can ever feel something like this again for someone else, but I'm going to look for him. Not now; I'm far too hurt right now. Maybe not any time soon. But someday.

If you hadn't betrayed me I'd be worried about betraying you by saying this, but as it is, I've got to look out for myself. I can only hope that I will love again as much as I loved you. But that man will also be a better man than you. I'll demand it.

Did we know each other in a previous existence? I thought so. Were we meant to be, and did you ruin that for us? I suppose I won't soon know, and that it no longer matters. And though I'm sure that many people have joyous reunions after death, I don't believe that the two of us will ever meet. The hopes I have are not those of seeing you again.

If you were here, I would expect the gravest of apologies. I probably would be outraged and find it hard to forgive you. To betray the feelings I had for you, as you did, seems almost the worst thing you could possibly do. Maybe you don't even understand that. Since you're not here, I'll have to do my best to forgive you anyway, and since I won't be able to extend forgiveness in person, you'll have to assume that at some point I found it within me.

But I don't know if I can yet.

I was having difficulty putting the words down on the paper. I had to finish, though.

I'm glad that at the very least, you can do no more harm to yourself or anyone else. Your loss grieves me doubly; not only have I lost the man I wanted to love forever, but it's just as much of a tragedy that someone who could have been such a good man chose to be the opposite. So I'm glad that you won't go any farther down dark paths, and that you won't compound my grief any further, even if it is what lasts forever.

Perhaps it really will last forever. I don't know. I hope not. But nothing can change what has happened. In the end, you truly became Luctus—Grief—for me, and for all the sweet feelings I had I'll never be able to remember you with happiness.

This is the last I can give to you—this last true and complete expression of my love and sorrow. I hope you'll know the value of that truth, and I hope you'll regret causing such sorrow.

And I hope the regret will be worth something to you.

Maria

I set down the pen.

Almost three pages worth of writing, on three sheets.

This letter was not to be mailed; I had a different sort of delivery in mind. Instead of marking an envelope, I folded each sheet of paper in turn first lengthwise down the middle and then along several diagonals, producing several basic paper airplanes much like what I'd used as a child. Having folded them all, I wrote To Bastian Greywall on the top of each.

One of my luxuries in my father's luxurious house was a fireplace in my own room. It often went unused, but since I'd returned home my mother had kept it lit and well-fueled while I stayed alone in my room to keep me warm and, if nothing else, to ward off the silence.

Coming to my feet, I gently lifted the first of the paper airplanes, then turned toward the fire. With a careful throw I propelled the aircraft forward.

It glided across the room, catching a minor air current here and there, dancing with the smallest of twists as it soared. As it flew from me I almost felt as if he really were reading it. It descended and, as a testament to my aim, landed neatly on top of the burning logs. Flames rapidly licked over it. In seconds, it had lost its shape, and within several seconds more the last of the white paper had charred and was mostly gone. The scant remains were soon almost indistinguishable.

I picked up the second, and threw it also, more gently than the first, but with equally true aim. I could imagine Bastian, the human Bastian, understanding my love for him and feeling equal melancholy for losing me. The paper was suspended gracefully, though traveling slowly; the speed with which it reached the fireplace seemed incongruous with the depth of sentiment it carried. It bounced upon landing and took a short moment before also catching fire, but lasted no longer than the first once ablaze.

Only one page left to deliver.

I raised and threw the third, with barely enough force to impel it adequately to its destination. I wanted to think, as it glided through the air, that it would carry the pain with it, that I would feel relief as it ignited and was consumed. But quite the opposite happened; while it flew I felt a tear run down my cheek, and when it struck the flames and began to burn, my own heart began to burn as well, and I couldn't bear to watch the plane disappear in the blaze. I averted my eyes, and only after taking a moment to recover emotionally I looked back, and I found that the letter was now entirely gone.

All I could do was sit down right where I was and sob. I don't know how long I stayed there. Disappointingly, as much as I wanted the passage of time to dull my inner ache, the minutes I spent there had essentially no effect. Sitting didn't help. Lying down didn't help. Pacing didn't help. And yet, I didn't want to do anything else, either.

However, the passage of time did allow me to recognize and appreciate a bit more of what I was feeling. Although my emotion for Bastian lingered, possibilities of a future with him were utterly shattered, and I knew I still had a lot of life to live. There was one more short letter that I needed to write.

Once again, I sat with pen in hand:

To the one who will stay with me,

I'm worth the effort, and I deserve something good. I'm hurt right now, but someday I'll be ready for you.

I want you to be ready for me. Be a good person. Be the hero I need. Don't settle for selfishness. Don't settle for any destiny other than the best, for both you and me.

Be true to me.

Be the best of good men.

Be what I know I deserve.

With hopefully the greatest love a woman can have,

Maria

I carefully folded the single sheet of paper into one final airplane, and stood to send it along an airborne course. But this letter wasn't for the pyre, wasn't for the dead. I carried it to my window, which I opened. This letter was meant to reach someone and needed to be let out to the open world.

A light gust of wind brushed past me into the room, carrying the scent of rain and trees.

I lifted the last paper airplane and sent it aloft, watching for only a few seconds before closing my eyes. I wanted to imagine it flying on endlessly, over forest and city and sea until it reached one man who would not only read the words but truly understand them, and feel the need to follow them.

Never mind that the paper was going to be destroyed in the rain. Let me live with my dream, I told myself.

Hoping for hope was no more of a balm than the simple passage of a few minutes, however. I again felt a twisting in my heart and then tears on my cheeks. I let them rest where they were as I stood at my open window.

Maybe the wind would be kind enough to dry them once they stopped.

9.3

I wondered about my father. Two days after I'd come home, my mother had received a phone call from a friend in Europe who had seen Lucard and spoken with him briefly, and who had decided later to check in with us out of concern. It was the only clue we had to my father's whereabouts; we'd heard nothing else. I didn't know whether the information was helpful or frustrating. I'd only briefly considering going out to look for him; before hearing the news I'd had no idea where to start, and now the task seemed almost impossible. So for now, I stayed where I was.

Hansen had tried to come see me but my mother let him know that I still didn't want to see anyone. When she brought food to my room again at lunchtime, she told me that he had come, and he hoped I would be feeling well enough for company sometime soon. I didn't know how soon that would be. Grant had called a couple of times also, but my mother had given him a similar message. She had also brought me a note a day ago that simply read, *"So it goes: Your mom says you're okay but we're still worried. Come see us soon."* That nearly shook me out of my reverie, but with the way I was feeling even Nova would have to wait. At some point I would move forward, and keep living my life much the way I had before, but not now. For now, I spent most of my time thinking about Bastian, though I didn't think about him the same way I had a short time ago.

My seclusion began to make my mother unhappy, so sometimes she looked at me silently as if to say, "You were strong. You did what was right."

I acknowledged that I'd played an important part. I'd stopped a dark plot. How long it would have taken for Bastian to find the Life Stone without me, or how the world would have reacted to an invasion of demons, I couldn't imagine, but I knew what I'd done to settle things. Perhaps someone else would find solace in that thought; I didn't. It was of no consolation to me. I simply knew what had happened, and what my role had been. That was it.

As my mother set down the lunch tray and withdrew, I was grateful for her kindness and understanding. More than anything else I was grateful for such good parents. Parents do so much for their children.

I wondered about Bastian's parents. I lamented the fact that I would never even know if they were still alive, and I wouldn't be able to tell them that their son had died. I didn't know how to bring such news properly and I wouldn't want to speak with them for long anyway, as I could surely have little of anything good to say about him, but every parent deserves to know what has happened to their child. Then again, they may well have been dead already. Darker thoughts began to creep in when I considered this, but I quickly decided that I shouldn't spend any time thinking them.

Of course he'd had parents at one time, though. He'd been a young child earlier in life, and had been as innocent and pure as any other. Clearly, at some point he had chosen a path of darkness, but he had once been something else. It pained me to think of decisions he had made, decisions I didn't witness but that had turned him from a creature of innocence into a malevolent villain. I gritted my teeth at the thought, wondering what might have been…wondering who he might have been, and what might have happened between the two of us had he chosen what was good and right.

One tear and then several ran down my cheeks and fell away. I clenched my eyes shut in an effort to stop weeping.

We live with hope. Sometimes people know and understand our hopes, and sometimes they are sacred to us alone and we keep them hidden away in a special place in our hearts. At times we hope for something for days, or months, or even years. If we pair our hope with faith enough to take action we often actualize our hopes and rejoice in them. We hope for companionship, for comfort, for the pursuit of dreams, for peace…and we have good reason to hope. But some events are beyond our control and sometimes the wind blows the wrong way or the person on whom we rely makes a choice we can't abide.

Sometimes, sadly, even tragically, we have to accept that our hopes will never be fulfilled—that with a decided finality, we have to give them up. Sometimes we can do nothing but relinquish our hope as it drifts uncontrollably away only to be replaced by despondency and grief.

Some things are hard to hold on to…and some things are forever lost.

End of Part III

The Patient Hyacinth
(twelve years earlier)

Hansen threw another rock into the water nearby. "You know, my dad's a hero."

"What?" I knew what heroes were like, and Hansen's dad was just normal.

"Yep. He's a hero. He kills dragons almost every day."

"No, he doesn't, Hansen. Dragons aren't real."

"They are too! My mom says so, and she doesn't lie! She says my dad goes out to kill the dragons and then comes back to the castle. That's our house."

"You don't live in a castle!"

"Well, it's got bricks. It's like a castle."

I still wasn't sure he was right.

"Anyway, my mom says so."

He had a point there. Maybe he was right after all.

I threw a rock of my own before speaking. It only splashed once and then was gone. "Is it hard?" I asked.

"To kill dragons? It must be. My dad is usually pretty tired when he gets home." He threw another rock, which also only splashed once just like mine. "I'd kill dragons every day for you, Maria."

I put my fists on my waist. "Well, of course you would! Boys are supposed to do that kind of stuff for girls!"

He threw another rock, and then another. "I don't know how they skip these things..." For good measure he found another rock and kicked it. It made it just barely into the water. "I'd better go home now," he said. "Bye!"

I said, "Okay. Bye, Hansen!" and watched him run away down a path. I thought I should go home, too.

I picked up my special diary from where I had set it. I hadn't written much in it yet, but I had something good to write now. I opened it and found a blank page and wrote, "BOYS KILL DRAGUNS."

When I was bigger I would be a mommy, and a boy would be a daddy with me. He would kill dragons, too. And he'd always be nice and never yell at me, and he would give me nice hugs, just like my dad was nice and gave nice hugs to my mommy.

But who would be my dragon killer? How would I know what boy was the right one?

I thought for a minute, and then I knew: the right boy would give me my favorite flower, a grape hyacinth. I had one right there with me that I had found earlier, with its bunch of purple or purple-blue flowers that looked like an upside-down bunch of grapes. The right boy would give me *this* flower! I held it up to the sky.

Yes. That was good. Flowers were important for girls.

I put the flower in my special diary and closed the book.

This was big news, and I wanted to tell my mommy, but I realized I couldn't, because the flower was in my special diary. Anything in my special diary was a secret. Maybe I could tell her just a bit, though. Just a little bit.

I held my special diary carefully and ran home.

It was a bright, sunny day.

Demons and Dark Essences:

Luctus

Questions for readers:

1. Maria's narration states that we want to be judged by others, and that's why we dress in the way we do. Do you think your appearance is a large part of your identity? What are you trying to say about yourself by the way you choose and alter your clothing, hair, and general grooming? How would you be affected by a drastic change in your appearance?

2. As Maria makes some decisions, such as lying to her mother or rejecting the affection of a boy, they cause her to feel guilt. She also feels guilt after realizing that she has misjudged others. Do her feelings of guilt inhibit her, or do they serve her in some good purpose?

3. Several characters make the mistake of placing trust in others who later betray them. Sometimes the betrayal causes physical pain or danger, or even loss of life; sometimes, the betrayal causes heartache. Do you put yourself at risk of being hurt emotionally when you trust others? Should you give trust and love to others even if you are risking a lot emotionally? Should you give that love and trust casually?

4. Maria lies to Abbott before going to pursue the Life Stone, but she decides that she doesn't feel bad about it. Eventually she sees that her actions have caused trouble for her and others, but many people lie all the time for the purpose of personal gain. Is it always bad to lie to others, and if not, when would it be the right thing to do?

5. Maria eventually confides in her mother and confesses to the things she has done wrong. By the time she does so, she has made many bad choices, and her resulting problems are also numerous. Do the wrong choices we make always catch up with us? Do the problems we create for ourselves grow worse or better with time? Do they grow worse if we commit additional wrongs in an effort to escape negative consequences?

6. Artemis Brown says that "the real way to succeed is to live well day by day, all the time for a long time, so that doing the right thing comes naturally to you." To know how to live well each day we have to heed the advice of wise people around us. Who do you trust to give you good advice on how to live well, and why?

7. Maria begins to feel a stronger desire to drink blood, but believes that to do so is wrong. We also sometimes feel natural desires to do what we believe is wrong. What did Maria do to avoid or remove temptation? How can we avoid or remove temptation to do things we believe are wrong?

8. As Maria begins to think that Amy is or will be jealous of her, she is blinded to her own jealousy of Amy. Put otherwise, she accuses someone else of a fault while ignoring the same fault in herself. How often do people in general make the same mistake?

9. Lucard wrote to Maria that he wanted to protect her from the dangers of the world while she was young, knowing that she would eventually be old enough that she'd have to deal with them herself. What dangers should parents shield young children from? Does growing older make it okay to invite those dangers into our lives, or does it just make us more capable of protecting ourselves on our own?

10. Maria and her mother Laura have a reserved approach toward physical romance. Laura had told her that even a simple kiss "and anything else that followed were a treasure" that are "unavoidably cheapened when shared with more and more people" and that she expected Maria to only give that treasure to someone she planned to marry. Most people take a very different approach. Is her mother wrong? As Maria encounters future romance, will it be difficult for her to follow her mother's advice?

11. Bastian vacillated between his aspirations for power and elegance and his love for Maria. Ultimately he gives in to desires that prove to be destructive and even fatal for him. While at his worst, he allows himself to manipulate and hurt the person for whom he has the strongest feelings. When is it right for us to pursue an identity that isn't already part of our nature, and what cost is acceptable if we become what we want?

12. Maria grows to love Bastian in a short time, sensing something different about him, and feeling as if she already knew him. She believes that Bastian could have and should have made different choices, and their relationship "should have been thrilling, deep, and lasting love". Was she simply a young, inexperienced woman with a strong crush, or do you believe that her conclusions were right?

Acknowledgements

Having written a real book for the first time, I feel a certain sense of accomplishment, and I'm thrilled about it, but I readily recognize that I couldn't have done it without help from family and friends. I took insight and correction from every one of the following people.

My greatest thanks go to my wife, Jeri Lynn, who not only checked my writing every so often while I was producing it, and also reviewed at least one completed draft, but who also wrote the short story that inspired me and which, with some modification, also became Maria's explanation to Grant about how her parents met.

Sandra read my first draft and provided the paintings of Maria and Greywall Castle that I used on the cover. Thank you, Sandy, for your feedback and for putting up with my relentless requests for a slightly different painting of Maria even though I ended up using one of your first.

Thank you, Robyn, for being one of the first to read an early draft and for providing a unique sort of reassurance when you informed me that you'd read it in only three days. It was nice to know that I was hitting the target.

Thank you, Ryan, for reading draft versions multiple times and giving many very smart and insightful thoughts back to me. I hope that I can do the same for you some day.

Thank you, Becca, for also providing useful feedback and helping me to put finishing touches on my first novel.

Big thanks to Dave for creating the dragon icon. It's everything I could have hoped for. I also really appreciated your help with the cover.

Aside from my test readers and artists, I'd like to thank everyone who has read this book. I hope you both enjoyed and found value in what I wrote. It's tricky to make something up and presume that it's worth someone's time to read, and I'm glad if you found it worthwhile. Also, I want to give extra thanks to anyone who buys this book for a friend! Remember that supporting someone's work encourages them, and enables them and others like them to keep producing that kind of work.

And speaking of that, hopefully it takes me less time to finish a second and third book to complete Maria's story.

17049168R00190

Made in the USA
San Bernardino, CA
18 December 2018